FUJINO
OMORI

ILLUSTRATION BY
SUZUHITO
YASUDA

© Suzuhito Yasuda

INTERLUDE   THEY BEGIN TO STIR   2

CHAPTER 7   POEM OF DESPAIR,
             POEM OF TRIUMPH   9

CHAPTER 8   THE VOICE OF THE HAMMER   98

CHAPTER 9   HELLO, DEEP LEVELS   166

CHAPTER 10   THE WHITE MAGIC PALACE   217

SPECIAL
CHAPTER   RECOLLECTION OF JUSTICE   236

CHAPTER 11   WHERE THE WILL TO KILL LEADS   242

SPECIAL
CHAPTER   REMINISCENCE OF JUSTICE   257

CHAPTER 12   FORLORN HOPE
             IN THE DUNGEON   262

CHAPTER 13   BEYOND A THOUSAND
             DARKNESSES   305

EPILOGUE   YOU'LL BE BACK II   401

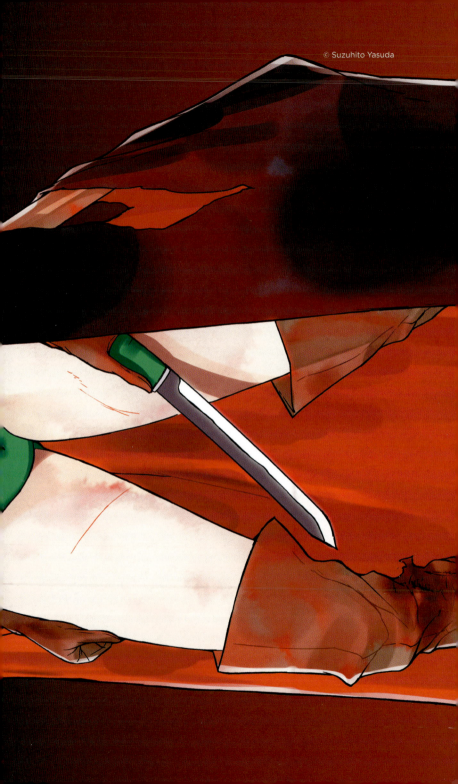

© Suzuhito Yasuda

Is It WRONG to TRY to PiCK UP GiRLS iN A DUNGEON?

VOLUME 14

FUJINO OMORI

ILLUSTRATION BY SUZUHITO YASUDA

YEN ON

NEW YORK

IS IT WRONG TO TRY TO PICK UP GIRLS IN A DUNGEON?, Volume 14
FUJINO OMORI

Translation by Winifred Bird
Cover art by Suzuhito Yasuda

DUNGEON NI DEAI WO MOTOMERU NO WA MACHIGATTEIRUDAROUKA vol. 14
Copyright © 2018 Fujino Omori
Illustrations copyright © 2018 Suzuhito Yasuda
All rights reserved.
Original Japanese edition published in 2018 by SB Creative Corp.
This English edition is published by arrangement with SB Creative Corp.,
Tokyo in care of Tuttle-Mori Agency, Inc., Tokyo.

English translation © 2019 by Yen Press, LLC

Yen On
150 West 30th Street, 19th Floor
New York, NY 10001

Visit us at yenpress.com
facebook.com/yenpress
twitter.com/yenpress
yenpress.tumblr.com
instagram.com/yenpress

First Yen On Edition: December 2019

Yen On is an imprint of Yen Press, LLC.
The Yen On name and logo are trademarks of Yen Press, LLC.

The publisher is not responsible for websites (or their content) that are not owned by the publisher.

Library of Congress Cataloging-in-Publication Data
Names: Ōmori, Fujino, author. | Yasuda, Suzuhito, illustrator.
Title: Is it wrong to try to pick up girls in a dungeon? / Fujino Omori ; illustrated by Suzuhito Yasuda.
Other titles: Danjon ni deai o motomeru nowa machigatte iru darōka. English.
Description: New York : Yen ON, 2015– | Series: Is it wrong to try to pick up girls in a dungeon? ; 14
Identifiers: LCCN 2015029144 | ISBN 9780316339155 (v. 1 : pbk.) |
ISBN 9780316340144 (v. 2 : pbk.) | ISBN 9780316340151 (v. 3 : pbk.) |
ISBN 9780316340168 (v. 4 : pbk.) | ISBN 9780316314794 (v. 5 : pbk.) |
ISBN 9780316394161 (v. 6 : pbk.) | ISBN 9780316394178 (v. 7 : pbk.) |
ISBN 9780316394185 (v. 8 : pbk.) | ISBN 9780316562645 (v. 9 : pbk.) |
ISBN 9780316442459 (v. 10 : pbk.) | ISBN 9780316442473 (v. 11 : pbk.) |
ISBN 9781975354787 (v. 12 : pbk.) | ISBN 9781975328191 (v. 13 : pbk.) |
ISBN 9781975385019 (v. 14 : pbk.)
Subjects: | CYAC: Fantasy. | BISAC: FICTION / Fantasy / General. | FICTION /
Science Fiction / Adventure.
Classification: LCC PZ7.1.O54 Du 2015 | DDC [Fic]—dc23
LC record available at http://lccn.loc.gov/2015029144

ISBNs: 978-1-9753-8501-9 (paperback)
978-1-9753-8502-6 (ebook)

1 3 5 7 9 10 8 6 4 2

LSC-C

Printed in the United States of America

VOLUME 14

FUJINO OMORI
ILLUSTRATION BY **SUZUHITO YASUDA**

BELL CRANELL

The hero of the story, who came to Orario (dreaming of meeting a beautiful heroine in the Dungeon) on the advice of his grandfather. He belongs to *Hestia Familia* and is still getting used to his job as an adventurer.

HESTIA

A being from the heavens, she is far beyond all the inhabitants of the mortal plane. The head of Bell's *Hestia Familia*, she is absolutely head over heels in love with him!

AIZ WALLENSTEIN

Known as the Sword Princess, her combination of feminine beauty and incredible strength makes her Orario's greatest female adventurer. Bell idolizes her. Currently Level 6, she belongs to *Loki Familia*.

LILLILUKA ERDE

A girl belonging to a race of pygmy humans known as prums, she plays the role of supporter in Bell's battle party. A member of *Hestia Familia*, she's much more powerful than she looks.

WELF CROZZO

A smith who fights alongside Bell as a member of his party, he forged Bell's light armor (Pyonkichi series). Belongs to *Hestia Familia*.

MIKOTO YAMATO

A girl from the Far East. She feels indebted to Bell after receiving his forgiveness. Belongs to *Hestia Familia*.

HARUHIME SANJOUNO

A fox-person (renart) from the Far East who met Bell in Orario's Pleasure Quarter. Belongs to *Hestia Familia*.

LYU LEON

Formerly a powerful elven adventurer, she now works as a waitress at The Benevolent Mistress.

CHARACTER & STORY

The Labyrinth City Orario——A large metropolis that sits over an expansive network of underground tunnels and caverns known as the "Dungeon." Bell Cranell came there to pursue his dream of becoming an adventurer. After meeting the goddess Hestia, he joined her familia and began to spend his days in the Dungeon, hoping to win the respect of his idol, the Sword Princess Aiz Wallenstein. Soon the supporter Lilly, the smith Welf, the Far Easterner Mikoto, and the renart Haruhime have joined *Hestia Familia* alongside him. When news of a murder rocks the Dungeon's resort town, the blame is pinned on Gale Wind, a black-clad figure with a bounty on her head. Seeking to clear Gale Wind—that is, Lyu Leon—of the crime, Bell and his party set out to find her. But then Cassandra has a nightmarish prophetic dream…

EINA TULLE

A Dungeon adviser and a receptionist for the organization in charge of regulating the Dungeon, the Guild. She has bought armor for Bell in the past, and she looks after him both officially and personally.

CHIGUSA HITACHI

Another member of *Takemikazuchi Familia*. A kindhearted girl, she has been friends with Mikoto and Ouka since childhood. Not naturally suited to fighting.

MIACH

The head of *Miach Familia*, a group focused on the production and sale of potions and other recovery items.

DAPHNE LAULOS

Former member of *Apollo Familia*, along with Cassandra. Joined *Miach Familia* after *Apollo Familia* lost the War Game.

SYR FLOVER

A waitress at The Benevolent Mistress. She established a friendly relationship with Bell after an unexpected meeting.

CHLOE LOLO

A catgirl waitress at The Benevolent Mistress who talks and acts like a goddess. Chases after Bell.

OURANOS

The god in charge of the Guild, who also manages the Dungeon.

AISHA BELKA

A daring, lustful Amazon in *Hermes Familia*. Formerly a member of *Ishtar Familia*.

JURA HARMER

A tamer and surviving leader of *Rudra Familia*, he detests Lyu. The man responsible for summoning the calamitous Juggernaut.

OUKA KASHIMA

The captain of *Takemikazuchi Familia*. With his shield in hand, he takes the lead in protecting his companions in the front guard. He and Welf fight like cats and dogs.

TAKEMIKAZUCHI

The deity of *Takemikazuchi Familia*. The god of combat and martial arts, he boasts tremendous skill in the art of war and has instructed Mikoto on a range of techniques.

NAHZA ERSUISU

Originally the sole member of *Miach Familia*. Jealous of women who get close to Miach.

CASSANDRA ILLION

Like Daphne, she joined *Miach Familia* after *Apollo Familia*'s defeat. She is quite attached to Daphne, who is caring toward her.

AHNYA FROMEL

One of Lyu's and Syr's coworkers at The Benevolent Mistress, she's something of a foolish catgirl.

RUNOA FAUST

A human waitress at The Benevolent Mistress. Although she seems to be a commonsense type, she has a troubled side.

FELS

A mage shrouded in mystery who answers to Ouranos directly.

TSUBAKI COLLBRANDE

A half-dwarf smith belonging to *Hephaistos Familia*. Currently at Level 5, Tsubaki is a terror on the battlefield.

TURK

A werewolf who lives in Rivira. Worked with Jura to set off the massive explosion on the twenty-fifth floor.

INTERLUDE
THEY BEGIN TO STIR

"It has stirred."

The elder god's soft-spoken words echoed through the darkness.

Ouranos's bulging eyes were fixed on the Dungeon spread beneath his feet.

"Stirred? Surely you don't mean...the Juggernaut?"

The reply came from a fist-sized crystal.

It was an oculus, and on the other side of the magic item was Fels.

The oculus was in the Chamber of Prayers beneath the Guild Headquarters. Ouranos—the god who prayed to the Dungeon—may not have been perfect, but he did have a grasp of the general situation. Or more accurately, he sensed the presence of a certain monster there.

The ruinous Juggernaut had risen again after an absence of five years. The presence of this "apostle of murder" that had massacred *Astrea Familia*, to which Gale Wind belonged at the time, was enough to fill Orario's founding god with extreme foreboding.

"Yes...it has strayed far from the zone where it emerged and is *descending the floors*."

That ruinous creature had begun to move.

And not merely within its own floor. It was crossing multiple floors, so many that Ouranos could discern its movements from the surface.

A terrifyingly rapid dive ever downward from the Water Capital where one would have expected it to emerge.

"I can't believe it...Considering its origins, the chances it would leave the floor where it spawned are...!"

Fels—who at the moment was accompanying the Xenos in the fight to capture the man-made dungeon Knossos—sounded puzzled.

For the Juggernaut to appear, the Dungeon had to suffer massive damage.

When that happened, the living Dungeon responded defensively by summoning its antibody. In other words, the point of the Juggernaut's existence was to obliterate any traces of the invading pathogen—adventurers—on the floor where it had spawned. Under normal circumstances, even if the monster's targets fled, it would never travel several floors to pursue them.

"...What is happening?"

The reality was that the delusions of a tamer were causing the monster to pursue a certain boy and elf.

But even an omniscient god, and the founding god of Orario at that, could not parse the details of what was happening in the Dungeon when it fell so far beyond established understanding. Ouranos and his companions on the surface were able to grasp only that an irregularity was occurring.

"And this response...a Monster Rex has appeared in the Water Capital? Did the Dungeon ignore the regular spawning interval and dispatch it...?"

Ouranos also noticed another action by the Dungeon that was impossible to ignore.

The face of the wizened god, who was mockingly called the "immovable one" by the other deities, twisted into an unmistakable grimace.

"What will you do, Ouranos?"

"...Send reinforcements to the Water Capital. Even if they are unable to resolve the situation, we need to know what is happening."

"But we are still fighting to capture Knossos. Few forces are available to have Loki Familia *take the lead. If you order a mission and the regular procedures are followed, they'll never make it in time!"*

The voice emanating from the crystal was filled with anxiety. Ouranos realized that when Fels said the troops wouldn't make it in time, the immortal mage was talking about the safety of *Hestia Familia*. Ever since the incident with the Xenos, Fels had been willing to risk everything for the sake of Bell Cranell.

The same was true of Ouranos himself.

"I will do all I can...even if it ends in failure."

The four torches surrounding the altar swallowed up the will of the deity.

From his throne, Ouranos turned his blue eyes toward the darkness above.

"The rest depends on whether there is anyone besides us who will take action…"

Crash!

A cup slid off the table with a clatter.

"Hey, Syr! Are you okay?"

"…"

The waitress Runoa rushed to the girl with the blue-gray hair, who was surrounded by ceramic fragments. The item that had fallen did not belong to the bar; it was instead the favorite cup of one of their coworkers.

It belonged to the elf who was no longer there with them.

Syr shifted her gaze from the smashed pieces of pottery to her hand. Drops of red blood were seeping from her slender fingers.

"…I'm sorry everyone. I'm going to step out for a minute."

"Syr! Where are you going, meow?!"

Syr ran out the back door, ignoring the words of the catgirl Ahnya. She and the other waitresses were left behind in the quiet bar, which hadn't opened yet.

"Think she went to look for Lyu, meow?" asked the catgirl Chloe as she turned over a piece of the cup in her hand.

"Can't think of what else she'd be doing…even though we have no idea where that girl could be."

Runoa, the only human of the three, frowned as she answered. Her words were devoid of conviction. The same went for the kitchen workers. But Mia, the owner of The Benevolent Mistress, did no more than watch and sigh as her employees went about their work completely distracted.

"Meow…It's all Lyu's fault, meow! The fact that Syr's acting strange and also Mia and the others being so worried, not to mention the gloomy mood around here—it's all her fault!"

Ahnya shrieked her words at the ceiling.

Before Lyu up and vanished, she had been tense for days on end, and her fellow waitresses suspected she had gotten wrapped up in something bad. It was only a hunch, but one based on a long friendship.

They couldn't explain it, but they all felt it in their bones.

"Excuse me, is anyone in there?!"

Just then, as if trading places with Syr, someone else arrived.

"Meeeow?"

"A goddess? A customer?"

"No, it's the boy's patron deity...Lady Hestia, meow."

The goddess, who could easily have been mistaken for a regular girl, was standing in the doorway of the bar. Judging by her panting and how hard her black pigtails were bouncing, she must have run there. Without stopping to properly catch her breath, she rushed up to Ahnya, Runoa, and Chloe.

"Were you guys close with the elf? Close enough to know what she's up to?"

"The elf...? You mean Lyu, meow?"

"Yes! And this is the most important question: Are you guys as absurdly strong as she is?"

"Just wait a second, Goddess. What are you even trying to find out after barging in here like that?"

"Yeah, meow. First you should explain why you're asking that question, meow."

As Ahnya tilted her head quizzically and Runoa worked herself into a fluster, Chloe alone coolly demanded an explanation.

Hestia, who had been leaning eagerly toward them, clammed up.

"...Look at this."

Instead of answering, she held out a letter. Ahnya took it, while Runoa and Chloe peered over her shoulder from either side.

"It's a letter my supporter sent from the eighteenth floor..."

The message contained an explanation of Gale Wind's current predicament and a request for reinforcements.

Although the three women were supposed to be no more than ordinary waitresses, the looks on their faces were as sharp as that of hardened warriors.

Crack!

A fracture raced down the hammer with a loud pop.

"Huh...?"

The cracked tool was in Welf's workshop in the rear garden of Hearthstone Manor, the *Hestia Familia* home. The woman who had been using the hammer to forge a sword, helping herself to it even though she wasn't its true master, stared in disbelief.

"Did it get too hot? No way, must be Welf's fault for not taking care of his tools with the proper smith's spirit! It's definitely that! It can't have been my fault...Is it my fault? Uh-oh, this is bad...He's gonna be so mad at me."

Clutching her head as she muttered, her curvy upper body wrapped in a single strip of bleached cloth, the woman was undeniably suspicious. She glanced back at the ruined hammer.

"Or is it...a bad omen?" she muttered.

As she stood staring at the hammer in the now-quiet workshop, the door opened behind her.

"What, the owners are back already? Or could it be a thief in the *Hestia Familia* home...?"

"Calm down. Just like Hephaistos kept you behind, we've been asked to watch the place while everyone's gone."

"Oh really? My bad, my bad. Now that you mention it, you do look familiar...the god Miach and his follower, if I remember right."

The woman let down her guard as Miach entered the workshop, Nahza following close behind. She laughed nonchalantly and was about to make small talk when she noticed their expressions and wiped the smile off her face.

With Hestia having run off to The Benevolent Mistress, Nahza was the one who spoke up.

"Um…I know it's a terrible bother, but can you do us a favor, Cyclops?"

The woman's nickname echoed through the room along with the word "favor."

Tsubaki Collbrande, captain and Master Smith of *Hephaistos Familia*, narrowed her patchless right eye.

CHAPTER 7
POEM OF DESPAIR, POEM OF TRIUMPH

No matter what I do, it's always the same.

No matter what I say, no one listens.

No matter how I beg, my pleas reach no one.

It's always the same.

The world always stomps on my hard work.

The world always jeers at my tragedies.

Even when I gather my courage and struggle, even if I scream at the top of my lungs, I always bump up against absurdity.

So many times, my desperate warnings have been ignored.

So many times, my determination has crumbled like a sand castle.

I have tasted defeat again and again.

Time after time, I have been hurled from the cliff's edge into the depths of darkness.

But what can I do? I'm surely cursed.

What can I do, what can I do…what can I do?

When did those words begin to invade my heart?

When did I start feeling a shade of resignation even in the moments when I tried to change the future?

No one trusts me.

No one even tries to believe me.

Not even my own familia members.

Not even her, whom I call my best friend.

So I gave up.

I didn't really go all out trying to change the future.

Just once, a boy appeared who believed my words.

I thought *this time I have to succeed*.

I took a step forward because I'd made some friends I desperately didn't want to lose.

But as usual, the world jeered at me.

Ahh, in the end, all was useless.

Who could blame me for thinking like that?
Faced with such despair, who could punish me and my broken heart?

Alone, the prophetess of tragedy drowned in sorrow.

It was clad in white.

Two rearing heads.

The huge, beautiful body brought to mind the phrase "dream dragon," but in fact, it was the embodiment of violence and destruction.

"The Monster Rex of the twenty-seventh floor—"

The dragon's double cry echoed forth. The two weaving heads blended hostility and murderous intent in perfect harmony.

"—The Amphisbaena!"

As a stunned prum looked up at the dragon, the Amazon beside her spat out the monster's name.

"OOOOOOOOOOOOOOOOOOOOOOOOOOOOOO!!"

Its immense roar thundered across not only the twenty-fifth floor but all three floors of the Water Capital. The members of the alliance backed away in unison when they heard the battle cry of the Amphisbaena, the floor boss that had emerged from the Great Falls linking the three floors.

The alliance had been formed by multiple familias to carry out an expedition, with *Hestia Familia* at its core, venturing into the lower levels for the purpose of uncovering the truth about the murder that Lyu, the Gale Wind, was being blamed for.

They had parted ways several hours earlier with Bell, who had joined the elite party that went on ahead to the twenty-seventh floor. After that, there had been a chain of explosions so great it seemed the entire Water Capital would be demolished, followed by the appearance of an irregularity in the Dungeon—the banquet of calamity—that had occurred only a scant twenty or thirty minutes earlier, although Lilly's party had been untouched.

Now it was appearing again in front of their eyes, together with a new Irregular.

"That's…a floor boss from the lower levels."

It was the next Monster Rex after the seventeenth floor's Goliath.

Chigusa, who belonged to *Takemikazuchi Familia*, stared at the monster in a daze as she spoke. It was looking up from the huge lake that was the twenty-fifth-floor plunge pool.

She had to crane her neck to take in the majestic form towering over twenty meders high. Dozens of times as wide as an orc, it truly lived up to the moniker "floor boss." Its entire body was white. The form encased in chalky scales was certainly huge, but it also evoked a certain magnificence.

The light in its eyes, however, was undeniably that of a monster—the glint of a heinous being that abandoned all logic to indulge its instinct to destroy.

"A two-headed dragon…"

The two heads, which seemed to move independently, were particularly noteworthy.

The long necks split apart at the point where they emerged from the body. Each ended in an unmistakably bestial face covered in dragon scales as large as breastplates. The pair of eyes set in the left head was blue, while the pair in the right was red.

As those whispered words fell from Mikoto's lips, not a single member of the party—not Lilly, Welf, and Haruhime nor Ouka, Chigusa, Daphne, and Aisha—could hide their shock.

"…Ah."

Daphne's face turned white. Her clenched fist opened audibly. She could hear the shattering of forgiveness after she had sacrificed so many lives to save her friends.

The dragon she faced was truly an embodiment of despair.

"_____"

Its roar—so deafening that even the persistent din of the Great Falls, the Dungeon's largest waterfall, could not drown it out—broke off, leaving the residual cries to echo through every corner of the Dungeon.

As dim light from the crystals of the Water Capital reflected off its white body, the two-headed dragon slowly trained its menacing glare on the foreign substance threatening its mother, the Dungeon. In other words, it was targeting adventurers.

"—OOOOOOOO!!"

Another ferocious bellow.

The blue-eyed head exhaled a horrendous breath.

Blue flames raced forth, singeing the air.

The sight was so beautiful that the onlooking adventurers felt chills run down their spines. Terrifyingly, the instant some embers touched the surface of the plunge pool, a tremendous gust of steam exploded upward. Ouka and the others stared in horror as the scorching flames marched toward them, vaporizing the water as they went.

"Scatter!!"

Aisha's scream, which didn't leave even the tiniest room for hesitation, spurred her companions into action.

They launched themselves away in that instant. Welf grabbed his backpack and forcibly pulled Lilly toward him, while Aisha hugged Haruhime to her chest, and Mikoto fled with Chigusa as fast as they could.

"Cassandra?!"

The healer alone lagged behind. She was in a daze, stock-still. Unable to move.

Daphne had already started to escape, but she quickly reversed course and grabbed Cassandra's arm. She was too late.

The blue light of the terrible inferno illuminated the two girls' faces.

What saved them from certain death was the vanguard's wall.

"Gyaaaaaaaaaaaaaaaaaaaaaaa!"

"Ouka!"

"Sir Ouka?!"

Fulfilling his duty as the party's tank, Ouka thrust forward his large shield.

The Level 3 adventurer had narrowly escaped death more than once in the course of venturing down to the lower levels. Now he used his mind's eye—which might also be called his quick wit—to protect the party. Instead of blocking the flames head-on, he held his shield at an angle.

Shoving the surprised Daphne and Cassandra out of the way with his back, he jumped aside and deflected the barrage of fire breath. His quick thinking exhibited the skills he had gained on the current expedition as well as his accumulated experience. But…

"Huh…?! But my shield worked so well in fending off the lambton…!"

Ouka gulped as he looked down at the hard valmars surface only to find it melting like wax.

Equipment destruction. Although Ouka had managed to ward off the immediate danger, his shield had not fully blocked his enemy's fiery breath. Any spots where the flames had skimmed across the floor or collided against the walls were left with gouges and melted pieces scattered about. Worse, the crystal columns had melted exactly like candles under the heat of the blue flames, and were collapsing with thunderous crashes.

In a panic, Ouka tossed aside his sizzling shield that still had blue flames dancing across its surface.

"That heat is unbelievable…!"

Every hair on Welf's body stood on end as he kneeled on the crystal ground and stared at the fiery dragon breath. Like the speechless Ouka, the smith who had forged the shield shuddered in horror.

Until a few moments earlier, the twenty-fifth floor had been slightly chilly due to its proximity to the great rush of water. Now it was so hot every adventurer present was dripping sweat.

"The breath of the Amphisbaena…those flames are *burning on the water's surface…*"

Just as Lilly said, the flames burned not only on land but on water, too. From the crystal shore to the steaming water, blue flames danced gracefully on everything that had been in the path of the dragon's breath. Lilly had read up on the two-headed dragon at the Guild before they set out, and now, as she knelt on all fours beside Welf, the very real, raw power of that horrifying monster was unfolding before her eyes.

The breath of the Amphisbaena was laced with a special type of flammable liquid produced in the dragon's bile duct. Thanks to its extremely hydrophobic quality, the substance repelled water, transforming the breath into a paradoxical river of fire. The Amphisbaena was born in a watery world, yet its primary weapon was fire; this was its special attribute.

Enchanting blue napalm.

Even on water, the blaze raged at unbelievably high temperatures.

It made for a surreal scene, but whatever or whoever was unfortunate enough to be in the path of the Amphisbaena's deadly breath would be instantly incinerated, leaving not so much as a dusting of ash behind.

A direct hit meant certain death.

"Don't let it touch you! You'll catch fire and keep burning! Recovery magic is useless!"

As Aisha shouted that warning, she set down Haruhime amid a swirl of blue sparks and picked up her *podao*.

Rivulets of sweat were streaming down her coppery skin—caused both by the skyrocketing temperature and her own panic.

We're gonna fight a floor boss right now?! What a nightmare! No way do we have the manpower to take down that piece-of-shit monster!

Level 4 second-tier adventurer or not, the current situation struck fear into her heart.

When she had belonged to *Ishtar Familia*, Aisha fought the Amphisbaena multiple times and always killed it. But that had been with a band of Level 3 Berberas, and even more crucially, the Level 5 Phryne had been there.

The monster was so fierce it usually required more than twenty Berberas working together to defeat it. Her current party was far weaker than *Ishtar Familia*. How in the world were they supposed to get through this?

They lacked the combat strength, plain and simple.

"Damn the guys up there for taking off!"

Far above her, on the cliff at the southern tip of the huge cavern, not a soul was to be seen.

Bors had stationed a group of adventurers at the mouth of the passage connecting to the twenty-fourth floor to watch for Gale Wind, but it looked like they'd turned tail and fled to a higher level. It wasn't surprising, given the string of irregularities topped off by the appearance of a floor boss.

Adventurers tended to put themselves first. It didn't make sense to hold a grudge against them for it, but Aisha couldn't help cursing as she glanced up at the cliff. If they'd been able to work together to pincer the dragon from both sides, they might have had a chance at breaking through.

What the hell?! If the Guild's information is right, the Amphisbaena shouldn't have appeared for another two weeks!

Lilly, the brain of the party, had collected all the publicly available information she could from the Guild before they left, but Aisha hadn't slouched on her intelligence gathering, either. Checking on the presence of floor bosses and the intervals at which they emerged was one of the most basic preparations whenever a party was setting off on an expedition. It was essential to thoroughly investigate what the potential dangers were on the planned route, including any irregularities, in order to eliminate as many risks as possible. Indeed, *Hestia Familia* had timed its expedition to specifically avoid the periods when lower-level floor bosses were expected to appear.

The moss huge, the lambton...it's been one Irregular after another!

"Shit!"

The bad-tempered Amazon scrunched her beautiful face into a scowl.

"Ms. Aisha! I think retreat is our only choice...!"

"Obviously! There's no way we can put up a real fight against that thing!"

Aisha returned Lilly's shriek from behind without taking her eyes off the two-headed dragon.

We can't go back into the maze on the twenty-fifth floor. It caved in after that last huge explosion. It's a long shot, but the only way we'll have a chance is by escaping to the twenty-sixth floor...!

Neither humans nor monsters could pass through the interior of the cliff now that the explosion caused by the Inferno Stones had destroyed it. Aisha glanced back at the gaping maw of a tunnel on the southeastern side of the cavern, which led to the floor below them.

The problem was that since the Amphisbaena was a mobile floor boss, it could use the large rivers that connected with the Great Falls to leave the cavern and enter the labyrinthine sections of the Water Capital. If they were driven into a corner, the second a jet of that blue napalm came shooting down a passageway, they'd all be toast—

Aisha's line of thought had gotten that far when she heard a dripping sound.

"…?"

Something was raining down hard.

When it hit the ground, blue sparkles scattered apart.

It sounded like hail.

Tiny motes of light danced around Lilly and the others, bouncing off their hoods, robes, and battle clothes.

"Crystals from the ceiling…?"

She peered up at the ceiling of the twenty-fifth floor far, far above. The whole surface area was carpeted in crystals, with huge roots emerging from the blue field here and there. They were the same roots Bell had seen when he first arrived on the floor, measuring five meders in diameter and radiating outward, a sign of the Colossal Tree Labyrinth above.

"OOOOOOooooooo!!"

The Amphisbaena roared.

Ignoring Aisha and the others as they pressed their hands to their ears, it looked up and let loose another cry.

The cavern shook. The showering hail of crystals intensified. Countless ripples spread across the plunge pool.

The roar sounded like an accusation.

Like the dragon was begging the Dungeon for something.

No one knew for what, though.

But the next moment, the ceiling of the twenty-fifth floor *creaked*.

"—"

As Lilly, Welf, Mikoto, Haruhime, Ouka, Chigusa, Daphne, and Aisha gazed at the ceiling and saw it quietly begin to crumble, all of them felt as if time had stopped.

Slowly and steadily at first, and then with irreversible force, the crystals rained down.

Fragments of the shattered ceiling were falling around them.

And then.

"The colossal tree is—"

The trunk had lost its support.

Like a proclamation of unending despair, the roots that had radiated across the ceiling *plummeted downward*.

"The cage of despair—"

Her face white, the prophetess of tragedy whispered as if she had finally realized everything.

WHOOOOOOOOOOOOOOOOOOOOOOOOOOOOOOOOOOOOOOOO OOOOOOOOOOOOOOOOOOOOOOOOOOOOOOOOOOOOOOOSH!

The roots tore through the air with a whipping noise and fell toward the plunge pool. On their way down, they scraped against the cavern walls and even struck the Great Falls with a horrible crash, as if the immense dragon was dragging its claws down the cliffs and waterfall. The iguaçu lurking behind the falls were swept up by the fallen debris. With no time to escape, the brilliant scarlet swallows were smashed flat and hurled into the plunge pool, the remains of their ruined wings scattered everywhere.

Like the iguaçu, Welf and the rest of the party had nowhere to run. All they could do was take up positions for battle, eyes wide.

The mass of roots finally smashed into the ground.

"~~~~~~~~~~~~~~~~~~~~~~~~~~~~~~~~~~?!"

As she violently bounced up and down from the impact, Lilly had the illusion that the entire floor was caving in.

A storm of crystal fragments flew from the walls and floor, shook the plunge pool, and were swallowed up in the waves caused by the burning blue flames.

Unable to withstand the shocks, the adventurers stumbled and lost their footing one after another. Gradually their blank minds rekindled and started to process their surroundings.

It took a few seconds to realize they were still alive.

And it took another few to become aware of the new environment that had been created.

"What—?"

An enormous dome rose from the center of the plunge-pool lake.

The strange object was actually formed by the enormous roots of the colossal tree. Like a crushed birdcage, the twisted heap had landed between the shore where Lilly and the others stood and the wall.

The entire twenty-fifth-floor cavern was carpeted by the fallen roots that had once stretched across the ceiling.

"The colossal tree from the twenty-fourth floor...fell?"

"Must be because the part of the twenty-fifth floor that had been holding it up was destroyed..."

Ouka's mutter answered Daphne, who still hadn't stood back up.

It wasn't that the entire twenty-fourth floor had collapsed. What they had witnessed was one portion of the Colossal Tree Labyrinth's roots dropping down.

And only the bottom-most part of the roots at that.

"Wait...! We lost our escape route!"

Aisha snapped her head around to check the southeastern shore.

A long, thin splinter that must have come from a massive root had pierced the wall and mercilessly demolished the connecting passageway. Which meant that the adventurers had indeed lost their way out of the cavern.

"Oooo..."

The two-headed dragon was undeniably still in the center of the lake. It was moving each of its heads in turn, without the slightest sign of confusion or distress.

The roots were woven together like a net, blocking their escape.

The dome-shaped lid now covering the plunge pool was indeed a cage.

"We can't escape…"

"It's…"

All color drained from their faces as Mikoto and Chigusa voiced their trapped companions' fears.

It was now impossible for them to leave the Water Capital. They couldn't even escape to the twenty-sixth floor. Their only option now was to face the dragon that was the embodiment of despair.

A compulsory battle demanded by the Dungeon.

"OOOOOO!"

"?!"

As if to say the stage was set, the Amphisbaena belched a stream of blue flames.

Lilly and the others reflexively jumped away from the hellfire that burned water and crystal alike. Flames flickered across the northeastern shore where they stood.

Again, the temperature on the floor skyrocketed.

Fires raged around them as if they were inside the devil's cookpot.

"Ready your weapons! We've got no choice but to fight!"

Not surprisingly, Aisha was the first to recover from the shock.

She brandished her *podao*, shielding Haruhime behind her.

"But…Lady Aisha…"

"Steel yourself! …I already made my peace."

There was no way to retreat. They had to fight.

That is, if they considered themselves true adventurers.

A moment after shouting at the rest of the party that they needed to prepare for the worst, Aisha grimaced.

Is this even remotely possible…?

The faces of the party members as they stared up at the floor boss seemed on the verge of losing all hope.

This was different from their encounter with the moss huge. Their lives were at even greater risk this time.

No one present was so stupid as to be oblivious to the difference in combat strength. The Amphisbaena had a potential equal to a Level 5. Aisha was unaware of this, but on paper, it was on the same level as the Black Goliath. A hundred upper-class adventurers had been present for that battle. Asfi, Lyu, and Bell had all been there. Right now, there were only nine of them. Even if the goliath's insane ability for self-regeneration made it stronger than this dragon, the party still had plenty of reason for succumbing to despair.

There was only one thing that was certain.

They were under attack by a mountain of absurdity that seemed like it had been sent specifically to kill them.

This would break them. Break their will, and their spirit.

It was almost as if the Dungeon was whispering to them. *Don't think you'll escape!*

Their will to fight was sputtering like a candle in the wind. Cassandra was the worst off. She simply stood in place, having resigned herself to her fate.

We don't have enough combat strength. We don't have enough fire-power. We don't have enough morale.

We don't have a pillar to rally around.

It was astounding how unprepared this party was for a fight with a floor boss.

Even Aisha wanted to throw in the towel.

"This is an ill-fated day," she muttered, thinking about how they'd already encountered so many Irregulars that she had never seen, even in the deep levels.

If only Bell Cranell were here.

She almost said the words out loud. Suddenly, her face flushed with rage.

Get yourself together, Aisha Belka! Since when were you the kind of spineless woman who relied on a man?

She denounced the passing thought, ashamed of herself. As a pureblood Amazon, she couldn't tolerate such whining.

She let out an indomitable battle cry, hardening her resolve.

But these guys...

She had fought this monster before. She had faced its brutal, absurd reality multiple times and overcome it. That, above all else, was her prime weapon against losing heart.

But the same could not be said for Lilly and the rest of the party.

They didn't have Aisha's strength or as much experience straddling the line between life and death. And without that, they couldn't hold back the encroaching despair.

Aisha had said something to Bell when they entered the New World on the lower levels for the first time a few days before.

If you stumble, the party stumbles. That's the kind of party this is.

She'd been mistaken.

The alliance and *Hestia Familia* were strong. They were tough enough to beat back adversity even when the boy wasn't with them.

But this was different.

They were staring into the jaws of death. The strength of the vessel was being tested.

The situation threw into sharp relief the importance of a figure like Bell who could act as the support pillar.

For them...Bell Cranell is a hero.

Or at least something close to a hero.

He was a weakling and honest to a fault, but when he gathered what courage he had and challenged hopelessness itself, he became a beam of light propelling forward everyone who knew him.

His tears wrung Lilly's heart.

His raging voice stole Mikoto's heart.

His back shrinking into the distance spurred Haruhime's feet.

But he was not with them now.

What became of troops who didn't have their hero?

In fairy tales, they were crushed by monsters like sacrificial victims.

If Bell were here.

If only Bell were here.

Aisha could see at a glance that those words were rising in Lilly's throat.

Bell Cranell was so important to them that not even Aisha could fill his shoes.

They needed a pillar to take the place of Bell.

A voice to spur them forward.

Right now, they had no pillar.

But…

…they had flames.

An instant later—*Bang!*

"‼"

Lilly and the others swung their heads toward the clang of metal being thrust against the crystal floor.

The redhead at the tail end of the party steadied his greatsword with both hands, his casual kimono still swaying.

Everyone's focus was on him.

Even the Amphisbaena stopped moving for a moment to train its eyes on him.

Still looking down, Welf sighed loudly. His face was dripping sweat, but when he turned toward Lilly at his side, his expression was nonchalant.

"Li'l E, I bet this is your first one."

"Um…?"

"Your first adventure without Bell."

Lilly's eyes went wide at his words.

"You might think that you can't fight without the strongman, that you can't stand up without your hero—but that's wrong, right? That's not the case, yeah? That's not how it is for adventurers."

Mikoto and Ouka held their weapons with trembling hands.

"It's about time we show Bell what we're made of! We've gotta prove we can take down floor bosses on our own!"

Haruhime and Chigusa gulped.

"If we tell him, 'We're helpless when you're not around'…well, that's just causing him trouble! Am I wrong?!"

They didn't have a pillar.

But they had a smith who had fought beside them and watched over them from the very beginning.

They had the flames of a furnace that rang with the sound of the hammer through thick and thin to arm them with weapons.

Welf smiled a resolute, fearless, and impudent smile.

"…Obviously! Lilly and her companions are not mere luggage!!" the prum snapped back loudly. "Lilly will stand side by side with him and play a part in the adventure!"

She pressed one hand to her small chest and hollered her big decision.

"I…I, too, refuse to be left behind. I will not go back to being a prostitute who only waits for him to save me!"

As she spoke, Haruhime wagged her fox tail.

"…I'm on board, too, Mikoto. We must not bring shame to Take-mikazuchi's name!"

"Yes!"

"Chigusa, I won't let Bell Cranell beat me!"

"Yes!"

Ouka, Mikoto, and Chigusa all shouted their battle cries.

"Oh, come on, you guys…aren't you a little too simpleminded?"

Daphne was the only one who hadn't said anything yet, and while her comment was spoken in a profoundly exasperated tone, she was visibly on the verge of tears. A moment later, she was smiling.

"I know, I know…We're adventurers, after all. If we're really pushed into a corner, we've gotta fight."

To Daphne, who strove to make decisions objectively, their rising morale felt like a sign—like a fair wind blowing them toward battle.

"Daphne…"

In front of her dazed eyes, Cassandra watched Daphne step into the battle line and draw her baton-like dagger, confirming her decision.

"…I'm in excellent condition, Ignis," she said.

As Aisha watched this go on, she gave the big-brother figure of *Hestia Familia* a silent word of praise.

The job of a smith was to bring fire to weapons.

And the job of adventurers was to use those weapons to kill monsters.

Flames tinged the faces of both adventurers and smith.

Ignited by the fire the smith had lit, the adventurers turned their eyes forward and took in the monster.

They met the eyes of the two-headed dragon awaiting them.

"OOOOOOOOOOOOOOOOOOOOOOOOOOOOOO!!"

"Forward!!"

Welf's roar matched the dragon's. Mikoto copied him.

It had begun.

The quest to resist despair.

"Kokonoe!"

The one who blew the battle's starting whistle was neither the floor boss nor the adventurers.

It was a certain magic user.

"Beloved snow. Beloved crimson. Beloved white light."

Before anyone else had even moved, she began to chant.

Haruhime had watched fights with a floor boss play out many times before.

It was a typical scene when she was a part of *Ishtar Familia*.

When the adventurers gathered everything they had to take on such a tenacious monster, her job as a sorcerer was to immediately invoke her magic.

Sorcery combined with firepower.

By conferring an overall level boost, she was able to improve the performance of the entire party.

Either Lilly or Aisha would direct her to the person she should buff, so she prioritized focusing on the chant. As she wove her spell, which was one of the longest chants, she began to summon the golden tails with all her strength.

"Hiya!"

The next to take action was Welf.

He swung his deep aqua longsword down from above his head.

He aimed the magic-blade ice gun at the water.

"?!"

The lake instantaneously froze. Four dragon eyes registered surprise as water transformed into a field of ice.

Ouka and the other adventurers had the same expression on their faces.

There had been no strategy meeting, and no one had told Welf to do it. He had simply concluded that in order to approach that massive floor boss and take it down, they'd need something to stand on. That was what made him bring down the huge magic blade that had the power to freeze everything in sight.

There could have been no better strategy for taking on the two-headed dragon. Normally, the preferred method was to fight Amphisbaena inside specific rooms where the waterways were dotted with numerous islands, providing places to stand. Large numbers of adventurers would go to these specific areas on the twenty-fifth, twenty-sixth, or twenty-seventh floors and lie in wait while others lured in the floor boss.

"Not bad!" Aisha cheered with a smile.

Her worry over the lack of natural footholds necessary for this battle had just been dispelled.

"OOOO!!"

The third to make a move was the Monster Rex itself.

As if to say it had no intention of letting the adventurers do as they pleased, it twisted its two necks and breathed out a stream of dreamlike blue napalm.

Cracks appeared all across the frozen lake as the blue flames began to melt it. The solid field of ice was quickly becoming a multitude of islands.

Now they had the ideal terrain for taking down Amphisbaena, just as Aisha had been hoping for.

"With me, brave conqueror!"

To round off the preliminary skirmish, the Amazon began her concurrent chant. She intended to draw the monster's attention until Haruhime finished the level boost.

The renart girl couldn't move at all while performing such a powerful chant. To make sure no attack reached her, Aisha quickly jumped onto one of the islands and approached the floor boss.

"OOOooooOOO!"

"—!!"

The dragon zeroed in on Aisha, who had begun to activate her impossible-to-ignore magic and was now acting as a decoy. The dragon's right head bellowed as if to spur its left counterpart, which responded by spitting out blue flames.

Aisha leaped out of the way in the nick of time, grimacing at the deadly heat, and circled the floor boss in a broad arc. Dodging the enemy's torrent of fire, she continued casting without pause before finally unleashing magic in place of a greeting.

"Hell Kaios!"

She slammed her *podao* down on the iceberg at her feet, launching a slicing wave that sped forward like a shark's fin. The dragon's second head moved quickly in response.

"HAAAAA!!"

Though the left head had spit out blue flames, what the right brought to bear was a crimson mist. A sickle-shaped band of dense fog protectively curled around the dragon's body. Not even a second later, the magic *podao* hurtled toward the monster's side.

The moment it made contact, the magical power clearly weakened. The wave swayed like a shimmering heat haze and grew smaller, but managed to break through the mist in the end. As it made contact, the floor boss's body made a popping noise.

The dragon scales were entirely unscathed.

"Huh...?!"

"The power of the magic dropped?!"

Mikoto and Ouka were stunned. Aisha replied to the confused pair without pause.

"It's the Amphisbaena's mist! Any magic that touches it gets diffused!"

This was the second dragon head's ability.

If the blue flames were the dragon's sword for eradicating its quarry, then the crimson mist was the shield that warded off its enemy's attacks. The effectiveness was obvious. It could neutralize even a second-tier adventurer's deadly attack that had slaughtered every kind of monster the lower levels had to offer.

Aisha sounded irritated as she shouted her next words.

"The only way to kill Amphisbaena is to strike it from close range!"

That was why adventurers typically chose rooms with many islands when they had to take it down.

Normally, voluntarily fighting an oversized water dragon over water would be considered suicidal. But because the crimson mist suppressed the magic that was so crucial to killing other floor bosses, adventurers were forced to engage Amphisbaena in close-range combat.

Their weapons couldn't reach the magic stones in the monster's massive body, either, which meant killing it with a single stroke was not an option.

"If we pounded it with magic, it would eventually open a hole in the mist or blow it away, but it's not worth it! At the very least, we cannot manage that!"

Lilly added what she'd learned about the monster even as she trembled before the living specimen.

The mist wasn't impenetrable. Each time it crippled incoming magic, the mist itself thinned out a little. But the dragon could replenish any openings with fresh mist from its right head. It was reasonable to liken the immense body of the Amphisbaena to a bottomless storage tank of mist. In all likelihood, a party's magic users would run out of Mind before the monster ran out of mist. Or they would be incinerated by the blue flames first.

The dual breath of the Amphisbaena was truly ideal for both offense and defense.

"So this magic blade won't work either…!"

Welf looked down at the Crozzo's Magic Sword he gripped in his right hand and smiled ironically.

"Grow. Uchide no Kozuchi!"

With that, Haruhime finished her preparations.

The five fox tails that had manifested as she performed the concatenated casting were now fully charged with level-boosting magic.

"Give them to Mr. Welf, Mr. Ouka, Ms. Mikoto, Ms. Chigusa, and Ms. Daphne!" Lilly shouted immediately.

The Amphisbaena had the potential of a Level 5. If a Level 2 adventurer took a direct hit from its attacks, the results would be fatal. Fortification of the front and center was essential. At the same time, Lilly's list left out the Level 4 Aisha and the rear guard made up of herself, the party's supporter, and Cassandra, the healer. The prum had decided on conducting a quick strike.

Lilly had stepped into the role of commander now that Aisha stood on the front line, so Haruhime quickly heeded her orders.

"Dance!"

The tails of light that had grown from Haruhime's lower back separated from her body and transformed into orbs of light. The Kokonoe enchantment, charged by the Uchide no Kozuchi spell, flew to Welf and the others, entering their bodies as though the magic was possessing them. The level-boost light orbs formed a chain.

But there were only four.

One tail of light was still attached to Haruhime's body. She pressed one hand to her chest, panting as she took out a magic potion.

If all five were sent out at once, I'd collapse. But if I hold one back for a moment…!

Haruhime had learned that lesson from their battle with the moss huge.

If she tried to use all of the Kokonoe magic simultaneously, she would suffer a Mind Down and crumple into a pathetic, useless heap.

This was a method she had come up with to sidestep that problem. By activating all but one of the magic tails and keeping the last bit of magic on standby, she could retain one tail's worth of Mind and avoid fainting. Once she recovered, she could provide the party with level boosts again. Plus, she could use the remaining tail as a spare in case of emergency.

She simply couldn't afford to collapse at this moment.

That much was plain to see.

She had discarded modesty and humbleness. What the party needed most in their current situation was her power. In order to stand a chance against the outrageously strong floor boss, she had to continuously produce that level-boosting light in order to support Mikoto and the others.

She felt guilty, but this was the only way she could manage.

Haruhime's eyes met Chigusa's, the one person among those named by Lilly who had not received a boost.

"I'm so sorry, Chigusa."

"It's okay."

What Chigusa meant was *I can still fight.*

Haruhime felt tears come to her eyes as her childhood friend smiled, one kindhearted eye peeping out from behind her swaying bangs. In her hands, Chigusa held a bow and arrow. She was part of the center guard.

Her tail wagging, the renart fixed her gaze on the battlefield, determined not to look away for even a moment, then focused on recovering.

"I didn't want to use this, but…this isn't exactly the time to be stingy, is it?"

Daphne chuckled hollowly as she stood beside Haruhime and watched the Amphisbaena thrash about. Looking reluctant but resigned, she began her own chant.

"*Follow blindly the sun in the sky. Blossom, armor of laurel, so that all will flee from thee.* "

It was a short chant. Drawing a circle in the air with her dagger, Daphne completed casting the spell.

"Raumure."

A film of deep green light enveloped her entire body. It was protection magic, similar to enchantments. The result was a small increase in her endurance and a large increase in her agility. It was the only magic Daphne had, and she didn't like to use it because it reminded her of a certain deity; she hadn't even used it during the war games, when her familia's very existence had been on the line.

"Ooraaaaaaaaaaaaaaaaaaaaaaaaaaaaaah!!"

With that, the pseudo–Level 3 adventurers, boosted by Haruhime's magic, charged forward.

Their statuses had risen dramatically. Including Daphne's magic, the party buffing was complete.

All their preparations had been made. They were about to shift from skirmishing and begin the main battle.

With a powerful battle cry, Ouka and the others moved from the shore onto the islands atop the water and rushed the floor boss.

Their boots stomped on ice and their new strength rocketed them into the air. Using the momentum granted by their temporary Level 3 status, Welf, Mikoto, and Ouka leaped energetically from one island to the next, scattering in three directions as the floor boss bore down on them.

Together with Aisha, who had already circled around to the dragon's back, they surrounded it, all aiming at different targets.

But…

"UOOOOOOOOOOOOOO!"

"HAAAAAAAAAAAAAAA!"

"?!"

As soon as the two heads let slip a double roar, the advancing trio found themselves instantly on the verge of defeat. Welf dodged the dragon's right head by a hairbreadth as it swooped ferociously down on him, while Mikoto and Ouka had to leap away from the left head's attempt to mow them both down. As the head swung horizontally, grazing the soles of their shoes, their fighting stances crumbled and the huge ice island they were standing on split in a V-shape.

A flurry of water droplets flew into the air, beating down on the three adventurers as they somehow managed to land on another island.

"It's so fast!!"

"But more than that...!"

"It never lets its guard down!"

Welf, Mikoto, and Ouka spoke with voices that trembled in fear.

The two rapidly undulating dragon heads each had minds of their own. Whether they were surrounded or caught in a pincer attack, the heads' combined situational awareness eliminated all blind spots. Moreover, the long, powerful necks braided with dragon muscles attacked with extraordinary speed and were able to strike at enemies approaching from any direction.

"—?!"

Without so much as a pause, the dragon's right head shot forth in dogged pursuit of Mikoto.

She had let her attention waver for a mere instant, not even long enough that it could be called a moment of carelessness. But even with her Level 3 status, she was still unable to fully escape.

This dragon-hammer was more than enough to prevent Mikoto from recovering.

"Watch out!"

"...! Lady Daphne!"

Daphne swept Mikoto out of the way without a moment to spare. Her outstanding precognitive ability warned her about Mikoto's impending danger, and by using the extreme agility gained by combining the effects of Raumure with Haruhime's level boost, she had managed to leap to Mikoto's side from her position in the party's center.

The dragon's attack missed its mark but shattered the hunk of ice where its intended prey had been moments earlier. Carrying Mikoto by the waist, Daphne landed on another shelf of ice and set her down.

"This may sound unreasonable, but you've gotta get used to this monster quick. I can't be rescuing you over and over."

"Right, of course!"

Dripping sweat, Daphne returned immediately to the battle line.

Mikoto stood up, a shiver of terror running through her as she realized that becoming distracted meant instant death in this fight against the floor boss. As she gazed at the dragon, she told herself to sharpen her senses even further.

"The dragon floor boss...I thought I understood how fierce it was even without seeing it up close, but this strength is unbelievable!"

The grand appearance of the white dragon shrouded in crimson mist alone struck awe into its opponents.

Though the menacing glint in the dragon's eyes threatened to overwhelm them entirely, Mikoto and her comrades flew at it once again. This time they attacked in unison from the dragon's front, left, and right. Thanks to Aisha stepping in to help, Ouka was able to escape the Amphisbaena's notice and finally land a successful blow, but the results were not what he had hoped.

"Eh?!"

A violent storm of sparks flew from Kougou, his huge battle-ax made from the high-quality ore varmath. The tough dragon scales had hindered his attack.

Penetrating a dragon's scales—which were among the highest quality drop items available—was one of the greatest challenges any adventurer could face. The combination of vicious attacks and this nigh-impenetrable defense was what gave dragons their reputation as one of the strongest monsters.

Completely unaffected by Ouka's assault, the dragon swung its two necks back and forth as if they were caught in a violent storm. The four attackers were forced to flee the scope of its assault, their protective gear already battered.

No sooner had they pulled back than a blue haze appeared around the dragon's mouth.

"The breath is coming!"

Daphne shouted the warning from one of the ice islands where she anchored the center of their formation, her dagger-style magic blade gripped in one hand. Chigusa ran behind her and loosed an arrow in an attempt to distract the white dragon, but it did not pause.

"~~~~~~~~~~~~~~~~~~~~~~~~~~?!"

New waves of blue napalm swept over the battlefield.

In the blink of an eye, an ice-float measuring ten meders across melted into nothing, and the surface of the lake ignited.

The blue napalm fueled by dragon-bile propellant did not rely on magic, but rather on pure firepower. For this reason, even Welf's anti-magic fire chant was useless against the monster's breath.

The billows of steam rising from the path of the blue flames had made the entire floor incredibly hot and humid. It changed the normally cool waterside environment into a sauna—or more accurately, into a cauldron of blue flame.

"I can't breathe..."

"My throat's burning."

Every time adventurers fought Amphisbaena, the Water Capital underwent this transformation. Aisha was used to it, but the others were different. This baptism by steam—despite the fact that it wasn't a volcano floor—was unpleasant even for upper-class adventurers and eroded their ability to concentrate. And when they did manage to collect themselves, they were still significantly weakened.

Standing near the blue flames that constantly consumed the oxygen in the air, Mikoto and Ouka groaned.

This crimson mist...it doesn't just block magic. It also interferes with attacks by reducing visibility. Combined with the heat and humidity...this is awful.

Daphne stood at a distance from the front line, carefully observing the Amphisbaena.

If they entered close combat, the mist veiling their enemy acted like a curtain blocking their view. Most likely, Ouka's first strike had been ineffective not only because the dragon scales were so protective, but because his timing was off, too.

We technically have footholds to stand on, but these ice platforms are unreliable compared to solid land...

Thanks to the water pounding down from the Great Falls on the north side of the cavern, the countless fragments created when the iceberg shattered were like unstable floating islands. The distance between them was constantly varying, so it was impossible for the adventurers to move as they pleased.

To start with, those two heads move way too quick for a humongous floor boss!

When they faced the goliath, all the adventurers needed to avoid taking lethal damage was being vigilant when they were directly in front of it. Plus, they were able to creep up close to attack.

But this battle with Amphisbaena was different.

Its speed seemed impossible for an ultra-large-class monster, and it skillfully used that speed to both gather information and intercept attacks. It was like an extra cherry on top of the potent blue flames that seemed to incinerate everything they touched and the misty barrier that blocked magic.

"Wish I could escape...even though I can't."

Thanks to the commanding roles she'd been pushed into ever since her time in *Apollo Familia*, Daphne couldn't help analyzing the enemy, and muttered her gloomy conclusion in spite of herself.

"GUaaaaaaaa?!"

"Damn, too shallow?"

Aisha had slipped past the enemy's sharp teeth with her usual confidence and landed a blow aimed between the protective scales, but she managed to draw only a few drops of blood. Fury at the Amazon who had hurt it seeped from the eyes of the floor boss.

The two heads roared in turn, and the next moment the dragon plunged under the water's surface.

Apprehension consumed the adventurers as they watched the monster disappear deep under the water.

The white dragon dove nearly to the bottom of the lake, glared up through the rippling surface with its four eyes, and then burst upward.

"—OOOOOOOOOOOOOOOOOOOOOOOOOOOOOOOOOOOO!!"

"Guoooooooooooooooooooooooooooooooooooooooo!!"

The two heads surged above the water followed by the massive body, which barreled straight for the adventurers.

Neither retaliation nor defense was possible. As Ouka and the others fled the hulk shooting out of the water toward them, they were overtaken by the tsunami it had created.

The water dragon—which reached its greatest potential in the water—was charging them. After achieving incredible acceleration underwater, both the force and the range of the incoming attack were on a different level compared to everything they had seen so far.

The shock waves even reached Daphne and Chigusa in the center, cowing them.

"Cough, cough...Argh!"

Their undine cloths now sopping wet, Welf and the rest of the front guard kneeled on an island and glanced up at the floor boss as it peered down at them.

The Guild rates them at Level 6 when they're encountered on the water, Aisha had mentioned before. The others were only just beginning to understand the meaning of her words.

The watery world that spread out on the other side of a single piece of ice was itself their enemy's most important weapon. It went without saying that if they were pulled into the depths, they would be brutally killed in the blink of an eye.

"Damn it's strong...Stronger than any monster we've fought before!"

"But we'll take it down! Right?"

"That's right. Here I go!"

Welf and Ouka returned the dragon's glare, hoisted their weapons onto their shoulders, and rushed forward to renew their assault.

"W-w-w-wait! Just wait a...!"

Meanwhile.

Standing on the shore behind the attacking members of their party, Lilly couldn't do a thing.

Her last action had been to tell Haruhime what to do with her level boosts. Since then, she'd felt like a lost child.

What in the world should we do about this thing...?!

A fight against a floor boss was completely different from an ordinary battle.

There was just too much information to take in. When they were in passageways within the labyrinth, Lilly had been able to handle the job of commander. But now they were in a cavern. The space was incomparably huge, and it included difficult waterfront terrain. The scale of it was alien to her, especially with that oversized dragon diving in and out of the water to attack them as it pleased. To top it all off, there were the countless ice floes, raging flames, and the final straw—the root dome surrounding them overhead and on all sides. Lilly wanted to ask someone if she was in a fairy tale.

·Lilly was still a commander in training. The current situation was beyond what she could handle.

What should Lilly do...?!

In the vast wilderness of her brain, the options were endless. She couldn't swiftly figure out the correct choice.

Far downshore, flames swirled around the ajura tree. It burned briefly, its fallen petals scattering to the ground. Lilly watched Haruhime press her hands to her chest and rest both elbows on the ground, desperately trying to recover. To Lilly, the renart seemed to mirror her feelings of anguish.

Sweat rolled down her cheek as she drank in this profound scene from the corner of her eye.

"Lilliluka! Keep it together!"

"!!"

It was Daphne, her teacher in the basics of leadership.

"What's most important for the rear, especially the commander, is insight and decisiveness! And composure! You must keep a cooler head than anyone else in the party!"

"I-I understand! But...!"

From the far side of the iceberg, Daphne cut off Lilly's cry with a shout of her own.

"The best commanders don't ask what they should do in a given situation. They ask how they can change the situation!"

"!!"

"Once you can do that, you're ready to graduate."

With that, Daphne took off running.

"We're short on people! I'm going to the front!"

She left command of the party entirely to Lilly.

The prum paused for a moment as she considered the unspoken trust that Daphne's decision rested on. Then her chestnut eyes flashed angrily.

The confusion had vanished from her mind. All she felt now was the will to fight blazing brightly in her heart.

The heavy pressure that came hand in hand with responsibility was gone. In its place burned the heat of an oath to not fail the party, to not let a single one of them die, and to fight alongside them.

Invigorated by Daphne's encouraging advice, Lilly's little head began to spin big plans.

There's the frozen plunge pool and the tree overhead...

First, she observed her surroundings.

We have four magic blades left, and the status of the party members who can use them is...!

Next, she scrutinized the cards in her hand.

Luckily—though that may have been the wrong word—the destruction of the maze meant no other monsters could find their way onto the shore. She was still within range of the blue napalm, but as long as Welf and the others were keeping the dragon occupied, she had time to think.

Eventually she settled on a strategy.

"Ms. Mikoto, do your chant!"

The other adventurers turned around at the prum's loud shout.

"Trade positions with Daphne and drop back to center! Everyone in the vanguard, please hold back the enemy with all your strength! Ms. Chigusa, continue providing support!"

Issuing a flurry of orders, their commander set her plan in motion. Her powerful, clear-cut voice had the authority to spur warriors to action. It was like a beam of light piercing the darkness. No one questioned her.

Mikoto nodded, Welf smiled, and Aisha licked her lips.

"Forgive my impudence as I beseech thee—"

Mikoto fell back to the center of their formation where Chigusa was and began her chant, as ordered.

Meanwhile, Daphne—who had a higher status than Mikoto to start with—adroitly filled the gap she had left, using the bird's-eye perspective she'd gained before to skillfully coordinate with the rest of the front guard.

"There's no one who fills in more smoothly than you!"

"Well, thank you, sir!"

"OOOOOOOOOOOOOOOOOOOOOOOOOOO!"

Welf and Daphne, who had faced off against each other in the war games, now ran side by side while trading banter. As the dragon's right head darted toward them at a downward slant, Daphne lured it as close as possible before pulling back. Meanwhile, Welf used his greatsword to slice at the monster's trunk.

Aisha and Ouka threaded between the crackling blue flames to suppress the left head.

"Bring forth the evil-crushing blade! Bow to the blade of suppression, the mythical sword of subjugation. I summon you here now, by name."

All this time, Mikoto was steadily building up her store of magic.

She had decided that staying in one place would be dangerous, so as she performed her concurrent casting, she constantly moved from island to island. It took everything Chigusa had to keep up and guard Mikoto, who was leaping and sprinting like a Level 3.

"!"

The Amphisbaena had noticed the adventurers' threatening movements.

As the monster attempted to aim its blue napalm at Mikoto, Aisha and the others intercepted the attack. The white dragon shook its two heads, as if annoyed at the tiny beings that hovered around ready to brandish their blades at the slightest opening.

"OOOOOOOOO!"

"AAAAAAAAA!"

"Shit!"

Perhaps having realized their current attack pattern was getting them nowhere, the two heads roared and then disappeared under-water. More icebergs cracked as the dragon's huge body banged against them, and Welf retreated with a curse.

His target wasn't visible anymore. He didn't know where it might pop up next. Would it target the chanting Mikoto? Or would it attempt to scatter Welf and the others on the front line? As electrifying tension ran through each member of the party, Lilly issued another command.

"Ms. Mikoto, use your Yatano Black Crow skill!"

"!"

Mikoto reflexively obeyed the divine revelation. Yatano Black Crow allowed her to detect previously encountered monsters. Thanks to her level boost, the dragon could not escape her notice even after diving underwater.

On the black map that unfurled at the back of Mikoto's mind, there was one crimson dot moving with extreme speed.

She had continued her concurrent chanting while using this other skill, so she simply pointed to indicate where they should direct their attacks.

"Northwest! Under Ms. Aisha!"

"!!"

Without missing a beat, Lilly screamed the information. As the prum's voice echoed into the corners of the yawning space, Aisha and those near her promptly leaped away.

Less than an instant later, the floor boss struck.

Ice fragments scattered and water sprayed into the air. The adventurers had successfully avoided the attack originating from underwater.

"*Shinbu Tousei!*"

Almost simultaneously, Mikoto finished her chant.

Its attack failed, their enemy was now fully exposed. This was a perfect opportunity.

But with astounding reaction time, the right head breathed a new screen of crimson mist. Ouka and the rest of the front guard scowled with frustration as the dragon donned its armor in the nick of time—but Lilly quietly issued her final command.

"Aim as far and as high as you can."

"Huh?" Mikoto muttered, but as she looked to where the prum was pointing, she heard ice cracking.

The noise came from directly above the floor boss.

From the cage-like root dome encircling them.

Mikoto guessed Lilly's intention and spoke the name of her spell.

"Futsu no Mitama!"

A sword made of deep purple light appeared, and concentric circles rippled outward from the Amphisbaena.

Mikoto had activated her gravity-controlling magic.

"UUUUUU..."

The gravity attack bearing down from overhead surrounded the Amphisbaena, but predictably, its armor-like mist weakened the impact. The most it could do was force the monster's neck down until it barely touched the water's surface. The field of gravity shaved away at the mist's density, but the dragon immediately breathed out more. The magic strike was not a lethal blow.

The floor boss shook its heads in apparent irritation.

"—GA?!"

Then, a series of fierce blows landed on the two heads. The rain of blows did not stop, continuously pouring down on the Amphisbaena without pause. Its mind went blank. There was no way for it to grasp what was happening.

"The colossal tree roots..."

"She brought them down with her gravity magic!"

The adventurers were watching the scene unfold from a distance. Ouka and Daphne were amazed.

The sword of light—a sign of the gravity being manipulated by Futsu no Mitama—had been deployed at its maximum range, appearing right by the root dome above the dragon's heads. In other words, the massive tree-cage overhead was within range of its power.

Pulled down by extreme gravity, the section of the root dome directly above the floor boss had collapsed in on itself.

The mist could only weaken incoming magic; it could not block a hail of tree roots. With the added force of the gravity, a mountain of roots measuring five meders wide hurtled down at the Amphisbaena.

"......?!"

One head of the immense floor boss was bludgeoned by massive amounts of debris. It was instantly stunned.

"You did it Li'l E!"

"Your turn now!!"

They were not the kind of adventurers who would let an opportunity like this slip by.

The dazed floor boss was like a sitting duck quietly floating on the water.

The attackers licked their chops at this ideal prey—an oversized, defenseless target.

Aim for the legs and bring it to the ground. That was standard practice when fighting floor bosses and other large-class monsters.

Lilly had done the opposite: *Aim for the head and bring it to the water.*

Welf and Aisha cheered their young commander, while Ouka and Daphne flew forward so they wouldn't miss their chance.

"UOOOOOOOOOOOOOOOOOOOOOOOOOOOOOOOOOOOO OOOOOOOO!!"

The instant Futsu no Mitama dissipated, Welf sliced, Ouka smashed, Daphne pierced, and Aisha shredded.

Dragon scales flew off under the onslaught of greatsword and battle-ax. Blood spurted from a shower of dagger thrusts, the blade working its way between scales. A hunk of flesh came away from one neck as the sharp edge of the *podao* bit deeply. Mikoto's sword and Chigusa's arrows joined the assault.

The huge body covered in countless large scales was injured, and the two necks suffered damage as well.

Not long after, the dragon recovered from its stunned state and roared in outrage at the all-out attack that the adventurers had launched.

"~~~~~~?!"

Its roar also served the dual purpose of summoning other monsters to the fight.

The adventurers jumped back from the thrashing dragon only moments ahead of multiple snake heads bursting out of the water.

"Aqua serpents!"

"And harpies, too?!"

"Looks like it called its friends!"

The long bodies of the aqua serpents emerged from the water between the ice-islands. The party cursed as a flock of harpies descended from above at the same time.

In all, six monsters had appeared.

The reinforcements were irritating opponents. But their number wasn't anything the party couldn't handle.

"We'll take care of these monsters first! Ms. Aisha and Ms. Daphne, distract the floor boss!"

Wasting no time being indecisive, Lilly directed the flow of the battle with her swift command.

Welf, Ouka, Mikoto, and Chigusa went after the monsters. Meanwhile, Aisha and Daphne distracted the dragon until the rest were exterminated.

"Dance!"

Just when she needed it most, Chigusa found herself on the receiving end of a level boost. When she and Mikoto looked up, they saw Haruhime moving on to the next part of the Kokonoe chant, plump beads of sweat rolling down her body. Mikoto's heart swelled to know her friend was supporting them, and she threw herself into a sword attack on the monsters.

"Push them back—!!"

The fierce clanging of sword attacks rang out, the song of the battlefield.

The adventurers wielded their weapons with all their might.

How strong these people are.

This was what Cassandra thought as she stared at the scene before her.

They keep on fighting…without giving in to the despair.

How brave they looked, their bodies covered in wounds and their cheeks bloody.

They fought with all their strength, not a single one cowering in fear.

I…

Cassandra couldn't do it.

Hopelessness was still wearing away at her heart. Terror had nested deep within her.

No matter what we do, it will happen again. It will happen again.

The words echoed incessantly in her ears.

She felt overwhelmed by her powerlessness to surmount the nightmare.

Even if she were to join the struggle, the world would push her off the peak of hope into the depths of the abyss. Terrified by the misery and heartbreak that would assail her when that happened, her hands and feet refused to move.

If this is the "cage of despair" then…does that mean this cavern where the floor boss appeared has already become the "coffin"…? We won't escape death in time…? It's no good, I can't think…

Some part of her heart wanted to ask a question: *Is it okay to give up on everything here and now?*

But just as if the wires connecting her mind and her physical body had been severed, her body refused to move as she willed it. She felt like she was watching a tragic play unfold.

Cassandra had left so many adventurers to their fates. She had offered them up as sacrifices to calamity. That, too, was a cancer that fed her resignation. *Shouldn't you pay for your sins with your own life?* her weak heart whispered to her.

She lost both her spirit and her will to fight.

Cassandra could not stand.

Cassandra could not face it.

"—Get it together!!"

"Ow!"

All of a sudden, something hit her on the side of the head and the world filled with stars.

"D-Daphne?!"

Her best friend was standing next to her with one hand clenched in a fist and her breathing ragged. The teary-eyed Cassandra was about to ask why Daphne was there, but she didn't have a chance.

"Pull! Yourself! Togetherrrrrrrrrrrrr!!"

She was interrupted by an intense demand. It was the most terrible yell Cassandra had ever heard. Haruhime, who was standing on the same shore, shook her tail in surprise at the furious voice.

A whimper escaped Cassandra's lips in spite of herself.

"You're a healer! What are you doing just standing here?! You guys in the rear are more important than anyone else in floor-boss fights! Do you think we can hold the line with you acting like this?! We don't even have enough people on the front line!"

In response to Cassandra's terror, Daphne went on a rant, her eyes bloodshot.

The sight of the healer neglecting her work apparently drove her mad, prompting her to leave the combat on the front and race over to bring down a hammer of righteous fury.

"And now I have to run all the way back over there! It's double the trouble! I didn't have time to spare in the first place!"

Cassandra leaned back to avoid the incensed Daphne. Then she noticed something.

Daphne was covered in wounds.

Red lines crisscrossed her arms and shoulders.

Her undine cloth was in tatters and her shoulders heaved as she breathed.

"Daphne…is this my fault…?"

"That's what I've been saying! Hurry up and get to work!"

Cassandra looked down, pale-faced, as she gripped the undine cloth wrapped around her. She didn't look up when she spoke.

"Why hasn't everyone given in to the despair?"

"Huh?"

"Aren't you all afraid of the despair that's going to swallow us whole?"

Cassandra knit her brows. She knew her real meaning wasn't getting across, but she asked anyway.

This was the Dungeon, the endless labyrinth. The fight she and her companions put up was nothing more than a speck of dust in comparison.

She was asking whether the embodiment of the Dungeon—the dragon that transformed hope into despair—failed to terrify them.

In response, Daphne, who already had a habit of glaring on a regular basis, glared even harder.

"Isn't it obvious just by looking at me?! Of course I'm afraid!"

"What?"

Daphne held out her arm, which was shaking even now. Then she continued ranting at the bewildered Cassandra.

"But I fight anyway! I fight to survive!"

She leaned forward, her voice full of determination.

"Despair sure is a convenient word, isn't it?! You know you might get in even more trouble if you try to fight! It's the best excuse for giving up instead!"

"?!"

"I was the same until a few minutes ago! But what choice do I have? Lilliluka and her friends stood up to fight, and I figured I wasn't ready to give up, either!"

No matter how difficult the struggle, Daphne wanted to return home alive.

Plus, in spite of herself, she had found a group of companions she was actually growing fond of, and she didn't want them to die. Her motives were as simple as that.

"You like them, too, don't you? It's hard not to like them, right?!"

"!!"

"So make yourself useful already! Heal someone! Protect someone! You're still alive and so am I! Don't let the word 'despair' beat you!"

Daphne's words were like a rousing slap to the face. She was telling Cassandra not to turn away from reality. It wasn't over yet.

Cassandra interpreted that to mean she shouldn't give in to the future that hadn't yet arrived, or to a prophecy that hadn't yet been realized.

Regardless of how hard or painful it was, she had to struggle with all her might until the very end. She had to because she was an adventurer, and adventurers never gave up on a challenge.

Yes! Even if despair awaits—

"—Look to the future! Rise up!"

Always.

Always, Daphne was spurring Cassandra forward. She didn't believe Cassandra's prophecies, but when Cassandra curled up in grief, she scolded her and pulled her back up.

Daphne was Cassandra's polar opposite, and Cassandra felt a combination of envy, curiosity, and admiration toward her. That was why she had become so attached to her. That was why she wanted to be her closest friend.

"…I…"

There was no time to waste—that is what Cassandra gleaned from Daphne's receding form as she rushed toward the battlefront once more. One look at her made it obvious she believed in Cassandra.

Still rooted in place, Cassandra gripped her crystal rod in both hands and pressed it to her forehead.

Just a little bit longer.

Just a little bit more.

She would keep resisting despair.

Cassandra had failed to save many lives. But those most important to her were still alive. She would do it again. She would challenge the tragic prophecy one more time.

"Heavenly light, once rejected. Merciful arms that save my shallow self."

Light shot up from her rod. The magic that was released sent out sparkling brilliance full of a warmth that banished the darkness.

"Lady Cassandra…!"

Haruhime, who had been watching the scene from the same shore, could not help smiling.

"Rescue my miserable companions in place of my words that cannot reach them. Oh sunlight, may you beat back ruin."

Chanting the spell with her eyes closed, Cassandra looked like a prayer maiden.

The prophetess of tragedy shunned by the world sang her song of resistance once more, and when she was done, she opened her eyes.

She set her sights on the central area where fighting had become most fierce. Summoning all her mental power and aiming as far as she could, she cast her magic.

"Soul light."

Sensing the spell sooner than anyone else, Daphne shouted.

"Recovery is coming! Everyone, gather around Ignis!"

Warm magical light poured down onto the ice-islands from the air. Ouka and the other fighters abandoned their positions and raced to a circular area measuring about ten meders across that had been illuminated.

In the blink of an eye, their bodies were fully healed.

"Yeeesss!"

"Ready to go again!"

Welf and Mikoto shouted with delight, energetically mowing down the monsters that flew toward them. Now that they had recovered from their exhaustion, their movements were as crisp as they had been at the start of the battle.

"I'm so sorry…so, so sorry! I'm rejoining the fight!"

Cassandra pressed her hands to her chest and shouted as loud as she could. Her words of atonement faded on the battlefield, which had reached a new level of ferocity. None of the fighters could even spare the breath to respond.

But she thought she caught a glimpse of Daphne smiling at her as she sliced through a monster that happened to cross her path.

"You've finally recovered! Ms. Cassandra, you really are slow!"

"I'm s-sorry!"

"I'm going to work you and Haruhime to the bone! Without you two, we won't be able to win!"

""U-Understood!!""

Lilly was her usual self—or rather, she was even more prickly than usual, which compelled Cassandra and Haruhime to answer sharply.

For some reason that made them both very happy, and they broke into grins.

"This is no time for smiles! We're changing location! The monsters have noticed us!"

""Yes, ma'am!""

The three members of the rear guard moved together to a different spot on the shore.

Though still embroiled in a pitched battle, the party was now at its very strongest.

"What do ye mean?! I demand an explanation!"

Dormul Bolster raised his voice. The dwarf, a member of *Magni Familia*, was in the eighteenth floor Under Resort, where he and his familia members were waiting. He leaned in closer to the adventurer who had collapsed before his eyes.

"I-I already told you, an Amphisbaena spawned in the Water Capital!"

"But there should still be half a month left before the next interval! Why would a floor boss appear now?!"

"No idea! We just heard about it from some guys who escaped the lower levels and came running back here like mad!"

The adventurers who had fled to the safety point of Rivira, the Dungeon's post town, were members of the hunting party pursuing Gale Wind. These particular underlings had been tasked with guarding the connecting passageways between floors to prevent the fugitive from escaping, on the orders of their leader Bors. After learning what was happening on the twenty-fifth floor, they had run a relay of sorts to get the information back to Rivira as quickly as possible.

"The guys who escaped from the twenty-fifth floor were half-crazy...! They said the Dungeon was 'crying' and the Great Falls were stained red...the only thing we know for sure is that there were a bunch of huge explosions and the labyrinth on that floor collapsed."

"Collapsed?! That stupidly gigantic maze?!"

Dormul stared in shock at the pale adventurer whose words had trailed off at the end.

The dwarves had suspected something strange was going on. Several hours earlier, they'd felt the ground shake. It hadn't been an earthquake, but more of an up-and-down motion that seemed to originate from the floors below.

"If the explosions caused the floor boss to ignore the interval... then what caused the explosions? Did Gale Wind and the main hunting party get into a flashy magic shoot-out or something?"

Next to the dumbfounded Dormul, the *Modi Familia* elf Luvis grimaced sternly as he swung his empty right sleeve.

There was no way Bors's underlings—who hadn't gone with the main party into the Water Capital and didn't know what Jura and Turk had done—could have a proper grasp of the whole situation. Of course, the same was true of Luvis, Dormul, and Dormul's familia. They had all stayed on the eighteenth floor.

They didn't even have any way of knowing that a calamity had caused a massacre.

"According to the guys who escaped, *Hestia Familia* was left behind in the cavern, with the floor boss..."

"What...?! Ye mean to say you lot abandoned them?!"

"Couldn't be helped! Who wouldn't run from a floor-boss fight when equipment and manpower are lacking?"

"And the monsters were acting weird! We heard them screaming all over, and just before we left, a pack of all sorts mixed together barreled right through the connecting passageway on the nineteenth floor that we were guarding!"

It seemed those monsters were headed for the Water Capital.

Dormul and Luvis fell silent as they listened to the adventurers relate this information. But everyone present had the same word at the back of their minds:

Irregular.

Something so extraordinary it made the affair with Gale Wind seem like a mere trifle was occurring in the Dungeon. Each of the experienced upper-class adventurers shared the same strong hunch.

"What do we do...? Send in support? Or return to the surface first and inform the Guild?"

"...Both. We can't do much if we don't know what's happening down there, and we can't find that out here in Rivira."

In contrast to the agitated Dormul, Luvis's response was wise as he assessed the situation.

Thanks to the hunting expedition, much of Rivira's population was away. Of the remaining upper-class adventurers, the members of *Magni* and *Modi* familias ranked highest. Bors's underlings waited for those familias to decide since their own minds had gone blank in the face of such an unprecedented situation.

"Above all, we must not abandon *Hestia Familia*! Shario, Alec, get your weapons!"

"Wait now, Luvis! What can yer bunch do in yer current state? We dwarves will go to Bell's party. Ye elves wait here!"

"Do you think a band of elves would desert those we are indebted to? Or are you saying we'd hold you back? You slow-footed dwarves are the real dead weight, I'd say!"

"Rubbish! Count on an elf to take my kindly words and twist them!"

The onlookers scrambled to end the budding argument between dwarves and elves that had broken out at exactly the wrong moment. But just then, another voice interrupted.

"What did you say about *Hestia Familia*?"

Everyone present froze at the sound of the strong voice that cut through their bickering like a sword.

"C-Cyclops?!"

"What's the captain of *Hephaistos Familia* doing here?!"

"What, a smith can't enter the Dungeon? Forget about that—just tell me what's going on!"

The smiling half-dwarf standing before them had dark skin and a patch over one eye.

Tsubaki had apparently arrived at that very moment in Rivira. Behind her were what looked like three female adventurers—two cat people and one human.

Luvis and his companions were curious about the newcomers, but as the first-tier, Level 5 High Smith had instructed, they shared what they knew of the situation.

"A floor boss, you say? And the twenty-fifth floor exploded? And on top of it all, monsters are acting strangely?"

"Look at us however you like, that's all we know!" Luvis snapped at Tsubaki, who was questioning him with a suspicious look on her face.

"What happened to Gale Wind, meow?"

One of the cat people had jumped into the conversation with no concern for propriety.

"Hey, who are you?"

"Just a curious cat this smith brought along. Now, answer my question."

The bewildered Luvis and Dormul examined what appeared to be Tsubaki's party once again. They were outfitted with lightweight equipment such as hooded robes and knuckledusters. They were in the Dungeon, after all, so their gear wasn't a particularly odd sight, but still, they seemed oddly *unlike adventurers*. Especially the human and the catgirl with the black fur. At the very least, they were unfamiliar faces in the middle-level base camp of Rivira.

It was ridiculous to use the phrase to describe adventurers in general, but these people didn't quite seem *respectable*.

I feel like I've seen this catgirl who just interrupted us somewhere before...

Luvis glanced at the one properly outfitted catgirl, who was wearing red-and-white battle clothes and carried a spear embossed in gold. She seemed familiar. But his train of thought was cut off by her impatient demand of "Tell me, meow!"

"Gale Wind hasn't yet been captured. We hear she's likely to be on the twenty-seventh floor, and that's where the elite hunters have headed...but to be honest, that's the least of their worries at this point."

"You're talking about what they call Irregular?"

"This place is a real monster's nest. Ah, I wish we could hurry up and get out into the sun again, meow!"

The human and the other catgirl reacted to Luvis's explanation as if it wasn't their concern. Just as Luvis and the others were wondering who the hell this motley crew was, Tsubaki interrupted.

"Right then, leave the twenty-fifth floor to us. We'll go take a look."

"Huh?! What's the meaning of this?!"

"Is there a problem? We're faster than you, so we're better suited to the job. All the more so because time is short. Plus...a former coworker I used to keep as a pet is with *Hestia Familia* now."

"W-wait! Hey!"

By the time Luvis and Dormul tried to stop them, Tsubaki and her party were already becoming distant specks. The adventurers watched in a daze as the four figures disappeared, leaving Rivira behind.

"Now we've done it. We're not in disguise like Lyu. Think they guessed we're bar waitresses?"

"In that sort of situation you ought to melt into the shadows, meow. If they don't remember your eyes and voice, you'll be okay, meow."

"I can't pull off assassin stuff like you can."

The party had crossed the marshlands on the eighteenth floor and emerged into a broad meadow. The catgirl Chloe, dressed in a hooded robe, and the human Runoa, wearing knuckledusters, chatted as the group advanced in a tight formation. Their casual voices were completely at odds with their superhuman speed.

They cut across the central zone of the eighteenth floor so fast the monsters lurking in the meadow didn't even notice them, and if they had, they wouldn't have been able to even come close to them.

"Man, are you still telling me you all are just a bunch of regular tavern waitresses or something? Alehouses sure must be mighty dangerous these days!"

"Well, it's not like we make a habit of partying with characters we don't know, meow..."

Still maintaining her speed, Tsubaki gave a childlike laugh. Chloe shot an indignant glance as she ran alongside her.

"You've never heard of The Benevolent Mistress? It's pretty famous."

"That's the place Mia runs, right? I'm always holed up in the workshop so I don't know about all that worldly stuff. I had no idea girls like you even existed! Forgive me, ha-ha-ha!"

"This lady sure is hard to work with, meow..."

These were the support troops Hestia had sent in. The party had been quickly thrown together in order to rescue Gale Wind and assist *Hestia Familia*. It was made up of the three bar waitresses Ahnya, Chloe, and Runoa, plus Tsubaki.

If someone in the know had seen them, however, their eyes would have bugged out at *the nearly first-tier party*.

"And what do you think about what that elf said, meow?"

Chloe glanced questioningly at Tsubaki.

"All I can say is, it's totally different from the story we heard before we left. I thought our job was to help Gale Wind escape if she'd been captured for something she didn't do."

The four of them had rushed into the Dungeon before they even finished introducing themselves. Chloe, Ahnya, and Runoa were there to rescue Lyu, whose life was at risk, while Tsubaki was there to lend a hand to Welf and his companions as they treaded a dangerous path. But now things were heading in an unexpected direction. Tsubaki knit her brows, sniffing something fishy.

"That's beside the point, meow! So what if we encounter monsters or adventurers get in our way? We'll blow them away and save Lyu, meow! Along with the white-haired boy and his party, too!"

Ahnya, who was running as fast as she could at the front of the pack, shouted back to Tsubaki. Her coworkers gazed at her as she twirled her long lance in one hand and ran like crazy, her battle clothes fluttering in the wind.

"Idiots sure have it easy, huh?"

"But we're the ones who have to clean up her messes when she dives in without thinking, meow."

"Ha-ha-ha-ha! I agree with that girl! The simpler the better!"

"Cyclops catches on quick, meow!"

Runoa, Chloe, Tsubaki, and Ahnya kept up the lively banter. Despite their relaxed, jovial tone, their speed hadn't reduced in the slightest. Every adventurer turned in surprise to stare as this strange group passed them by on the way to the Central Tree leading to the nineteenth floor.

The battle with the floor boss was a test of endurance.

The monster's massive, seemingly tireless body didn't even flinch in response to minor attacks. Even a concentrated barrage of magic—one of the keenest weapons available to adventurers—could not take the beast down in a single shot. As long as the levels of the adventurers involved were not overwhelmingly superior, fighting Amphisbaena tended to be a waiting game. Lilly's alliance party, made up of fewer than ten members, should have been at an insurmountable disadvantage.

But they were determined to overcome adversity. They were making an all-out effort to tip the scales and achieve victory.

"Hiyo!" the magic blade shrieked.

Welf—greatsword in his left hand and magic blade in his right—launched his attack. The supply of stable islands on the lake was dwindling, but now the bluish ice blade that had once made a certain first-tier dwarf moan transformed the lake into a field of ice for the second time. The floor boss was in the line of fire, and it turned its head at the flapping ice wings.

"HAAAAAAAAAAAAAAAA!!"

Naturally, the Amphisbaena offset the attack with its crimson mist.

But Welf's attack was so powerful the dragon was forced to use the mist as a shield rather than a suit of armor encasing its entire body. The dragon's irritation was evident as its right head roared at the young smith and breathed out more mist.

The floor boss's white body was marred by frostbite.

"Mr. Welf! The Amphisbaena is a water dragon, so ice magic blades won't affect it much! Please hold off on more of those attacks!"

"I know! …This blade is at its limit, too."

Welf glanced down at the weapon in his right hand. With a popping sound, a web of fissures sped through his magic blade Hiyo.

As she watched, Lilly realized time was running out; they had to up the intensity of the fight.

"Ms. Haruhime, support please! Ms. Cassandra, heal Ms. Aisha first and then focus on Ms. Mikoto and the others on the front line!"

"Grow. That power and that vessel. Breadth of wealth and breadth of wishes."

"Rescue my miserable companions in place of my words that cannot reach them."

Two chants seemed to melt together behind Lilly.

Haruhime and Cassandra had been supporting the front line by constantly casting spells. Without a magic user to provide artillery fire in their current party, these two unquestionably held the fate of the battle in their hands.

Haruhime in particular played a key role. She was already entering her third round of level boosts. Normally during battles she was mostly a tagalong, but now she was truly proving her worth. The adventurers were rapidly draining their magic potions, too—and that worried Lilly.

If this thing does what that Black Goliath does…I'll be mad enough to cry!

She couldn't help comparing the Irregular they'd fought in the past with their current foe.

When a Monster Rex was able to regenerate, it was a nightmare terrible enough to crush anyone's willpower. As a commander who incessantly yelled out orders to limit the damage they suffered, Lilly knew that better than anyone. The fight on the eighteenth floor had been truly hopeless.

But the water dragon she was looking at now didn't have that secret weapon. Or at least she didn't think it did. That would be unthinkable. Lilly offered a silent prayer as she continued to issue orders.

The Amphisbaena doesn't have a secret weapon. What's scary is the blue napalm. If it catches us with that, the situation will immediately take a turn for the worse.

The other person thinking furiously was Aisha.

This two-headed dragon's most terrifying weapon was its hellish flames that couldn't be stamped out, which made its attacks fatal. Allow a hand to catch fire and the only result would be tragedy. Welf and the others were taking extreme care to avoid the blue napalm, but the loss of even one fighter would undermine the entire front line.

Now how many vials of that fire-quenching potion did I pilfer from Asfi just in case…?

Several methods did exist for extinguishing the blue napalm flames.

The most well-known was the anti-napalm healing solution produced by Amid Teasanare, the Dea Saint of *Dian Cecht Familia* and the greatest healer in Orario. It was much sought-after for expeditions in the lower levels because it not only snuffed out flames, it also healed the skin they had burned. The item had contributed enormously to the efforts of upper-tier adventurers because it had opened the door for them to conquer the Amphisbaena.

What was less well-known was that Perseus had developed a similar magic item.

Asfi belonged to *Hermes Familia*, which lied about both its official level and the floors it had reached. The first time the captain of *Hermes Familia* laid eyes on Amphisbaena, she set about developing an antidote with the greatest trepidation.

Only members of *Hermes Familia* were permitted to use the secret

item. It didn't help with recovery, but it was universally acknowl-
edged to put out flames. Plus, unlike the anti-napalm heal, it could
be used to extinguish all sorts of other flames.

"Yah!"

"UUU...!"

The cavern had turned into an oven fueled by the wavering blue
flames, but Aisha ignored the sweat dripping off her as she lunged
at the Amphisbaena with her *podao*. Unable to hide its flagging
strength, the dragon swung its neck away to avoid taking serious
damage but writhed at the assault on its scales.

One more push and the balance would crumble. Aisha was sure
of it.

The effects of Haruhime's Uchide no Kozuchi last fifteen minutes at
most. The interval before she can activate her magic again is a little
over ten minutes...so if we can just get through the next ten minutes,
we can count on another level boost!

Aisha had looked after Haruhime when they were both prostitutes,
and they'd worked as a pair on the battlefield, too. She knew all there
was to know about the renart's magic. By cleverly manipulating the
length of the magic's effectiveness and the waiting interval, it was
possible to have an extra person fighting with a level boost for about
five minutes. The burden on Haruhime would increase, but this time
she'd simply have to push through.

Aisha glanced back at the shore. Despite the distance between
them, Haruhime sensed Aisha's gaze and nodded as if she understood her intention.

I like the look on her face these days.

Aisha smiled briefly at Haruhime's determined expression.

The girl who had once lamented the real world was nowhere to be
found.

Most of all, for me—

Then Ouka yelled.

"It dove in!"

The dragon had disappeared underwater again, sending up a wave
in its wake.

The threat of attacks coming from underwater would have sent a chill down the backs of most adventurers. But this party was different.

"Mikoto!"

"It's moving west! South…no, east! Lady Lilly, get out of the way!"

Thanks to Mikoto's Yatano Black Crow skill, they had the upper hand.

By moving quickly, Lilly was able to narrowly avoid a strike from the Amphisbaena, which had emerged exactly where Mikoto said it would. Several smaller monsters suffered the impact of the attack instead.

A figure sped across the landscape, timing its approach to the instant when the floor boss showed its face.

It was Mikoto, whose detection skill verged on premonition.

She drew her longsword, Shunsan.

Although it was hard to maneuver due to its great length, there was no better weapon for fighting a large-category enemy. The sword was also ideal for performing her special move.

Golden glimmers of light from the level boost swirled around the god of martial arts' disciple. She leaped forward, twisting her hips as she drew the sword.

"Zekka!"

Spirit and technique melded perfectly in the attack that burst from her scabbard. The blade sliced a dragon scale in half and tore deep into the neck of the floor boss's right head.

"OOOOOOOOOOOOOOOOOOOOOOOOOOOOOOOOOOOOOO OOOO!"

The Amphisbaena screamed as fresh blood rained down from the center of its neck. The blow was unquestionably fierce, and Welf cheered at the sight of it.

Yup, with Eternal † Shadow here, we can even head off those damn underwater attacks!

Mikoto was an all-rounder who fought in the vanguard and could detect as well as track enemies. She was bringing her full potential to bear in this battle.

The party had insanely powerful magic blades capable of not only devastating attacks, but even of creating terrain to stand on.

On top of that, they had Mikoto's detection skill.

Combined in the right way, those two assets gave a party of fewer than ten adventurers the upper hand in a water fight with an Amphisbaena.

Mikoto was as crucial to winning this battle as Haruhime.

We're so good we can even knock out the other monsters in our spare time!

Because the massive explosions had caused parts of the Dungeon to collapse, the monsters inside hadn't been able to reach the cavern. That, too, was a great advantage in this battle. Normally, part of the party would be occupied taking care of monsters other than the Monster Rex, but that wasn't the case now.

Aisha's *podao* sliced through an aqua serpent, bringing the number of visible monsters below five.

"Hey…do you think this might actually work?" asked Daphne, fighting back-to-back with Aisha. The Amazon nodded.

"Yeah. With these magic blades, it seems we can even win a fight in the cavern."

The wounded Amphisbaena was clearly drained. The proof lay in the fact that the blue napalm the dragon had been breathing out so fiercely in the early stages of the battle was now coming in ragged puffs.

At this point, a water dragon would normally have stopped fighting and hidden at the bottom of the lake until it recovered. From the adventurers' perspective, that would have been the worst possible outcome.

But from the dragon's perspective, the prey might escape in the meantime. In a real emergency, they could scale the cliffs leading to the twenty-fourth and twenty-sixth floors.

This floor boss had ignored the basic interval for its emergence, and it was also ignoring its ordinary behavioral patterns to prioritize slaughtering the intruders. At least, that's how it appeared to Aisha. As long as it was worrying about the possibility of their escape, it most likely wouldn't rest for long.

Lilly and the rest of the rear guard were moving constantly along the shore to avoid coming under attack as they supported Welf and the others who were maneuvering around on the icebergs. In an emergency, Lilly could use her own dagger-type magic blade to fend off the enemy. Meanwhile, Welf's group was intermittently launching assaults on the floor boss.

Everything was coming together in perfect harmony.

The wind was blowing in their favor.

This party, even with its scant number of fighters, could take down an Amphisbaena.

We can win.

Aisha was sure of it.

She was *too sure of it.*

This was the Dungeon. The endless labyrinth.

And she had forgotten that the Dungeon was anything but predictable.

"…"

Four bloodshot dragon eyes glared at the scene.

The accumulated damage…the lost blood…and worst of all, these inferior adventurers who had the nerve to oppose a dragon despite their puny stature.

Everything about the situation fueled the Amphisbaena's anger, until its huge body burned with rage.

"AAAAAAAAAAAAAAAAAAAAAAAAAAA!!"

"UOOOOOOOOOOOOOOOOOOOOOOOOOO!!"

Both heads roared at once. Then the dragon dove underwater.

Welf and Ouka shivered as its massive fin split the water, sending up a storm of droplets.

"Again?"

"Mikoto, we're counting on you!"

"Got it!"

She activated Yatano Black Crow. There was no way the massive underwater motion beneath her feet could escape her notice. She tracked the monster's direction and was about to relay the information to her companions—when suddenly she froze.

"......"

Time stood still for Aisha at the same moment.

The adventurer's instincts she had honed so well rang in alarm.

In the past, Aisha had always lured the Amphisbaena into more favorable terrain before fighting it, so she hadn't realized.

Indeed, none of the battle-hardened adventurers who had taken down the Amphisbaena in the past knew.

No one had seen what an Amphisbaena would do if they fought it in the cavern of the Great Falls and drove it into a corner.

They didn't know what irregular behavior it would use to annihilate its enemies.

It's heading for the waterfall—

The water dragon's track cut across Mikoto's detection net.

Without a backward glance toward the adventurers, it charged straight at the waterfall on the cavern's north side. It was moving *with the same terrific force it had when it ascended from the twenty-seventh floor to the twenty-fifth.*

An instant later, it shattered the ice and collided with the Great Falls, raising a massive spray of water.

Welf, Lilly, Haruhime, Ouka, Chigusa, Daphne, and Cassandra watched as the white form ascended the huge waterfall.

Only Mikoto and Aisha had managed to guess their enemy's intentions.

Even they were too late.

Having reached the top of the waterfall, the Amphisbaena *leaped into the air.*

"........."

The cavern went silent.

Even the roar of the waterfall ceased.

In this hushed world frozen in time, the adventurers saw the dragon dancing far overhead.

The wingless monster was floating in midair.

And then the terrifying roar of the falls broke through the frozen flow of time.

The Amphisbaena began to descend.

*   *   *

"UOOOOOOOOOOOOOOOOOOOOOOOOOOOOOOOOOOO
OOOOOOOOOOOOOOOOOOOOOOOOOOOOOOOOOOOO
OOOOOOOOOOOOOOOOOOOOOOOOOOOOOOOOOOOO!"

The moment Welf's scream ended, the floor boss plunged into the center of the lake.

The root dome exploded with an impact that seemed to shatter the earth itself.

Not only the twenty-fifth floor but the entire Water Capital shook as a mass of debris—incomparably more than what had fallen from the colossal tree earlier—hurtled to the ground.

The impact sent up a tsunami that overturned everything resembling an island of ice.

Aisha and everyone else who had narrowly escaped the dragon's body slam were thrown into the water.

As the tsunami reached the shore, it swept the rear guard up and threw them against the wall.

Even the blue flames that had been flickering on the shore and water were swallowed by the violent waves and drowned in the frothing water.

Like wine overflowing from a glass, emerald blue water poured into the twenty-sixth floor without slowing down.

The tremors opened an alarming lattice of cracks across the entire cavern.

"Ahhh—"

Mikoto was closest to the center of the floor boss's dive-bomb attack. It had clearly targeted her. Buffeted by aftershocks and chunks of ice, she fell through the water's surface and downward into a cerulean world.

Blood streamed from a head wound, tinting the water a hazy red.

Mikoto grew groggy.

As if to deal her a parting blow, her eyes delivered bad news.

A school of huge fish was rapidly approaching.

—*Raider fish!*

Unlike the aqua serpents, they could not emerge onto land. They jetted toward Mikoto as if they had been waiting for prey to fall into the water.

One bared its long, sharp fangs and sank them into her right shoulder.

Owwwwwwwwwwwwwwwwwwwwwwwwwwwwwwwwwwwwwww!!

Another latched onto her left arm, and a third bit at her right foot.

As the hideous monsters swarmed in an attempt to make a meal out of her, she felt as if they were violating her. Her tender body spurted blood, and even the undine cloth she wore seemed to cry out as it was shredded.

Her silent screams only came out as countless bubbles while her body sank with the throng of monsters to the bottom of the lake.

The last thing she saw was the massive stomach of the dragon rising toward the water's surface directly above her.

"Cough, cough! …Shit!"

Welf grabbed onto one of the few remaining islands and burst through the water with great force. He took a deep gulp of air, then spit out a stream of water and curses.

The cavern was a terrible sight.

The water was still as rough as a stormy sea, and its level had definitely fallen. The ice platforms had been broken into thousands of pieces that made it hard to tell that they were once used as bases for launching attacks on the floor boss. The root dome directly overhead was a wreck, a yawning skylight in its center. Even the four walls of the cavern were laced with cracks, as if they had been smashed by a meteorite.

The Dungeon had already been battered, but this was unprecedented damage. Ripples overlapped across the water's surface as countless crystal fragments continued to tumble down from the ceiling.

"Huff, huff…!"

"This is insane…!"

Daphne, Chigusa, and Ouka grabbed onto floating ice chunks and root fragments and popped their heads out of the water.

Every member of the party was torn up with bruises and cuts. Some had even lost their weapons.

"Ms. Cassandra…!"

"Uugh…!"

Those on the shore had suffered just as much.

Cassandra lay sprawled on the ground. A chunk of ice had collided with her back when she shielded Lilly and Haruhime. Lilly's backpack was hanging from a dripping wet crystal cluster.

The formation that the adventurers had so painstakingly built in pursuit of victory was utterly demolished.

"Mikoto…? Where's Mikoto?!"

Chigusa was the first to notice that one of their party was missing.

As Welf and the rest of the vanguard clambered onto one of the few remaining ice platforms—a large island that had been flipped upside down—Chigusa, now without her bow and arrow, peered back and forth.

"No way…Mikotooo?!"

No sound came in response to her shriek.

But Daphne saw a geyser of red bubbles stain the water's surface. She stood stock-still, her face twisting as she realized the fate Mikoto had met.

"OOOOOOOOOOOOOOOOOOOOOOOOOOOOOOOOOOO!!"

"This bastard…!"

At the same moment, the two-headed dragon burst through the water's surface, its eyes crazed.

From her perch on an ice chunk, Aisha hurled a stream of abuse at the beast.

The two heads mercilessly pursued the adventurers, their offensive line now broken.

The left head breathed out blue napalm.

"Ah?!"

"Moooove!"

As the adventurers leaped out of the way, the left head followed them, and soon the water was scored with blue flame. Their enemy wasn't really aiming. Aisha jumped from island to island, while Daphne dove headlong into the water.

In a berserking rage, the water dragon continued to shoot flames in every direction, as if it was intent on burning down everything in sight. Crystals melted as the searing waves swelled, and what little remaining air in the cavern thinned.

The moans of winged monsters filled the air. Though they tried to escape the swirling blue sparks by fleeing deeper into the labyrinth, chunks of crystal falling from the ceiling knocked them into the sea of blue flames.

The adventurers gripped their throats and shuddered.

Fire had spread to the wreckage of the root dome, creating a cage of flames.

The top floor of the Water Capital glowed blue.

And then the dragon shot a stream of blue flames at the northeastern shore where Lilly, Cassandra, and Haruhime stood.

"…"

Lilly had only just pulled Cassandra to her feet. She watched the flames race toward them. As the hot light illuminated their faces, they froze.

There was nowhere to run.

It was over.

Lilly and Cassandra were on the verge of succumbing to the azure death, when—

"Oh!"

A shock reverberated through their backs.

"Wha—?"

"Ms. Haruhi—?!"

Lilly's eyes met a pair of green eyes gazing back at her.

Cassandra shouted as the slender hands pushed her out of the way with the power of the powerless.

Not a second later, the renart disappeared behind a veil of flames.

"Ms. Haruhimeeeeeeeeeeeeeeeeeee?!"

A sea of flames covered the shore.

The hellfire swallowed Lilly's scream.

"—Haruhime."

From a distance, Aisha was witnessing a scene she had hoped never to see.

She ran to the northeastern shore as if drawn by an invisible force and then stood rooted to the ground before the fiery expanse.

She did not see Lilly sink to the ground from her knees, or Cassandra curl into a ball.

For the first time, the second-tier adventurer left herself exposed to attack. But it didn't even matter.

The two-headed dragon had already resolved to extinguish all life in the cavern.

"OOOOOOOOOOOOOOOOOOOOOOOOOOOOOOOOOOOO OOOOOO!!"

The wild stream of flames did not subside. They seethed like an act of the gods.

The remaining adventurers looked up at the dragon as its dual roar pealed.

"So this is the end…!"

Standing in the shallows where he had fled the flames, Ouka gripped his battle-ax, Kougou, in one hand.

Welf glared at the dragon as blue flames raged behind it, distress coloring his sweaty face.

Behind her bangs, tears streamed from Chigusa's eyes as she thought of her two friends now absent from the battlefield.

"…Mikotooooooooo! Haruhimeeeee!"

Ouka poured the emotions ravaging his chest into his cry, burning with anger.

Anger at the floor boss for committing such an atrocity. Angry with himself for not being able to protect them.

Within the mists of despair, this warrior who had lost his childhood friends burned with anger.

"Haruhime…that bastard's gonna pay!!"

So did Aisha.

With Lilly and Cassandra still sprawled on the ground beside her, she clenched her teeth and turned back toward the dragon.

As an ordinary woman, her clenched fists were trembling. But as an Amazon, her instincts refused to let her succumb to sorrow. She wouldn't allow herself to reveal any weakness by sobbing. In a sense, it was a type of desperation.

Plastering over the loss that gripped their chests with the anger they felt, the adventurers glared up at the floor boss.

Ouka and Aisha.

As they turned their eyes away from despair and threw themselves into a battle without hope of victory, each in their own way was thinking of the two lost girls. These thoughts coalesced into the will to die as heroes in battle—to take down the dragon even if they paid for it with their own lives. A hellfire as fierce as the blue flames consumed the two of them.

The fire of their tenacity.

And then…

"Descend from the heavens, seize the earth."

…a song…

"Grow."

Only they heard it.

"_____"

Only the man and woman who had not lost their will to fight heard the songs of the two girls echoing from the depths of the hellfire.

That's—

Ouka saw it.

As everyone else stood frozen, only he who held fast to his determination to fight till the end saw it.

Only he saw the band of light that ever so slightly blurred the water's surface, nearly hidden by the glow of the blue flames.

Only he saw the particles of light forming a silhouette among the swirling sparks.

A sword—

The next instant he dashed forward.

"—Smith, shooooooooooooooooooooooooooooooooooooot!!"

The enraged scream shook Welf's hands into motion.

As if the vision he glimpsed in the corner of his eye of Ouka sprinting forward spurred him on, or irritated him, or pushed him to compete, he gripped the hilt of his sword with both hands.

Stop ordering me around! I believe you.

Precisely because they always swore at each other and butted heads, Welf was able to act.

Precisely because he was Ouka's partner in crime, although he would never admit it, he was able to swing the blade.

"Hiyo!!"

A missile of ice shot forward.

The battle cry of the magic blade quenched the blue flames as it raced ahead, leaving countless icicles in its wake.

"HAAAAAAAAAAAAAAA!!"

The Amphisbaena interpreted this action as a threat. Its right head exhaled a powerful gust of crimson mist. A storm of billowing snow met a flood of mist. Azure battled crimson.

Welf squinted as more cracks spread through the magic blade.

Finally, the ice broke through the mist and froze part of the dragon's body. The dragon narrowed its eyes and prepared to unleash its counterattack of flames from the other head.

At that very moment…

"Shinbu Tousei!"

The spell rang out clearly.

"—"

"—"

It was a song they never should have heard.

A song of invitation that should have *echoed underwater* and vanished in bubbles.

Yet there was no question about what they heard.

Adventurers and dragon alike recognized the song.

The band of light on the water's surface became concentric circles imprisoning the dragon.

The particles of light hovering in the air fused together to form a deep purple sword of light that looming above its head.

The two-headed dragon was extremely wary of the magic blade. It breathed out mist to form a shield in front of it.

There was no armor of mist protecting the rest of its body.

The magic blade shattered with a loud crack and the mist vanished.

In the same instant, *she* roared.

"Futsu no Mitama!!"

The wavy underwater world reflected the scene that had taken place several minutes earlier, like the fragment of an illusion.

"Forgive my impudence as I beseech thee…"

The shoulder that monster fangs had sunk into was screaming.

The left arm missing a large chunk of flesh was shrieking.

The right leg that, even now, was on the verge of being pulled off was howling.

The wounds were deep. The bleeding wouldn't stop. Her consciousness kept flickering in and out.

Sinking to the bottom of the lake as monsters tore at her flesh, Mikoto could no longer fight.

And so she sang a prayer.

"I call upon the god, the destroyer of any and all, for guidance from the heavens. Grant this trivial body divine power beyond power…"

As her consciousness sank into darkness along with her body, the words faltered and became fragmented.

The only image remaining in the back of her mind was that of her companions.

"Saving, purifying light. Bring forth the evil-crushing blade!"

She sang a song of exorcism to sweep away evil and call upon the light.

"Bow to the blade of suppression, the mythical sword of subjugation."

A song to sweep away the poison of despair and call to the spirit-sword of the god of combat that would lead to freedom.

She sang to deliver this to her companions.

"I summon you here now, by name."

That was when it happened.

"Mikotoooooooo!"

A scream rippled the surface of the water, and she thought she heard the voice of Ouka calling her name.

And then the whole world glowed with white heat.

We haven't given up!

We won't give up!!!

Neither he nor I have given up yet!

That warrior who always fought with such courage!

That brave, strong man who fought on and on to protect his companions!

Still, still!!

Mikoto gritted her teeth.

With her one good arm, she lifted the best fist she could make.

"Descend from the heavens, seize the earth!"

She squinted as light returned to her eyes and then spit out a roiling stream of bubbles.

She was too groggy to properly guide her attack.

Underwater, she could not even see her enemy.

But if she aimed straight up, where that massive form hovered…

…She could *trap it.*

"Shinbu Tousei—"

Concentric circles formed at the bottom of the lake.

The raider fish grew uneasy as her magic flowed.

Mikoto roared toward the sword of light that had materialized above the water's surface.

*   *   *

"*—Futsu no Mitama!!*"

Receiving its grand order, the deep purple blade pierced the floor boss and deployed a field of gravity.

"~~~~~~
~~~~~~~~~~~~~~~~Aagh?!"

A tremendous force fell upon the Amphisbaena.

Because it had not been aware of Mikoto's underwater chanting, it never had a chance to evade sustaining a direct hit. And with its armor of mist gone, it had no way to fend off the gravity-controlling magic.

The force was so great it shattered the dragon's scales as it brought the two heads low, forcing its necks toward the water.

Even the center of the lake was drawn downward by the relentless pressure of the unnatural gravity.

"Gyaaaaaaaaaaaaaaaaaaaaaaaaaaaaaaaa?!"

Directly beneath the dragon, Mikoto, too, was crushed by the gravity she had created with her magic. An endless geyser of bubbles escaped her clenched teeth.

A human's fragile body would be destroyed by the spell long before it would affect the massive monster.

—Can't win.

It seemed like the world was caving in as her vision narrowed.

Her slender fingers snapped with a dull popping sound.

Her internal organs deformed and a film of blood escaped her lips.

But Mikoto did not attempt to deactivate her magic.

If I stake my life on it—it can't win!

Silently screaming her readiness to face death, she set her very life ablaze.

The overwhelming gravity pressed her body against the bottom of the lake where cracks were appearing one after another.

The raider fish were caught in the field of gravity along with Mikoto. Their eyes popped from their sockets and their flesh was crushed with an eerie sound. As one of the massive fish loosened its teeth from her right shoulder, she pushed her hand up against the gravity toward the water's surface as if she were reaching for victory.

"OOOOOOOOOOOOOOOOOOOOOOOOOOOOOOOOO!"

—I won't let it escape! No matter what, I won't let it get away!

Beyond the water's shimmering surface, Mikoto's bloodshot eyes caught sight of her enemy's form.

She believed in her companions who were outside this watery world.

In her heart, she held onto the image of her friend, the warrior who had called her name.

"UOOOOOOOOOOOOOOOOOOOOOOOOOOOOOOOOOOO!!"

He raced forward.

Crushing crystals underfoot, Ouka headed for the purple field of gravity in the center of the cavern.

"Mikoto, don't let goooooooooooooooooooooooooooooo!"

Ouka leaped onto the wreckage of the root dome.

The roots of the colossal tree were ragged from the multitude of assaults it had endured. Now blue flames were spreading along the lattice of wood, creating an ever-expanding tangle of fire. As the flames licked closer, they burned the intertwining layers of roots. But Ouka neither hesitated nor questioned his next move. Surrounded by swirling sparks, he charged ahead through the only opening.

He raced down the last remaining route, a single unburned root—and jumped.

As Welf stared in astonishment, Ouka swung his great battle-ax down and dove into the field of gravity.

"Gu—ooooooooooooooooooooooooooo!!"

The world blurred before Ouka's eyes as a monumental force pulled him downward. From his position directly above the dragon trapped within the gravity's field, he fell rapidly toward its body.

Even with the level boost, he did not have the strength to sever the Amphisbaena's heads. And so he borrowed the power of Mikoto's gravity-controlling magic and turned himself into a guillotine.

"!!"

The instant before Ouka executed his attack, a scene from the past flitted across his mind.

Mikoto and Chigusa were not the only ones to receive training from Takemikazuchi before the expedition. Ouka, too, had sought a new special move befitting Kougou, the battle-ax for which he had taken out a loan to buy from Welf.

In the dim predawn light, he had lain sprawled with arms and legs outstretched in the large courtyard, battered and exhausted.

Above him stood the martial arts deity who had hammered the battle skill into him.

It was simple yet perfect, a daring technique that required him to use every ounce of his powerful, huge form's potential.

Only Ouka could pull it off.

"If you use your skills at the right time with the correct breathing, you can become a set of fangs with the power that can slay even a dragon."

Ouka was sure those had been the god of combat's very words.

He whirled halfway around.

Fighting the pressure of gravity, he exhaled air from deep within in his lungs. Instantly it changed into sparks.

Like a set of all-engulfing fangs, Ouka unleashed his lethal move on the dragon's right head as he bore down on it.

"Kokuu! Devouring Tiger!"

His ax fell.

"—Gaa?!"

A roaring flash of silver light hurtled across the dragon's field of vision, pierced its scales, and split its flesh.

A fountain of blood sprayed out, blooming in the air.

The crimson-eyed head separated from the long neck.

At almost the same moment, the field of gravity vanished, its power spent.

"OOOOOOOOOOOOOOOOOOOOOOOOOOOOOOOOOOOOOO
OOOOOOOOOOOOOOOO!"

The adventurer fell, the dragon's remaining eyes bulged, and a massive icicle hurtled into the air.

Deprived of its other half, the left head roared.

This is—

Aisha heard it.

"That power and that vessel. Breadth of wealth and breadth of wishes."

Aisha had heard that chant more times than anyone else in the world, and only she was able to pick out the clear, beautiful voice that uttered it.

"Until the bell tolls, bring forth glory and illusion."

It was coming from the very center of the terrible ocean of flames.

Surrounded by those flames that returned all to ash—Haruhime sat and sang.

The Goliath Robe.

After the renart pushed Lilly and Cassandra out of the way but just before the blue napalm swallowed her up, she had thrown the robe over her body and dove facedown onto the ground.

It was the first and only tactical move ever executed by this magic user who didn't know how to fight. The robe was an indomitable wall that blocked not only blunt force trauma and piercing attacks but also lightning and wind; in the same vein, the floor boss's river of fire could not burn it.

—I feel like I'm going to burst into flames!

Still, the fatal blazing inferno was alive and well. The world of flames that incinerated people and monsters alike was truly hellish. The robe's wearer may have been protected from catching fire, but the supernatural heat hounded her without mercy, melting her consciousness like wax. The tongues of flame seemed to mock her as they licked at the exterior of the robe, sending rivulets of sweat down her beautiful white skin. She felt as if flames would erupt from her slender throat.

—No, no! It's fine even if I burn! Even if I turn to ash!

All the same, she sat cross-legged beneath the robe with her eyes closed and sang.

As long as this song rises from what remains and reaches them!

She poured all her remaining mental strength into the spell.

As she did, she envisioned the face of the woman she knew was waiting for her song.

"All you have to do is sing."

Several years earlier, Aisha had said those words to Haruhime during an *Ishtar Familia* expedition.

Although Haruhime had been to the deep levels, she knew almost nothing of the Dungeon's terrain. That was because the Amazons always stuffed her into a sturdy basket, shut her inside, and carried her along with them.

She was treated exactly like a weapon or an item.

The Berberas would take her out when they needed her and use her for their own ends.

In fact, they did not require Haruhime to do more than act like any other tool. There was no point in asking her for anything else.

"We don't expect anything else of you. Just focus on your singing."

All she could do during those battles was stand rooted in place while watching blood and flesh fly as tears filled her eyes. She could barely keep herself from fainting.

A cloistered noblewoman had no place in the brutal world of the Dungeon.

All she could do was chant. Urged to use the mysterious power hidden within her, her quivering lips had no choice but to utter the verses no matter what state her mind was in.

"Finish your chant even a second late and one of us dies. Here in the deep level, that's how it is."

It was a harsh fate.

The sturdy Amazons would fall one after the next, their limbs ruined. Even Phryne, a first-tier adventurer, was often wounded so badly she vomited blood. The powerless Haruhime was dragged to the battlefield, wanting nothing from it herself, then forced to take responsibility for the lives of others.

For an innocent girl who knew nothing of the world's violence and cruelty, it was a living nightmare.

It would be a lie to say she hadn't hated them.

"Well, I'm sure you must hate us.

"It's fine even if you let us to die."

That was all Aisha had said to her.

Her body half covered in blood, her eyes turned away, those were the words she tossed in Haruhime's direction.

"AAAAAAAAAAAAAAAAAAAAAAAAAAAAAAAAAAAA AAAAAAAAAAAAAAAAAAAAAAAAAAAAAAAAAAAvAAA AAAAAAAAAAAAAAAAAAA?!"

Its right head sliced off by Ouka's special move, the Amphisbaena was wild with rage.

As long as it still had one head left, the dragon would continue to go berserk. And now that the gravity field was no longer active, nothing restricted its movements anymore. Its remaining eyes were bloodshot from top to bottom. The left head opened its mouth so wide it seemed ready to split.

The blue light within its maw glowed brighter than ever before.

It had drawn up every last drop of dragon-bile propellant to unleash one enormous final blast of blue napalm.

Welf and Daphne attempted to follow up Ouka's attack and slice off the remaining head but they wouldn't make it in time.

This breath attack, powerful enough to immolate the entire cavern, would hit first.

Lilly and the others stared, still as statues, at the glow of impending destruction.

The symbol of obliteration was searing itself into the eyes of the adventurers.

And then.

Aisha took action.

Perhaps she acted out of instinct, or perhaps because she was guided by some greater force. But in the midst of the most extreme of extreme situations, when neither a mad rush nor a chanted spell could stop the insane flames, Aisha leaned forward.

Like a black panther crouching low as it gathered strength, she got into position for a charge.

"How could I ever choose to let you to die?"

Haruhime's voice as she answered Aisha was hoarse and damp with tears.

That was because she had no resolve, weak and timid creature that she was. She could not stand up to the heavy pressure of life.

But the people standing on that battlefield were people she wanted to save, even if she could.

I will sing until my body disappears from this world.

And so she pledged herself.

She sang and sang.

"Grow."

And after singing day after day after day, her spell had *gotten faster*.

"?!"

The heightened power of the magic astonished the prum.

The singing voice sent shivers down the spine of the healer who had used her own magic so many times.

The giant hammer of golden light that formed in the exact center of the sea of flames filled the dragon's eyes with shock.

As the spell sped up, it left the blue flames in the dust.

Accelerated casting.

The pinnacle of magic's basics.

Spells woven faster than the wind could rescue companions and bring the fortune of victory.

Haruhime could do nothing besides chant, but this was the one real skill she had cultivated over time. It was the one polished and refined ability that belonged to this magic user, who had been used so by others so much. After casting hundreds and even thousands of times, the speed of her casting—and that alone—surpassed that of upper-class magicians.

"*Confine divine offerings within this body. This golden light bestowed from above.*"

Haruhime's song raced through the cavern.

Throwing aside the safety she usually sought, she prioritized speed above all else, shaking off caution even if it meant she might cause an Ignis Fatuus.

Yes, all she was good for was casting.

If that were the case, then she would stake her very body and soul on casting faster than anyone in the world so that her spell would reach the brave adventurers.

"*Into the hammer and into the ground, may it bestow good fortune upon you!*"

She opened her eyes wide and saw the warrior woman, facing away from her as she stood before the sea of blue flames.

"*Grow!*"

In that same instant, Aisha—her body bent forward—took off running without a backward glance.

"Give it to me, Haruhimeeeeeeeeeeeeeeeeeeeeeeeeeeeeeeeeeeeeeeeeeeeeee!!"

As Aisha roared her request, the hammer of light fell upon her.

"*Uchide no Kozuchi!*"

The spark ran toward Aisha, igniting a great burst of light particles.

Imbued with the glow of the level boost, the Amazon roared and shot forward at a speed that stretched the boundaries of what was possible. Her tawny body had become an arrow of golden light.

Kicking up crystals like they were gravel, she bore a hole through the dancing sparks. As the dragon filled its lungs with blue flames, she took aim at its eye.

"—"

Wild with fury, the dragon finally realized its error.

Normally, as the left head prepared its fiery attack, the right head fended off enemies. But now the right head was gone. Nothing remained to protect the left head.

The Amazon charged like a lunatic.

Her speed and the distance she covered would have been impossible for a Level 4, but not for a Level 5.

There was a way.

A single path led across the lake.

A towering bridge of ice, laid down by Hiyo at the price of the magic blade's complete disintegration.

"Ooooooooooooooooooooooooooooooooooooooooooooooooo ooo!!"

"AAAAAAAAAAAAAAAAAAAAAAAAAAAAAAAAAAAAAAA AAAAAAAAAA?!"

The roars of the adventurer and the dragon layered atop each other.

Intent on incinerating the warrior woman and the rest of the cavern along with her, the dragon prepared to release the fiery breath. It had reached the critical point within its throat.

But the combined light of Aisha and Haruhime was swifter.

A flash.

Aisha leaped into the air, a brilliant comet's tail slanting upward past the center of the floor boss's neck.

One of the enormous scales shattered, exploding outward. Aisha's blade tore deep into the flesh of the thick neck underneath.

An instant later, the propellant that had built up in the dragon's throat and mouth erupted from the wound she had opened.

"~~~~~~ Aaagh?!"

Like a broken water main, the blue napalm gushed out and caught fire.

Burning in its own flames, the Amphisbaena writhed as if it had fallen into purgatory. Worse than misfiring, the extra-large blast of dragon breath had set off a massive explosion. The floor boss screamed as its flowing gushing fed the flames.

"Come, reckless conqueror!"

Aisha did not stop.

"Oh brave warrior, oh strong hero, oh covetous, cruel champion."

The moment she rebounded onto an ice chunk floating in the lake, she took off running again and leaned into the Amphisbaena a second time. She attacked the dragon with a torrent of swift, wild slices to prevent it from escaping into the water, even as she intoned her concurrent chant.

"Prove your desire for the queen's girdle."

She kicked off one of the huge icicles formed by Hiyo, kept moving, and flew at the floor boss with a freedom and speed that rendered her invisible to Welf and the others watching from the shore.

All they could see was a path of golden specks trailing behind her. This was a war dance truly worthy of the name Antianeira. She answered the water dragon's moans with the final words of her chant:

"My famished blade is Hippolyta!"

An epic leap.

She flew into the air directly above the burning body of the dragon. As she descended toward her enemy's trunk, where its core was buried, she lifted her *podao*. Then, with all the power she and Haruhime could muster, she swung it down.

"Hell Kaios!!"

The *podao* struck the dragon's body, discharging magical glittering light.

The sword strike's crimson wave landed squarely on the monster's body, ripping into its flesh and burrowing deep inside. Forging its way through the river of dragon blood, it reached the large, deep-purple crystal buried within and shattered it.

"_____?!"

Its magic stone destroyed, the Amphisbaena's form disintegrated and a riot of azure flames bloomed.

Ash erupted as the remaining blue napalm detonated.

The cavern thundered with the powerful explosion. For an instant, everything was engulfed by the flash of heat.

As she watched this scene from within the sea of flames, the ren-art smiled faintly and collapsed facedown onto the ground.

"Ms. Aisha?!"

The moment the flash ended, Lilly—who had thrown her slender arms over her face and curled into a ball to avoid being blown backward by the explosion—shouted the Amazon's name.

In the blizzard of ash, where flying fragments of drop items and purple crystal drew parabolas in the air among countless hovering sparks, she had glimpsed Aisha falling into the lake.

When an adventurer chose to carry out an extreme close-range attack, there was no way to avoid getting caught in the aftermath. Lilly and the others who watched Aisha conduct her assault stood pale and silent with fear...but before long, the warrior broke through the water's surface, her long hair dripping.

"..."

As her beautiful limbs and bare coppery skin came into view, they saw that she was covered in burns. Still, given the scale of the explosion she had weathered, the gleam in her eyes was surprisingly bright. She walked slowly through the shallows, particles of light still coating and protecting her body.

Embers of lit blue napalm flickered on one arm, and she was dragging her *podao* behind her through the water; the palm of her hand was stuck to its hilt.

The onlookers snapped out of their daze and ran to her, but she brushed them off and headed straight toward the sea of flames that engulfed the shore.

"Haruhime..."

With her left hand, she pulled out a vial of Perseus's fire-quenching potion, ripped off the cap, and poured it over the flames on her other arm. Smoke billowed as the item did its work. She used the rest of the potion to subdue the fire directly in front of her before walking into the weakened flames. From above, it must have looked like a rut was being drawn through the wild sea of fire.

Aisha arrived in front of Haruhime, who lay facedown under her fireproof robe, and cradled the renart in her arms.

"...Aisha..."

"You've mastered it, haven't you...my dumb little fox."

Aisha smiled down at the girl. Haruhime's eyelids fluttered open as she lay in Aisha's embrace. Filled with joy, she smiled weakly and rested her head limply against Aisha's chest.

The pair returned along the path Aisha had used earlier and were greeted with tears of joy by Lilly and Cassandra. Although the Goliath Robe had absorbed so much heat that it burned both of Aisha's arms, for the moment she hardly even felt it.

"You saved me, Haruhime..."

The renart had closed her eyes again, but she still heard the words Aisha whispered into her ear, like an older sister celebrating how much her younger sister had grown.

"Mikoto! Ouka!"

Meanwhile, Chigusa had crossed the iceberg to the epicenter of the Amphisbaena explosion and dove into the water, which was now thick with ash. Using the site of the gravity spell to guide her, she had set out to rescue the two missing adventurers.

She quickly found Ouka and Mikoto, who had wounds all over her body, and pulled them to shore. Then she ran over to Cassandra.

"Hey! This is crazy, I mean it *was* crazy, but are you okay?!"

Meanwhile, Welf was lending a hand to Ouka.

"Grab my hand, big guy!"

Flames still flickered here and there in the cavern, so the adventurers gathered on a piece of ice in the center of the lake.

"Everyone's alive..."

"We brought down the floor boss all by ourselves!"

Casandra and Lilly couldn't contain their happiness as they set about using their remaining items to heal the rest of the party.

Mikoto had deep wounds on her shoulder, arm, and leg, and all her bones had been broken by the gravity spell. Her eyes were closed and she was unconscious but breathing. Haruhime had suffered a Mind Down and was barely aware of her surroundings. As for Aisha, she might have used the fire-quencher and other potions, but her Level 4 toughness was on full display given how she was still able to stand on her own two feet.

"It's too soon to celebrate…but you guys did well."

They had beaten the floor boss by the narrowest of margins, and Aisha's praise was genuine. As if to give shape to the adventurers' outstanding achievement, some Amphisbaena bile, a valuable drop item, washed up on the ice float. Welf and the others smiled at Lilly as she began to collect some as soon as her sharp eyes noticed it.

The group was on the verge of giving a collective shout of victory when a loud bang interrupted them.

"‼"

The Dungeon had not given them so much as a moment to bask in the warm afterglow of victory before rearing its head once again.

"What's that?"

"The floor is swaying…?‼"

As Welf and Chigusa cried out in confusion, the floor began to crumble with an ear-piercing screech.

First there had been the explosion so massive it demolished a section of the labyrinth, and then the fall of the root dome followed by the Amphisbaena's dive, and finally the barrage of blue napalm. The cavern simply had not been able to withstand the savage battle, and now it began to disintegrate in earnest.

"Hey, doesn't this seem bad?!"

This was the Dungeon's angry howl, or perhaps its sorrowful cry. In either case, massive clumps of crystal began to fall from the ceiling with terrible crashing sounds, raising waves in the plunge pool wherever they landed. The pale-faced, panicked adventurers used their weapons to bat away this atrocious downpour.

"Ahhhhhhhhhhhhhhhhhhh!"

The scream did not belong to anyone in their party. When they turned around, they saw a party of four adventurers standing on the crystal bridge that skimmed the top of the Great Falls on the north-western side of the cavern, where it connected with the maze inside the cliff.

One was a werewolf. It was Turk, the very same adventurer who had fanned the flames that kindled the hunt for Gale Wind in Rivira. He was also the ringleader of the plan to blow up the twenty-fifth floor.

"You lied to us, Juraaaaaa!! We never knew it would turn out like this!"

"Those idiots…!"

The band of four must have escaped the devastation that had destroyed an entire part of the Dungeon and managed to reach this cavern. Aisha found it galling to have to watch the people who were responsible for causing this terrible situation incoherently complaining about it.

Seized by terror, the four adventurers flew down the crystal bridge in a haphazard attempt to flee.

They landed high above Aisha and the others, onto the root dome that still capped much of the cavern. Although the blue napalm fire had already spread there, Turk led the fleeing adventurers onto it without thinking. When some of the flames spread to the backpack of one of them, the wearer burst into a ball of fire, screaming until death came.

"I don't wanna die, I don't wanna die!! I sure as hell don't wanna die here!!"

Dripping with what could have been either tears or sweat, encircled by smoke and flames yet still clinging fiercely to life, the band of minor villains made it to the cliff on the west side of the cavern and began crawling up it.

Ironically, this scene helped Aisha's party discover a way out.

"They crossed over the roots of the colossal tree…! Does that mean we can use the connecting passageway now?!"

Generally speaking, ascending or descending the towering crystal cliff was not a realistic option even for first-tier adventurers. But at the moment, because of the dome, climbing up the cliff face was relatively easy. If they scaled the height and emerged onto the path leading along its edge, they would be able to escape from the passageway on the southern tip of the floor.

This was the sole signpost pointing toward a way out of the crumbling cavern.

"We can't exactly afford to be picky right now…! If we stay here, we'll be buried by crystal debris!"

At best, their chances of climbing the cliff with the injured members of the party on their backs was fifty-fifty.

The only route left across the still-burning dome was on its south side. Seeing how the flames advanced toward their exit route by the second, Aisha screamed for them to withdraw.

"Let's get out of here! Climb the western cliff!"

"Wait!! Mr. Bell is still somewhere below us!"

It was Lilly who protested.

Her small finger was pointing to the southeastern cliff—in other words, to the precipice that rimmed the Great Falls and led to the twenty-sixth floor. She was suggesting they could still enter the maze by descending that sheer wall.

"I'm against it, too. We've gotta rescue Bell before we split!"

"I understand how you feel…but…!"

"In this condition, Mikoto and Haruhime…!"

Welf had weighed in on Lilly's side, only to be countered by Ouka and Chigusa.

As Chigusa supported her childhood friend, who was limp as a corpse and still hadn't opened her eyes, she held back tears.

"You guys…! Are you idiots?! Look at our situation!"

Due to her position and experience, Aisha's words carried more weight than those of anyone else in the group. Now she shouted back at Lilly and the others, her face contorted with distress.

Like Ouka and Chigusa, she had no desire to abandon Bell. In fact, she wanted more than anything to rescue this male who had caught her fancy. But with the party in its current condition, immediately after a fight-to-the-death with a floor boss, Lilly's proposal was suicidal. Mikoto and Haruhime could no longer fight. Most of their weapons and items were broken or used up. They were in no state whatsoever to go searching for a missing companion.

Above all, Aisha was thinking of the renart still cradled in her arms.

As Aisha weighed the girl against the boy and was about to tilt the scale toward the girl, a weak hand reached up from her arms and stopped her.

"Lady…Aisha…please…forget about me, just…!"

"…!"

"Please, help Sir Bell…!"

Aisha bit her lip as she looked down at Haruhime fighting so hard to cling to consciousness.

"We cannot abandon Mr. Bell!"

"But if we stay on this floor…!"

Lilly, Welf, and Haruhime wanted to stay behind.

Aisha, Ouka, and Chigusa wanted to pull out.

The party was split.

Everyone has lost their cool. Even Lilliluka and Antianeira!

Daphne stood in the middle of these two extremes.

Her heart pounding and sweat dripping down her face, she forced herself to remain objective. Only she, who still didn't know Bell and his familia very well, could do so.

Staying here is impossible! This is insane! We have to get out immediately!

Naturally, she came down on the side of retreat. It was a no-brainer.

Given the supremely irregular situation that left the floor itself on the verge of crumbling, remaining in this part of the Dungeon was out of the question.

I'm sure this is the only floor that's going to crumble. The twenty-seventh floor is two floors down! It should be fine! Bell Cranell of all people should have a good chance of surviving…!

She didn't really believe that, but Daphne used this rationalization to put the safety of the party first.

That was the job of the commander, and that was the responsibility that now fell on the shoulders of Daphne Laulos.

Opinions are split three to three. If I cast my vote in favor of retreat, things will tip in that direction!

Daphne knew that in a tight fix, the weight of the majority was decisive.

She would make sure the concern Lilly and Welf felt for their familia member didn't lead them in the wrong decision.

With a resolve tinged by unease, Daphne prepared to speak.

"The cage of despair...shall become a coffin...tormenting thyself..."

However, a string of disjointed words spoken by the girl standing next to her stopped Daphne in her tracks.

"The colossal tree is on fire, the floor is crumbling...the cage of despair has become a coffin...is this place, this situation what 'tormenting thyself' means?"

Everyone stared at her.

As the unending rain of crystals beat down on her and the light of the blue flames illuminated her face, the girl continued to mutter her soliloquy.

"...Cassan...dra?"

Her upturned eyes did not see the present world.

She was staring at another place, at events happening in another time, as if she was being guided toward something.

"Now is the time of prophecy. This is the crossroads, the fork in the road, the place where fate diverges—"

Daphne's gaze was fixed on Cassandra, who had gone into a trance like a shrine maiden receiving an oracle.

The coffin is a symbol of death. But if I still have time to be tormented, then that's the same as saying a death-filled future isn't inevitable yet. On the other hand, if we make the wrong decision after being tormented, the prophecy will consume my life.

Meanwhile, Cassandra had sunk deep into her own thoughts.

The seventeen lines of the prophecy floated in a sea at the bottom of her heart. As the prayer that went by the name of a nightmare shifted with dizzying speed, her perception of time stretched to its limit.

In a world cut off from her surroundings, the prophetess of tragedy drowned in a sea of verse as she tried to grasp the true meaning of the oracle.

In other words, the thing tormenting me right now in this "coffin"—is the decision itself?

This was the action Cassandra must take. It would determine the future of the party.

Certainly, two choices had split the party: remaining or retreating.

Cassandra knew the group's decision would determine their fate.

Do not forget. Seek naught but the light of the reviving sun.

Gather the fragments, consecrate the flame, beseech the sun's light.

Take heed. Such is the banquet of calamity...

Reviewing their situation, it was clear they had already plunged into the fourteenth line, given the coffin reference. That left the last three lines of the prophecy.

The seventeenth line is simply a conclusion wrapping everything up, so I'll ignore that for now. But there's no question the other two lines are a warning to avoid annihilation!

The line beginning with "Gather" clearly didn't match their current predicament of choosing between two alternatives, so she set that aside as well.

That meant she had to minutely scrutinize the line telling her to "seek naught but the light of the reviving sun."

Does "light" mean...hope? And I'm supposed to choose the option that relates to "the reviving sun"? But what is "the sun"? Where is this thing "the sun" represents? There is no "sun" in the Dungeon!!

I don't know, I don't know, I don't know!

What should she choose? What should guide her decision?

What do I even want?

I don't want these people to die.

I want to go where he is.

Without letting anyone die, I want to go to whatever horrible place he's been forced to go.

As the static of her emotions cut into her thought process, Cassandra stood before the two choices confronting her.

Retreat or remain?

The twenty-fourth floor or the twenty-sixth?

Up or down?

The path along the cliff on the west side, or the sheer precipice to the east?

"_____"

Suddenly, a jolt of electricity shot through Cassandra's body.

The light they sought…was that the single choice that would leave them alive?

The reviving sun…there was no one and nothing here on this watery floor that represented the sun.

Did that mean it wasn't something she could see with her eyes? Not a person? Not even a physical object?

A suggestion, an abstraction, an allegory.

A metaphor.

The reviving sun…the sun disappearing and then appearing again, so the sunset *and—*

Cassandra turned around as if she'd been stung, and that's when she saw it.

The connecting passageway to the twenty-sixth floor, on the *southeast side.*

The cave that should have been destroyed by the root cage.

Repeated shocks had deformed the terrain to the point that now, between the root and the ground, a *gap just large enough for a person to squeeze through had opened.*

"—Oh."

The light flickered.

Everything before her eyes blinked in and out like sparks.

The pieces of the prophecy clicked together with an audible sound in her mind.

The light of hope that would allow them to escape despair and destruction had been delivered into her hands.

"To the east!!"

The moment she arrived at her conclusion, Cassandra screamed it out.

"Huh?"

"Everyone, go east! To the twenty-sixth floor, quick!!"

She tried to urge on the startled party. She had thrown concern for appearances to the wind and was shouting wildly, which threw everyone into confusion.

"Cassandra?! What are you sayi—?"

Daphne, her face pale, attempted to stop her reckless friend, only to be interrupted.

"I was wrong, Daphne! I was wrong!! The prophecy wasn't talking about a person or a time!"

"?!"

"The 'reviving sun' represents a direction! I'd been misinterpreting the words all along!"

The oracle of tragedy interrupted Daphne with more revelations about her prophetic dream.

During their time on the twenty-first floor, Cassandra had tried to deduce the meaning of the line before. She'd guessed that the warning had something to do with things or people related to Apollo, or that the sun might have even represented daytime.

But she had been wrong.

The "reviving sun" was a metaphor for the sunrise, which was essentially the disappearance of the sun at night and its reappearance in the morning. The prophecy was actually referencing the direction from which the sun rose.

"This floor has already changed from a 'cage of despair' into a 'coffin'! The only way for us to escape the foretold death is to go east, toward the reviving sun!"

When she thought about it, her mistake was really quite simple.

She used to be a member of *Apollo Familia*, so it was only natural that her old patron deity had come to mind, and that had restricted her thinking, blinding her to the possibilities. She'd made things unnecessarily complicated.

Only when presented with the two choices of the western and eastern routes did she finally comprehend the verse.

"I still don't know what the 'sun's light' is supposed to mean! And I have no idea what the 'fragments' to collect are, or how to consecrate the 'flame'! But going east is our only choice! Hurry everyone, head to the twenty-sixth floor!!"

Cassandra had understood at last, but...

"What are you talking about?! And at a time like this!"

Daphne snapped angrily at her. *She didn't believe her.*

"Stop talking nonsense! Drop it already!!"

Cassandra's heart cracked when she saw how her friend glared at her. To Daphne and the others, Cassandra's desperate plea seemed like nothing more than a string of illogical words. Disorganized, incoherent rambling.

No one believed what she said—this was the curse of the prophetess of tragedy.

Doubt fills the eyes of her companions.

The world twisted in on itself, changed shape, then shrieked and jeered at Cassandra.

She felt as if her teary eyes were going to burst into pieces and her knees were about to give out.

It's always the same.

No matter what I do, it's always the same.

No matter what I say, no one listens.

No matter how I beg, my pleas never reach anyone.

It's always the same.

The world always tramples on my hard work.

The world always jeers at my tragedies.

Even when I gather my courage and struggle, even if I scream at the top of my lungs, I always bump up against absurdity.

So many times, my desperate warnings have ended with inaction.
So many times, my determination has crumbled like a sand castle.
I have tasted defeat again and again.
Time after time, I have been hurled from the cliff's edge into the very depths of darkness.
But what can I do? I must be cursed.
What can I do, what can I do…what can I do?

………Is that really true?

When did those words begin to invade my heart? When did I become so discouraged?
When did I start feeling this tinge of resignation? When did I start to lie?
When did I stop fighting?
When did even I stop believing everything and anything? When did I fall into despair?
Have I truly reached the point where I will even look away from my closest friend as she stands here in front of me?!
It's always Daphne who breaks my heart.
And then—

"Don't let the word 'despair' beat you!"
"Look to the future! Rise up!"

It's always Daphne's words that give me courage!
The light in the altar of her heart began to glow.

Concealing the words that repeated themselves in her heart, she returned her friend's penetrating gaze and faced the mocking world.

Cassandra clenched her fists and shouted.

"Listen to me, Daphne!"

"‼"

She leaned toward the stunned Daphne, focusing only on her as she screamed her next words.

"I'd given up! No one ever believed me in the past, so I assumed no one would believe me in the future, either!"

Pressing her right hand to her chest, she laid bare her true feelings.

The rejection, shock, and despair that had plunged her to a pit of dejection. Reliving all those memories of the past was pure pain for Cassandra.

"I was always afraid! I was in agony! I was sad and I didn't want to be hurt anymore!"

But still the words kept coming.

"I was scared and I never said what was really important!"

When Bell appeared before her, she felt like she had been saved.

She had stayed by his side, whispering into his ear, living in the fantasy that he accepted and believed her.

But that had merely been dependency.

She hadn't done anything.

Not once had she truly stood up to the world that imposed tragedy. She had never sincerely confronted the curse of prophecy that dwelled within her.

She had never genuinely tried to speak *those* words.

"I don't care if this is the only time you ever listen to one of my dreams! Just listen!!"

Don't give in to despair.

Resist the curse that's trying to rip us all apart.

Don't give in to the weak self that is terrified of rejection and despair.

"Daphne, believe in me!"

The power of her words reverberated through the crumbling cavern.

Her outstretched hands grasped Daphne's right hand and squeezed it as if in an embrace.

Their eyes met.

Cassandra's eyes gleamed with her ardent plea. Daphne's wavered like a rippling pool of water.

For a brief moment, their hearts were one.

And then…

"…You can't expect me to actually believe your dream!"

Daphne forcefully shook off Cassandra's hands.

Cassandra's teary eyes opened wide as they filled with more despair than ever before.

—Then Daphne continued.

"Everyone! To the east!!"

She had announced her decision.

Turning toward the surprised adventurers, she sided with those who wanted to hold out.

"...Huh?"

Then she turned back toward the dazed Cassandra.

"I don't believe in your silly dreams!"

Daphne pouted, her cheeks bright red. Then she stuck her pointer finger toward the other girl and yelled at the top of her lungs.

"What I believe in is Cassandra Illion!"

Daphne hadn't believed in the prophecy.

She had believed in her friend.

It only took Cassandra a second to understand what she was saying. But it was a very long second.

Fresh tears spilled from her eyes.

Blushing, Daphne grabbed her friend's right hand and took off running.

Cassandra held tight to Daphne's hot palm.

"Quick! Hurry!!"

Daphne shouted as she ran with Cassandra toward the eastern passage. The rest of the party followed on reflex. They accepted her choice because her vote had tipped the scales.

"Run! Ruuuuuuuuuuuuuuuuuuuuuuuuuuuuuuuuuuuuuuuuuuuuuuun!!"

The roar of the crumbling floor drowned out the scream coming from Aisha, who was bringing up the rear.

A torrential downpour of massive crystal chunks pursued the adventurers as they leaped from one ice-island to the next. With a crash, the burning root dome collapsed into the lake.

The singing of wild waves, the dancing of blue flames, and a chorus of demise. Turning away from the Dungeon's requiem, Daphne and the rest of the party cut across the cavern and raced down the eastern shore.

Their destination was the passageway connecting to the twenty-sixth floor.

Reaching the tiny gap that had appeared between the root and the ground, they dove into it one by one.

"~~~~~~?!"

An instant later, the entire cavern caved in on itself with a terrific roar.

The plunge pool was obliterated by the wreckage of crystals thundering into it. Inside the cave, the adventurers were blown back by the backdraft.

"Gyaaaaaaaaaaaaaaaaaaaaaaaaaaaaaaaaaaaaaaaaaaaaaaaaaaaaaaaaaaa aaaaaaa?!"

In the middle of it all, Turk and his companions—who had chosen the western route—were caught in the collapsing debris and fell from the crumbling cliff face.

Not a soul was left to attend to them. They were cruelly crushed beneath the avalanche of crystals, forced to pay the ultimate price for their destruction of the Dungeon.

"Whew…we made it…"

"If we had tried to go back to the twenty-fourth floor…"

Lilly and Chigusa were panting and pale as they stood up. When they looked back at the cave connecting to the twenty-fifth floor, it was already half crushed, the passage completely blocked off.

"Daphneeeeeeeeeeeeeee!!"

"Stop hugging me! This isn't over yet."

Surrounded by her companions who had so narrowly escaped death, Cassandra was wailing and clinging to Daphne, her cheek pressed to her friend's as they crouched side by side. Daphne blushed as she struggled to peel Cassandra off.

"Thank you, thank you…! You believed me…!"

She wrapped both arms around Daphne's neck like a baby, sobbing and smiling at the same time. She couldn't help but weep tears of joy now that her friend had finally believed in her.

Perhaps out of embarrassment, Daphne pouted.

"All right, enough fussing, you two! Stand up! They're coming!"

The sharp reprimand came from Aisha as she ran past them. The pair looked up and saw a horde of monsters racing toward them from the path straight ahead that split off toward the twenty-sixth floor. *Still alive, are you? We won't let you get much farther,* they seemed to be saying.

"Bad luck always brings friends…!"

"Stop babbling, big guy! Now that we've come this far, we're absolutely going to reach Bell for sure!"

Ouka held up the battered Kougou, and Welf stood ready at his side with a spare magic blade. Daphne and Cassandra leaped up as well. Without even having time to fully relish the fact that they were still alive, the adventurers scrambled into battle positions.

The vanguard dashed forward, having handed over the still-unconscious Mikoto and Haruhime to their comrades bringing up the rear.

With the Amazon's *podao* leading the way through flying monster blood, the adventurers continued their battle.

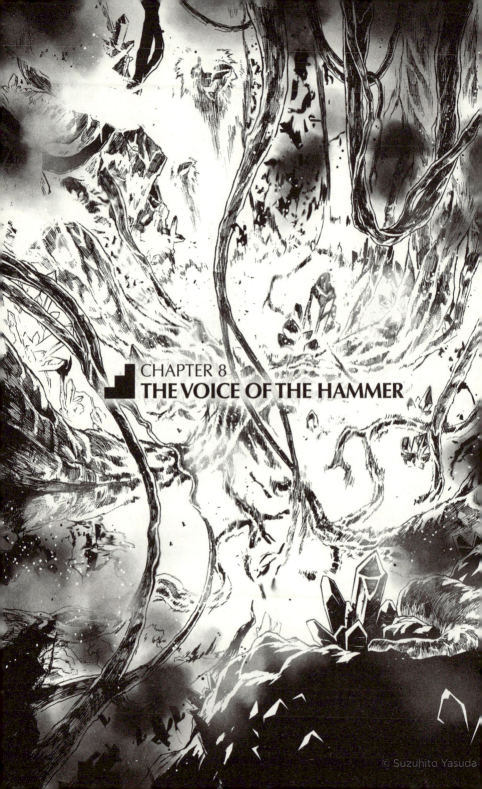

CHAPTER 8
THE VOICE OF THE HAMMER

© Suzuhito Yasuda

They were too late.

Even Ahnya, who was universally recognized to be dim-witted, understood that as she confirmed the scene with her eyes.

"What is this?!"

"...Is the Water Capital always such a hellish landscape, meow?"

Runoa was shaken, and Chloe's voice was heavy.

They were standing at the edge of the cliff outside the passageway that led to the twenty-fifth floor.

A terrible vista sprawled below them.

Rising from a raging sea of blue flames was the wreckage of what appeared to be the burned-out roots of an enormous tree. The plunge pool was filled in with a mountain of crystal debris huge enough to easily bury any living thing that might have been in the yawning cavern. The waves of blue napalm showed no sign of subsiding, sending waves of heat and billows of scalding steam toward the band of adventurers. Chloe had not exaggerated when she described the scene as hellish.

The cavern's walls and ceiling, too, appeared as if they had been crushed to pieces in the jaws of a dragon.

The once beautiful watery paradise was nowhere to be seen.

"Looks like a floor boss went wild in this cavern...I bet you've never seen anything like this before, have you?"

Even the Level 5 Tsubaki couldn't help narrowing her one good eye as she looked down on the decimation. Their surroundings bore the sure signs of a fierce battle rather than a natural disaster. But how much time had passed since the fighting broke out? Hours? Half a day? Had the Amphisbaena been defeated?

Only one thing was clear:

Tsubaki and her companions had arrived too late to help the adventurers who had fought here.

"Well...Lyu should be on the twenty-seventh floor, meow! Let's get down there quick, meow!" Ahnya shouted, giving her head a good shake to clear away the swirling questions. Given her own stupidity, she realized it wouldn't do much good to stand there trying to think her way through things.

Clearly, there was nobody left in the hellfire below them. Whether on land or in the water, anything inside that inferno wouldn't have been able to breathe. That, or they had been buried alive. It was certain that searching for survivors would be a waste of time.

They had heard in Rivira that the hunting party pursuing Gale Wind had been on their way to the twenty-seventh floor. Encountering this Irregular made Ahnya anxious. The face of her elven coworker rose in her mind as she urged the others on.

"That's all well and good, but...this whole place is in shambles! There's nowhere for us to walk! What do we do?!" Runoa asked, frowning. Tsubaki tapped the back of her sword against her shoulder as she answered.

"Looks like our only option is to descend this cliff face."

"What? You're not serious, meow...?"

Chloe stuck her tongue out in dismay.

"There aren't any monsters in the cavern now, meow! As long as they're not pestering us, we can do it, meow! Plus...my older brother managed to go down all by himself! If he can, we can, meow! A-at least, I think so!"

Ahnya's unconvincing argument echoed hollowly across the cavern.

"Oh, damn it all, guess we're going for it!" Runoa finally said.

The four women nodded at one another and leaned boldly forward.

Pushing through the hot steam, they stepped off the cliff's edge. Without using their hands, they raced straight down the near-vertical slope. Whenever the rocks began to noisily slip out from underneath their feet, they jabbed their weapons deep into the cliff face to support themselves.

Although they nearly fell countless times, the advancing line of adventurers held one another up, heading for the twenty-sixth floor.

"Shit!!"

Welf's spare longsword sliced a merman in half.

But even as the bisected half-fish monster died, a new merman crushed its corpse underfoot in pursuit of the smith, who responded with more curses.

"Is this a joke? They're endless!" he shouted.

"These numbers aren't normal!"

"They're coming from the s-sides and behind us, too!"

Ouka and Chigusa returned his shout.

The party was currently on the twenty-sixth floor. Having narrowly escaped the crumbling cavern, they were now facing one battle after the next. They encountered an unending stream of monsters. It was possible that due to the unprecedented destruction on the twenty-fifth floor, which had thrown the interior maze into chaos, the monsters seemed to have grown more sensitive to the presence of invaders.

The adventurers' breathing was ragged as they met the swarm of aquatic monsters that ferociously bore down on them.

"We shouldn't bother with them! It's a waste of precious energy!"

Even as she shouted, Lilly's arrow threaded the crowd of jostling mermen before piercing the eye of their leader. Such shots from supporters or commanders, who normally did not directly participate in the fighting, were rare. The merman leader in the center of the swarm screamed and for a moment neglected to direct its troops.

The adventurers seized the moment to flee the scene.

"This is no joke! At this rate, we'll never have time to search for Rabbit Foot…!"

Glancing at Aisha, who was handling monsters approaching from the sides, Daphne confirmed the escape route. Just then, a devil monster jumped down from overhead and she swiped it away with her baton-like dagger. Paying no heed to the spray of fluid produced by the hideous monster's wound as it rolled across the floor, Daphne dashed forward.

A drop of something—sweat from nerves or heat, she didn't know—rolled down her narrow chin.

"How many times are you going to say that?! When we came to the twenty-sixth floor, we made up our minds to meet up with Bell!"

"I know, I know! We can't go back to the twenty-fifth floor now that it's destroyed! And believe me, I get that you don't want to abandon your friend! I've given up convincing you all otherwise! But still, this is…!"

Daphne returned Lilly's shout with equal irritation. Even her eyes seemed ready to groan in distress as she surveyed their surroundings.

The twenty-sixth floor had clearly suffered damage as a result of the cataclysm on the twenty-fifth floor. The walls and ground were cracked, suggesting that they hadn't been able to safely withstand the pressure from above. The water running down the center of the passage had overflowed and was thoroughly soaking their feet. The sprinkle of falling crystals conjured ugly visions of the whole ceiling collapsing in the near future. The labyrinth could easily cave in on them at any moment.

The viscous howls of either confused or excited monsters further fanned the party's anxiety.

"In our current state, and without the slightest clue to his location, our chances of finding him are basically zero!"

"Sheesh!"

Every time Lilly wanted to prioritize looking for Bell, Daphne always cut in with the reality of their situation.

The wretched condition of the party after the fight with the floor boss was a serious concern. How were they supposed to search for a lone adventurer on such an immense floor?

"Anyway, since this is our first time on this floor, we need to be putting safety first…!"

Even though the twenty-sixth floor was considered a part of the Water Capital, it was irrefutably a completely new world for most of the party. Despite that, they had totally ignored the usual standards for clearing a new floor and were barging straight ahead. It was enough to make Daphne—who approached Dungeon exploration with the watchwords "steady, cautious, and timid"—want to faint. She thought it was absolute madness to leap without looking into the maw of the demonic Dungeon.

But even as she exchanged shouts with Lilly, Daphne could not afford to stop running. It was obvious that the moment she did, she would be crushed underfoot by the onrush of monsters.

"Moving forward is our only option! We can't go back to the twenty-fourth floor until the Dungeon has repaired itself, and we don't even know if it *will* repair itself! Just pray we bump into him!"

Currently the party was proceeding down the floor's main route.

Aisha, who was constantly keeping track of the party's morale, tried her best to ease Daphne's anxiety.

Plus, though I hate relying on other people, Gale Wind should be on the same twenty-seventh floor, where we'll find Bell…!

She had other things on her mind, too—namely, the elf who had been accused of murder in Rivira. For Aisha, the question of whether she was actually guilty no longer mattered much. If they were able to meet up with her and Bell and gain her cooperation, even by force, a way forward would open up, albeit a rash and potentially deadly one. It was precisely the presence of that idea in the back of her mind that had convinced Aisha to change course and bet her life on their current reckless advance.

It was a pity that an irregularity so extreme it would rip Aisha's schemes to shreds awaited them at their destination, the twenty-seventh floor.

"More monsters…!"

"Even for an Irregular this feels like too many!"

As Chigusa carried the unconscious Mikoto on her back and Cassandra shouldered Haruhime, Ouka and Welf scowled at the newest swarm that had just appeared. They were at the front of the party, and now the adventurers were being forced to change course.

"It's like every monster in this place is after us...!"

Chigusa's panted speculation was by no means an exaggeration.

To the contrary, she had hit a bull's-eye.

All the monsters on the floor—or rather, the entire zone—had rushed in the party's direction, searching for prey. As if to confirm her fearful guess, a huge form burst through the water's surface.

"ROOOOOOOOOOOOOOOOOOOOOOOO!!"

"What?! A kelpie?!"

"But that's a twenty-seventh-floor monster!"

Lilly's astonishment was even greater than Aisha's wide-eyed surprise.

Kelpies. These horse monsters with blue pelts and manes as well as finned bodies were able to gallop through the water just as if they were on land. As Lilly said, they normally appeared on the twenty-seventh floor. Their beautiful outward appearance belied a potential that was among the greatest of any in the Water Capital.

"It came up to this floor?! And in these conditions...?!"

Overwhelmed by the magnificence and power of her enemy, Lilly was continuing to shout in confusion when she was interrupted by a chorus of roars coming from deep in the maze.

"AAAAAAAAAAAAAAAAAAAA!!"

"OOOO, OOO!"

"GUAAAAAAAAAAAA!"

A lamia, an afanc, and a dodora were loudly announcing their presence. All were monsters that normally appeared for the first time on the twenty-seventh floor.

"A huge swarm of monsters? No, a mass migration...?! It can't be!" Daphne shrieked.

All the monsters were red with blood, shreds of scarlet flesh hanging from them.

All of it belonged to adventurers. Upper-class adventurers who had joined the hunt for Gale Wind only to be crushed by the fangs and claws of calamity.

This tragedy had unfolded unbeknownst to Aisha and her companions. Now, after devouring the corpses of various adventurers and becoming drunk on enormous quantities of gore, the monsters had grown more ferocious and brutal than ever.

More blood. More flesh. Another feast.

In search of fresh offerings, the massive swarm of monsters had left the demolished twenty-seventh floor behind them and poured into the twenty-sixth floor.

"What in the world is going on?"

"Ask the Dungeon! That's what's messing with us adventurers like this…!"

Of course, Lilly and the others had no clue about any of that.

Aisha, who had hoped to find refuge at a safety point, swore in frustration when she realized her plans had been foiled.

Fortunately, because the Dungeon was prioritizing the repair of the twenty-fifth floor, no new monsters were currently being spawned on any of the Water Capital's three floors. Nevertheless, there were still far too many for the party to take on.

Sensing impending doom closing in from all sides even as they fought the kelpie directly in front of them, the blood drained from their faces.

"—!!"

"Whoa!!"

Welf's knees quaked at the sight of the kelpie thrashing wildly and flinging its blue mane around. This was an incredibly strong specimen. Its potential might even have exceeded Welf's and Ouka's statuses. The level boosts that had provided them with divine protection that led to victory so many times before were not available.

Facing this twenty-seventh-floor opponent, the party was finally beginning to hit a wall they could not scale with the skills of Level 2 adventurers like Welf and Ouka.

"Argh!"

Caught up in the monster's attack, Welf was thrown backward. He had been able to somehow prevent a direct hit with his longsword, but now his back was against the wall. It had been cracked before, but it distorted under the latest impact, sending fragments flying as the crystal moaned.

"Shit...!"

Welf, still exhausted from the fight with the floor boss, gritted his teeth and was trying to stand back up when...

"—?"

Clank, clank!

A chunk of wall rolling across the floor with a clatter drew his attention.

The lustrous steely blue was not the color of the tiresomely abundant crystals of the Water Capital.

This was a natural Dungeon ingot, glittering with the sheen of rare metal.

The ingot resembled a garnet the size and shape of a misshapen fist, with fragments of crystal clinging to it. It seemed to have fallen out of the wall's interior, perhaps due to the extensive damage the floor had suffered.

In true smith's fashion, Welf stared in disbelief at the ore that had rolled to his feet.

"No way...this is adamantite!"

He gasped as he realized what variety of rare metal it was.

"What are you doing, Ignis?! Get back on your feet!"

"Oh, right!"

Aisha, who had just cut down the kelpie, yelled at him impatiently.

As Welf stood up in relief, he reflexively picked up the ingot before running to catch up with his companions.

"Uoooooooooooooooooooo!"

"!!"

Just then, someone cried out. Someone who did not belong to their party.

The sound came from a human form surrounded by monsters farther down the main route.

"Is that...someone who went to the twenty-seventh floor?!"

Aisha's earlier prediction had proven true. Welf and several other members of the party ran to the stranger, quickly drove away the monsters, and rescued the intended victim.

"You're Rivira's…"

"Mr. Bors!"

Welf and Lilly were right. It was indeed the hulking adventurer Bors Elder, his whole body heaving as he breathed.

He was a wretched sight.

His brawny figure was covered in wounds from head to toe. His battle clothes were stained red with blood, although no one could tell how much of it belonged to him and how much came from the monsters he had killed. The patch he usually wore over his left eye was missing. So was his weapon, which they guessed he must have lost somewhere along the way. It was unbelievable that he had made it this far without one. His hands and gloves were torn and reddish black, evidence that he had fended off the monsters by flailing wildly and slamming his fists against their tough shells and scales.

"Y-you, you guys are…*Hestia Familia*…? You…survived…?"

Bors turned from one member of the party to the next in a daze.

There was no trace of the leader of Rivira's usual arrogance or overbearing self-importance. Instead, he spoke as if he was still delirious after just waking from a nightmare.

"Are you alone? Where's the rest of the hunting party?"

Filled with a terrible dread, Aisha questioned this returnee from the twenty-seventh floor. Bors responded in a barely audible whisper, his face clouded by an uncharacteristically dark expression.

"…I'm the only one left. Everyone else…they're all dead."

"What?"

"What are you saying…? Do you even know how many upper-class adventurers went with you?!"

"They can't all have been wiped out!"

"Were they killed by Gale Wind when they tried to attack her?"

Chigusa was the first to break the silence with her whisper, followed by Daphne, Ouka, and Aisha shooting out questions in rapid succession. They weren't outright denying Bors's claim, but their faces were taut with doubt and disbelief.

Several hours earlier, they had witnessed the twenty-seventh-floor plunge pool turn crimson. The "lower reaches of Hell's river" had turned that huge body of water the color of blood.

"It was an Irregular…a monster I've never seen before took my followers and…"

"…The great calamity."

Cassandra turned white as Bors, eyes unfocused, recalled his encounter with a creature not of this world.

Only Cassandra understood that this was the "calamity" her prophecy warned of.

"—Mr. Bors?!"

Just then, Lilly interrupted with an ear-shattering shout.

"What happened to Mr. Bell?!"

"Rabbit Foot got taken out, too…one of his arms was blown clean off, and the bones in his neck were…I'm sure he…"

"?!"

"And Gale Wind, too!…That elf who was fool enough to protect me…! Everyone, and I mean *everyone*, got killed! That monster slaughtered them all!!"

As she listened to this tragic tale, Lilly's chest heaved as if she had been run through by a sword. Meanwhile, the more Bors talked, the more emotional he became.

As if he had lost heart. As if he had lost hope.

"It's a lie…a lie, a lie, a lie! Bell can't die! He can't leave Lilly alone!!"

"Calm down, Li'l E!"

Welf held down Lilly's fist, which seemed to be on the verge of punching Bors while her other hand gripped his shirt.

The smith's heart was hardly calm, either. From the annihilation of the upper-class adventurers to the death of Bell, the information that suddenly confronted the party was like shackles binding their feet. They all froze, but only Lilly's screams echoed down the passages.

"OOOOOOOOOOOOOOOOOOOO!!"

"—?!"

Of course, the monsters didn't care the least bit for their feelings. Their wild war cries once again reached the adventurers, who had momentarily forgotten their current situation. A second later, a pack appeared from around a bend in the passage and charged toward them.

"Run!!"

Aisha creamed a command. Her companions shook off their shock and complied. Obeying their own instincts screaming for survival, they defied death once again.

"UOOOOOOOOOOOOOOOOOOOOOOOOOOO!!"

To the adventurers, the monsters' roars sounded like an evil sneer.

Retreat was out of the question, yet moving forward held no hope for them.

Ahead of them lay only the corpses of countless adventurers.

The party had broken out of the "coffin" and overcome "despair," but what awaited them now was the "banquet of calamity."

The reverberations of monsters running in pursuit of their prey transformed into phantoms howling "Give up!" Beneath the dim phosphorescence, the deformed shadows streamed past as if they were dancing wildly in rapture. The beasts seemed bent on crushing the weak hearts of the adventurers.

"Damn it!!"

With a curse, Welf swung his remaining magic blade at the pack of monsters charging straight at them. Flames shot forward with no heed for the watery surroundings, charring the monsters as they howled in their death throes.

And then he heard the dagger cracking.

"...!"

The last Crozzo's Magic Sword was beginning to crumble.

Welf panicked as he watched it fracture. Ouka grimaced as well. The moment they lost that last magic blade was the moment the party itself would collapse.

Not long after, they arrived at a crossroads where a number of routes intersected. At the same time, howling monsters appeared from passages in every direction.

The·adventurers had no idea what to do as certain death drew near. Suddenly Aisha shouted:

"Shrimp, take out the stink bombs!!"

"What…?! The Malboros?! But they won't work on water monsters…!"

"Not for their noses, for their eyes!"

"!"

Realizing Aisha's intention, Lilly stuck her hand into the side pocket of her backpack and pulled out five stink bags—their entire supply of Malboros. She threw them down the four passages toward the approaching monsters.

"UUUUU?!"

As the minority of monsters that did have a sense of smell writhed in discomfort, the remaining majority groaned in confusion. A curtain of haze made up of the green particles released by the bombs enveloped them. Like some kind of strange pollen, the stinking dust filled the entire intersection, causing a chain of collisions. The monsters forgot all about the adventurers—who had slipped away in the midst of the chaos—and began tearing at one another in outrage.

Aisha's plan had not been to use the Malboros to keep the monsters away, but rather to create a blinding smokescreen by ripping open the bags.

"Now's our chance!!"

Just before the stink bombs split open, the party had turned tail and dived into one of the few passages that wasn't completely filled with monsters. They continued to run as fast as they could, moving farther and farther from the main route. After putting quite some distance between themselves and the monsters, they emerged into a large room.

"…!! It's a dead end…"

The room was a cul-de-sac.

It measured around thirty meders on each side and had no water-ways in it. What had once been a field of crystal lay in ruins, perhaps due to the shocks of the destruction on the floor above. There was only a single opening for entry and exit, meaning they had no escape route.

"Uh-oh…"

They had to get out quickly.

The same words were on everyone's lips, but they were panting too hard to speak them.

The combination of the battle with the floor boss and the continuous harassment they'd been dealing with since then meant the entire party was in desperate need of rest. They had to have at least a moment to catch their breath. More than anything, the very real possibility that Bell could be dead was throwing their minds and bodies out of sync.

We're still in a hopeless fix…we haven't escaped ruin. Is the prophecy still continuing? Or have we parted ways with it? Did I make the wrong decision?

Meanwhile, Cassandra was wandering through her own maze of unanswerable questions.

She didn't know if they were still following the trajectory of her prophetic dream, or if they had strayed off its path. Gloomy thoughts bubbled up ceaselessly in her mind, robbing her of the willpower to even to lift her face.

No one could lift even a finger, never mind take decisive action.

"—Bors. Tell us exactly what you saw."

As the party sunk into a state of near mental paralysis, Aisha broke the silence.

"Tell us all the details you know about the monster that attacked Bell Cranell…not your pessimistic guesses, but exactly what happened."

"…Rabbit Foot's arm got pulled off, and he suffered a blow to the neck. No question those were fatal injuries. But I saw Gale Wind use recovery magic, too. He could…still be alive."

"…!"

Under Aisha's sharp gaze, Bors relayed what he had seen without embellishing the account.

As they listened to his words, Lilly and the others shuddered. Light returned to their eyes. The transformation surprised Cassandra.

"Listen to me. Our plans haven't changed. We're still heading to the safety point. Getting there might leave us a hairbreadth from dying, but we're going to find Bell Cranell. Even if it costs you your life, you're going to help us, Bors."

"H-hey?! Didn't you hear me?! I said there's a horrible monster on the twenty-seventh floor!!"

"Who cares? There's no way back anyway."

"I...I'm not going! I'll be damned if I head into that hell again!"

As Bors screamed in protest, Aisha grabbed his battle clothes threateningly.

"If you understand how indebted you are to Bell Cranell and Gale Wind...then man up."

The Amazon's words were quiet but weighty. Bors stood dumbfounded for a moment, then glared angrily at his feet. He didn't nod in agreement, but he didn't argue any more, either.

This woman is truly strong. It's not just the strength granted by her status, but that emotionally fortitude...Even in a pinch like this, she hasn't given up.

Cassandra gazed at the black-haired powerhouse. Despite being covered in sweat and blood, Aisha was beautiful. Her words had not only stemmed all argument from Bors, but had also unified the will of the party. The proof was in their faces, which were no longer clouded by hopelessness. Aisha had successfully revived the will to fight that had nearly buckled under the news of Bell's possible death.

Neither Lilly nor Daphne, their commanders, had been able to do that. Only Aisha, who was stronger and more battle-hardened than any of them, had what it took. As Cassandra stared at that powerful figure, she wished that she could be equally as strong.

"If we're going anywhere, we better backtrack out of this room quick."

Daphne spoke slowly. Her words sounded heavy, as if she were driving reality home.

"We may have shaken the monsters, but the route to this room was practically a straight shot. If we don't get out of here, we'll be crushed by a headlong rush of monsters..."

But what was next? What would happen if they managed to slip past the mob of monsters? How many more battles were awaited on the long journey to the twenty-seventh floor?

The unspoken questions flashed back and forth in the adventurers' glances. Not even Daphne had an answer.

Their hearts and minds were united, but their situation hadn't improved one bit. They still didn't have a solid plan to turn back the hordes of rampaging monsters or otherwise shake them off for good. Once again, a veil of silence descended on the room. They could hear the howling monsters. As death crept ever closer, anxiety tormented the party.

Lilly and Daphne racked their brains trying to come up with a way out. Ouka and Chigusa laid Mikoto and Haruhime down on the floor, frowning as they held their limp hands in their own. Aisha and Bors kept their sharp gazes fixed on the passage beyond the entrance, watching for enemies. Cassandra frantically tried to interpret the last part of the prophecy.

—*What should we do?*

Last of all, Welf stood rooted to the ground by mental anguish.

How can we get to Bell? How are we supposed to get through this?

Like Lilly, he was racking his brain for a way out of this impasse.

He turned the seemingly impossible problem over in his head again and again, searching for a solution.

If only we had some magic blades...!

Instead of a solution to their crisis, all he could muster was wishful thinking.

I'd already made the decision to stop weighing my pride against my friends...That's right, I did, I did stop! But I still don't have the magic blades I need!

He could only curse his stupidity for using them all up. It was either that or his own incompetence was to blame for making weak blades that crumbled so quickly. All he felt when he looked back on his past actions was regret.

Is there anything I can do to help these guys? What can I offer as a smith to repay these adventurers?!

Welf shut his eyes tight and searched for an answer.

He clenched his fists and asked what use he was to the world.

Lady Hephaistos...what should I do?

He was being a wimp. A total wimp.

But he couldn't help asking.

When he was really, truly in trouble, that goddess, that pillar of strength always had the words he needed.

If she were looking at his spineless self now, at this Welf Crozzo who couldn't do anything, what would she say?

It made him nauseous to foist his responsibility on a woman like this.

But for the sake of his friends, he tossed away his shame and his concern for outward appearances and sought the help of that exalted presence in his heart.

Here in this Dungeon, what can I do...?!

And then—

"As long as you have a hammer, metal, and a good flame, you can forge weapons anywhere—"

He heard the voice of the goddess he revered.

He saw the supreme light he must aim for.

Divine revelation pierced his mind.

"—"

His eyes popped open.

His arms trembled.

The words that Hephaistos, the goddess of the forge, had spoken in the past rose vividly in his mind.

Welf jerked his head up as if someone had punched him, then looked around.

He was in a room with only one entry and exit.

Lilly's backpack was stuffed with tools.

Lastly, he had the flame magic blade that was already starting to disintegrate plus the ingot gripped in his hand.

The glow of heat still flickered deep within the cracked blade, and the nugget of metal glittered like steel.

Welf looked down at his hands and gulped.

An instant later—he made up his mind.

He clenched his teeth so hard they nearly cracked, widened his eyes with fierce intent, and gripped the magic blade and adamantite ingot with all his might.

He took a step toward his companions.

"Hey, you guys."

His resolute voice echoed through the quiet room.

All eyes were on Welf.

"Will you put your lives in my hands?"

Every one of them stopped moving and stared back in shock.

Every one of them choked on his words, confused and unable to discern what he intended to do.

"...Smith, you must be kidding."

Ouka, his voice shaking, was the only one who guessed Welf's plan.

Welf gazed steadily back at his companions and spoke.

"I'm going to make magic blades right here."

Time stood still.

"...What?"

"I'm saying that I'm gonna forge new magic blades here in this room."

Welf held back his emotions as he answered the flummoxed Cassandra.

Magic blades would be born here in the Dungeon.

Here in this crucible of monsters that might attack at any moment, he would set up a smithy and work the metal. Although his face dripped sweat, his eyes were unclouded as he announced his intention.

"That's impossible!"

It was Lilly who explosively shot down his idea.

"Stop saying idiotic things!! What are you thinking?! The very idea—to forge weapons in such a dangerous area of the Dungeon that isn't even a safety point!"

While Aisha and the others stood frozen in place, Lilly, who had known Welf so long, panned his idea.

"Where are your tools? Your furnace? Where will you gather the raw materials you need?!"

Although Lilly had decided his idea was unreasonable, Welf answered her in a low, calm voice.

"There's a hammer among the tools I brought for maintenance. A hearth, too. And this magic blade will provide the flames."

Lilly was at a loss for a response. She glanced at her backpack. As Welf had said, everything was there. He himself had pulled together a full set of tools for their expedition. It was a moveable blacksmith's workshop, and he'd already used it to repair their tools and make the Goliath Scarf.

"Plus, I picked up some materials a minute ago."

Daphne and the others gaped as he held up the misshapen chunk of adamantite, which shone dully in his hand.

"Listen, the only way we can get out of our current fix is with magic blades. If we're gonna blow away those damn monsters and make it to the twenty-seventh floor, our only option is to rely on the power of the Crozzo blood…!"

Welf's mental anguish was clear as he laid out his thoughts.

"Once I start working, I won't be able to fight. You'll have to protect me until the magic blades are done…*I'm asking you to put your lives in my hands.*"

An unnatural stillness descended on the room, as if it had been cut loose from the rest of the world. The crystal fragments scattered around the floor gleamed blue. Lilly, Chigusa, Daphne, and

Cassandra were stunned, their eyes unsteady. Aisha and Ouka simply stood there tight-lipped.

"You, Ignis…are you in your right mind?"

The first to squeeze out a few words, his eyes twitching, was Bors. *I've never met a smith as crazy as you*, the head of Rivira seemed to be saying. Welf returned his question with an irate scream.

"What's it matter if I'm crazy?! We have no other choice! Are you gonna believe in me or not?! Answer me!"

Welf looked around at the adventurers, before finally resting his eyes on Aisha.

The second-tier adventurer held the real decision-making power in the party.

A moment passed before she answered the smith standing in front of her.

"…Can you do it?"

That was all she asked.

Before he replied, Welf closed his eyes and once more turned inward to his own heart.

You have a hammer.

You have metal.

The only question is, has your fire been lit?

"Of course I can!"

It was blazing.

The flame of Welf's heart burned hotter than ever.

He opened his eyes and shouted at the top of his lungs.

"As long as you have a hammer, metal, and a good flame, you can forge weapons anywhere. That's what it means to be a smith!!"

The determination and commitment in his voice made his audience quiver. Aisha ignored her breathless companions and laughed.

"Well then go ahead!"

Ouka, who had been quiet up till then, laughed as well.

"Yeah, forge us some blades!"

With that, Lilly stared up at the ceiling, Daphne fended off a fainting spell, and Chigusa squeezed her hands together in a sign of faith.

"Son of a bitch," Bors said, slamming his fist onto his knee as he smiled spitefully.

To show her respect for Welf's decision, Cassandra screwed up her courage and nodded at him.

"Our lives—"

Acceptance, resignation, resolution.

Ouka spoke for all of them, though the emotions each carried were different.

"—are in your hands."

As his fellow adventurers gazed at him with trust, Welf grinned back at them fearlessly.

Welf took his bandana from around his neck and tied it around his head.

This was the process, or rather the ritual, by which the ordinary Welf became a smith.

He brandished the remaining magic blade.

The furnace glowed vermilion, shining brightly as it began to give off heat. He didn't have any proper fuel like coke, so he used the Amphisbaena bile Lilly had collected. It caused a small explosion when it came in contact with flame, but the furnace stayed lit and began to violently heat up. He had reinforced his portable hearth with drop items they'd picked up along the way, such as the blue crab shells they had intended to use as proof of completing their mission, and the lopsided dome contained the heat well. It would be able to perform the job of melting adamantite, one of the hardest metals around.

Having given up its last burst of power, the dagger fell to the ground in countless pieces. Welf clutched the weapon's skeleton in his palm and crouched before the blazing furnace.

"Here I go."

Gripping the hunk of metal between his tongs, he carefully but swiftly thrust it into the fire.

"Get into battle formation! Don't let any monsters approach Ignis!"

As the flames roared, the others followed Aisha's command and formed a semicircle around the lone entryway. Aisha, Ouka, Daphne, and Bors made up the front line, while Lilly took command and Chigusa supported the formation from behind. Farther back, Cassandra the healer stood watch over Mikoto and Haruhime, and farther back still, in the center of the large room, was Welf.

Charged with reviving the party, the High Smith could not fight. The others had to halt the advancing monsters so he could concentrate.

"Huff...puff..."

The sound of shallow breathing filled the room. The adventurers were panting despite not even catching a glimpse of a monster yet. It wasn't simply due to the heat radiating from the glowing furnace, which dampened their cheeks with sweat; Lilly and the others were all on edge as they watched Welf glare into the flames.

The contents of the furnace melted swiftly in the fierce heat. At the perfect moment, Welf slowly extracted the hot metal. The adamantite had been transformed into a red candy-like material, bathing the deep blue crystal walls of the room in crimson as it cast intense heat. The shadows of the adventurers stretched long on the floor, swaying unsteadily.

Welf set the metal on an impromptu surface, grasped the hammer in one hand and the tongs in the other, then held his breath.

The room went completely silent.

The smith focused his mind and swung the hammer down hard.

"Huff!!"

Clang! Clang!! A loud, metallic clanging rhythm began.

"Even the idea of forging in the Dungeon...!"

Daphne pressed her hand to her mouth.

"This can't be happening...!" she moaned at the unbelievable scene.

They had indeed entered unknown territory.

Most adventurers and smiths would have called it idiotic.

The deities would have held their sides and laughed with glittering eyes at this adventurer's journey into the unknown.

If he succeeded, it would be an incredible accomplishment.

If he failed, it would be an unprecedented act of folly.

Their corpses would be buried here, their disgraceful deaths the laughingstock of future generations.

Welf was attempting an act of barbarity that even the master smith Tsubaki Collbrande had never hazarded.

—Forging weapons in the Dungeon.

Producing magic blades deep within the labyrinth itself.

"Huff!!"

Welf exhaled loudly as he hammered the blazing red adamantite. Sparks swirled as the rhythmic pounding continued. Each time the hammer crashed against the metal, Chigusa and Cassandra jumped. The whole world seemed to vibrate from the unrelenting pounding.

Unsurprisingly, the deafening metallic clanging began to attract monsters as it rang out in the Dungeon.

The sound of the hammer was like a countdown to ruin.

And then it began.

"OOOOOOOOOOOOOOOOOOOOOOOOOOOOOOOOOOOOO OOOOOOOO!!"

Accompanied by a chorus of roars and the pounding of countless feet, a huge, motley swarm of monsters came into view far down the passage. The whole pack they had dodged at the crossroads was now rushing toward them.

"Hell Kaios!!"

Aisha activated her magic instantly. She had been chanting as she waited, and now the jumble of monsters struggling to beat one another down the narrow passage became fodder for the slicing wave attack.

"Take these shields and hold at the front of the entrance! We can't let the monsters into this room!"

Obeying Lilly's command, Ouka and Bors positioned themselves between the passage and the room to form a wall that would hold back the rush of monsters.

The single entryway would limit the number of monsters that

could enter at one time and reduce the maximum momentum of their charge. This was one tactic for taking on a large horde of monsters in the Dungeon. The flip side was that if even one got inside and started a melee, the adventurers wouldn't stand a chance.

Defending the "gate" with their lives was an absolute precondition for Welf's success.

"Uwaaaaaaaaaaaaaaa!"

"Bastards!"

Ouka braced himself as the monsters began to throw themselves against the spare shield he was holding up. Despite putting his whole body into a defensive stance, the impact forced him to take a step back. Next to him, the Level 3 Bors desperately held them off with his own borrowed shield as he jabbed randomly with the expandable silver lance Chigusa had handed him.

"You don't have to kill them! Just cut off their feet!"

"I can't even aim!!"

"We need support…!"

Aisha and Daphne sliced at the enemies from the sides of the "wall," while Chigusa stepped in with Shakuya, Mikoto's throwing knives, and Lilly supported them with shots from her Little Ballista. At the back of the formation where Mikoto and Haruhime lay, Cassandra struggled to keep her wits about her as she activated her recovery magic whenever Daphne or the other fighters were at risk of falling out of the battle line.

With the smith's iron melody ringing in their ears, the adventurers intercepted one monster after the next.

"…!"

Bang, bang, bang!

As if mirroring their anxious hearts, the falling hammer drew an arc through the air again and again.

The dangerous heat seared Welf's skin. The combination of the magic blade and the dragon bile had created temperatures far higher than normal, scorching his undine cloth and bathing him in sweat. The instant a drop of moisture fell from his chin onto the hammer, it evaporated with a sizzle.

The flurry of sparks was proof of his strength, though it needed no outside confirmation.

The precision with which he hit the center of the metal each time stemmed from his dexterity.

His whole body burning, Welf threw every bit of physical strength, courage, and skill he had at the hunk of metal.

But, but, but...

"Crap...!"

He couldn't properly shape it according to his wishes. In fact, the metal seemed to ignore his will as it morphed into an uneven, bumpy shape. He felt as if it was a living being with a capricious mind of its own.

Adamantite was among the finest of rare metals. It was exceedingly hard, which made processing and forging difficult. Even famous High Smiths struggled to control it.

He'd gained experience working with dir adamantite, a lighter, processed version of the metal, when he made Bell's armor. But this pure ore was resisting his attempts completely.

His skill level clearly fell short. That, or he lacked the experience required. The wildly leaping flames and the intense resistance of the metal were all signs that he was not in control.

"You've gotta be kidding me...!"

Complaining didn't help, of course.

Welf's hands shook as the adamantite stubbornly refused the hammer.

Impurities were transformed into countless sparks that flew into his face as he reheated the metal and began to beat at it again.

There's no time. I can't stumble. I have to finish fast.

Nevertheless.

Wish my heartbeat would pipe down.

It sounded slow, lingering in his ears unendingly.

For every three times I bring down the hammer, my heart only beats once—

Welf was at the center of a maelstrom of time.

Each time he swung his hammer, time seemed to melt away. The burning red metal consumed his focus.

How long have I been working on this?

How many hours? Half a day? Or a single minute?

Where am I?

The process for making a magic blade differed from that for a regular sword, but neither could be drastically shortened. If he wanted to make a weapon strong enough to break them out of their current fix, he had to achieve mastery within limited time.

This anxiety verging on obsession thrust Welf into the darkness of the forging process.

I'm giving it all the strength and skill I can muster.

All my craftsman's pride, self-worth, and will.

So why isn't it coming out how I want?!

"GAAAAAAAAAAAAAAAAAAAAAAAAAAAAAAAAAAAA AAAAAAAAAAAA!!"

"Gyaaaa!"

The monsters' roars were coming more often now. The counterattacks Ouka and the others undertook sounded weaker. Welf wondered if they were okay, but he didn't have the leeway to look away. If he took his eyes off his work even once he could fail. And failure here meant death. Distraction invited distraction. It was the worst possible cycle, eating at him mentally and physically.

As he struggled, he began to sink into an uncomfortably warm, bottomless abyss. It was a miracle that his hammer hadn't missed its mark yet.

"Huff, puff, huff...!"

As large drops of sweat rolled down his face while his breath seemed to come out scalding, the world disappeared into the pounding reverberations of his heartbeat.

He couldn't even tell right from left, up from down, front from back.

Within the blackness before his eyes hung the brilliant red metal and his hammer.

At this moment in time, they were his entire world.

For the first time in his life, he experienced an extreme vision.

I hear a voice.

The world was wrapped in darkness.

In the gap between despair, anxiety, and an individual's will to resist those feelings, Welf heard the ingot speak.

"Listen to the metal's words, lend your ears to its echoes, pour your heart into your hammer."

He had learned that from the Crozzo family as a young boy.

These words expressed the spirit of his grandfather and father, whom he had once hated.

They were the starting point for Welf's rebirth and the cornerstone of everything; now they delivered to him the voice of the metal, the question of the hammer.

Listen.

To what?

Why do you swing me, your hammer?

To forge weapons.

Why do you forge weapons?

To survive.

Wrong.

That's not what I'm asking. That's not what you need right now. Listen.

Why do you forge weapons?

"—"

The questioning voice of the hammer became Welf's own voice as he asked himself why, plumbing the depths of his heart.

"Mr. Welf!"

From the depths of the darkness, Welf heard the prum's desperate plea.

"Smith…!"

From beyond the darkness, a man moaned.

"Mr. Crozzo!"

From beside him, the girl whom he had told not to call him by his family name was doing exactly that.

The war cries of the adventurers and the voices of his friends shook him.

I...

I...

I...!

"I forge weapons for my friends."

For Bell.

For the people here in this room—his comrades.

"To save my comrades who believe in me!!"

The weapons he forged with someone particular in mind contained a special power. They sparkled brighter than any other weapons.

Yes. This was the truth. It was obvious. Why had he forgotten?

For his friends.

So they could go save Bell—

"I!!"

The hammer struck metal with a loud clang. The hammer screamed as it bounced back into the air. The melody changed.

The tempo of the hammer was freer, stronger.

The adventurers heard the difference as they continued to hold off the braying monsters. When they looked up in surprise, they saw that Welf's eyes were burning crimson as if they had melded with the flames.

Changing, changing, changing.

The adamantite—hardest of all metals that had no reason to obey Welf's hammer—was taking on a new shape.

As if yielding to the will of one man, its war cry rang out, its crystalline structure shifted, and the silhouette of a blade began to emerge.

"Whew!!"

Welf's blood boiled with excitement.

His racing blood harmonized with the roar of his heart, pushing open a new door.

We'll never get out of this with regular magic blades.

We'll never overcome danger if our magic blades have an expiration date.

We'll never escape the jaws of death with magic blades destined to fall apart.

So what should he do?

The answer was clear.

He had to overcome.

He had to overcome the idea of regular magic blades, right then and there.

He had to make a weapon that went beyond magic blades—a new generation of weapon, a *stable* magic blade.

He had to twist the destiny of the magic blade itself to create a self-contradictory weapon.

On that fateful day in the past, he had declared his intentions to his grandfather, Tsubaki, and Hephaistos.

He had sworn that instead of simply crafting Crozzo's Magic Swords, he would forge his own weapons—Welf's weapons. He would fulfill that promise here and now.

Right here and now, he had to go beyond being Welf Crozzo.

"Excellent!!"

He didn't have a theory.

But he had an idea.

A vision had started to come into view.

No—that wasn't accurate. The hint he needed had been beside him all along.

It was the goddess's blade.

The masterpiece that the goddess of the forge had crafted was viewed as heretical, but it also represented the hope of Welf's ideal—and it had been in that boy's hand the whole time.

Bell, wait for me!

Bell had run so fast and soared so high that he shocked humans and deities alike.

And Welf—well, he'd be damned if he just stood by and watched the distance between them widen relentlessly.

I won't leave you alone!

I refuse to abandon you. I'll walk by your side no matter what it takes.

No.

I'll walk a step or two ahead of you.

I'll surpass you, and Hephaistos, too!!

That's why—!!

I'm aiming for the heights, beyond this cursed blood of mine.

I'm going past that abominable curse to the source of virtue and merit.

The skin of Welf's clenched fist tore, seeping blood that sizzled in the flame.

But the Crozzo blood did not evaporate. Instead it became a haze of heat that intermingled with, and then entered the adamantite.

This cursed blood—the bloodline of the dead that Welf had inherited—became blindingly white-hot as it tried to answer the young smith's will.

As his mind ran wild in an unconscious state devoid of a sense of self or idle thoughts, it crafted a design acknowledging the fundamental laws, heeding divine providence, and overturning logic itself.

As he spoke with the adamantite, Welf infused it with the plan he had drawn in his mind.

"It won't hold!!"

At that very instant, the sound of metal being ripped apart thundered through the room.

"Eyaaaaaaaaaaaaaaaaaaaaaaaaaaaaaaaaaaaaaaaaaaaaa!"

Daphne's shout was followed by Bors's howl as he and his wrecked shield flew into the air.

"_____!!"

With roars that sounded like declarations of victory, an avalanche of monsters spilled into the room.

What began to take place afterward was a portrait of hell.

Intent on trampling the adventurers whose battle line had crumpled, the monsters set upon them from every direction.

"Form a circle! Don't show the monsters your backs!"

The party just barely managed to obey Aisha's blurted command and form a circle, but it clearly wouldn't last long. The monsters pressed further into the circle second by second, its circumference shrinking as if it were being steadily shaved away.

Soon, they were forced back to where Cassandra was guarding Mikoto and Haruhime. Aside from the central area, the entire room was filled with monsters.

"Aaaaaah…!"

Concentric rings of monsters surrounded the adventurers. Cassandra felt the strength draining from her body as she stared out at them.

The fighters were still repelling their enemies' fangs and claws, but just barely. The moment they had lost control of the room, their morale had flagged.

Their faces smeared with blood and sweat, the party was on the verge of accepting utter destruction.

Cassandra stiffened as despair breathed down her collar for the umpteenth time, and was about to press her eyes shut.

—?

But as she did, she realized something.

That sound—

The hammer had gone quiet.

The melody of the forge, which had continued up till that point no matter how fierce the howling of the monsters, had stopped.

Cassandra looked over her shoulder, unsure what this change meant.

"—"

And then she saw it glittering.

Whoa—!

"Ouka!"

At exactly the same moment, razor-sharp claws shredded Ouka's shoulder, and at long last, he collapsed. Chigusa screamed his name as several bloodthirsty mermen flew at him.

Their black shadows engulfed Ouka, who had stopped breathing.

Their hideous fangs bore down on his fallen form—*and then they burst into flame.*

"…What?"

"GYAAAAAAAA!"

As jaws of fire devoured the pack of mermen, time halted for Ouka, Lilly, and the monsters alike.

The flames had come from the center of the room.

Their source was the patch of ground inhabited by a single man, whom Lilly and the others had protected.

Everyone looked in his direction.

Like Cassandra, who was staring wide-eyed and unable to pull her gaze away, each of them processed what they were seeing.

"—"

The smith stood tall.

Though his undine cloth flapped in waves of heat, its hems singed, he stood quiet and calm.

In his left hand, he held his bandana.

In his right hand, he held a gallant crimson longsword.

"—OOOOOOOOOOOOOOOOOOOOOOOOOOOOOOOOOO OOOOOOOOOO!!"

The monsters had regained their destructive instinct. Shaking off their confusion, they flew at the adventurers, intent on initiating another bloodbath.

"Can you give me a hand?"

"What?"

From all directions, every monster in the room flew at him.

Welf was standing next to Cassandra with no means to block them on his own.

"I can't do it by myself—would you grab hold of this?"

Cassandra peered into his eyes and grasped the hilt of the magic sword he held out.

Monster fangs and claws drew close.

The adventurers took their stances.

Welf wrapped his hands around the same hilt Cassandra was gripping and pointed the tip of the blade toward the ground.

"Here we go!"

For Welf, this was the beginning.

It was a mere foothold for reaching the level of mastery that the deity of the forge had achieved.

He puffed out his chest as he spoke.

To save his friends, and to carve his will into the world, he roared the weapon's name for all the Dungeon to hear.

"Shikou—Kazuki!"

He thrust the blade into the ground.

Instantaneously, huge crimson flames leaped upward.

"OOOOOOOOOOOOOOOOOOOOOOOOOOOOOOOOOOOOO OOOOOOOOOOOOOOOOOOOOOOOOOOOOOOOOOOOOO OOOOOOOOOOOOOOOO!"

Precisely as the monsters prepared to launch themselves toward Ouka, Chigusa, Lilly, Daphne, and Aisha, flames erupted from directly below.

Neatly avoiding the adventurers—or rather, protecting them with a formidable wall—the flames leaped up in overlapping circles like a flower of fire. They had traveled through the ground from the tip of Welf's sword and blossomed explosively the moment they reached the monsters' feet.

The group of adventurers standing at the eye of the storm was dumbfounded by the power of the flames and the waves of heat they radiated. Beyond the crimson haze, they heard mermen, kelpies, blue crabs, and lamias howling as they burned.

The inferno was so powerful it immolated even water monsters normally resistant to fire attacks. Blasting in all directions around the adventurers, it looked as if the sun had descended into the Dungeon.

"—Ah."

A flash of light shot across Casssandra's brain.

That most hideous of nightmares replayed in her mind alongside lines from the prophecy. In the dream, Lilly had died with her guts spilled everywhere; Haruhime had drowned in a sea of blood, torn to pieces; the bodies of Mikoto, Chigusa, and Ouka had been piled atop one another; Aisha, carrying the body of the renart, had teetered from exhaustion before finally getting swarmed and then devoured by multitudes of monsters; and a blood-drenched, hollow-eyed Daphne had drawn her last breath.

The prophecy clearly referred to death, and the images had depicted annihilation—but Welf alone had not been included.

"*The hammer shall be shattered...*" *Welf had lost his arms and legs in a cruel vision.*

Certainly, his arms and legs had been severed in her dream.

But that was all.

In the prophecy, too, Welf was the only one whose certain death had not been hinted at with words like "flowers of flesh" or "torn to pieces."

What if he lost his four limbs *but still remained alive*?

The last remaining piece of the prophecy, the warning in the sixteenth line, connected everything.

Gather the fragments—The fragments were Welf's four limbs. This suggested Cassandra, the healer, would restore them.

Consecrate the flame—This was a metaphor for lighting a fire in the furnace in order to refine the magic blades.

And finally, *beseech the sun's light*—the answer to this puzzle was already plain to see.

"A great sun...no, it's *blooming crimson lotus flowers in the shape of the sun.*"

An inferno in the shape of a sun had formed to protect the adventurers in their circular battle formation. And that "sun's light" had indeed incinerated countless monsters.

Heal the smith, watch over him as he worked at forging, and blaze a new trail with his magic blade.

That was the full meaning of the sixteenth line.

Cassandra's actions had changed the future, and as a result, Welf never lost his four limbs. Neither had Daphne and the others died.

Cassandra had won out over fate without losing a single one of her companions.

—She had managed to prevent the prophecy from coming true.

The prophetess of tragedy, fully understanding for the first time, stood rooted to the ground as the flames illuminated her face. Her hands still gripping the hilt of the magic sword, she looked at the face of the young man beside her.

Welf gazed out at the towering flames and slowly parted his lips.

"That's right...this is the beginning. The beginning of my quest for supremacy."

For Welf, it *was* the beginning.

It was a mere foothold for reaching the level of mastery that the deity of the forge had achieved.

The sword hilt he still gripped tightly was no more than a masterful forgery born through imitating Hephaistos's creations.

That's why he had partly dubbed it Shikou, or First Height. It was a name that contained his ambition to reach true mastery as well as signaling the start of his journey to realize that goal.

It was the beginning of his climb toward the peaks—the first of a series, worthy of commemoration.

The strength of this new type of magic blade depended on the magical power of its user, and for that reason, it would never run dry. Its life span was not determined by a predetermined expiration date.

This sword was not fated to crumble; it had shaken off that destiny. It was a Welf's Magic Sword—the only one in the entire world. This weapon's strength was not only directly in proportion to its user's strength, it would continue to develop as its owner grew. Just a moment ago, Welf had added the magical power of Cassandra, a healer, to his own in order to increase the sword's attack strength.

Welf's magic blades would never shatter again.

Never again would they corrupt the pride of the person who used them or the dignity of the smith who created them.

They would accompany their user through life, developing together like a part of their own body, forging a bond that only death could separate.

"...Hey, you guys."

The braying of the flames had faded and the room was quiet again. As Daphne and then all the others slowly turned to face him with incredulous eyes, Welf addressed them.

"I'm ready to give back the lives you put in my hands."

He pulled Kazuki from the ground and hoisted it onto his shoulder.

Daphne's eyes happened to meet Welf's at that exact moment, and she blushed.

Cassandra smiled at the smith, who looked exhausted but at peace. Ouka also recovered from his stunned state and turned up the corners of his mouth.

"You did it!!"

He, Aisha, Bors, and even Lilly joined in praising the smith.

Welf grinned faintly in return, then grew serious. They had to get moving, and fast.

Leaving behind immense heaps of ash that had once been monsters, the adventurers dashed out of the room.

"—?"

Just as that party took flight, elsewhere, Tsubaki raised her head.

"What is it, meow?"

"Oh...nothing, it's just..."

For once, Tsubaki had no ready answer for Chloe's question. It was simply a feeling—or rather, the sixth sense of a smith. She tried to put her premonition into words, but quickly gave up and shook her head. If she didn't focus on her immediate surroundings, she would undoubtedly trip up.

"OOOOOOOOOOOO!"

The passage in front of her eyes was packed with monsters. Starved for blood, they roared incessantly.

This was the twenty-sixth floor.

Tsubaki and her companions had made it partway through the ordeal of descending the cliff, but as soon as they got past the twenty-fifth floor, harpies, sirens, and other winged monsters appeared, forcing them to give up on that route. They'd decided instead to enter the twenty-sixth-floor maze before they were hurled against the Great Falls.

"Zaa!"

Tsubaki guided her sword boldly and skillfully through the wave of grotesque beasts dashing toward them.

Silently, almost like magic, multiple monster heads were sent dancing through the air. The terrible flash of silver sliced the long body of an aqua serpent in half, then switched direction to sever the head of a crystal turtle.

The blade she held in her hands was Benishigure, a magnificently crafted naginata-style polearm without a single nick on its blade. She had forged it herself, a first-class weapon that reigned unchallenged over all others. It flashed through the air like swirling flower petals, sending down a rain of fresh blood worthy of its name, which meant Scarlet Winter Shower.

Any monster standing in Cyclops's path was soon stained red and deposited atop the growing mountain of corpses.

"Out of my way~~~~~~~~~~!!"

The fighting style of the three waitresses rampaging in front of Tsubaki was equally extreme. Befitting their employment at The Benevolent Mistress, which had its own interesting history, their combat skills could not exactly be described as average.

While Ahnya mowed down a pack of mermen with one swing of her golden lance through their torsos, Chloe cut a fast-rolling crystal urchin into slivers with her assassin's blade. At the same time, Runoa's merciless knuckledusters tore through the intestines and chest of a kelpie rearing up to strike, transforming it into a mass of ash.

They were making quick work of the lower-level monsters. But no matter how many they slaughtered, the flood was endless.

"We don't know much about the Dungeon, but wow!"

"Yeah, is it always such a crazy party down here, meow?"

Runoa and Chloe kept fighting the unending battle as they spoke. Tsubaki and Ahnya, too, wielded their respective naginata and sword as they answered.

"If things were always like this, the place would be littered with the corpses of adventurers!"

"This is an Irregular for sure, meow! I've never seen the Dungeon like this!!"

Their expressions were racked with anxiety as they struggled to contain the deluge of monsters, never mind stemming the tide. They were thinking of *Hestia Familia*, believed to be in this zone, and Gale Wind, whose location was still unknown. This was not an easy situation to break out of, even with Level 5 Tsubaki in their party. What might have happened to a group of adventurers lacking similar strength?

"The monsters are howling like crazy…!"

Even Runoa, who knew little of the Dungeon, could sense something unusual was happening as battle cries echoed from every corner of the floor. It was as if the Dungeon itself was running wild because it couldn't get the situation under control.

"…I've got the feeling there's a really nasty monster around here, meow."

"What? What do you mean?"

"Just a hunch, meow. Still…my tail's quivering. Might be on this floor, might be above or below, but there's something nasty nearby, meow."

Chloe narrowed her eyes in irritation as Tsubaki glanced back at her. As if to back up what experience told her was true, her ears moved constantly and the fur on her slim tail stood on end. Ahnya and Runoa seemed nervous as well; their time together with Chloe had taught them to trust her as someone who was as sensitive to danger as a stray cat.

What they didn't realize was that by entering the twenty-sixth floor, and therefore dividing the attention of the monsters, they'd miraculously lightened the burden of the other party also fighting on that floor.

Unbeknownst to them, their struggle had allowed that certain other party to break through the wall of monsters and enter the twenty-seventh floor.

That said, how could Tsubaki and the others have possibly known that they had just ushered the other party into an even more harrowing situation?

"…! A scream?!"

Just then, Ahnya's ear's stood straight up. Amid the war cries of the monsters, she had made out the sound of a human voice.

"The twenty-seventh floor!"

"We made it!"

Welf and Lilly shouted excitedly the second their feet hit the flat crystal ground on the far side of the connecting passage. The labyrinth here didn't look significantly different from what they had seen on the twenty-fifth and twenty-sixth floors. The size of the crystal columns and the passageways themselves, however, was generally larger.

"Stop spacing out! We're gonna keep moving!"

Aisha didn't even give the party a second to catch their breath before hurrying them along. She was determined to reach the lower-level safety point as soon as possible.

"Monsters incoming!"

"Out of my way!"

As a great swarm of monsters hurtled toward them from the distance, Welf pushed Ouka out of the way and leaped to the vanguard.

"Kazukiiiiiiiiiiiiiiiiiiiiiiii!!"

He swung Shikou Kazuki through the air. It spit out a dramatic tongue of dancing flame that burned the entire swarm to a crisp.

"He did it again...!"

"Seems a lot stronger than his old blades!"

Cassandra and Daphne stared in shock at the vista of decimated enemies. That's how unprecedented the war cry of this new magic sword was. Aisha smiled to herself, a storm of sparks flowing around her as she took on the monsters popping up from side tunnels while Welf handled the main route.

A magic blade that never shatters...! He's crafted us quite the weapon, hasn't he?!

The scarlet-and-crimson sword glittered brilliantly against the backdrop of their surroundings. It had played a starring role on their journey to the twenty-seventh floor as well. They'd lured the monsters into cramped passageways and then torched them en masse. There wasn't even a need to chant when monsters tried to approach during the downtime between magic-blade attacks. As long as they had the timing right, the monsters never got a chance to draw near, and if a couple did happen to escape the flames, Aisha and the others could easily take care of the leftovers. Plus, they were free of the anxiety they'd always felt from not knowing when a Crozzo's Magic Sword would shatter.

In the party's current heavily wounded state, Welf's magic sword had drastically reduced the burden of fighting and turned the hopeless prospect of reaching the twenty-seventh floor into a reality. Aisha silently commended the smith's achievement in such a tough spot.

Still, she had some concerns.

Instead of eventually shattering...I guess they consume the user's Mind like spells do.

She could already see the exhaustion lining Welf's face. It wasn't possible to constantly summon such overwhelming firepower. Conducting this many attacks entailed a rate of Mind depletion that completely dwarfed the strain of using anti-magic fire.

"Ignis, hang in there!"

"I know!!"

As Aisha hollered at the sweat-drenched Welf, she silently swore she wouldn't be caught dead carrying a male adventurer on her back, and redoubled her own efforts. Swinging her *podao* again and again, she cleared a way forward for the party with a ferocity equal to Welf's magic.

"—Oh no!"

"Don't tell me this was the main hunting party…!"

They had been following the paths up and down inside the multi-level maze for some time when they stumbled upon a horrific scene.

Chigusa went pale and Ouka groaned as blood-spattered crystal walls, still-wet pools of blood, and half-eaten arms and eyeballs sprang into view. Most likely, they had been killed by the monster Bors had spoken of, each corpse belonging to a victim the beast had hunted down. The water nearby was dyed light pink, as though some of the bodies had been dragged inside.

The scene hinted at the sort of atrocious banquet that had taken place here. Aisha examined the space, oddly glad Haruhime was currently unconscious.

"What the hell showed up here…?!"

As they stood stock-still while taking in the aftermath of a string of murders that stretched into the distance like footprints, each member of the party tried to imagine what monster could have carried out this massacre on the hunting party.

Had it really managed to kill so many adventurers?

Was it still on the twenty-seventh floor?

Had Bell and Lyu managed to survive their encounter with this calamity?

As those idle musings crossed her mind, Aisha glanced at Bors, the only member of the group to have actually seen the monster. She was worried he might once again be consumed by terror, but that was not the case.

"…I can't hear it."

He was simply in shock.

"What?"

"That hopping sound…that sound it makes when it moves, I can't hear it anymore…!"

The calamity played a certain melody of death—an omen of destruction bouncing ever closer, as if it were ricocheting off the floors, walls, and ceiling. Bors had experienced that hell firsthand. The calamity on legs had instantly located and lashed out at them, no matter where they tried to hide, and he was disturbed that there was no longer any sign of it.

"Is it really…gone? Could Gale Wind and Bell have killed it?"

Aisha didn't know how to interpret the words Bors mumbled in a daze. Was he expressing a real hope or unfounded optimism? She didn't know, so she decided to keep moving.

"Bors, take us to the last place you saw Gale Wind!"

"Right!"

Whether the monster was still there or not, every second was precious. Aisha chose action over stagnation. She pushed Bors to the head of the party and told him to lead the way.

"…n't…don't."

The moment they set out, however, Aisha heard a strange voice.

"Don't…go that way."

"…?"

The warning came to her in fragments between the sounds of the party's pounding feet. The words were spoken haltingly in human language.

She checked around but saw no one. The only things reflected in her eyes were dimly glittering crystals, bloody weapons scattered on the ground, and water running alongside dry land.

Only she had heard the voice. It sounded urgent and tearful, as if it was desperately trying to hold them back. Although she sensed those emotions, however, her only choice was to ignore the warning.

That was because she knew the rest of the party would not stop until they found Bell.

"Here it is…!"

Finally, they reached an enormous room with both an abundance of solid land and numerous waterways. The entire space was scarred by traces of a terrific battle.

"What…is…this?!"

Enormous crystal formations were lying about, webbed with cracks as if something had crashed into them with incredible speed. Deep fissures ran through the ceiling, walls, and floor, which were perforated with deep, cave-like holes. Some of the crystal columns looked like they'd been melted by the extreme high heat of a flare.

Every corner of the room bore scars.

"What could have possibly caused this kind of damage…?" Daphne wondered aloud. Beside her, Ouka stared around in a daze.

The adventurers didn't need to say it aloud to know that a huge battle had taken place here, and that it had been a fight to the death with a monster far more powerful than any of them.

The problem was that neither winner nor loser remained in the room.

There was no pile of ash to show that a monster had been slain, nor did they see the tragic remains of an adventurer who had met a cruel end. The noisy gurgling of the waterways crossing one another was all that remained on the wrecked battlefield.

Welf and the others walked to the center of the room, but found no clues there, either.

As if pulled by some invisible force, Lilly approached a patch of land where the fighting had been so fierce it had changed the very direction the water flowed in.

Among several holes in the ground, she saw one vertical shaft that was larger and deeper than the others. It looked like it had been carved out by something spinning, and seemed to continue all the way through to the floor below them. As Lilly stared wordlessly down the hole, she felt as if it led all the way to the deepest depths of the Dungeon. Like the chamber's other scars, it was slowly healing and closing itself up.

—It can't be.

Suddenly, Lilly thought of the lambton, a deep-level monster she would never have expected to meet in this watery zone.

The possibility seemed outrageous, yet alarm bells were ringing in a corner of her mind.

"Where the hell did all the corpses go? I saw those guys kick the bucket myself…Did those damn monster eat them, too…?"

Clearly still fearing the hideous creature he had encountered, Bors closely examined the copious amounts of gore left behind by the missing adventurers.

He was the only one who knew exactly what had happened here. The rest of the party peered around as he spoke.

Who would be on a battlefield where neither winners nor losers remained, where all who had fought had disappeared? Of course it would be looters who stomped on the dignity of fallen warriors. Bandits who devoured towering piles of corpses to satisfy their hunger. But this devastated battlefield was not home to any loping hyenas on its land or any circling vultures in its skies.

What it did have was corpse fish lurking in its waters.

"?!"

Splash, splash.

Suddenly, multiple forms broke the water's surface and *swam into the air.*

"Fish monsters…? Floating in the air…?!"

Ouka gaped as the piscine bodies floated through seemingly empty space.

The bodies were made of stone. They were purplish black and ranged in length from one to two meders, with eight protruding appendages resembling fins. Where a pair of eyes should have been was only a single goggling eyeball.

The ragged scraps of human flesh stuck between their sharp fangs answered the question of where the corpses had gone.

"Voltemeria!"

Aisha, who had been to the twenty-seventh floor before, grimaced.

The voltemeria was a rare monster found only on that floor. Its potential ranked among the highest in the Water Capital, right alongside the kelpie. Its stone body was exceedingly resistant to physical attack, while its powerful jaws and sharp fangs could crush even the heaviest armor donned by adventurers. Its ability to swim through the air distinguished it from all other aquatic monsters.

With a composition similar to that of light quartzes, which also were present on the twenty-seventh floor, the fish monsters were able to float approximately three meders aboveground. Their speed, however, far exceeded that of the floating crystal monsters; voltemeria lunged at adventurers like menacing demons swimming in air just as they would in an underwater battle. Instead of "living fossils," adventurers usually referred to them as "flying fossils."

Normally voltemeria only inhabited areas where multiple waterways met and formed deep pools. But the smell of blood from the massacre had drawn them here.

Now, they were leaping incessantly from every waterway in the room.

"There's so many…!"

"We're surrounded…!"

The endless splashing the voltemeria caused as they flew into the air upset Cassandra, and her alarm quickly spread to Chigusa. They could easily count thirty of the floating fish in front of them.

This is bad.

Daphne paled as she took in the scene.

Their advance through the twenty-sixth floor had been an exercise in risk-taking. They had holed up in various rooms and survived monster attacks by limiting the front they presented to only the entryways. But now they were under siege. The monsters were using the massive chamber to their advantage to attack from all directions, including from overhead and underwater. There were far too many for the party to take down one by one.

On top of that, the fish could move through *both air and water.* Even with Welf's magic sword, there was no way to wipe out an enemy that crept up on them from both directions.

"Ignis, can you burn them all?"

"Do I have a choice?"

Welf spat out his response to Aisha like a curse. He was on the verge of a Mind Down. Aisha could tell from one glance at his harrowed face.

The party realized that for the third time, they were staring into the jaws of death. They had lost track of Bell and Lyu again, and with it went all indication of what was the correct way forward. The party's physical stamina and their will to go on were both dwindling.

"..."

The stone voltemerias made no sound. They simply rolled their single eyes ceaselessly in their foreheads, signaling that they would never let their prey escape.

The school of monster fish encircled the adventurers exactly like a snake coiling around its prey or a pitch-black tsunami about to swallow them whole. From outside the room, they could hear a thundering mixed chorus of other monsters. Faced with the Dungeon's infinite pool of resources, the adventurers nearly sunk to their knees.

"—!!"

The next instant, the taut thread of tension snapped and the monsters flew toward them.

The merciless siege had begun.

Predictably, Welf's magic sword was the first weapon to intercept this school of voltemerias so numerous it could have been considered a monster party on its own. Kazuki's breath of fire annihilated ten of the monster fish, but another thirty bore down on them from a different direction.

Frantically fighting for their very lives, Bors and the others struck back. They sliced, ripped, jabbed, and crushed, struggling desperately to protect their wounded companions and rearguard members currently in the center of their circular formation.

But it was no more than the final struggle of a cornered animal.

"Shiiiiiiiiiiit!"

Lilly's stores of items were long exhausted, and Cassandra's Mind had been drained to the last dregs. Welf's fingers were already slipping from the hilt of his magic sword. Ouka's brute strength, Daphne's quick wit, Chigusa's weapon handling, and Bors's tenacious grip on life were all on the verge of running out. Even the ever-flowing stream of curses from Aisha's mouth was beginning to run dry.

They killed monster after monster, but still the throng came. One of the fish clamped its jaws hard on Daphne's shoulder. The girl vomited blood. Ouka pried it off her with brute strength. Next came his turn to feel sharp fangs sinking into his arm. Cassandra and Chigusa screamed. Lilly lost hope in her own meaningless commands.

Then a singular darkness blacked out their vision.

A wall of flying fish had surrounding them.

The adventurers were about to be smashed flat by voltemerias. The purplish-black wave was about to swallow them. It was precisely the "cage of despair" that the prophetess of tragedy had sought to avoid.

And then, like a fatal blow, the adventurers glimpsed a sight so horrible it broke their spirits.

"But that can't…"

From outside the room, an avalanche of monsters led by a lamia thundered in.

The assorted species roared their individual terrible cries.

The adventurers gasped at the overwhelming numbers they faced.

"Is this the end…?"

Someone muttered the words, and all understood their horrible meaning. The voltemerias set upon the discouraged adventurers with renewed vengeance.

"—!! Haruhime?!"

"Cassandra?!"

Fangs of death bore down on the rear guard.

Having broken through the front line, the monsters closed in on Lilly and Cassandra, who were respectively guarding Mikoto and Haruhime. As their bodies slammed against Cassandra, she went flying together with Haruhime. The renart was hurled onto the ground some distance away, while Cassandra looked up to find herself staring into a hideous maw.

Her pupils contracted.

She was staring directly at death.

Daphne was shouting something.

Cassandra shut her eyes in the face of her inescapable demise.

And then—

A lamia flew at her from the side and tore the oncoming voltemeria to shreds.

"—Huh?"

The claws drew a bloody arc through the body of the floating fish.

As Cassandra froze on the spot, the lamia mowed down the other voltemeria near her with its long snakelike lower body.

"aaAAAAAAAAAAAAAAAAAAAAAAAAA!!"

The lamia thrashed and screeched in a shrill voice.

Other monsters followed suit. Unbelievably, the pack that had just barged into the room began attacking the voltemeria.

Time seemed to stand still as the adventurers watched the monsters begin to slaughter one another.

"Infighting?!"

"What is going on?!"

Daphne and Ouka whipped their heads back and forth, watching the fight in confusion. In no time at all, the battle had turned into an all-out melee. The adventurers stood like statues, unable to make sense of the scene before them.

"…Wh-what the…?"

"…"

Lilly was in a daze behind the still-stunned Cassandra, gazing at the monsters attacking the voltemerias.

The newcomers were terrifyingly strong.

Their faces were stained red with what looked like gory makeup.

They were *carrying weapons*.

"__"

Lilly's eyes practically popped out of her head.

The lamia—the same one that had just rescued Cassandra—noticed Lilly's gaze and shot her an adorable secret wink.

It was not the unfeeling blink of a monster's eye, but more like the sort of wink a human would give a dear friend.

Lilly's chest filled with an emotion so strong she could hardly breath.

"—The Xenos!"

She was practically weeping as she screamed the words.

"Greetings once again, good people of the surface!"

No sooner had she cried out than a form danced through the air and landed at her side.

This figure wore a hood and robe that covered the entire body. Lilly recognized this as a disguise meant to impersonate an adventurer.

She remembered those monster eyes that were so warm and kind.

"We have come to rescue you!"

Under her hood, the harpy Fia shook her deep red hair and smiled brightly at the teary-eyed Lilly.

"Are you well, Miss Lilliluka?"

The next moment, another small monster arrived at Lilly's side, having just used a battle-ax far too large for its size to split a voltemeria in half. It was Lett, the gentlemanly red-cap goblin. He, too, was wearing a robe to disguise his true identity.

"Why are you here...?" Lilly asked, still unable to quell her surprise.

"Fels ordered us to come! Rei and several of the others are on a separate mission at the moment, but the rest of us rushed here under Lido's command!"

Such was the Will of Ouranos when he had learned of the irregularities in the Dungeon. The Xenos had received the wizened deity's mission during their assault on the man-made dungeon, Knossos, and had split into two groups accordingly. Rei had taken charge of the group that remained in Knossos while Lett's group had taken the secret passage on the eighteenth floor into the Dungeon and headed straight for the Water Capital based on the information Ouranos had provided. Taking the shortest possible route and using any means available, they had even barged straight through the adventurers' line of defense to rescue the rear guard.

In fact, the monsters that had caused a huge panic among the adventurers returning to Rivira were these very Xenos.

They had done it all to rescue *Hestia Familia*, whom they believed had gotten pulled into the maelstrom of a certain calamity's return.

If an outsider had seen Lett and Fia in their costumes, they wouldn't have been the least bit suspicious, but Lilly lost all words at their explanation.

"We made a pledge to Mr. Bell! We promised to come running to your aid if you should ever find yourselves in trouble!"

They had only made it in time because they were Xenos.

Even the support troops Lilly had requested would have been too late to save them from this scene of tragedy.

Only the monsters that *Hestia Familia* had shaken hands with, forged a relationship of trust with, and ultimately saved from certain death could have made it in time to rescue them from imminent danger.

"We have come to pay back our debt to our irreplaceable friends!"

And there was one more reason.

There was the bond that Bell had woven.

Just as that young boy had saved Lilly, he had also saved the Xenos, and now they were here to return what he had freely offered them.

There was no way to stop the tears spilling from Lilly's chestnut eyes this time.

"B-but, how did you get here? How did you find Lilly and her companions in this immense Dungeon...?"

She hurriedly rubbed her eyes dry.

Fia answered with a smile.

"We have Helga and Aruru to thank for that!"

"Meep!"

As Cassandra lay slumped on the ground, a white al-miraj strad-dling a hellhound appeared before her. Ignoring her shock, the fluffy white monster raised one hand energetically, as if to say, *Hello again, old friend!*

"Y-you..."

The wide-eyed Cassandra had seen these faces before on that unforgettable day when these very same armed monsters had appeared on the surface and plunged Orario into complete chaos.

Obeying a prophetic dream, Cassandra had secretly protected the hellhound and the al-miraj.

"Meep! Meep!"

"Woof, woof!"

Cassandra yelped as the al-miraj threw its arms around her and the hellhound licked her. She was about to faint as the white rabbit monster buried its face in her cleavage and nuzzled her breasts. As it looked up at her with its red eyes, she couldn't help flinching a little.

"Did you...come to find me?"

The little round eyes glittered as the al-miraj rubbed its face against her chest. Cassandra took that as a yes—but an instant later, a shock ran through her, taking her breath away.

"That dream I had...with the jet-black wave and the rabbit charm..."

It had happened about twenty days earlier, just before the battle on Daedalus Street. She had seen a prophetic dream that led her to shelter the al-miraj.

In the dream, a jet-black wave had swallowed her up. Just as she was on the verge of death, she had taken out a rabbit charm she'd received beforehand and managed to escape. At the time, she'd taken the black wave as a representation of the black minotaur. Because she protected the al-miraj, she'd avoided being attacked by the frightening beast.

But now that she thought about it more closely, that interpretation seemed odd.

If she hadn't protected the "rabbit" like the oracle had dictated and gone to the place it had told her to go, she wouldn't have encountered the minotaur in the first place. Maybe Daphne had been right when she'd gotten mad and told her she was acting in a play she wrote herself.

In other words, the destruction she avoided by protecting the al-miraj hadn't taken place that day.

Cassandra looked around in a daze.

The voltemeria were black. And when a mass of them crowded together, they looked exactly like a jet-black wave.

Could it be that the dark wave that swallowed her in that dream wasn't the minotaur but rather the school of black flying fish?

Had the "rabbit charm"—that is, the al-miraj—grown used to her scent when she cared for it for days on end and then used it to locate her in the Dungeon?

Squeezing the fluffy white monster with her right hand as it gently pawed her cleavage, she realized that she had only just evaded the fate laid out in the prophetic dream moments ago.

"Can prophetic dreams be redundant...? Was the vision of that day a warning to avoid the destruction of today?"

Cassandra looked questioningly at the al-miraj and the hellhound who seemed so overjoyed to see her.

Meanwhile, Daphne—who was totally overwhelmed by the unexpected turn of events—wasn't paying attention to Cassandra, who had mustered up her courage and was about to furtively hug the monsters.

"...Nope, can't do it!"

"Meep?"

Well intentioned or not, it seemed that she still wasn't ready to go that far.

"You guys..."

On the verge of a Mind Down, Welf could only manage a few

mumbled words. But as he watched, a troll, a lamia, and a deadly hornet wiped the floor with a huge school of voltemerias while totally ignoring the adventurers.

"Wh-what…the hell is going…on?"

"Are these…the armed monsters we heard about?"

"I thought *Loki Familia* wiped them out on Daedalus Street!"

Bors, Chigusa, and Ouka were hopelessly confused. Daphne was still frozen, unable to understand what was happening. The monsters appeared to be protecting the adventurers, or rather prioritizing their fierce battle with their own kind as they ignored the adventurers. Bors, Chigusa, Ouka, and Daphne couldn't manage much more than a freaked-out response, let alone a coherent reaction.

But Welf understood what was happening.

A gargoyle flew over his head, noticed Welf's stare, and glanced back at him before turning away like a rude person. Suddenly, savage air combat commenced. Completely overpowered by the Xenos with its huge, nearly indestructible stone wings, the voltemerias fell one after the next.

Below the gargoyle, a certain lizardman was fighting his own battle. With countless ground-battle victories under his belt, the proud warrior sliced through several furious flying fish with one swipe of the scimitar in his right hand, while pounding still more with a bold swing of the longsword in his left.

As he sped in front of Welf, the lizardman turned up the corners of his fang-filled mouth.

He looked like he was about to smile.

—*Guess who else is here?*

That's what the indomitable glint in his narrowed reptilian eyes seemed to say as he glanced across the room.

Welf followed his gaze and jumped in surprise.

A figure in a black robe was dashing across the battlefield—

, "…Ahh."

Haruhime's eyelids fluttered as something moved against her cheek.

She felt very groggy, almost like some gauze draped over her ears was muffling the sounds around her.

The one thing she knew for sure was that she was on a battlefield.

Perhaps due to the persistent aftereffects of the Mind Down, an extraordinary exhaustion and lethargy weighed down her arms and legs. But she had to sing. She understood her role as a sorcerer. She could not afford to remain lying down.

Haruhime whipped her body with the lash of her will. She needed to summon strength in her limbs and bring a chant to her lips. She had to grant that miraculous light to her companions. But right as she was thinking that she should stand up, and fast, like Bell had done on that day in the past—somebody took her in their arms.

"…?"

As she realized that her body was being gently supported, she opened her eyes.

She saw a pair of amber eyes, and then a face filled with a warm red light.

It looked exactly like the face of the girl Haruhime had been thinking of ceaselessly since they parted.

As soon as her hazy vision came into focus, Haruhime's lips spoke the girl's name.

"Lady…Wiene…?"

In response to the feebly whispered words, the dragon girl's face blossomed into a smile, her blue-white hair swaying.

"Yes, Haruhime."

Tears fell from Haruhime's green eyes at the sound of the vouivre's voice.

"I've come to save you!"

"Ah…ahhhh…!"

Still kneeling, the Xenos drew her close in her slender arms. Haruhime found holding back her emotions an impossible feat.

She had never stopped thinking of this girl who felt so much like a sister or a daughter. Not a day had passed when she did not think of her. Her tender feelings at seeing Wiene again swept away any thought of exhaustion. She wrapped her own arms around the dragon girl and pulled her close. Wiene nuzzled her tear-stained face against Haruhime's.

"I wanted to see you so much, Haruhime!"

"Me too...me too!"

"I didn't cry the whole time! I didn't want to make you worry!"

Like Fia, Wiene was wearing a robe that concealed her head and body. Her beautiful voice sounded like birdsong to Haruhime's ears.

"But...now I can't stop crying!"

Haruhime felt as if her heart would burst. The dragon girl's smile was as pure as the clear tears rolling down her cheeks.

They embraced once again.

"Ms. Wiene...!"

"Wiene has been taking part in our various activities, and when she heard you were in trouble, she said she wanted to come no matter what."

Lilly had been watching the reunion unfold in happy surprise. As Lett explained the dragon girl's motivations, she sensed the truth in his words. She thought back warmly on the days she had spent on the surface with Wiene. She truly had become a part of their familia.

"What is going on in here, meow~~~~?!"

Just then, she heard an oblivious voice shouting at them from the room's entryway, accompanied by the sound of a monster being brazenly kicked aside.

Ahnya and her party had arrived just a few steps behind the Xenos.

"We found the adventurers, but..."

"The monsters are killing one another, meow?!"

The panting Ahnya was startled out of her wits by the scene they found inside the room. Runoa and Chloe also gaped at the ferocious battle between the various monsters—that was to say, between the voltemeria and the Xenos.

After the band of four heard Lilly's scream, they had followed

Chloe's hunch to the twenty-seventh floor, where they caught a glimpse of a terrifyingly strong parade of armed monsters from behind. Sensing the monsters might be up to something based on their single-minded march into the floor's depths, Ahnya and her companions had decided to follow them. Whenever they lost sight of the parade, they simply followed the sounds of fighting before eventually ending up in this room.

"Ms. Ahnya…! Lady Hestia really came through for us!"

Lilly was the first to guess the meaning of their arrival, silently cheering her patron deity's response to her request for support from the surface.

Meanwhile, a certain half-dwarf was advancing toward a certain young man as if drawn to him magnetically.

"Welf…"

"Tsubaki?! Why are you…?"

Tsubaki stopped in front of the confused smith.

Her former colleague was in tatters. He was gasping for breath, covered in wounds large and small, and seemed ready to collapse at the slightest nudge.

But for the moment, she didn't care. All her single eye could see was the sword in his hands.

"That magic sword…"

It was a crimson longsword. Not a Crozzo's Magic Sword—a Welf's Magic Sword.

Her right eye opened wide with a level of emotion Welf had never seen in it before.

She was not so unsophisticated as to ask what it was, however.

To the contrary, she found herself momentarily dumbstruck. One glance at the sword's gleam told the master smith what Welf had achieved.

"Heh-heh-heh, ha-ha-ha-ha-ha-ha-ha!! So you've finally gone and don't it, eh, greenhorn?"

Her roaring laughter was hardly appropriate for a battlefield. As Bors and the others peered crossly at her, only Welf returned her gaze with clear eyes.

"You tried your hand at it even though you didn't know how far the heights of mastery go! You aimed for the peaks of the heavens!"

"..."

"I said you were an idiot, but to think you were actually an idiot even among idiots! And all the more a fool for giving unnecessary advice! Ahhh, what a cheeky bastard! A unique pleasure, this is!"

Tsubaki's words were neither insults nor criticisms, but instead the expression of pure delight.

They were a sign of the rivalry she felt toward this boy who had exceeded her expectations.

And they were proof that she had accepted him as a part of her tribe.

"Congratulations, Welf Crozzo. You're finally one of us."

Then she added, "And...welcome to hell."

Her praise was genuine; the master smith celebrated Welf's achievement from the bottom of her heart.

"I'm in a good mood. Leave the rest of these monsters to me."

"...! Wait, Tsubaki, those monsters are—"

"I know, I know. I'll only take down the ones that aren't armed."

Tsubaki turned away from Welf, licking her lips at the arrival of a fresh school of voltemeria that the waterway had carried to her side. Unable to hide her excitement, she grinned as she set upon them like a demoness.

Ahnya, Chloe, and Runoa threw themselves into action and joined Tsubaki in slaughtering the voltemeria for the sake of the paralyzed party they had come to save.

A bitter battle between monsters, adventurers, and Xenos had begun.

"Lido! Lidooooooooooo!"

A soprano voice pierced the ceaseless sound of fierce fighting. The lizardman looked up to see the Xenos mermaid Mari popping her head out of a waterway. He hurried to her side.

"Mari, you're here of all places?! Then you must know what happ—"

"Bell! Bell went below!"

Mari tearfully interrupted Lido's human words.

"Bellucchi? Mari, you were with him?!"

The surprised lizardman quickly made sense of Mari's halting words, gleaning that Bell and an elf had been sucked into a wormhole and taken to a level somewhere below them, only to be followed by the "apostle of murder" that had recently spawned. The report matched up with what they'd learned about the "calamity" from the wizened god via Fels.

"UOOOOOOOOOOOOOOOOOOOOOOOOOO!!"

The Xenos whipped their heads around toward Lido as he bellowed a war cry. That call was a message to monsters that humans could not understand. Having received his information, the lamia and several other Xenos howled back at him and immediately raced out of the room.

"The armed monsters have...!"

"One minute I think they're fighting among themselves, and the next they're taking off. What exactly is going on, meow?! I don't understand one bit, meow!"

Chigusa and Chloe watched in shock as the eccentric monsters hunted down the last few voltemerias before suddenly rushing out of the room.

"Mr. Lido has—?!"

"He said that Mr. Bell and an elven adventurer were taken to a lower level by another monster!"

Lett, still wearing his adventurer disguise, had remained behind with Fia. He relayed what they had just learned.

"It seems that an apostle of our mother, the Dungeon...a huge monster chased after Bell and the elf!"

"...! And what floor are they on?!"

"We don't know! But if the god Ouranos's guess is right...they could be in the deep levels."

Lett's words left Lilly speechless. Her mind went completely blank at the prospect of this worst-of-all-possible news.

"And Lido had a message for you...'If you want to come, then come. We will take you there.'"

"!!"

Lido's call to action startled Lilly. She perfectly understood what he was trying to say.

"Ms. Ahnya!"

"Meow, meow, meow? The white-haired one's supporter is calling...?" The catgirl raised her voice as she turned toward Lilly without moving. The prum ran up to her.

"What level are you, Ms. Ahnya?"

"What kind of question is that, meow? More importantly, where is Lyu—?"

"Oh for goodness' sake! Just answer my question!!"

"Meow? Level Four! Chloe, Runoa, and I are all the same level as Lyu, meow!"

Frightened by Lilly's bloodshot eyes and indignant expression, Ahnya answered reflexively. Lilly's heart pounded at her answer.

"—Then we can clear the Water Capital!"

The very next instant, Lilly shouted a command to the party.

"It is highly likely that Mr. Bell and Ms. Lyu were carried through a wormwell hole to a lower level! We'll all head to the safety point and regroup! From there we will go to rescue Mr. Bell and Ms. Lyu!"

"What...?!"

Bors and the others stared at Lilly in a daze as she shot out her orders.

"No arguments!!"

The little commander proclaimed her decision like a tyrant.

The mysterious waitresses from The Benevolent Mistress *are actually Level Four fighters! And Tsubaki, the captain of* Hephaistos Familia, *is Level Five! If we work together with them and the Xenos, we can make our way through the twenty-eighth floor and beyond...!*

Lilly noted the fighting ability of Ahnya and her companions on her mental battle map, calculating whether the strategy she envisioned was feasible.

She had guessed the intention behind Lido's message correctly.

The Xenos planned to rescue Bell together with Lilly's party. Most likely they would maintain a certain distance from the adventurers as they searched for Bell and Lyu, relaying messages back and forth via bestial howls that Lett could interpret for them. This is what Lido meant by saying the Xenos would take them there.

Starting with Lido and Gros, who both had Level 5 potential, the Xenos had high fighting ability. Including Tsubaki's party meant they had more than enough strength for the battles that lay ahead. Plenty to break through the lower levels. All Lilly and the other Level 1 and 2 adventurers had to do was provide support.

It was clear that an unexpected opportunity—a kind of opening— had materialized. But could they properly execute the strategy needed to take advantage of it?

We might.

No. We're absolutely going to make it work!

They would take up the challenge to defeat the Dungeon and find the boy and the elf.

Nearby, Daphne and Cassandra were debating their next move.

"You mean we're looking for the wormwell's hole? But we have no proof Rabbit Foot was even taken down there, let alone any assurance they're alive..." Daphne argued.

"L-let's go with them, Daphne!! Let's save Bell and Lyu!"

"Oh geez! Fine, I'll come along! It's not exactly a question of logic now that we've come this far, anyway."

Daphne tried to voice her doubts about Lilly's plans, but when Cassandra eagerly leaned forward to convince her friend, Daphne gave in and responded in a detached manner.

Meanwhile, Bors was looking for a way out. As usual, he was putting his own safety first.

"I'm not obligated to go along to the end...!"

"What are you talking about? A Level Three fighter like you is valuable to us. We're going to squeeze every drop of strength out of you until you're bone dry!"

"You've gotta be kidding me!"

Aisha laughed shamelessly, having effectively denied him any chance to escape. At the same time, Tsubaki's party was renewing its commitment to saving Lyu.

"I don't really get it...but if Lyu's down below, then I'm going, meow!" Ahnya said.

"In the Dungeon, the lower you go the worse it gets, right? Whew, I'm already exhausted."

"It's a losing proposition if we're not getting compensated for this quest, meow...And we're not even adventurers."

"Ha-ha-ha! We're all in the same boat now!"

Tsubaki's laugh swept away Runoa's and Chloe's lingering pessimism.

Chigusa and Ouka, on the other hand, were still thinking about the scene they had witnessed on Daedalus Street, when a certain vouivre had rescued the children.

"...I feel like those armed monsters...*were intentionally helping us...*"

"...And those guys hiding behind robes who seemed to be adventurers...Smith, you better explain all this later!"

"Not sure I can explain it very well!"

Brushing aside their questions, Welf threw his two companions an annoyingly calm smile.

That same vouivre was still standing beside Haruhime.

"Let's go, Haruhime! Let's save Bell!"

"Yes, Lady Wiene!"

The dragon girl reached out her hand, and Haruhime squeezed it firmly.

As Lilly looked around at the determination and high morale apparent in the faces of her companions, her little chest grew warm with emotion.

We can do it...! With this party, we can make it to the deep levels!!

There was just one problem left.

"From here on out it's a battle against time. We've got to find Mr. Bell while he's still okay!"

"...!"

"Progress in the lower levels is slow. It'll take us at least a day or two to reach the deep levels...!"

Lilly responded to Lett's muttered concern by clearing her throat.

Without proper equipment, they would only be able to function in the lower levels for a limited amount of time. They didn't have a second to spare. They had to advance at top speed if they were going to rescue Bell and Lyu. She momentarily pushed away the anxiety, uncertainty, and fear she felt swirling around her and issued an order.

"We're off!"

The adventurers began to run.

They left the room and flew into the main route leading to the next floor.

The Dungeon could not stop them now.

The war cries of the Xenos thundered ahead of them, as if they were welcoming this advancing front of courage.

【DAPHNE ‧ LAULOS】

BELONGS TO: *MIACH FAMILIA*
RACE: HUMAN
JOB: ADVENTURER
DUNGEON RANGE: TWENTY-SEVENTH FLOOR
WEAPONS: DAGGER, RAPIER, WHIP
CURRENT FUNDS: 570,000 VALIS

Lv. **2**

STRENGTH: D505   DEFENSE: E478   DEXTERITY: B707   AGILITY: C698
MAGIC: F370   IMMUNITY: I

《MAGIC》

【RAUMURE】
- PROTECTION MAGIC
- INCREASES DEFENSE AND SIGNIFICANTLY INCREASES AGILITY
- EFFECTS ARE PROPORTIONAL TO THE USER'S MAGICAL POWER

《SKILL》

【HELIOS PASSION】
- SLIGHTLY INCREASES AGILITY
- WHEN BEING CHASED, TEMPORARILY GRANTS USE OF THE DEVELOPMENTAL ABILITY "ESCAPE"

【LAUREL WREATH】
- GREATLY INCREASES DEFENSE WHEN EXHAUSTED OR NEAR DEATH
- USER MAY CHOOSE THE ACTIVATION LOCATION. MODIFIES SKIN AT TARGET LOCATION

《FENCER LAUREATE》

- A BATON-LIKE SLENDER SHORTSWORD MEASURING 60 CELCH IN LENGTH.

- APOLLO SPECIAL-ORDERED THE WEAPON FOR DAPHNE. MADE IN THE FAR EAST, ITS ORIGINAL NAME WAS KEIKAN KENJIN.

- MADE OF SACRED MOON-TREE SAP AND BLUE STEEL. DURABLE AND LIGHT, IT SUPPORTS ITS USER'S MAGIC.

- ALTHOUGH DAPHNE WOULD PREFER TO GET RID OF IT, THE WEAPON'S PERFORMANCE IS EXTREMELY HIGH, SO SHE STILL USES IT ALL THE TIME.

- DAPHNE FEELS NO LOYALTY TO APOLLO, THE DEITY WHO FORCED HER TO JOIN HIS FAMILIA, BUT HER FEELINGS TOWARD HIM ARE COMPLEX, SINCE HE ALLOWED HER COMPLETE FREEDOM DURING HER TIME UNDER HIM. ACCORDING TO HER, SHE'S SOMEWHAT GRATEFUL TO HIM BUT HATES HIM EVEN MORE.

【CASSANDRA · ILLION】

BELONGS TO: *MIACH FAMILIA*
RACE: HUMAN
JOB: HEALER
DUNGEON RANGE: TWENTY-SEVENTH FLOOR
WEAPONS: WAND, SHORT ARROWS
CURRENT FUNDS: 111,111 VALIS

《HOLY CRYSTAL ROD》

- A MAGIC WAND THAT RAISES THE MAGICAL POWER OF SPELLCASTERS AND HEALERS. WORTH 1,200,000 VALIS.

- THE QUEEN'S MACE OF SUNSHINE THAT APOLLO GAVE CASSANDRA WAS SO SOPHISTICATED THAT IT WAS BASICALLY IMPOSSIBLE TO FIGURE OUT HOW TO USE, SO UNLIKE DAPHNE, CASSANDRA RELUCTANTLY BOUGHT HER OWN WEAPON, THE HOLY CRYSTAL ROD. SHE HAS SINCE REPAID THE LOAN SHE TOOK OUT FOR IT. MAGIC WANDS ARE TYPICALLY MORE EXPENSIVE THAN FRONTLINE WEAPONS.

- WHEN CASSANDRA CONVERTED TO *MIACH FAMILIA*, SHE HAD THEIR EMBLEM CARVED ON THE ROD.

- AS AN ASIDE, CASSANDRA ASSUMES CURE EPHIALTES IS FOR REVERSING THE EFFECTS OF POISON; SHE DOES NOT REALIZE IT ALSO CAN REVERSE THE EFFECT OF CURSES.

STATUS

Lv. **2**

STRENGTH: H101   DEFENSE: H189   DEXTERITY: G248   AGILITY: F341
MAGIC: D588   HEALING: I

《MAGIC》

【SOUL LIGHT】
- WIDE-AREA RECOVERY MAGIC
- AREA OF EFFECT VARIES ACCORDING TO AMOUNT OF MIND USED

【CURE EPHIALTES】
- DISPELS HARM

《SKILL》

【FIVE-DIMENSION TROIA】
※ INDECIPHERABLE
※ EVEN THE NAME OF THE SKILL IS NOT WRITTEN IN HIEROGLYPHS; THE CURRENT NAME IS BASED ON MIACH'S INTERPRETATION

《RABBIT CHARM》

- A PROTECTIVE CHARM MADE FROM THE FUR OF AN AL-MIRAJ. LOOKS EXACTLY LIKE A RABBIT'S FOOT. CASSANDRA MADE IT HERSELF.

- TERRIFIED BY THE PROPHETIC DREAM SHE HAD IMMEDIATELY BEFORE THE BATTLE OF DAEDALUS STREET, CASSANDRA MADE THE RABBIT CHARM MENTIONED IN THE PROPHECY. NATURALLY, SHE OBTAINED THE FUR FROM THE XENOS AL-MIRAJ.

- ARURU AND HELGA FOLLOWED THE SCENT OF THE CHARM HANGING AROUND CASSANDRA'S NECK AS WELL AS CASSANDRA HERSELF. LITERALLY AN ITEM OF PROPHECY.

- INCIDENTALLY, IT'S A SECRET THAT THE PROPHETESS OF TRAGEDY FELT A BIT GIDDY AFTER BELL WAS NICKNAMED "RABBIT FOOT" IN A BITTERSWEET TWIST OF FATE.

THIS IS AN ABSOLUTE SECRET.

【WELF ⬩ CROZZO】

BELONGS TO: *HESTIA FAMILIA*
RACE: HUMAN
JOB: SMITH
DUNGEON RANGE: TWENTY-SEVENTH FLOOR
WEAPONS: GREATSWORD
CURRENT FUNDS: 4,000 VALIS

《PORTABLE FURNACE AND SMITH'S TOOLKIT》

- A SET OF TOOLS WELF ASSEMBLED FOR THE PURPOSE OF CONDUCTING MAINTENANCE AND REPAIRS. HE SPENT QUITE A LOT OF HIS CAPITAL ON PREPARATIONS FOR THIS EXPEDITION, AS DID BELL AND THE REST OF THEIR PARTY.

STATUS

Lv. **2**

STRENGTH: H118   DEFENSE: H123   DEXTERITY: H143   AGILITY: I71
MAGIC: I72   SMITH: I

《MAGIC》

【WILL-O-WISP】
- ANTI-MAGIC FIRE
- CHANT: "BLASPHEMOUS BURN"

《SKILL》

【BLOOD OF CROZZO】
- ABILITY TO PRODUCE MAGIC SWORDS
- STRENGTHENS THE MAGICAL PROPERTIES OF MAGIC SWORDS DURING THEIR PRODUCTION

《SHIKOU KAZUKI》

- MAGIC LONGSWORD. FLAME ATTRIBUTES.

- THE NOTABLE FIRST WEAPON IN THE SHIKOU SERIES THAT WELF PLANS TO DEVELOP FURTHER.

- BECAUSE IT RUNS ON THE USER'S MAGICAL POWERS, THE WEAPON HAS NO PREDETERMINED LIFE SPAN AND THUS ESCAPES THE FATE OF ORDINARY SELF-DESTRUCTING MAGIC SWORDS.
  ITS LEVEL OF POWER ALSO CHANGES IN TANDEM WITH THE USER.
  A COMPLETELY NEW TYPE OF MAGIC SWORD THAT STANDS APART FROM EVERYTHING WELF HAS MADE BEFORE.

- HEPHAISTOS ONCE SAID THAT, AS A SMITH, SHE CONSIDERS THE HESTIA KNIFE A WEAPON ON THE PATH TO HERESY BECAUSE IT GROWS ALONGSIDE ITS USER. ON THE OTHER HAND, AS A SMITH OF MAGIC SWORDS, WELF SEES SHIKOU, A SIMILAR WEAPON, AS A START ON THE PATH TO RIGHTEOUSNESS.

- EXCLUSIVE TO TIMES WHEN WELF USES SHIKOU, THE MAGIC BLADE WILL RESONATE WITH THE BLOOD OF THE SPIRITS AND BECOME EVEN MORE POWERFUL THAN ANY OF CROZZO'S MAGIC SWORDS.

© Suzuhito Yasuda

CHAPTER 9
HELLO, DEEP LEVELS

The deep levels? …Is it scary down there?

I asked that question once.

I wanted to hear the answer from that flower so far beyond my reach.

To the girl I look up to so much.

What does the world look like from the heights where that swordswoman who bears the name of first-tier adventurer stands?

How perilous is the stage where my idol stands as she pursues her adventures?

I asked her out of curiosity, or maybe because I wanted to get a little closer to her.

When I was there, I felt for the first time that monsters…that the Dungeon was frightening.

We were up on the city walls, surrounded by blue sky.

I couldn't see past her golden eyes.

She answered me with the gaze of an adventurer who had risked her life many times.

It's not the kind of thing you can understand by only hearing about it…but if you go there, you'll understand.

She spoke very clearly.

If…one day in the far, far future you're able to go there, then…

I'm trying to remember that conversation.

What did she tell me that day?

For some reason, I can't seem to remember the words.

My ears are ringing.

The sound is like the shrill cry of a child who's just woken from a nightmare.

A cry of reason, screaming in denial of reality.

The shriek of my instincts assaults the depths of my mind.

"The deep levels…"

The whispered fragment of a thought falls from my lips and melts into the darkness.

Stillness pierces my ears.

The pounding of my heart thunders through my whole body.

The gloomy blackness of the maze embraces me.

A strange milky color seems to stick to the walls, and the ceilings are so high I can't even see them. The scale of the labyrinth is so enormous it seems impossible.

I'm on the thirty-seventh floor.

I am in the abyss that all adventurers fear—the deep levels of the Dungeon.

"………"

My neck feels frozen in place, so I move just my eyes to look around.

I don't see any monsters nearby. No telltale sounds or signs of them, either.

I squint into the dimness, barely able to make out my surroundings.

My current location is a tremendously large room. The distance from the center of the chamber, where I am, to the walls must be at least four hundred meders. Aside from a couple of specific places like the Great Wall of Sorrows on the seventeenth floor and the pantry, I've never been in a Dungeon room this big. The phosphorescence illuminating the walls is weak as candlelight.

Right next to me is the dead body of a huge serpent.

It's the lambton, otherwise known as a wormwell, that expired after we sliced our way out of its belly and crawled through a fountain of blood. That was after it swallowed us on the twenty-seventh floor and burrowed its way down here with us in its belly.

"……! …Ah…"

I stare with one wide eye at the huge corpse.

My mouth opens and closes of its own accord, severed from conscious thought.

My tongue is all tangled up, unable to form words.

I can produce only a dry rasping sound as if I've tried to take a breath and failed.

—This has gotta be a lie. It can't be real.

Wormwells normally show up on the thirty-seventh floor.

Did it take us back to its own nest, of all places?

Did it really burrow through ten floors' worth of rock?

Did its homing instinct carry it here as it teetered on the edge of death—here to the deep levels?!

This is so weird!

It's totally ridiculous!

Unprecedented!

I've never heard of anything so harsh!

This is bad...really, really bad...!!

My thoughts keep swirling with one particularly apprehensive word.

I'm dripping sweat and my body feels unnaturally hot.

The deep zone.

The Guild has designated this place the "True Deadline."

It's the most dangerous place in the whole Dungeon. I am definitely not ready to play a role on this stage—especially not solo!

Especially not in my current condition...!

"Ms. Lyu...!"

I check the elf lying limp in my arms.

She's battered from head to toe after being swallowed by the wormwell and exposed to its toxic stomach acid. Patches of her long cape and battle clothes have been burned away, revealing her bare white skin, which is marred with countless burns. Her right leg, wrapped up in her cape, is bent at a strange angle. It's broken.

My own skin has been burned all over by that same caustic acid. My left eyelid melted and is stuck shut, so I can't open it. As I continue looking around with my one good eye, I pull Lyu a little closer to protect her—or maybe to cling to her.

I grip her narrow shoulders with trembling fingers that refuse to obey me anymore.

"Ms. Lyu, Ms. Lyu…Ms. Lyu…!"

Like a little child crying for his big sister, I call her name over and over.

I can't think. My mind is a blank.

This is the worst possible Irregular. We've been hurled onto the thirty-seventh floor. We're at the mercy of the darkness.

Alone, isolated, detached, completely cut off. I'm incredibly uneasy. Cold. Lonely. Sad. In pain. My emotions are a mess.

I'm quietly spiraling in a deadly panic.

The only thing I can do is beg my lone traveling companion, the elf, to wake up.

That's when it happens.

Pitter-patter.

Fragments of stone are falling.

"—"

I freeze as the little pieces of something dribble onto my head.

I peer up as if my gaze is being pulled toward the ceiling.

The fragments of stone are still falling from the vault of darkness, which blocks my view of the ceiling. I can't figure out what's happening based on such limited visual information.

But sound is another matter.

I definitely heard a noise.

A noise like *something* was speeding violently toward this floor.

Like a certain object was hurtling down the hole we came through—

The moment I become aware of that possibility, the blood drains from my head.

That enormous form rises again in my mind's eye.

The shell that repels magic.

Those all-destroying claws.

And those pure red eyes that glint like fresh blood.

No way—

Is the monster we fought on the twenty-seventh floor chasing us down the hole the wormwell dug?

So it can kill us?!

Shudders rack my body, but in my heart, I know the truth.

The dying words of that man called Jura—the final unrelenting command of that tamer—have led the monster to us.

My heart beats faster as I think back on the circlet with the scarlet stone fastened to its colossal body.

"Hiii…yaaaaaaaaaaaaaa…!"

The fuel of anxiety has been thrown onto my blank mind.

Run, run!

Escape that monster!

That sole desire is enough to get my frozen mind and body moving again.

I force energy into my limbs and stand up, still supporting Lyu. The second I do, it suddenly feels like someone lit my body on fire. My abrupt movement revived all the agony that was momentarily numbed.

My open wounds drip blood onto the floor. My seared skin is screaming.

Worst of all is the incredible pain of my left arm.

Heat is radiating from that arm, which was wrapped in the Goliath Scarf while I used it to block the monster's claws throughout the length of our battle. I feel like I'm about to vomit. My eyes are tearing up and my legs are shaking. My spirit is on the verge of collapsing.

Still, I grit my teeth and push off the ground with my boots.

I take a step forward.

With each step, I push aside exhaustion and pain to propel my body forward.

I can still move.

I can still run.

Even now, I can still…!

As stone fragments continue to trickle down from above, I gather my meager strength and set off. Supporting the unconscious Lyu with my shoulder, I make a mad dash across the room. But just before I reach the opening that leads to the passage—*crash!*

Something leaps out of the hole.

"!!"

Casting a purplish-blue glow, it hurtles from far overhead into the ground.

The room shakes and rumbles.

When I turn around, I see its deformed, one-armed silhouette swaying. There are the familiar reverse-joint knees and bony body encased in a shiny purplish-blue shell. At three meders or so tall, its huge form makes me think of the phrase "a dinosaur fossil wearing armor." The left arm ends in those destructive claws one could easily mistake for fangs.

Across the dimness separating us, I can see its two red eyes glowing eerily.

No question about it.

It's the ultra-destructive monster from the twenty-seventh floor.

"—"

Whirl.

Like it's pinning us with its gaze, the monster rotates its neck.

Its glowing red orbs meet my eyes.

"—oOOOOOOOOOOOOOOOOOOOOOO!!"

"?!"

As soon as it roars, I turn on my heels and dive into a passage, leaving the room behind.

I can hear it thumping after me, raising a hellish commotion.

"*Gasp…!*"

I dash aimlessly down the complex passages of the labyrinth. If it catches up to us, we're done for. If I turn into a dead end, it's all over. If I encounter another monster, that'll be it. The only thing I can do in this worst-case scenario is pray.

I change directions over and over, dashing down branching passages as I try to give my enemy the slip.

But the monster's footsteps don't fade.

If anything…they're getting closer by the second!

"Huff…huff…huff!"

My lungs are on fire. The sweat won't stop. My throat is burning.

Since I'm carrying Lyu, I'm going so slowly I want to cry. I can hardly lift my feet. My whole body is screaming out in pain. All the same, I flee from the monster with all the strength I can muster.

My brain isn't working right. Questioning voices rise and vanish like bubbles at the back of my mind.

I've driven this thing into a corner once. Should I turn around to face it and put an end to my anxiety?

What good will running away now do?

Isn't it a bad plan to keep running from an enemy who will, without a doubt, chase me to the edge of the world?

Am I just buying time before I have to commit to a decision?

But no, it's no good.

I can't do that right now.

Right now, I just have to run!

I'd be willing to bet on it. If I fight this monster this instant, either Lyu or I will die.

The monster will fight with everything it's got and considering how my body is so badly burned by the wormwell's poisonous acid, I won't be able to put up much of a fight. The situation is totally different from the battle on the twenty-seventh floor.

I absolutely cannot fight that monster right now!

Determined to escape, I squeeze my left hand into a fist and unconsciously start to chime.

"—!!"

After making a couple more turns in the maze, the monster has managed to close the distance between us to the point where I can clearly see it. It's bouncing in every direction off the floor, walls, and ceiling of the Dungeon at top speed. Even though our fight should have also left it in bad shape, this monster's instinct must be urging it to kill its prey at all costs.

The gleaming red eyes pierce my back. I can hear the claws of destruction making scratching sounds.

Sensing that the threat of the ever-growing bloodlust barreling toward me has reached a critical point, I swivel halfway around and thrust out my left hand.

"!!"

The monster has noticed.

The chime.

And the particles of light seeping from the Goliath Scarf wrapped around my left hand as I charge.

Fear fills the red eyes and it screams in fury.

I've charged for twenty seconds.

My face distorts as I shout.

"Firebolt!!"

A huge bolt of electrical fire hurtles relentlessly forward.

Within the enclosed space of the passage, the turbid stream of flames demolishes walls and ceiling alike as it charges ahead.

From the corner of my eye, I see the monster flex its left leg backward and bound into a side passage the instant before electrical fire swallows it up.

A second later, the firebolt explodes violently in the passage. Since I was unable to fully absorb the kickback from firing, the shot went up at a slight angle into the ceiling. The passage shatters.

"Whoa!"

I'm thrown back by the wind and dust from my shot's explosion. As Lyu and I fly backward, the bedrock above rumbles and begins to fall, as if the whole tunnel is about to cave in. The sound of cascading rock echoes through the floor.

Finally…it stops.

Having rolled across the floor and landed facedown, I manage to look up at last. As the dust clears, I realize the broad passage has been completely blocked by milky white boulders. We can't return the way we came, but neither can the monster pursue us.

Did we actually…get through this?

"Huff, puff…aah…!"

It's a stroke of pure luck.

Same goes for the fact that we weren't crushed by the falling rock. I'm fairly sure we won't get off so easy twice.

I give myself a second to calm my ragged breath, then attempt to peel myself off the ground with shaking hands. I fail several times. The aftermath of my skill Argonaut has totally drained my physical and mental strength. I'm a wet noodle. Worse, I'm on the verge of fainting.

It hurts, it sucks. I'm suffering.

For a second, a powerful desire to let my strength fade away washes over me.

To lay here facedown on the ground and close my eyes.

Overwhelmed by this total mental collapse, I'm drifting between two desires, when—

"Mr....Cra...nell...?

"!"

I jump at the whispered words.

When I shift my gaze toward Lyu, who's laying faceup on the ground, I see that her eyes are slightly open. The hazy sky-blue irises peer around until they find me.

"Ms. Lyu...!"

Instantly, I kick away the desire that was sweet-talking me into giving up. I'm *able* to kick it away.

I can't let anyone die. I don't want anyone to die.

Just like I felt with Weine, but with everyone this time.

After all, I promised I'd become stronger for that exact reason...!

I curse at myself for letting whines and complaints momentarily control me. I bite my lip and get up for real this time.

I drag myself over to Lyu and sink to the ground on both knees.

I lift her battered body in my arms.

"...What is this place?"

"It's...the thirty-seventh floor...the deep levels."

I can't hide my despair as I answer Lyu's feeble question. Stumbling again and again over my words, I explain as simply as I can that we were swallowed by the wormwell, carried to a different floor, chased by the same monster we battled before, and for now have escaped. Her eyes glint with understanding, perhaps because memories of the twenty-seventh floor are coming back to her.

She squints at me, clearly having guessed just how bad our current situation is.

Most likely her astounding physical strength is gone now, along with the spirit that sent shivers down my spine.

She just stares at my face with its one crushed eye.

"Uuu…!"

"Ms. Lyu?!"

Grimacing, she brings her hands protectively to her body.

She is as exhausted and horribly injured as I am. If I take her broken right leg into consideration, she might even be in worse shape than me. Huge beads of sweat cover her skin.

"Please heal yourself! Use your magic on your own body…!"

I don't have any items with me. I lost them along with my leg holster in the battle with the monster. Given that, I beg Lyu to use her recovery magic.

"…"

Maybe she's still groggy, because she keeps peering at me with her half-open eyes. Eventually she parts her lips very slowly.

"I sing now…of a distant forest…A familiar melody…of life…"

Haltingly, in a raspy voice, she begins to chant.

Finally, as if she's wringing out her last drops of strength, *she places her hands on my face.*

"Noa…Heal."

The surprised look in my eyes can't stop what happens next. A warm glow like dappled sunlight filtering through treetops envelops my face.

I scream at her.

"No!! Not me! Please heal yourself! If you don't, you'll…!"

Even as I'm screaming, the wounds on my face are closing and the pain is ebbing from my closed eye. The healing power centers on my neck but also flows to my wounds and burned skin. My energy level even flickers up slightly from zero.

Having seen my right eye open, Lyu lets her hands drop like a marionette whose strings have been cut.

"Why did you heal me?!"

"…I can't…I can't move on my own…I'm useless…"

"…!"

"That was the last of my mental strength, too…"

Struggling to breathe, Lyu brings her hands to her broken right leg.

"So it makes sense…to heal you, to let you live."

"That makes no sense whatsoever!"

I yell angrily at Lyu, who for some reason is smiling despite our situation. I hate the faintness of that smile. I'm angry at her for being noble at a time like this. I don't want to hear the words her lips are forming.

She's probably right.

We're wounded from head to toe, utterly exhausted, and completely alone. We have no physical or mental strength left, and not a single item. We are facing obliteration. That darkness called death is poised to swallow us.

In exchange for saving my life, she is about to let *something* else go.

"Mr. Cranell…leave me…"

But just as she's about to say the definitive word, we hear something.

Clack-clack-clack-clack.

A sound comes echoing toward us.

It's a dry sound, like a broken marionette abruptly laughing.

"" ___ ""

That sound is clearly abnormal.

It's not a human voice, but it's not a Dungeon noise either.

My eyes are drawn to the darkness beyond the reach of the phosphorescence, in the opposite direction of the cave-in.

Something is there.

Something is lurking in the darkness.

A drop of sweat falls from my chin onto Lyu's tense face.

A moment later, the thing that made the sound silently appears.

"Wha—?"

The instant I see it, I second-guess my eyes.

A white mask is floating in the darkness.

There are two twisted horns and two black holes hovering in space.

It looks like—

The grim reaper...?

I'm thinking of death's messenger from imaginary tales—the skeleton wearing a black robe and carrying a sickle.

Death has come for us as we suffer. At least, I have that illusion for a second.

But there's that sound again—*clack-clack-clack.*

The mask bounces up and down like it's crowing.

Like a monster gleeful at finding prey.

"—"

I gulp.

I was wrong.

It's not a mask.

It's a skull.

It's not the grim reaper.

It's a *monster.*

"?!"

I grab the hilt of the knife at my hip and draw it.

Shielding Lyu, who can't move on her own, I stand and raise the Divine Knife.

The monster clacks its mask like it's laughing at me.

It's a first encounter worth noting.

My debut battle in the deep levels—and maybe my final battle—is with a sheep.

A skull sheep, to be exact.

It's a midsize sheep-like monster that appears in the deep zone, measuring around 140 celches high. Both the face with its two empty eye sockets and the rest of the body are made of bones, as the name suggests.

They belong to a larger family of skeleton monsters. Even though they don't have flesh, skin, or organs, large numbers of these highly unusual monsters manage to wander around the thirty-seventh floor.

A typical example are the spartois. The appearance of these skeleton warriors is so shocking that even lower-tier adventurers who can't make it past the middle levels know about them.

I might as well call this milky white maze a den of the undead.

"...?!"

As I dredge up the facts I learned from Eina before leaving on the expedition, I run my eyes over these monsters that defy the laws of biology. The skulls seem to float before me in the dusky passage. As to what's below, I don't have a clue. That's because the rest of the bones are covered by skin.

Skull sheep are different from other skeleton monsters in that a long, wide skin reaches all the way to their feet, so just the bony hooves are visible. This skin is about as far from clean as you can get. It's dark and torn here and there so it looks like they're wearing a ragged old robe. It makes sense that I mistook this thing for the grim reaper.

As far as I can see, only one skull is floating eerily in the darkness.

"..."

The monster aims its empty sockets in my direction. Now and then it shakes its skull, sending its strange clacking melody through the Dungeon.

I'm paralyzed by tension, unable to decide whether to wait for it to make a move or strike first myself.

Suddenly, the eerie noise stops.

The skull approaches until it's right before my eyes.

"?!"

No sooner did I hear the sound of hooves striking the ground than it was on me.

The reason is the skin covering everything. I couldn't see it pawing the ground or preparing to move, and that caused my blunder.

I was depending too much on visual information, so I missed the signs of its rapid approach.

Below the twisted horns, the jaw hangs open. I can't read any emotion whatsoever in the mask of bone, but the countless fangs are hideous.

Snapping out of my daze, I abruptly bend to the side.

"Whoa!"

The skeleton sheep jumps over my head, which is touching the ground. Its surprise attack having ended in failure, it lands with a clatter. I jump up and lunge forward to protect Lyu, who's lying on the ground.

I'm just getting ready to make an offensive move, when—

"What...it's gone?!"

My enemy has disappeared without a trace.

All I can see is the still-smoking aftermath of the cave-in, and beyond that, dusky darkness.

What the...? It vanished?!

"Wrong...the skull sheep's robe...!"

From her position at my feet, Lyu groans the name of a drop item.

I jump a little.

She's right. The skull sheep's skin doesn't just cover its body. It also helps the sheep blend in with the duskiness so pervasive on this floor, like a human hunter wearing camouflage clothing. In other words, skull sheep can conceal themselves in the darkness.

First they terrify their prey with the eerie sound of their bones, then they silently creep up and devour them. That's why adventurers have nicknamed them death hermits!

Where is it, where is it...where's it gonna come from?!

I swivel my head back and forth. All I see is darkness. My enemy must have covered its face with its baggy hood, because I can't see a thing. My confusion serves its spying perfectly.

My thundering heartbeat interferes with my sense of hearing, which is all I have to rely on, and steals my calm as well.

Just when I've reached peak anxiety, Lyu speaks up again.

"Right...!"

"!"

I hear the hood being flipped back and bones creaking.

I escape its strike by a hairbreadth, but it's a bad start.

The sheep grazed my right arm, and the draft it sends my way makes the abrasion burn. I say graze, but a significant chunk of my arm was torn away. Its robe fluttering, the skull sheep ignores my gaping and lands on all four hooves.

"Oww…!"

The moment I look back, gripping my forearm…I wish I hadn't.

The monster's fangs are making a clacking sound as they chew. Bits of my stolen flesh are hanging from the joints in its jaw and neck, which are stained red.

There's no question I feel terror at this horrifying monster—no, at the Dungeon itself.

"—!"

The skull sheep can't hide its raging bloodlust. It shakes its body several times, then lowers its head so it grazes the ground. It's crouched low, and I'm guessing its hooves are planted firmly beneath the robe.

My adventurer's instinct flashes red.

The next instant, bumps rise on its skin.

"What?!"

The bumps are caused by protruding bones. Missiles aimed at its prey pierce the inflated skin from the inside.

Three "bone lances" speed toward me.

They're spikes—no, stakes!

I'm not able to completely evade this long-distance attack that my enemy implements by elongating a part of its skeleton. The lances gouge flesh from above my right shoulder and my left armpit.

"Ouch!"

I avoid being pierced like a kabob, but I still stagger, at which point the skull sheep charges forward like it's intent on finishing me off. Retracting its elongated bones, it paws the ground and flies at me. Those sharp, bloodstained fangs are about to sink right into my neck!

"Yaaaaaah!"

"!"

Just before my flesh is ripped open, I thrust out my left arm. The sheep latches on to that instead, knocking me over. My back slams against the ground.

"Mr. Cranell!"

Lyu's shout twines around the monster and me, who are tangled together. I can tell right away that she's surprised.

That monster's fangs aren't sunk into my flesh.

I made it bite my left arm on purpose.

The arm with the black band wrapped round it.

The Goliath Scarf. This protective gear is so hard it even repelled the claws of that monster on the twenty-seventh floor. The sharp fangs clack up and down, trying unsuccessfully to crush the scarf. For the first time, I sense an emotion—perplexity—coming from the skull sheep.

Groaning from the pain that I nevertheless feel in my left arm, I thrash all four limbs to shake off the monster.

I've been struggling hard for a couple of seconds when the skull sheep shivers and stops moving.

Its stomach was exposed beneath the robe. The Divine Knife gripped in my right hand has slipped between its ribs and…crushed the magic stone glittering as it floated in the hollow cavern of its trunk.

"*Huff…puff…huff…!*"

Ignoring the pile of ash that cascades over me, I stare up at the ceiling, panting.

That was a single fight.

And I'm this wiped out.

These are…the deep levels.

"…!"

This is impossible. It sucks. I can't do it.

If I run into another monster in this condition…

Obeying my instincts, I dig out of the ash and pick up Lyu.

Once again, I support her on my shoulder and set off.

We've gotta get away from here…!

If we don't hurry, other monsters attracted by the sound of the fight will soon arrive.

If one of them engages me in battle, I won't be able to do it. All the energy I regained through Lyu's recovery magic is gone. We've got to escape somewhere and let this exhaustion pass.

I run forward desperately.

Blood is dripping from the fresh wounds the skull sheep gave me.

I've been bleeding buckets since our fight. If I'm not careful, I'll get dizzy. If I hadn't ranked up to Level 4 and gotten this incredible toughness, I'd already be a useless mess.

But with every step forward, my mind and body are cruelly reduced.

My left arm is killing me. I wish I could cut it off. The word "ruin" is flashing in my head, as if to foretell my coming end.

But I press on.

To survive, I press on.

Like a defective marionette, I continue to move forward.

"…Mr. Cranell…stop…"

Lyu sounds like she cannot stand being carried along on my tortured procession any longer.

"Put me down this instant and go on alone."

"!"

She's acting like she's a mere piece of luggage.

Like all she'll do is slow me down.

That's what goes unspoken in her whisper.

I furrow my brows as deep as they can go.

"I don't want to!"

"Mr. Cranell…"

"I'll never leave you behind!"

I'm insisting on it like a stubborn child. Lyu turns her pained eyes toward the ground.

Abandoning her isn't an option.

If I did, I'd stop being Bell Cranell.

I'd never be able to rescue anyone again!

I scream out the words my raging emotions dictate:

"Do you think I stand a chance of surviving alone in the deep levels?!"

"..."

"Take that fight just now. I'd have been in big trouble without you!"

Blood rushes to my head. The words won't stop even though a monster might hear me.

But at the same time, my instincts seem to unconsciously understand the situation. To survive, I have to convince her that her presence is crucial. So I keep on yelling even though it uses more of my precious energy.

"I need you because you know about the deep levels! I need your experience!"

As I'm screaming, I realize something. What I just said makes sense.

True, I have the knowledge of the deep levels I gained from studying with Eina. But there's a big gap between knowledge and experience. Right now, that gap determines the difference between life and death. The fight with the skull sheep is proof.

Any adventurer knows how scary it is to see a new floor for the first time. I have no compass to guide me through the terrible sea of the deep levels.

To survive, I must have a lantern to light the way, a captain to lead me forward.

"...!"

Lyu's eyes are wide open. She presses her lips closed and won't say a word.

My bet is she's weighing the options—the merits of freeing me from her weight versus the merits of becoming the brain that leads me forward.

After spending some time in mental anguish, she speaks quietly.

"...I'll watch for monsters. You focus on moving us forward..."

"Ms. Lyu...!"

"Just as you said...it seems there's still a use for me..."

Light has returned to the sky-blue eyes that were so full of resignation. The shadow of death has lifted from her tattered body. Her petite lips form an ironic smile, as if to say, *Fine, it was a rash decision. I lost my cool.*

For my sake, she's given up. I can't help yelping with glee.

"Mr. Cranell…please head for a room…a dead end, as small as possible…"

"A room…?"

"We'll hole up for a while…If we damage the walls…no new monsters will be born…and we'll be able to get some rest…"

"…!"

This battle-hardened second-tier adventurer gives precise orders. Her suggestion startles me, but she's right. If we hole up in a room, we'll be freed from this forward march that risks death at any moment.

We have a direction now. A way forward has opened up.

Following Lyu's orders without question, I start to search for narrow passages.

…But our actual situation hasn't gotten any better…!

We'll still be wiped out if a pack of monsters finds us. If one spawns from this wall in front of us, it's over. This exhaustion is stubborn. If I let my attention waver, my knees will collapse under me.

If we get to a room, what next? Even if we rest, then what? Is there a way back from the deep levels? A way to return to the surface alive?

I turn my back on these dark whispers eating at my heart, close my ears, and put all my energy into escaping. I focus on putting Lyu's words into action. If I don't, I won't be able to move.

My face lit by the faint phosphorescence, I feel my way along the milky white wall. Lyu grimaces as if even the vibration from my shoulder pains her. Our breaths intertwining, we wander through the Dungeon.

"…?"

I wonder how much time has passed. Has it only been a few minutes?

Suddenly I narrow my eyes.

There's something ahead of us on the left.

A dim light is blinking from a narrow passageway.

At first, I think a monster must be moving back and forth in front of the light's source, blocking it. But the instant I realize the pattern is regular, my eyes pop open.

Is it...flashing?

"No way...Is that a magic-stone lamp?"

That kind of flashing light is out of place in the Dungeon.

But it is familiar on the surface. My incredulous whisper turns to certainty.

No question about it. This light isn't natural phosphorescence, it's...man-made!

"Ms. Lyu, it's a magic-stone lamp! There's a person down here, an adventurer!"

"...Yes, that light...is..."

Lyu responds to my delirious shout with a surprised whisper of her own. Monsters don't carry lamps! There must be a human up ahead!

With a little cheer, I squeeze into the passage branching off to my left. I've forgotten all about the pain that was tormenting my whole body. My step has a spring to it now.

Adventurers have been rescued from the brink of obliteration by other adventurers more than once. Most of the time, they'll fight together on an emergency basis even if they don't get along in regular life. I've heard about these outlaw morality stories, and now I'm one of them.

What good luck!

Imagine meeting another adventurer in a place like this!

If they're down here in the deep levels, the party definitely must be upper tier. Could it be *Loki Familia*? Or maybe *Freya Familia*? That would be great! Anyone would be great!

Now we'll be saved! Now we'll be freed!

Me, and Lyu, too!

"Hello! Hello! Please, save us!!"

I gather my energy and shout toward the blinking light.

We turn the corner. Just a little longer. The blinking grows brighter. Just a second more now. I can see the entrance to the room. That's my goal!

The tension is leaving my face. The relief is unending. Perhaps to hide her joy, Lyu remains silent. I see a human form beyond the blinking light and unhesitatingly stretch out my hand.

"Please, save—!"

I step into the room with a smile on my face.

That smile cracks with an audible noise.

I hear someone gulp.

Belatedly, I realize it's Lyu.

Time stops.

"—"

Certainly, there are people here.

People surrounding the magic-stone lamp blinking in the center of the room.

They're definitely adventurers. I can tell from their weapons and protective gear.

But I can't tell what race they are. I can't tell their age or facial features, either. After all, they don't have flesh or skin.

Their slender fingers are white as plaster statues.

Their once-beautiful blond hair is dull.

The faint but distinct smell of rotted flesh hangs in the air.

These are the corpses of adventurers, *turned to bleached bones.*

One leans against the wall, its pitch-black eye sockets staring at us. Another, wearing a long, flared battle skirt, lies on the ground with its hair fanned out. Another slumps with its hands clasped around a dagger that pierces the red, dried-out clothing, as if the adventurer sank the blade into his own chest.

Certainly, there are people here.

Or rather, there are things that were once people.

Here lies the tragic end of adventurers who succumbed· to the deep levels.

"……Huh?"

I totter into the room as if I'm being pulled forward.

The blinking lamp is nearly broken. Like it's been lying here for months. The three silent skeletons tell the same story of passing time.

There is no adventurer to save us. Of course not. How did I think they would save us in the first place? What was I expecting of corpses that cannot answer my call nor move to help us? Did I think they would take my hands and dance? The idea is so ridiculous tears come to my eyes.

Lyu's expression has not changed. Her mouth remains clamped shut, as if she had half expected this.

Suddenly, my eyes meet the empty sockets of the skeleton leaning against the wall.

Welcome! Join us!

My ears deceive me.

This is the goal you longed to reach.

"………Ah."

Strangely enough, it *is* just what we were looking for: a room with a single doorway. A dead end.

I feel like the world is crumbling.

I pull Lyu close and drop to the ground on my knees.

"That's…"

I hear a fatal, soul-destroying sound.

Such little time has passed since I decided to try to make it through with Lyu.

A thread of hope has been dangled before our eyes, then yanked cruelly away.

If this is the work of the Dungeon, then she is a crafty, dirty trickster.

She crushes my will with unparalleled perfection.

Her mocking laughter rings in my ears.

This will be your fate, too.

Just like these adventurers, defeated and abandoned by fate.

"Mr. Cranell…"

Lyu sounds dejected.

I can't respond. I have no idea what sort of awful expression must be on my face. As if to announce that its role has come to an end, the blinking magic-stone lamp darkens for the last time. The tool that led us to the side of its owners has ended its life.

Darkness descends on the room.

For the umpteenth time, the darkness of despair arrives.

And then—

As if to pull us to the brink of death as we sink into despair, the clacking begins.

"—"

Feeling for a moment like a scythe has been held to my neck, I turn.

In the darkness beyond the single doorway float three sheep skulls.

The monsters have followed the footprints of their prey.

Once again terror rises in my frozen brain. The darkness has exposed my cornered heart.

Clack-clack-clack, clack-clack-clack.

These grim reapers are calling to us from beyond the darkness.

"...Ay aw..."

Lyu grimaces and I pull her to me as tightly as I can, shivering in fear. The masks floating in darkness slowly approach.

"Stay away..."

I wring a faint whisper from my throat. A voice of rejection, of fear, and of entreaty.

"Stay away..."

They are merciless. They crush my prayers brutally beneath their hooves.

The flock of monster sheep steps forward from the darkness.

The taught thread snaps.

"Stay away!"

The moment I give in to my exploding fear and scream out, the skull sheep kick the ground. With a terrible energy, the three skeletons prepare to charge the room.

I raise my right hand and thrust it toward them.

"Firebolt!!"

I concentrate all my mental power into the word.

Frantic to sweep away the death that is bearing down on us, I shoot off five bolts of electrical fire.

Two of the shots miss their mark and smash the wall of the maze, while the remaining three explode violently into the skull sheep.

"—?!"

They shriek at the Swift-Strike Magic's direct hit.

As the electrical fire pierces their dark robes and splinters their bones, the monsters roll on the ground in anguish. And then they flee, as if the wildly dancing sparks have frightened them.

"—ah."

At the same time, the last bit of strength drains from my body.

A Mind Down. It's what happens when you overuse magic.

My reserves of mental strength have finally hit rock bottom.

While I've managed not to faint, I literally can't move a finger.

Unable to relish the relief of having chased away the immediate threat, a fatal despair washes over me.

"Mr. Cranell…"

Someone is calling me.

But who is it? Who is beside me?

This is bad.

I can't hear. I can't think. I can't feel.

Why am I here?

What was it I had to do?

"Mr. Cranell…"

I'm wandering in a maze. A maze with no exit. An endless tangle buried in darkness.

I don't know front from back. Left and right are no longer clear. I can't comprehend where I am.

The sensation in my hands and feet fades.

The sound of my short breaths grows distant.

The borderline between reality and illusion disappears.

"Mr. Cranell—"

A darkness where no light penetrates erases my existence.
The darkness obliterates me body and soul.
I'm losing sight of myself—

—*Slap!*

There's a dry sound.
It takes a minute to realize it came from my own cheek.
"Please calm down."
The throbbing in my right cheek brings my sense of self back from the darkness.
I look up in a daze.
I see a pair of sky-blue eyes.
She is gazing at me imposingly.
"...Ms....Lyu?"
Sound returns. Sensation returns. Reality returns.
Her name returns and I call it.
She slapped my cheek. Now she nods.
"It might be hard, but listen. First, you need to calm down. Breathe slowly."
I feel warmth spreading from the hand placed on my shoulder. I obey her instructions.
Breathe in, breathe out.
Once more.
My lungs, which had been hyperventilating, relax.
Cool air flows into my brain and calms it.
The mist steadily clears.
"Mr. Cranell. You don't have to be depressed anymore."
Lyu has been quietly watching over me, choosing just the right moment to speak.
"We may have stumbled upon the corpses of fellow adventurers, but *that doesn't change our situation in the least. So there's no need to grieve.*"
I open my eyes wide at her words.

We've been in the worst possible situation from the start—the depths of the depths. Things haven't gotten better, but they haven't gotten worse, either.

To the contrary, we've found the kind of room we were searching for. We've made progress. Lyu is telling me very clearly that there is absolutely no need to lose hope.

…And I have to admit, she's right.

But I question her sanity, or rather the strength of her will.

How can she have faced those rotted adventurers and still be so unruffled?

"Mr. Cranell, take five minutes."

"What…?"

"Please sleep for five minutes."

Lyu cuts off my surprised protest and brings her outstretched hands before my eyes.

"W-wait, what do you…?!"

"I'll guard you. I'm telling you to take a nap."

"…?!"

"Take those five minutes to restore your strength as much as possible."

She's speaking very clearly. Finally I accept her command to rest.

But what's she mean by five minutes?

"Here in the deep levels, and especially in our situation…five minutes is the limit."

Any more is impossible.

Right now, we have to be on high alert for monsters. Resting for more than five minutes would be unacceptable.

I gulp at the finality in Lyu's tone.

I realize what she's saying is insane. How much can I possibly recover in five minutes? No matter how superhuman adventurers may be after they level up, can five minutes mean anything?

As I struggle to vocalize my doubts, Lyu answers them.

"To work toward recovery anywhere and anytime…this is the gift of the adventurer."

"!"

I'm startled.

Her words remind me of the words my idol spoke on top of the city walls.

In the Dungeon, you have to be able to sleep anywhere, anytime.

It is very important to be able to recover your physical strength quickly.

So…my mettle as an adventurer is being tested right now.

I admit I'd only half believed her advice up to this point, but now I realize…she was one hundred percent right. Trust Aiz to hit the nail on the head.

My renewed admiration for her notwithstanding, for some reason I have a vision of her glancing guiltily aside. What's up with that?

"Fortunately, your magic damaged the room. It's not likely any monsters will be spawned in the next five minutes."

Lyu looks around.

The firebolts I used to get rid of the skull sheep caused some damage near the doorway. Large rocks lay in a pile near the door, forming a low impromptu barricade. That's the only entrance or exit, so assuming the Dungeon prioritizes repair over spawning new monsters, it's the only thing we have to guard.

"Will you be able to restore yourself in mind and body in five minutes? This is a turning point for you—no, for us."

We were in a life-and-death situation to start with. Five minutes might seem like a drop in the bucket, but aside from accumulating these short rests, there's no way we'll return alive.

It's only five minutes of rest, but it *is* five minutes.

Whether you interpret that as heaven or hell is a question of perspective.

Which perspective do I take? I honestly don't know. What I do know is that I'm feeling less despair and sorrow than I did before. It's thanks to Lyu that I can even be thinking about this right now. Each one of her words carries so much weight. Her valiant voice ringing out in this realm of suffering gives me courage. It gives me a tiny glimmer of hope.

"…"

"..."

Still on my knees, I look Lyu in the eye and nod.

I should trust her.

With the last of my energy, I head to a spot by the wall, avoiding the adventurers' corpses as I go. With a thud, I drop awkwardly to the ground and lean against the cool wall.

"You sleep first. I'll rest after you do."

"...Okay."

Taking advantage of the kindness of her words, I prepare to close my eyes. I'm about to sleep beside the corpses of my fellow adventurers. I'm seriously unsure if I can rest in a place like this. But just before I shut my eyes, Lyu's quiet blue gaze meets mine.

"Sleep well..."

Her delicate lips smile faintly. That smile reassures me, and I am able to sleep. I slip gently out of the waking world.

Five minutes...will that be enough?

The instant Bell closed his eyes, Lyu's smile vanished. Sweat drenched her body.

Five minutes.

Accurately speaking, that was the minimum amount of time Bell needed to rest. According to Lyu's diagnosis, it really was cutting it close.

True, his firebolts had damaged the room. But not widely enough. It hadn't reached a level she could call safe. Normally she would demolish walls in all four directions, but with her leg broken that wasn't possible. She simply didn't have the strength.

The question was, could they stay still in a room in the deep levels for five minutes without being attacked? The odds were slim.

Watching the Dungeon begin to repair itself, Lyu shut her fears deep inside her heart.

I must not make him worry more than necessary...not after what he's done to protect me. If he doesn't rest, he'll break down...

Why had Lyu lied to Bell? Because she had no other choice.

With his mental strength completely sapped, he could not move. His physical strength was depleted as well. He was on the verge of losing his very sense of self as the horrible reality avalanched down on him. Rest—even a tiny bit—was essential if he was to take action after this. How could she have told him to demolish the room before sleeping?

She had only had one choice: to risk their lives and rest here.

This is the first turning point...

If they surmounted this one, how many more awaited? She tried to smile mockingly at her inability to answer that question, but failed. She didn't even have the mental or emotional space to mock herself.

For the next five minutes, she had to fight alone.

With her battered body, she had to protect the boy and fight the sprawling darkness of the maze.

Futaba is my only weapon...I can throw those two shortswords, which means I can chase away two monsters...After that, I'll have to stop them with this body of mine...

She pulled the two shortswords from her hip and thrust them into the ground beside her. She wanted to be able to throw them the instant an invading monster appeared out of the dimness beyond the doorway.

Since her right leg was broken and she could not move, she prayed that she would not have to use these weapons.

"Oooooo..."

Somewhere in the distance she heard a battle roar. A shiver shook her shoulders. Although she knew it was pointless, she quieted her breath.

She glared into the darkness and prayed over and over: Do not come. Do not appear.

Every time she moved in the least, her right leg screamed in pain and she breathed out loudly.

...Am I really this anxious just because I'm not talking to Mr. Cranell...?

The dusky darkness of the deep levels ate away at the heart of even that feared adventurer called Gale Wind.

That was what made this zone so aggravating. There was infinitely less light than in the middle levels. Darkness infiltrated every corner. And darkness makes people exceedingly anxious. It destroys their personalities and destabilizes information. All of that is doubly true when one is cornered—exactly like Bell and Lyu were. It also numbs all sense of time.

The three hundred seconds seemed endless.

How many had already passed?

How many did she still have to get through?

She asked the internal clock she had developed on expeditions. She bit her lip at its answer. Long. So long. Not even thirty seconds had passed.

She knew that her eyes were hollow.

She struggled even to control her ragged breathing so it did not interfere with Bell's rest.

The eerie silence that slowly spread through the room made her imagine horrible things.

Weren't cracks about to spread through the wall she was leaning against?

Wasn't a monster about to utter its newborn cry and then rip her head off?

And what about that passage beyond the doorway? Wasn't a pack of monsters on its way down it this very moment?

Lyu dug her fingernails into her forearm as she battled back these delusions.

"…"

She looked timidly to the side so that she wouldn't have to keep facing the darkness, facing reality. Bell was sleeping. His chin was resting on his chest, so she couldn't see his eyes. He looked as if he'd taken his final breath. But no, he was alive. He was definitely alive.

He'd obediently followed her instructions and thrown himself into a brief nap.

He was losing hold of himself…but that's to be expected in this situation.

Lyu did not think Bell was pitiful for becoming frenzied. To the contrary, he was holding himself together remarkably well given their extreme situation. He was in the deep levels for the first time, and starting from despair to boot. There was no way to break through and no hope. What's more, he was out of mental and physical energy. Anyone's will would waver under those circumstances. It wouldn't even be surprising for an ordinary adventurer to snap and take their own life.

Lyu glanced quickly at the skeleton with the dagger in its breast.

"…He's really gotten stronger…" she whispered.

She felt an urge to touch his bloody, dusty white hair. She wanted to gently comb her fingers through it. But she couldn't. She didn't have the space to do that.

Instead, she praised him sincerely and with deep emotion. At the same time, her conscience pained her. After he was done resting, she would have to give him a harsh command and force him to obey.

She would have to make him commit an act of daring barbarism.

She would have to do it to save him.

"*Only you* will be saved…"

The rotted adventurers were the only ones who heard her whisper.

Bell had been wrong.

Lyu had not rejected death.

She had chosen self-sacrifice.

She would use her own life to save his.

That was the resolve that supported Lyu.

If only we can escape the deep levels…there will still be difficulties, but he might be able to get through them on his own…Yes, as I thought, we must aim for the connecting passage to the thirty-sixth floor…

She thought about what it would take for him to return alive from this Dungeon.

The lower levels were different from the deep levels. He would still be in the terrible position of having no items left, but at the very least his chances of surviving would improve greatly.

If only they could escape this devil's lair—

—I'm begging you, Alize and everyone. I don't care what happens to me. I will follow in your footsteps to pay for my sins. But please, save the boy…

Lyu looked down as she prayed to her departed companions.

Only to the visions in her memory did she expose the weak self that also existed within her strong, noble self.

She squeezed her eyes shut like a weak little girl.

As she did, a roar came from the doorway.

She jerked up her head. Three masks of bone hung in the dimness.

New skull sheep. The hermits who feasted on death had appeared again.

Reality reminded her that clinging to her departed companions would do no good.

Lyu bit her lip and grabbed the shortswords sticking up from the ground.

Three at once—

It wasn't possible. She couldn't handle all three. One would get into the room.

With a pained noise, she aimed for the skull sheep and threw the swords.

One hit the bull's-eye. A moment later the second blade pierced its target. Two of the monsters collapsed to the ground.

But that was all.

The third monster dashed toward her and was about to enter the room—when a white blade blossomed from its head.

"!!"

A glittering white knife had been thrown at the sheep. The thrower was right next to Lyu.

Bell had opened his eyes and thrown Hakugen.

The lifeless bones collapsed with a clatter.

As Lyu watched in surprise, Bell lowered his right arm, which he had used to throw the knife.

"…Ms. Lyu."

Her slender ears trembled at his whispered words.

"Five minutes are up."

The meaning of his simple words only sunk in after a moment.

It seemed that Bell's body had somehow unconsciously kept track of the time even when he was asleep. He was no doubt wary of his surroundings as well. The ability to keep watch while asleep was indeed an adventurer's skill, but Lyu was surprised to see Bell had mastered it.

Or perhaps his teacher had trained him in this craft.

"...I'm sorry for failing to properly serve my role. I wasn't concentrating."

"No, it's fine."

Bell smiled awkwardly at Lyu's meek apology. Although she could still see traces of exhaustion in his face, he looked completely different from five minutes earlier. His voice was much stronger as well.

She guessed that the fog had cleared from his mind. Five minutes wasn't enough to do much for his physical or mental strength, but still, it was meaningful.

"Please take your turn and sleep now, Ms. Lyu."

"...All right, if you insist."

They had survived his five minutes. A heavy weight was lifted from Lyu.

Exhaustion suddenly overwhelmed her. Her eyelids grew heavy as lead.

She, too, was at her limit.

"Mr. Cranell...please destroy those walls so no monsters are spawned."

"Got it."

With that, she rested her weight against the wall. A deep sleepiness surrounded her like a cradle. She did not resist.

Her mind went blank.

Leon, Leon.

She heard a familiar voice.

She heard the voices of her familia.

She fell into the world of sleep as if at their invitation.

"—Leon, are you listening?"

Lyu looked up with a start.

A pretty girl with smooth red hair and green eyes was standing in front of her, eyebrows raised.

"You have some nerve to daydream when your captain is talking to you!"

The redheaded girl was speaking briskly and jabbing her finger into the air.

Lyu looked at her intently before finally opening her mouth.

"Sorry, Alize. I wasn't focusing."

She apologized contritely.

She didn't question the fact that the redhead was standing before her.

"Well, as long as you realize what you did!" the girl said, smiling brightly.

Oh. This is a dream.

Lyu knew right away.

The proof was that her body wouldn't do what she wanted it to. Her lips said words unrelated to her will, as if they were merely retracing an old memory.

The dream was replaying a day from five years ago.

It was set in a place that was very important to her, at a time when the familia she loved so dearly was still alive.

"When did our noble elven lady become such a sleepyhead? And while standing, too…such skills are far beyond me!"

"…Kaguya, I'm not sleepy. And stop talking like that. It's extremely irritating."

"Stop teasing her, Kaguya. Even the strongest adventurers can't help acting that way at that time of the month. She's a girl, after all!"

"Lyra, that's crude. Anyway…it's not th-th-that time of the month!"

Lyu was talking to a human with black hair and a prum with peach hair. Her expression was sour and her voice raised. If Bell or his friends who only knew the Lyu of today had seen her face at that moment, they would surely have been surprised.

She was young, and her expression was extremely vulnerable.

She only let her friends see this inflexible, youthful side of her.

She was full of things the Lyu of today had lost.

"Oh, so you're on your period, Leon! I'm sorry, I didn't realize. But when you're in the Dungeon you can't whine like that. Try to hold up as best as you can!"

"Don't you take her seriously, too, Alize!"

Lyu finally exploded at Alize, who not only winked saucily at her but also stuck her finger in the air again. Her female familia members laughed loudly as the elf blushed to the tips of her ears.

Astrea Familia.

Led by the goddess Astrea, the familia symbol was a sword of justice and a pair of wings.

During the dark days when evil spread through Orario, *Astrea Familia* fought alongside *Loki Familia* and *Ganesha Familia* to preserve peace in the city. All eleven members were female, and all were strong-willed, brave, and heroic warriors who inspired fear. Male adventurers fled barefoot from the members of this small, elite band.

"All right ladies, pull yourselves together. Let's talk about justice. The battle against the Evils is reaching its climax. It's time for us to revive our initial enthusiasm for the fight!"

Among all the brilliant members of that familia, Alize Lovell shined the brightest. She was their captain and Lyu's friend, the one who had invited her to join the familia. Her hair, which she wore tied in a ponytail that perfectly fit her cheerful personality, was the color of the setting sun. Described kindly, her words and actions were candid and straightforward; described unkindly, they were presumptuous and unthinking. The first time Lyu met her, she had barged into her confidence, going as far as to say, "Your name is Lyu? That's hard to say! I'm going to call you Leon from now on!" She was to thank for the fact that everyone in the familia aside from their patron deity, Astrea, called her that.

But Lyu respected Alize.

She was always focused on the future, impartially kind to everyone, and more honest than anyone else she knew.

In truth, Alize was Lyu's first friend.

"We're supposed to talk about justice? I'm not sure what to say..."

"The easiest definition would be that justice is doing good without compensation..."

"But isn't doing good without a goal the same as being self-satisfied?"

"If you have a goal, then it becomes calculating. That's far from real justice."

"Ultimately, justice is only a convenient tool. It's a weapon used to attain a goal, or a colorless flag used for justifying violent words and actions."

"Wait, take that back. The sword and wings of justice that we pledged ourselves to are nothing like that."

"Uh-oh, here comes Lyu the theorist!"

At Alize's urging, all the members of the familia had gathered in a room of their home for a discussion. The passionate debate was starting to create an explosive mood. Alize looked around the room and nodded generously.

"—Right, let's wrap up the discussion on this topic! Even the deities can't give a perfect answer to this question, so of course we won't be able to, no matter how hard we try! Yes, it's impossible!"

Alize was exactly as slap-dash and irresponsible as the situation required.

Her familia members looked at her with irritation as she put an end to the topic she herself had brought up.

"Anyone can talk on and on about justice. Instead of searching for the 'real' justice among the endless constellation of possible definitions, let's beat the villains who act under the banner of false justice!"

"!"

"When the evil of falsehood is gone, harmony and order will be born. The people will be so happy! I'm quite sure that is what justice means for us as members of *Astrea Familia*!"

Sometimes, she said the most surprising things in a nonchalant way.

"Justice is not something to carry on our shoulders. It is something that will crush us one day. It is not something to boast about. That's like pushing ill will on people!"

"Alize..."

"Justice is something to hide!"

Her familia members stared at her, the tension gone from their shoulders, and raised their eyebrows as if to say, *There she goes again!* Like their patron deity, Astrea, Alize was more popular and trusted than anyone else in the familia.

"Once again, you've prostrated yourself before my wisdom, I see! Hee-hee, I am good, aren't I?"

She also had a tendency to say unnecessary things. This time, the looks aimed at her as she put one hand on her chest and closed both eyes proudly were chilly.

Ah, I miss those days!

That was the thought in Lyu's mind as she watched this scene unfold.

Everything she sought was there.

If she could return, she would.

"All right, on to the main topic! I've learned from the Guild that Evils activity has been detected in the lower levels."

The second Lyu heard those words, her mind went cold.

"By Evils...do you mean *Rudra Familia*?"

"Yes. During that nightmarish fight on the twenty-seventh floor last year, the familias on the Guild side suffered heavy damage, but the Evils were hit even harder. Most likely they're only able to take action in that zone now."

"The strategy that time was heavy-handed, thanks to *Loki Familia* leading the counterattack. It really depended on the bravery of our familia."

Lyu's mind quivered at the memory of this conversation between Alize and the others.

It was the day before it happened.

The eve of calamity.

At the time, she had no idea what awaited them.

But the Lyu of the present knew everything.

"We in *Astrea Familia* will survey the lower levels. It's good if we find something, better if we can stop our enemy's plans, and fantastic if we can capture *Rudra Familia*."

No, no.

Jura and others in *Rudra Familia* had intentionally spread that information. Guild members with links to their faction had leaked it. As a result, *Astrea Familia* would head to the Dungeon and encounter the calamity.

"Don't you smell a trap? Just like the nightmare on the twenty-seventh floor..."

"Even if that's case, our only choice is to go. We will go so that a tragedy like that does not occur a second time."

Alize shook her head as she responded to the words of their prum companion.

Lyu had respected her direct gaze full of proud justice, but now it reflected the predetermined fate that made her so hopeless.

Alize, it's no good!

No matter how loudly she screamed, her words went unheard.

No matter how desperately she called to them from within her immobilized body, the dream proceeded according to the script of her memory, leading Alize and the others toward despair.

"We'll leave after the meeting. Get your things ready."

It's no good!

Stop, Kaguya and Lyra!

All of you—you must not go!

She screamed in vain. Alize turned away and walked out of the room.

The other familia members followed, and the dream-Lyu went along with them.

Only Lyu's present-day consciousness remained.

Wait.

Slowly, their home melted away and was filled with white light.

All that remained was the image of their backs walking away from her.

They continued ahead without looking back.

Beyond the light, to the far shore of the light.

They left Lyu behind like a painting on the wall.

Wait.

Kaguya, Lyra, Noin, Neze.

Asta, Lyana, Celty, Iska, Maryu.

She called their names to no avail.

All of them walked farther and farther away.

They left only Lyu behind.

Without realizing what she was doing, Lyu desperately reached toward the back of the red-haired girl.

Alize.

She could see the figure beyond the light, but it did not turn toward her.

"Alize…"

A soft whisper escapes her lips.

I can't help hearing.

We are in the room with the corpses of our fellow adventurers.

Just as Lyu instructed, I damaged the walls in all four directions. I stabbed, ripped, and gouged them over and over with the Divine Knife. This will definitely prevent monsters from spawning. I retrieved Lyu's shortswords and Hakugen, too.

I overheard her whispered word when I had finished all that and sat down next to her.

I look at her face, my own mouth shut tight.

She looks sad as she meets this person in her dream.

"…"

I turn my eyes back to the scene in front of me.

I hear and sense something. When I look at the doorway, I see a mask of bone.

The skull sheep are back in pursuit of our lives. Or maybe a flock of them is wandering around out there.

There's only one…in which case…

"…If it comes over here, I'll shoot at it."

I raise my right arm and thrust it out.

Gathering up the little mental energy my rest gave me, I concentrate magical power in my right hand.

No way am I going to let it know I'm tired. I stay sitting, but do my best to put on a tough-guy front.

The skull sheep looks at me with its hollow eye sockets as I aim my "gun," then disappears into the darkness as if in retreat. It probably felt threatened by my magic.

If we were on the upper or middle levels, I'm sure a monster would have charged ahead unthinkingly. I've gotta give these deep-level monsters some respect for their intelligence. They're a whole lot of trouble to fight, but it seems they're good tacticians, too.

I let out a long breath and glance back at Lyu.

…*I don't think I've ever seen her this unguarded before…*

Her eyes are closed. Her body is battered. Maybe because of our circumstances, her bloody, dusty face has an ephemeral beauty to it. She looks like a wounded fairy sleeping beside a spring under the light of the moon. I've got to watch over her. That's why I'm sitting so close.

Her warm shoulders, so close I'd bump into them if I moved even a little…look sweet to me. Circumstances be damned, I can't help it.

These narrow shoulders have fought so long.

Bloodied and feared, Gale Wind threw herself into the stormiest of battles.

"Alize…"

She whispers the same name again. She's calling it out like a little girl.

To think that such a gallant, fierce warrior can also be so weak.

I'm not even sure which one is the real Lyu.

I…just want to protect her.

I want to protect this girl who would never intentionally show me her weakness.

I feel like that desire is bringing back my strength.

"...Alize...wait..."

Five minutes are up.

But I'll just let her rest a little longer.

I'm sure it will be okay.

I let her sleep and continue my watch.

I let her sleep so she can keep on speaking just a little longer to the dwellers in her dreams.

Not much later, Lyu opens her eyes.

The same old gallant elf is back. I don't say anything about what I saw.

She's probably a little less exhausted, like me. Some of the color has returned to her face.

Now it's time to act.

"To those who seek thee, deliver the mercy of healing...Noa Heal."

Warm light spills from Lyu's hands and encircles her right leg. Although I can't say it's back to normal, the leg with the hilt of her knife bound to it as a splint does heal. She gazes discontentedly at it.

Now that our mental strength has returned a little, we're making quick use of Lyu's recovery magic. I managed to convince her to use it on herself by flatly refusing to let her heal me. At the very least, she had to fix that broken leg. It was just too exhausting to support her as I ran. That's what I told her, and finally she listened.

Her insistence on putting me first for so long reminds me how stubborn she is. Anyway, moving fast will still be hard, but at least now she can walk on her own.

"First we'll take stock of our situation."

"Right."

I look Lyu in the eye. We're both kneeling. We've got an eye on the doorway to watch for monsters as we speak in low voices.

"I'm not sure what part of the thirty-seventh floor we're currently in. We're both injured and tired. We're in an extremely hopeless situation."

In other words, there's no telling what might happen. I nod gravely.

Needless to say, not knowing where you are in the Dungeon can be fatal. Basically, wandering around without knowing if you're going forward or back is a shortcut to death.

The fact that we rested doesn't change our horrible situation. We're still way too weak to fight deep-level monsters. If I could, I'd take a bath in elixirs and then dive into bed.

"We don't have much by way of treatment, either. All we can do is nurse our sorry selves along with my magic."

We just used her magic on her leg, so we can't use it again for a while. Which reminds me—I gave up on healing my wrecked left arm. When we were talking about whether to heal her leg or my arm, she ripped off the scarf that was wrapped around it and gasped. From the shoulder down, it was such a mangled mess of flesh and bone that even I didn't want to look at it.

But I can still move it. Which means I'll be okay.

Of course, it still hurts so bad I want to die, and this disgusting sweat won't stop.

When we get back to the surface, I might have to get a fake arm.

…I'm not smiling.

"We lack adequate equipment as well. To put it bluntly, we have nowhere near what's needed to explore the deep levels. And we're short on items."

I touch my ragged pouch, which escaped the wormwell's stomach acid, as Lyu continues her pessimistic assessment. For weapons, we've got Hakugen, the Hestia Knife, and Lyu's two shortswords. Plus the Goliath Scarf, although I doubt it will do much more than serve as a protector and substitute bandage for my left arm.

My protective gear was shredded by the monster's claws and then melted by the lambton's acid. It barely even exists anymore. We're so poorly equipped it makes me dizzy.

Lyu continues.

"As for outside help…we'd better not count on that. Even if your familia is able to follow our footsteps, it will be impossible for them to make it to the deep levels."

We jumped from the twenty-seventh floor to the thirty-seventh. That kind of irregularity can't be expected of any adventurer. My only faint hope lies in Mari, who witnessed part of our battle. But even if she manages to make contact with Lilly and the other adventurers, how long would it take for a rescue party to reach the deep levels?

Days? A week?

As for the possibility of running into other adventurers exploring the deep levels…we'd better forget about that, too. That kind of overly optimistic idea isn't real hope—it's just a poison that destroys your spirit.

I glance at the adventurers turned to bleached bone and settle on a resolve resembling resignation.

I hope Lilly and the others are okay…

Suddenly I think of my friends. Since they stayed on the twenty-fifth floor, they probably weren't pulled into that horrible monster's massacre.

For the time being, I chop down that shoot of anxiety that grows bigger the more I think about things. If we don't get out of here alive first, I'm not going to be able to check on anyone's well-being.

"Based on our current circumstances…our best option is to head for the connecting passageway to the thirty-sixth floor."

Having laid out all the things that we have to worry about, Lyu moves on to our plan for moving forward.

"You mean escape to the lower levels? But even if we make it there…"

"I know. Our safety is not guaranteed. We'll be forced to make it through those levels, too."

The first safety point in the deep levels is on the thirty-ninth floor. That's a distance of two floors from here.

It goes without saying that the lower you get in the Dungeon, the bigger the floors are. The thirty-seventh floor is big enough to hold all of Orario. Rather than going down two floors, it will take much less energy to go back to the lower levels. We can't use the hard-labor approach of heading for a safety point on a lower level, like we did as a strategy of last resort that time in the middle levels. To start with, that stunt relies on a maze structure resembling a vertical channel.

"However, we'll have a better chance of surviving than if we stay in the deep levels. In the lower levels, there are berries and fruits that we can eat…Dungeon crops. It's a far better option in terms of food and water."

Makes sense. I nod to indicate my understanding.

At the very least, we won't have to worry about nutrition. Plus, the monsters should be less fierce and fewer in number. Compared to the deep levels, the lower levels are actually *easy*.

"From here on out, our mental strength is our lifeline. Obviously, we should avoid fighting monsters as much as possible, and use magic primarily for protecting ourselves."

Even if we use her recovery magic when her mental strength returns, we need to stockpile our energy and keep our cards close. Reckless use of magic or skills is prohibited.

That is, if the lower levels let us be that conservative.

"For now, we need to collect the items and equipment necessary for moving through the lower levels."

Water, too, if we can.

With that, Lyu ends her speech.

I don't have any arguments. I mean, what choice do we have?

Now, how do we get those essential goods? I'm about to ask her that when I notice something.

All expression has vanished from Lyu's face.

"Ms. Lyu?"

Her lips open and then close.

I glimpse hesitation and inner conflict in her cold face.

She seems to hesitate for a second before speaking. As if she's about to touch on a taboo.

She shifts her blue eyes away from mine.

"…?"

She glances at the corpses.

For some reason, I get a bad feeling about this.

For some reason, my hair stands on end.

Finally, she opens her mouth.

"We're going to *strip the dead* of their equipment."

Her words pierce my ears.

"…What?"

I don't get what she just said. The words don't make sense.

As I make an idiotic face, she repeats herself.

"…We'll strip the equipment from the corpses and use it."

Her low voice seems to be talking both to me and to herself.

As soon as I understand what she's saying, I shout in protest.

"W-wait a second!! You mean *loot* the dead…?!"

Desecration of the dead.

Normally, there's an unspoken rule among adventurers that if a body is found, it must be taken to the surface. Violating that rule to steal from corpses is the worst kind of barbarism.

Grave robbing, scavenging from corpses, banditry…detestable phrases swim in my head. Eventually I erupt in sweat. My eyeballs are unnaturally fixed in place. My tongue is instantly dry. When I try to express this unspeakable feeling to Lyu, she cuts me off mercilessly.

"They lost to the Dungeon, and we will use them. They are our predecessors in death, and we will beg of them a way out…We are not in a position to choose our methods."

Her dark determination echoes through the Dungeon.

I gulp.

She's serious about this.

"…I'll do the woman. You do the men."

She stands up.

Dragging her right leg, she walks to the woman in the long, flared skirt, kneels, and really does begin to search her.

"…?!"

She mercilessly rips apart the already tattered skirt, severs the belt with her knife, and rummages through the red pouch. As if the skeleton is crying out, a piece of its arm drops from the cuff of the sleeve, and the golden blond hair fans across the floor.

Please stop!

I don't want to see you like that!

I do not voice the screams of my heart.

My eyes fall on Lyu's face, her wide eyes shifting uneasily, and it dawns on me.

There's no way she's not hesitating. There's no way she's not trying to avoid this. No, Lyu is even more guilt-stricken then I am. She's vomiting invisible blood.

There could be no more loathsome act for an upstanding elf than the desecration of the dead. She is crushing her pride underfoot and donning a mask of cruelty to humiliate the dead.

She has done it to survive. She has done it for herself—or for me?

To do her duty as a leader of adventurers?

As I watch Lyu calmly strip the corpse of its possessions, I can't hold back my muddled emotions. I narrow my eyes and clench my fists, as if I'm about to start crying.

"‼"

I reprimand my useless legs and suddenly rush toward the adventurers-turned-skeletons.

My eyes meet the black sockets of the corpse leaning against the wall. I squeeze them shut for a moment.

I place my hands on its armor and pull it off without hesitating.

That's enough to make the world waver before my eyes.

My breathing is ragged. My head is swimming. Something hot is surging up from my stomach toward my throat.

No, don't vomit. This is a survival situation. Parting with bodily fluids will only bring me closer to death. I press my hands over my mouth and force the burning fluid back down.

The scene before me grows blurry. No, tears are no good either. I can't spare a drop of water.

This is why. This is why. This is why I clench my teeth and desecrate the dead.

I'm sorry. Forgive me. I can't die yet. As I strip the adventurers' equipment I repeat these tearful words over and over again in my heart. I steady my arm when it flinches as if electrified by the touch of the thin white hand bones, and I steal the sword and the protective gear.

This is what it means to be an adventurer.

This, too.

When forced to the border of life and death, you scavenge from corpses.

I knew this job wasn't all roses and gallantry. I thought I understood that already. But maybe a part of me was still naive.

Hardening my resolve at this point...is just sophistry...

But all the same—I want to live.

I promise to make up for their stolen lives by seizing life myself.

I desperately repeat these comfortless words to the corpses, but the bones say nothing in response.

Still, the sword I have stolen from them tells me that if I am an adventurer, I must overcome this.

That, at least, is what its sharp gleam in the darkness seems to be saying.

"Huff, puff...!"

Panting with both hands planted on the ground, I look up.

Spread in front of me are the possessions left behind by the adventurers—that is, their equipment and items.

There is a longsword with a nicked blade, a cracked wand, several daggers, a piece of side armor, a magic feather pen, several unappealingly discolored potions, a moldy piece of bread, and some other small things. There's quite a lot here, but one item in particular draws our attention.

"A partly completed floor map..."

The corpse leaning against the wall had been gripping the sturdy roll of cloth in its hand.

The X in one corner probably represents their base, which is to say, this room. From there, a red line traces a complicated maze.

Quite a large area has been completed. As I look at the map I can see that again and again they ran into dead ends but continued on with their mapping project, despite the discouragement they must have felt.

I am sure that they, too, were stranded in this place, wandering in search of a way out.

And in the midst of that aim, their strength ran out.

"I cannot guess at their bitter disappointment…but this map will be an enormous help to us."

I nod in strong agreement to the words Lyu mutters as she looks down at the map spread on the ground. We must pick up where their line breaks off and continue to map this floor.

We must draw the line that leads us home.

"…Ms. Lyu, does the information on this map look familiar…?"

"No…the thirty-seventh floor is too big. I haven't covered it all. At least, I don't remember a maze shaped like this."

I had hoped that she could at least place our current location within the floor overall, but unsurprisingly, the outlook is not bright. Still…

"I've been to the deep levels many times. I do remember the main route."

"That means…"

"Yes. If we can get close to the main route…I can lead us to the connecting passageway."

Lyu looks up at me, and I see a glint of light in her eyes.

It's extremely small, but I do see a little hope.

"About these possessions…let's bring as much as we can. We don't know what we'll need."

"Got it…"

I look away from the map and take in the pile of equipment and items.

I repair the torn backpack with a bootlace and begin packing it. I even put in the items that look too dilapidated to use, like the sooty, dented canteen and the empty vials. Lyu trades her tattered clothes for the ripped battle clothes of the female adventurer. I can't help blushing and looking away, even though it's hardly the time to think about that kind of thing.

I look at their possessions once again…and notice that there's still some food left, despite the mold and rot. Given that, it's hard to believe starvation or thirst were the direct causes of their deaths. But while there are plenty of potions left, I don't see any antidotes. I don't imagine an exploration party would neglect to bring them along…which means they used them all? Could their cause of death have been an abnormality in their condition sparked by poison?

It seems plausible. After they were stranded for whatever reason, they probably made this room their base while searching for a way out. But before they could, a monster poisoned them. They managed to hole up in here, but were unable to treat the poison with the items they had left…

As one companion died and then another, perhaps the remaining adventurer was driven crazy by the darkness of the deep levels and took his own life.

I can't help glancing at the skeleton that until a moment ago had a dagger sticking from its chest.

"…Mr. Cranell."

Seeming to have noticed something, Lyu turns the map over and hands it to me.

The cloth was originally a familia emblem, most likely a flag. Without paper to create a map, they had been forced to draw on the proud symbol of their familia. But it's too damaged to make out which familia it belonged to.

However, in one corner, there are some red letters written in Koine.

"Deepest apol…re…honorable…sorr…Mo…Mother…unable to return."

I read out their last words, some of which are blotted out by dirt. As we imagine the last days of this party of three, both Lyu and I feel the same sorrow.

"…"

"…"

Just before we leave the room decked out in their protective gear and weapons, Lyu and I stand before the three adventurers and close our eyes. We have laid them in the center of the room with their hands crossed on their chests. We silently apologize for what we have done to them and offer up a prayer.

It only lasts a few seconds.

This is the Dungeon, the den of monsters. We cannot afford to linger in sentimental reflection.

We leave the room with a final word of farewell and gratitude to these nameless adventurers.

CHAPTER 10
THE WHITE MAGIC PALACE

The White Palace.

That is what the thirty-seventh floor is called. The walls are a strange milky white and the scale of the maze is infinitely grander than the floors I've been to before. All the passageways and rooms are huge, easily ten meders across in most places. The ceilings are no joke, either, although I can't see how high they are thanks to the darkness.

The Ring Walls are especially distinctive.

In the center of the floor there's a staircase leading to the next floor, and five rings resembling huge castle walls surround it as if to protect the imperial throne of the staircase. This layout doesn't exist on any other floor. Adventurers must make their way through the intricate mazes between the walls, or else go up and down countless times as they head for the central staircase.

I wasn't exaggerating when I said all of Orario could fit in here.

Many parts of the floor are still unexplored and unmapped, and they say that if you get lost in here you'll never get out. That perfectly describes our current situation. We've got to break out of this unbelievably huge White Palace.

We must escape this maze of horror.

"SHAAAAAAAAAAAAAA!!"

A robust arm covered in blue scales flashes a blade.

The lizardman warrior thunders threateningly as I narrowly dodge its powerful attack, which has trimmed several white hairs off my head and left me drenched in cold sweat.

The lizardman elite.

As its name suggests, the monster is a higher-rank version of the lizardmen that appear in the Colossal Tree Labyrinth. Its abilities are on a totally different level. The scales are blue rather than red, and as hard as armor, leaving no offensive or defensive vulnerability whatsoever. Its hands skillfully wield nature weapons—two axes made of a milky white stone that resembles bone. Although their threat level varies across individuals, the Guild rates them between Level 3 and Level 4. They specialize in close combat.

"GRUO!"

"JAAAA!"

The battlefield is a square room. I face two enemies.

Since she can't yet move with total freedom, Lyu is forced to kneel behind me as the rear guard, waiting on the sidelines of the battle. I take on both lizardmen at once, protecting her at the same time.

I can sense my enemies' potential viscerally, but I'm careful not to get pulled into an unnecessary counterattack. Taking an oblique stance, I hold the longsword in my right hand and gradually inch backward, tolerating the lizardmen's attacks as stoically as I can. I feel Lyu's sky-blue eyes watching over me from behind. I focus my attention on my enemies' movements, saving up my strength.

Lyu has imposed a condition on my advance through this deep level.

I must prioritize the conservation of energy above all else. It is essential that I avoid wasteful movements, and whenever possible *kill monsters with one strike.*

In other words, a single lethal blow.

I've got to aim for the magic stone in the monster's chest!

"Yaa!!"

The instant one of the lizardmen gets tired of waiting and raises its stone ax above its head, I transition from defensive position and unleash a lightning attack.

Lunging forward on my left foot, I thrust my right arm forward like an arrow!!

"GAA?!"

The sword of the dead adventurer pierces the center of the monster's unguarded chest.

I feel the blade striking something hard—the magic stone.

Its eyes bulging, the lizardman convulses and then crumbles in a pile of ash.

"Haaaaaa!"

I turn on the other monster, confused now that it is left alone. Anxious not to let the opportunity slip by, I thrust the sword forward immediately. The tip pierces my enemy's chest, but...

"?!"

"Gu...GAaa!"

Although blood gurgles from its mouth, the monster does not turn to ash. Instead, it rolls its bloodshot eyes at me menacingly.

I've failed to smash its magic stone. My aim was off!

My anxiousness was partly to blame, but more than that, my lack of skill. The longsword is lodged between two scales, and I can't pull it from the monster's flesh. I lose hold of it as the lizardman elite thrashes around. Terrifyingly, it charges toward me still pierced by the blade.

Spinning halfway around, it swings its massive tail toward me from the left.

I block with the Goliath Scarf, which is still wrapped around my left arm.

A second later, a numbing shock reverberates from my arm to my brain.

My left arm has become my Achilles' heel. Even though I blocked the monster's attack, the pain is so extreme it immobilizes me, leaving me wide open. And a deep-level monster is not about to overlook that opportunity.

It roars in fury and raises its stone ax.

"Oh, no, you don't."

The moment before the lizardman splits my head open, a flying dagger stabs it in the right eye.

"GUGAAAAA?!"

"!"

The support came from Lyu.

Gaping in surprise, my next act is entirely reflexive. I pull Hakugen from my hip, swivel toward the writhing lizardman elite, and dive at it.

"?!"

The glittering white longknife pierces its chest.

Stabbed by both a sword and a knife, the lizardman elite finally expires. The dagger and longsword tumble to the ground as it turns to ash.

"Mr. Cranell, more are coming!"

"…?!"

I don't even have time to take a breath.

Many footsteps are pounding toward us from far down the passageway. There are too many. If we fight here, we'll be surrounded!

I grimace and wipe away the sweat, forcing my mind to shift from battle mode to escape. I grab the longsword and the dagger off the ground and pass the latter to Lyu. We can't afford to waste any weapons. I catch up with her, pull her arm over my shoulder, and hurry out of the room.

After we leave the room where the adventurers' corpses lie, we're only able to successfully battle monsters for a short time. We use the map to avoid dead ends and head toward a larger passageway, but our first battle lifts the curtain on unending waves of angry monsters.

Since the thirty-seventh floor is so huge, the total number of monsters—that is, the absolute number that can appear here—is extraordinary. Even the intervals are short, giving adventurers no time to rest. The one saving grace is the fact that the monsters are spread out in the overly large maze, but if you have the bad luck to encounter a cluster of them, you end up in the situation we're in now.

"OOOOOOO!"

"!"

We're being pursued by lizardman elites, skull sheep, and lots of other monsters. One fight calls forth the next. One battle cry invites another. If a battle lasts more than a few seconds, the deep-level monsters detect it with their keen senses and gather around the prey.

Lyu told me to avoid fighting as much as I could…but it's impossible!

We've already fought *fourteen battles*. I stopped counting how many monsters we faced after *thirty*.

Is this par for the course in the deep levels?

This must be a joke!

"—OOO!"

A loup-garou wielding a stone-sword nature weapon lopes across my field of vision.

It's a medium-category monster whose short trunk measures from 120 to 130 celches. I almost mistook it for a cobalt at first glance, but it has the head of a wolf rather than a dog. Compared to the low-level monsters in the upper zones, it's far more sinewy, and capable of violent attacks out of scale with its small body.

If animal people on the surface get wind of a werewolf-type monster, they'll beat it to a pulp. That's because they've caused more than their share of tragedy by invading the surface. Most of the time when a village gets ransacked on a moonlit night, it's by a pack of these loup-garous. Even I used to shiver at stories of these beasts when I was a child.

Werewolves in particular loathe these warlike wolf-monsters as if they were vipers!

"AOOOOO!"

"WOOOOF!"

"...?!"

One kicks off the wall and attacks me from overhead, while another creeps along the ground to attack my feet. Wielding milky white stone blades that look like knives, the two wolves attack wildly at the same time. Sparks fly from the longsword I swing overhead even as my left thigh is lightly ripped. I'm suddenly on the defensive thanks to their extreme agility, which is outstanding even compared to other deep-level monsters. Landing a single deadly blow on their chests is out of the question.

Cutthroat close combat.

That's another reason the thirty-seventh floor is called a "palace."

In addition to the undead, the place is full of warrior-type monsters.

From the lizardman elites to the loup-garous and spartois, all of them are specialists in hand-to-hand combat who bring brute strength, agility, and mastery of nature weapons to their fights.

They'll plunge even adventurers who excel at skill and tactics into a bloodbath.

They are true guardians of the palace.

And this is the kind of place Aiz and her familia members spend their time in...!

They're fast and strong.

Way faster and way stronger than any monster in the lower levels.

It's not that I couldn't beat them one by one. Their biggest weapon is their numbers.

It takes at least three blows to kill one—one to fend off the attack, another to push them off balance, and a third to bury the knife in their chest. Only then do I finally bring down one monster. And once that's over, another three are crushing the last one's corpse underfoot to attack me.

This is impossible—I can't kill them all!

"Mr. Cranell, over here!"

Perhaps sensing I've reached a limit, Lyu shouts urgently to me.

No sooner has she done so than a dagger passes through one of the loup-garou's ears and pierces its skull. Taking advantage of the moment, I spin around at full force. Dripping sweat as a lizardman's stone sword grazes my back, I race to Lyu's side.

"OOOOOOOOOOOOOOOOOOOOOooo!"

Naturally, packs of monsters are also chasing us.

We can never fully escape. We'll be crushed. What in the world could Lyu have in mind?

She's at the end of the passage as I retreat pitifully toward her. Now she turns the corner and hides.

"We have no choice...I'm using this," she whispers.

I look at her questioningly.

She reaches down to her hip and pulls a brilliant red stone from her pouch. I realize with a start that I've seen one of those before.

"Mr. Cranell, fire please."

—An Inferno Stone!

The moment she pokes her head around the corner and throws the stone at the approaching monsters, I reflexively raise my right hand.

"Firebolt!"

As I release the electrical fire, Lyu reaches around the corner and pulls me back with her slender arm—that is to say, her Level 4 arm.

Ignited by the electrical fire, the Inferno Stone sets off a tremendous explosion.

"~~~~~~ ~~~~~~~~~~~~~~~?!"

The shock waves and back draft reach us around the corner, drowning out the screams of the monsters.

When the waves of heat finally recede, I timidly peer around the corner and see, beyond the lifting smoke…a cracked hallway littered with the corpses of monsters killed by the explosion.

"…Ms. Lyu, you just used…"

"Yes, an Inferno Stone I confiscated from that dwarf."

Shaking from the stink of burned flesh, I nervously look back at Lyu. She's frowning.

We're talking about the incident on the twenty-seventh floor when I first made contact with her.

Lyu was stealing something from the vanquished dwarf, who was a friend of the tamer called Jura. I realize now it must have been an Inferno Stone, which they used to destroy the floor.

"I never guessed the Inferno Stone I stole from Jura's crew would save us…"

As she notes this terrible irony, Lyu for once can't hide her hatred. Although she said she didn't have a choice, I get the sense that her feelings are complicated.

In any case…the explosion seems to have stemmed the tide of monsters. Most likely it wiped out any that were near us. The passageway is suddenly quiet.

"…How many Inferno Stones do you have left?"

"Five."

In other words, we only have five more outs from tight spots…

I can't think of anything to say. Partly, I'm silent out of helplessness.

"Mr. Cranell, I need a little time. I'm going to do some mapping."

"Okay…"

"Please stand guard."

Lyu peers warily around, then sits down in the middle of the shattered passageway and takes out the map. Dipping the feather pen—a magic item called a Blood Feather that allows the use of blood in place of ink— into one of her wounds, she picks up where the interrupted map left off. As a result of getting into so many battles, we've strayed far from the part of the maze the deceased adventurers noted down. Lyu's hand never pauses, as if the complex route we took is imprinted in her mind.

"You can even make maps...?"

"Simple ones. I'm nowhere near as good as specialized thieves and cartographers."

I could never pull off what this second-tier elf does with such ease.

...I've been depending on her.

Far from protecting her, I've been letting her rescue me from the start. Honestly, I can't even imagine where I'd be if she wasn't by my side.

As I watch her draw the red line with perfect accuracy, I drop to the ground with a thud.

I can't hide it. This series of battles has completely drained whatever energy I'd regained. How will I ever get through the deep levels like this...?

"Mr. Cranell, you're still doing unnecessary things. Try to be more efficient."

"..."

Lyu is still working on the map. She doesn't even raise her head as she offers this cool advice. My face grows instantly hot—from shame and regret.

"I know, I know! But I can't!"

I forget our surroundings and shout my answer.

"The whole situation is impossible! The monsters are so strong and fast! The more upset I get the less I can fight!"

I cover half my face with my right hand, drowning in irritation and despair. Lyu looks up silently.

"If things go on like this..."

I won't be able to protect myself *or* Lyu…!

"…I'm sorry."

I end my tirade with a pitiful whispered apology. Then I slump on the ground and groan.

As I'm staring at the ground with a bitter frown…Lyu finally speaks.

"Mr. Cranell. You are not acting like an adventurer."

Her voice hasn't changed at all, but her words are totally out of place.

"Huh…?"

"You're doing a good job. From your perspective, this is a completely unknown world. It's natural for you to be confused and unable to perform well. Even if you're Level Four now, that's still true beneath the surface."

"…!"

"If you were a normal adventurer you would be screaming that I'm being absurd right now."

She's not blaming me, and she doesn't sound hopeless. She's simply telling me in a calm voice what she's thinking.

"You're too hard on yourself. That's what I meant when I said you're not acting like an adventurer."

"Ah…"

"If you gain a bit more confidence…you'll be a much stronger adventurer."

She smiles faintly. I can't take my eyes off her face, which is clearly visible even in the darkness.

She sets the feather pen down, hesitates for a moment, then squeezes my pinkie.

"Watch your enemies well and gauge them. Deep-level monsters are highly intelligent. Most likely they will execute tactics much more advanced than monsters you've encountered previously."

"…Okay."

"Your right arm tends to float up when you get flustered. Relax your shoulder and aim for the magic stone."

"…Okay."

"Rely on me in the rear guard more. Right now, I'm your party."

"…Okay!"

Encircling someone's pinkie with your pointer finger and thumb must have a meaning among elves. I feel calm now, like the tide has receded. Lyu's words penetrate straight into my brain. The warmth of her fingers clears the haze from my heart.

"Do you remember what I told you aside from aiming for the magic stone?"

"…Use the terrain?"

She nods and looks me straight in the eye.

"We'll fight again now, and I want you to remember everything I just told you. You can do this."

Even in our dire situation, Lyu's words are like magic. They open my eyes to many things. They make me *remember* many things.

I need to become aware of myself again.

I may have changed when I met the Xenos and when I lost to my greatest rival, but that doesn't mean I'm a full-fledged adventurer. However much I've grown, however much my status has risen, I've still only been doing this for five months. I'm still a novice. There's so much I can't do yet.

I'm still totally green.

But the flip side is that I can become stronger.

Even starting now. There's no limit.

This woman really is amazing…

It was the same when we were confronted with the dead adventurers. She wiped away my anxiety and guided me forward.

I'm determined to become stronger so I can protect this guide of mine from the deep levels.

"…You're like my teacher, aren't you?"

Before I realize, I've spoken the words on my mind.

Of course, I'm studying under Aiz, whose fighting style mine resembles, according to a certain first-tier adventurer. Still, I can't help smiling at the relationship that might have existed.

"…That might have been a possibility."

Lyu widens her eyes just the slightest bit and smiles at me.

Our situation is still as awful as ever. Nevertheless, we're able to smile at each other.

"Mr. Cranell, let's get ourselves back in shape."

After a moment, Lyu switches gears and puts on her usual well-defended expression.

I nod. My self-doubt has cleared, but I won't be able to beat monsters in my current state of exhaustion. Glancing around warily, Lyu puts away the map and takes out something else: a vial with garish purple liquid sloshing revoltingly inside.

"Drink this."

"..."

It's one of the potions of undetermined vintage that we got from the dead adventurers.

I sweat as the solemn Lyu holds out the weirdly discolored liquid to me.

Do I really have to drink this?

"This is no time to demand perfection. Drink."

She speaks curtly, as if she's read my mind. She sounds just like a strict, serious teacher who never bends the rules...

"It doesn't matter if it's spoiled."

"Ms. Lyu..."

"It will still work...I think."

"Ms. Lyu?!"

I can't help protesting when she lets slip that disturbing "I think."

But it looks like I'll have to drink up. After all, Lyu has to save her recovery magic for emergencies. I'm sure lots of adventurers lost in dungeons or ruins have eaten rotten food or used spoiled items to survive...!

I drink the spoiled potion, grimacing as I do.

"Blech...!"

The tingling in my mouth and the disgusting smell invading my nose make my voice sound weird.

The potion is sweet. But after the sweetness comes bitterness...!

With a bizarre gurgling sound, my internal organs start to move around strangely. I double over, gripping my stomach to somehow tolerate this sensation.

"You should be fine because of your immunity…"

Come on, don't say "should"…!

Tearing up at Lyu's words, I drink down the last dregs of potion. Fortunately, it doesn't give me diarrhea or make me vomit.

Abilities, or I should say adventurers, are amazing…

And hey…my strength is back.

Physically, I feel better than I have since coming to the Dungeon, although my nerves are frayed from anxiety and overstimulation. But even my wounds close up when I sprinkle a few drops of the potion on them.

I can fight again.

"Let's go."

"Right."

We quickly check over our equipment and stand up.

Keeping an eye out for danger, we dispose of the magic stones in the corpses of monsters killed in the explosion in order to prevent them from being used to create an enhanced species. We pick up the singed daggers, too, although one is no longer usable.

In contrast to the potion and food, the equipment we got from the skeletons is in excellent condition. When upper-tier adventurers go into the deep levels, they take with them weapons and protective gear forged by High Smiths that can withstand long use with almost no deterioration in performance.

Gripping the longsword in my right hand, I lend Lyu my shoulder and start walking, my side armor clanking.

The White Palace maze is peaceful.

It's easy to overlook because each passage is so enormous, but the number of intersections and staircases going up and down is also immense. The sheer number of choices we have to make reminds me of Daedalus Street. In that sense, the structure of the thirty-seventh floor may be strangely orthodox.

Unlike the Colossal Tree Labyrinth and the Water Capital, this is a genuine maze. It's a chalky labyrinth designed to confuse and trap thieves who invade the royal palace of the Dungeon.

"Ms. Lyu...are there any especially dangerous monsters on the thirty-seventh floor?"

"Right now every monster on this floor is a threat to us...but if I had to name two, I'd say the spartois and the peludas."

We're whispering back and forth as we advance cautiously down a dimly lit passage. In contrast to the battles of a few minutes earlier, the maze is quiet now. I don't sense any monsters nearby or hear any battle cries. We haven't had any encounters since we used the Inferno Stone. But even as we pray for this to continue, both of us know it's only the calm before the storm.

"Rare monsters aside, spartois are the most skilled of all warriors when it comes to close combat. They're especially dangerous because they're spawned with weapons made of bone. Some individuals even carry javelins."

Still keeping watch for monsters, I compare what Lyu is telling me with the book knowledge I already have. To get through the deep levels, I've got to root out all sources of anxiety in my mind. That's why I asked Lyu about the scariest monsters.

"Peludas attack with poison. Most likely the immediate cause of death for those adventurers we found in the room...was poisoned darts from a peluda."

"...!"

"If we run into a spartoi or a peluda, we should flee if at all possible."

I tuck Lyu's words away in my heart even as I fight back the panic they stir up.

I've made a point of asking Lyu about her experiences when she was an adventurer, and she's told me as much as she could. Greedily, desperately, I've stored it away, even as I look around with increased wariness.

The White Palace...

I turn the name over in my mind, thinking how apt it is.

The slightly repellant milky white color of the walls and floors lacks the splendor of a palace, but the incomprehensible scale is definitely fitting for a natural castle. The "palace" of the underworld may be just the right name for it.

As for the difficulty of conquering this White Palace, the Guild has set the requirement for the thirty-seventh floor at Level 4. When I think about that, I realize that Lyu and I do meet that standard. Plus, Bors said that Lyu was at the upper limit of Level 4. She herself told me *Astrea Familia* had made it to the forty-first floor. Our ability definitely isn't unsuited to this floor.

That is, if we weren't in our current situation.

"Ms. Lyu. Do parties of two ever explore the deep levels…?"

"Not likely. Aside from Ottar, the Warlord, even first-tier adventurers wouldn't come down here solo. It's not that kind of place."

"…Not even *Loki Familia*?"

"It's probably different if you're Level Six…but you've got to have at least a three-man cell—no, a four-man cell. Plus you'd want a healer."

Lyu sounds like she's anticipating what I want to ask.

Even *Loki Familia* and *Freya Familia* can't afford to be careless down here.

Not even the Sword Princess.

I feel as if my lungs just froze.

"Mr. Cranell, do you have a general picture of the thirty-seventh floor?"

Lyu cuts into my silence with a question of her own. I nod, mentally unfurling the map of the deep levels that I received permission to view with Eina.

The perfect analogy for the thirty-seventh floor is a box with a round cake inside.

The box is the floor itself, and the cake is the maze—that is, the White Palace where we currently are. The palace is made up of the five Ring Walls. The walls are numbered, starting with the First Wall in the center, the Second Wall beyond that, and so on. The mazes between the walls have names, too.

The centermost area inside the First wall is called the Throne Zone, and that's where floor bosses appear. Moving out from there is the Knight Zone, the Warrior Zone, the Soldier Zone, and the Beast Zone. Despite these names, there isn't a big difference in the type of monster likely to appear in each part of the maze. However, since the area grows smaller and the maze more intricate as you move inward, the number of encounters and surprise attacks also naturally increases. In addition, data suggests that battles are more intermittent in the outer rings, although that isn't necessarily the case since monsters can move from one area of the maze to another.

The all-important staircase to the thirty-sixth floor is outside the Fifth Wall, on the far southern tip of the "box." In other words, we have to get out of the White Palace.

On the route we plan to take, there's no chance we'll run into the floor boss at the center of the maze. That's the one saving grace in our current horrible situation. If we had to take on a floor boss, well…I might lose heart altogether.

"This is…"

We run into a number of monsters wandering the maze, and I fight them according to Lyu's instructions. We're still not on the route the other adventurers had noted on the map. Eventually, we enter an open space. An enormous wall towers before us.

"…A Ring Wall."

Even without having seen the real thing before, I know at a glance what it is.

Within the milky tint of the maze, the curved wall is a pure, unclouded white. You could easily mistake it for clear ice—no, for white crystal. It looks a bit like the Great Wall of Sorrows on the seventeenth floor, where the Goliath appears, although this one is incomparably bigger.

The wall extends as far as I can see to the left and right. It's so perfectly uniform it hardly seems like a natural structure. Because of the darkness, I can't tell how high it is. But I'm sure that if I searched all the countries in the world, I would never find a castle wall this monumental.

"…No question about it, this is the Third Wall."

Lyu's words shake me out of my daze. Still leaning on my shoulder, she squints up at the magnificent wall.

"Each of the Ring Walls has a subtly different color. The only one that's pure white is the Third Wall, in the middle of the five rings."

She sounds very confident. At her urging, we walk up to the wall. She quietly presses her palm against its surface, ignoring my terror at being so close to a maze wall, which is an extremely risky place for surprise attacks since a monster could spawn at any moment.

With her hand still against the wall, she moves along it.

"…It's very slight, but the wall is curving inward toward us."

"…! That means…!"

"Yes, we're between the Third Wall and the Second Wall…in other words, in the Warrior Zone."

If the wall is curving toward us…that means we're *encircled by it.*

We just figured out where we are.

The Warrior Zone at the approximate midpoint of the White Palace!

"I'm not yet sure of our exact location…but it's incredibly important that we were able to figure out the general area of the thirty-seventh floor we're in."

I nod, unable to hold back my excitement. My eyes meet Lyu's sky-blue ones, which give me the go-ahead to start moving along the wall. We have no time to celebrate. We have to find another passage before the monsters realize we're here.

All we know so far is our general location. We still can't pinpoint this exact spot.

All the same, it's a step forward. It's progress.

A beam of light has shone into the endless expanse of the maze. That's what I try to make myself believe. As I step forward, I tell myself this path leads toward hope.

We can survive…we can return to the surface! Our party of two…!

I focus my energy into the shoulder that is supporting Lyu's slender form.

The discrepancy between the two adventurers' outlook had not faded.

How much can I help him grow before I'm gone?

Lyu was deep in thought as she stole a glance at Bell's face, which was filled with renewed hope that they would return alive. Although he did not know it, she was mulling over what would happen after her life was offered up in sacrifice.

It's poor strategy to expect to sacrifice one's life from the start, but...I need to be ready for that moment whenever it comes...If I hesitate, both of us will die.

Like Bell, Lyu prayed that she would survive their ordeal. Of course she did. There was no harm in both of them returning alive.

But she also knew that the deep levels were unlikely to allow them that luxury.

Although their equipment had improved a bit through their desecration of the dead, their situation was still far from solid. After all, why should the Dungeon let weak, injured prey escape its jaws?

She expected circumstances would force her hand.

Undoubtedly, a situation would arise in which she must sacrifice herself.

Before that happens...I have to teach him how to survive.

Lyu planned to pass on all she knew to Bell in the time she had left.

Even after escaping the deep levels, he had to be able to survive alone until help arrived.

It was a good sign that he was seeking information from her so actively. Plus, because the Dungeon forced him to put what he learned into practice immediately, he was absorbing everything extremely quickly.

He's stronger now. Much stronger than before. Even if he's struggling right now...as he gains experience, the unknown will become known and he'll be able to adapt.

She didn't doubt that.

He really was stronger now. So much so that she hardly recognized him.

He had pushed the Juggernaut into a corner all by himself. A number of factors had contributed to his success, but nevertheless, it was an extraordinary achievement.

The sight of him fighting so hard against despair and ultimately breaking through had given her hope. She had seen the light of white flames that must never be allowed to die out.

...Even now he is pursuing his ideal. He is pursuing a future in which both of us survive.

The boy was brilliant. So brilliant he blinded her.

Once she, too, had shared his unclouded gaze. She had pushed forward believing in a better future.

She doubted that she was capable of pursuing an ideal anymore.

Rejoice, Kaguya...I'm like you now.

As she walked forward through the dim, milky white maze, Lyu cast a self-mocking smile at her departed friend.

Visions of those days rose in her mind.

As the adventurer Lyu looked ceaselessly around for monsters, the part of her that was already cut free from the present soared into the past.

"Take it back, Kaguya!"

It was a day long ago, and Lyu was shouting emotionally.

She and a fellow member of *Astrea Familia* were in a room in Stardust Garden, their home in Orario, butting heads.

"And why, exactly, do I have to take back what I said?"

The beautiful girl who smiled cheerfully back at her had long, straight black hair. Her island-style clothing and pretty hairpin suggested her origins in the Far East, while her graceful words and carriage were those of a sheltered girl of gentle birth. Still smiling, she tilted her head questioningly at Lyu's passionate insistence, as if to say, *Why all the fuss?*

"You're telling me that the minority should be ignored in the name of the bigger picture? Is that the justice Lady Astrea wants?! What good is peace at the cost of such a sacrifice?"

Lyu was younger then, her words colored by the upright character of the elf race. As Kaguya listened, she lowered her arched eyebrows, only to narrow her eyes like a fox.

"Idiot! You're so shallow it takes my breath away!"

"What…!!"

"Why…do you think…people call you a useless little elf?!"

Kaguya snorted, her refined manners of a moment earlier vanished like smoke.

Lyu wanted to explode at the way the other girl was talking to her so slowly, like she was a stupid child.

Gojouno Kaguya.

She was a Level 4 adventurer and the vice-captain of *Astrea Familia*. Her swordsmanship and skill in hand-to-hand combat far outstripped any other member of the familia. She and Lyu were constantly competing with each other to see who could advance faster.

Although she did not like to talk about her background, she was rumored to have grown up in a noble family in the Far East. Her long, silky hair reached to her waist and was cut straight across her forehead in bangs. When she wore a kimono and smiled, she was a veritable picture of a Far Eastern woman.

As soon as she opened her mouth, however, the illusion crumbled. She had a notoriously dirty mouth and not a shred of class.

Lyu felt like fainting from embarrassment when Kaguya would cross her legs so everyone could see up her clothes or walk around in her underwear when the weather was hot even if guys were around. She was just like Cyclops from *Hephaistos Familia*, which made Lyu wonder crossly if this was the only kind of woman the Far East produced.

"I adore Lady Astrea. If she hadn't made such a deep impression on me, I wouldn't be in this familia. I have the highest respect for her."

"Well, then…!"

"But that has nothing to do with the application of her concept of justice to real life," Kaguya said, cutting off Lyu's attempt at protest. "Is it easier for you to understand if I put it like this? Don't think we're strong enough to rescue the whole world."

The look in her eyes was sharp, and her tone cold.

"Leon, you're a strong fighter. Strong enough that I think of you as a worthy rival. But you're still the greenest member of this familia."

"Wha…!!"

Lyu lunged toward Kaguya, eyebrows raised incredulously at the sudden insult.

"I'm not picking on you because you're an elf. I'm saying you have a stronger spirit than any of us. But if you're right, then why did Shakti's younger sister, Adi, die?"

The hand that was reaching toward Kaguya froze.

"She died right before our eyes, didn't she? She was killed by the Evils with that nonsensical self-detonating bomb."

It was a dark time in the Labyrinth City.

Rudra Familia and other evil forces had reared their heads in Orario, bringing destruction and suffering.

Chaos and confusion had swirled in the lawless city as the bandits rampaged. The blood and tears of the powerless citizens had flowed without cease, and those with the strength to stop the evil were forced to make sacrifices.

"Look at the city. The cries of her people still have not stopped. We have had to make sacrifices even to reach this point. How can we scream for a justice that doesn't have a single blemish?"

"...!"

"You think we can save everyone? I don't think so, idiot."

Kaguya stroked the two daggers at her waist as she spit out her last words. But she was neither angry nor hopeless. Instead, she was coolly describing their harsh reality.

"The justice you speak of is no more than a convenient ideal. There comes a day for every person when they must make a choice. You and I, as well."

She turned her black eyes away from Lyu as if she'd lost interest.

"I think you need to learn a little more about the real world."

With those parting words of mockery, she turned away. Left alone, Lyu could only clench her fists—not in irritation at Kaguya, but in anger at herself for not being able to argue back.

"Looks like you two were getting into it again."

The voice caught Lyu off guard. It was Alize, who poked in her head from the hallway as if she just happened to have been walking by. Lyu looked away as the redhead came into the room.

"It's a good thing for you two to exchange ideas, but could you keep your voices down a little next time? Me aside, Lady Astrea overheard you. You'll only add to her pain."

"..."

"Of course, she'd probably just encourage you to talk things through. Anyway, sounds like Kaguya won again? You're much too upright. You make it easy to pick on you."

Alize smiled as she teased the dejected Lyu, who kept her eyes glued to the floor as she spoke.

"I...can't accept it. Even if I'm an idiot and Kaguya is right, I just can't swallow the idea of expecting to make sacrifices from the start…It's no different from giving in to the Evils. We might as well proclaim our own powerlessness and forget about working for justice!"

As she spoke, her emotions bubbled up and she couldn't help raising her voice.

"Please calm down, Leon."

Alize squeezed Lyu's pinkie.

Her pointer finger and thumb encircled the elf's slender finger. As she did, Lyu's feelings grew strangely clear.

That was what always happened.

Alize was always able to make Lyu feel as calm as a quiet sea. It was as if the girl's green eyes were sucking her in.

"…Did you hear what Kaguya said?"

"You mean about having to give something up? Yes, I did—why?"

"What do you think of it? Do you agree with her that sacrifices must be made?"

Before she realized it, she was asking Alize her opinion. Alize answered without pause or self-doubt, thrusting her narrow chest forward proudly.

"Of course it's better if we can save everyone. I think you were in the right!"

Lyu was shocked. Alize was breezily confirming the resolution that Lyu had arrived at through questioning herself. As she blinked in surprise, Alize continued.

"But I'm not sure if that's the correct answer."

"Huh…?"

"I don't think everything will go smoothly just by charging toward your ideal head-on."

After all, that could lead to paying a heavy price and making even more sacrifices. Alize did not deny what either Lyu or Kaguya had said; she viewed things not from an individual perspective, but rather from that of natural law.

"I've heard that when Kaguya was in the Far East, she went through a lot. I suspect she saw things you and I can't even imagine."

"…You mean the political strife in the East?"

"She may have spoken harshly because of those experiences…perhaps she said those things in order to protect what is truly important to her."

The captain of the familia was looking deep into Kaguya's heart.

"I don't think there is a right answer. There is only what we do to fulfill our wishes and how hard we struggle. There is only what we are able to leave behind on the altar of the ideals we cannot reach. Even I, in all my perfect purity and correctness and wisdom, can say no more than that."

Lyu wasn't sure if that last bit was spoken in jest or seriousness, but Alize smiled after she finished talking.

"But ideals are important, aren't they?"

Like pure, graceful flowers.

"They may be no more than beautiful words, but we should still strive for them, no matter how we are laughed at or mocked. If we don't, then we will become weak creatures willing to accept any outcome whatsoever."

Alize's eyes were completely earnest as she spoke those words. Lyu remembered them even now.

"If we don't pursue our ideals, the things we obtain through compromise will be insignificant."

That's what I think.

That's what I believe in.

Alize had said it quite clearly.

"I don't know if that's the right answer. But giving up is wrong. The ideals you pursue are filled with happiness."

"…"

"That's why it's meaningful to pursue them."

Each of Alize's words struck deeply in Lyu's heart.

"…What if someone really does fulfill their ideals?" Lyu asked.

Alize laughed like a child.

"Don't you know? Those are the people we call heroes."

CHAPTER 11
WHERE THE WILL TO KILL LEADS

© Suzuhito Yasuda

The battle cries of monsters echo like thunder.

Ignoring the sweat dripping down my body, I respond to the threatening chorus with a cool-headed swirl of attacks.

We are on a sprawling battlefield in the deep levels.

After making our way through the maze for a while, we've taken up positions at the top of a staircase.

The decision was based on one of Lyu's conditions for battle:

Always use the terrain.

Like the mazes in the Water Capital, those between the Ring Walls on the thirty-seventh floor are multilevel. The ceilings of the rooms are terrifically high, and to move forward you have to go up and down endless staircases. Right now, we're fighting monsters from the top of one of those staircases.

It goes without saying that the monsters have a hard time attacking us from below and an equally hard time fending off our attacks from above. We have the geographical advantage—that is, we're using the height differential to our benefit.

"Yaaa!"

"GAAA?!"

I swing a white stone cudgel down on a loup-garou that's left itself momentarily exposed. To the wolf-headed monster on the step below me, it's like the nature weapon—which I stole from the beast itself—is being swung down from high above my head. Even though it tries to shield with its arms, the cudgel smashes its head and body, reaching its magic stone.

Without even waiting to see its body crumble into ash, I toss away the cracked nature weapon and immediately draw the sword of the dead adventurer. I thrust it accurately into the magic stone of the skull sheep that was on me in an instant, almost as if I predicted its attack.

Watch your enemies well.

Lyu had told me to watch and gauge the monsters.

That would allow me to act tactically, but more importantly, to make up for injuries and other physical handicaps with my wits.

"OOO, OOO!"

"UUUU...!"

When I watch them carefully, I can see that the monsters below us are at a loss for how to attack.

The passageway and the stairway we're standing on are unusually narrow for the thirty-seventh floor, which allows us to limit the number of enemies we're fighting at one time to two. The corpses are piling up to the tune of their enraged howls.

All we have to do is give the monsters that approach carelessly a good kick.

That's what I do to a lizardman elite that charges up with an irritated howl. A sound kick to its jaw sends it flying backward, knocking down the other monsters on the staircase as it tumbles down and ultimately breaks its neck.

My right arm tends to float up...

That's something else Lyu told me.

I watch the wave of monsters ascending the staircase and very intentionally—without fear, panic, or strain—wait for my opportunity, then—strike!

"GUGAA?!"

My thrust lands in the center of the monster's abdomen. The loup-garou screams and transforms into a mist of ash.

You can do it. You can see. You can attack. You can fly.

If I put Lyu's advice into action, I can fight.

Compared to battles on flat land, the monsters' movements are far more limited here.

I make a mental leap.

Their limited range of movement means I can lead them in whatever direction serves me best.

And being able to lead them means my predictions *can get pretty close to premonition.*

I look over the monsters clamoring to approach me, take aim, and act.

"—Haaa!!"

I cut downward at a slant from the neck of the lizardman leading the charge, sending him flying. Instantly two loup-garous dodge the corpse and come at me. I reverse my swing and plunge the blade into the chest of the wolf-monster on my right. As the one on my left swipes its sharp claws toward me, I easily repel it with the Goliath Scarf wrapped around my left arm.

A jolt of pain shoots from my arm up to my skull. Ignoring it, I swing the sword around in a tight arc. Even if I'm not able to kill my enemy with one stroke, I'm trying to keep my movements as minimal as possible. The loup-garou is coming at me from the side now, and my sword slices off its leg, knocking it off balance. Immediately I hit it with the pommel.

Blood flies from its nose as my powerful blow lands on its face in midair. It ends up skewered by something that was meant for me.

It's a bone lance, one of the long-distance projectiles from a skull sheep that snuck up from behind. The sheep freezes for a second as its attack misfires into the loup-garou, and I take that opportunity to throw my sword at it. I glimpse the weapon piercing its skull and magic stone even as I'm taking up Hakugen with my now-empty hand.

I glance up at the loup-garou that's jumping silently over my head as if to say, *I see you*, ignore the surprise in its eyes at being *led into my trap*—and slice it in half with Hakugen.

I've just turned four or five monsters to ash as if I had planned it all out in advance.

"UOOOOO!"

Here comes number six.

I'm not going to be able to stop this loup-garou alone.

So...

"GUGEI?!"

I leave it to her.

Lyu throws a dagger from her position in the passageway behind my back. Her timing is impeccable: she throws exactly when I step out of the path of the blade. As the monster writhes, its eye pierced by the dagger from my incredible party-member in the rear guard, I plunge my knife into its chest.

I flew—I used it.

Leading the enemy.

It's something Aiz taught me.

They're always most off guard right before their final blow.

The instant before they attack is your best opportunity.

So you guide them into attempting a lethal blow.

At the time, we were talking about one-on-one encounters. But thanks to Lyu's instruction, I've broadened it to encompass all enemies. I'm calculating backward from my final blow as I watch and gauge all of their movements. Then, by using the terrain, I purposely draw them to me and limit their options.

I'm reading the entire battlefield and manipulating it.

My training with Aiz has linked up with Lyu's advice.

The teachings of the Sword Princess and Gale Wind have intertwined.

The second I realized that, the world expanded before me.

This momentary feeling of omnipotence seems to have given me power.

Unfortunately, I don't have time to relish the experience.

But now I know I can grow even stronger.

That conviction glows in my chest, and before I know it, my throat is vibrating.

"AAAAAAAAAAAAAAAAAAAAAAAAAAAAAAAAA!!"

"…Excellent."

As Bell's monster-rivaling war cry rang in her ears, Lyu whispered a word of admiration for the boy's current fighting style.

This is growth…no, it's a major leap. But can he grow still more?

It wasn't just that he was absorbing things quickly.

Lyu could see that he tended to conscientiously and earnestly put her advice into action. While he excelled at fixing his weak points, however, he didn't seem able to do more than she told him.

What to make of that?

Right now, he was listening to her advice and applying it.

He didn't leave basic knowledge alone, either; he thought about how to develop it on his own. Although Lyu didn't know it, it was very similar to what he had done to develop Argo Vesta from his own skills. In that case, he'd thought and experimented on his own. That was essential in an adventurer.

There had been signs this was coming. The dramatic events leading up to his advance to Level 4, including meeting the Xenos and encountering his worthy opponent Asterios, had changed him. Now, the extreme conditions of the deep levels were forcing him to take another leap.

If he didn't become stronger, only death awaited.

Thrust into this hell, the cruel jaws of death were forcing him to grow.

Lyu squinted as if she were looking at a blindingly bright light.

"—!!"

"!"

She was watching him slaughter a monster when she heard it—the howl of monsters from far down the passageway behind her.

It was a swarm of lizardman elites.

"Ms. Lyu?!"

He turned toward her, shouting in surprise.

The passage they were in now had no tunnels branching off it. They were trapped in a pincer attack. Afraid for Lyu, who was still kneeling and unable to move freely, he started toward her, but she stopped him with a sharp command.

"Mr. Cranell, focus on your own enemies!"

"But…!"

"I can't support you anymore. I won't have time to keep an eye on you."

These were the deep levels. She simply could not keep leaving the battles to Bell while she played backup.

She had known all along that in a two-man cell, a time would come when the rear guard had to step up and fight. Now that time had come.

Her face was calm despite the beads of sweat caused by the pain in her leg.

"I can't drag you down. I have to fight, too."

Lyu turned her back on Bell and took up a battle stance.

With monsters pressing up toward him, Bell didn't have time to hesitate. All he could do was continue fighting atop the stairs and trust in Lyu below.

"UOOOOOOOOOOOOOOO!"

She placed her hands on the blade at her waist as the lizardmen approached.

It was the steel sword she had taken from the deceased adventurers. It was beautiful, most likely forged by a smith drawn to the weapons of the Far East. Made from materials gathered in the Dungeon, its blade was as sharp as ever.

Holding it by her left hip, Lyu dropped to one knee as she faced the pack of monsters.

"…?"

The lizardmen looked suspiciously at the elf kneeling on the ground.

She was perfectly still, with both hands on her scabbard. To the monsters, it was strange behavior. They paused for a moment before their statue-still prey, then charged all at once.

The lizardman at the fore strode toward her, intent on splitting her in half with its longsword nature weapon.

Even someone unfamiliar with swordsmanship would have been able to tell that she was waiting for it.

As the monster flew recklessly toward her, Lyu unleashed her response.

"—Yaaa!!"

"GUAA?!"

Lyu shook, and there was a flash of silver.

No sooner had the lizardman entered striking range than she

swiftly drew the sword and struck her enemy. A huge cloud of ash filled the air. The other lizardmen gaped in confusion at the remains of their companion who had been cleaved clear in half, magic stone and all.

"Kaguya…I borrowed your trick."

Lyu had used a quick-draw, a skill her departed battle companion from the Far East had prided herself on. With her leg injured, Lyu was nearly immobilized. She'd therefore given up on moving around and instead focused on countering attacks. It was the only fighting strategy left open to her.

As she replaced the sword in its sheath, the confused lizardmen charged toward her, howling. Squinting at them, she drew the sword again and tore into their magic stones before their stone swords could reach her. No matter how many times they attacked, the result was always the same: As soon as one stepped within range, she struck it. Because the passage was so narrow, only two could attack at once. And she was skilled enough to defend herself with a sword in each hand, so that the mountain of ash grew twice as fast.

The flashing silver assaults that she performed with every part of her body except her right leg fell within the territory of slashing attacks.

If Kaguya were here she'd probably say I was putting her to sleep…

She'd learned the skill from her friend, but she was nowhere near as good as the original. Still, she was threat enough for the deep-level monsters. The moment they drew near in an attempt to break through, the flash of her sword did them in. It was almost like magic. The certainty of her blows made the monsters flinch and hesitate in their attacks.

And the more they hesitated the better. The more time she could buy for Bell the more of his own enemies he could do away with. By now he should be capable of taking them down without her support.

Her strategy worked precisely because she was dealing with highly intelligent deep-level monsters.

But just then—she jumped.

"‼"

An ill-omened sound turned her heartbeat into a fire alarm. Even before she saw the deep rift split the wall directly next to her, she'd leaped away. No sooner had she done so than a huge arm popped out of the wall and swung through the air precisely where Lyu had been standing.

"…! A barbarian!"

Lyu grimaced at the large-category monster that had spawned. It had two twisted horns and sharp fangs and claws. The warrior monster was as fierce as a lizardman elite or a loup-garou. The infuriatingly timed surprise attack of the barbarian made Lyu stumble in her quick-draw stance, and now it followed up with another blow.

"HAA!"

"Eee?!"

A long tongue snaked from its mouth.

Unable to move quickly, Lyu could not fully avoid the lick. Her strength slipped.

War cries immediately thundered out.

Headed by the barbarian, the lizardmen were charging toward Lyu. Just as the monsters lit by the phosphorescent glow were about to swallow up the elf—

"UAAAAAAAAAAAAAAAAA!"

"GYA?!"

Bell raced to block them.

Having finished off the opponents on the other side of the stairs, he executed a flying kick with all his might. Its chest bones cracked from the force of the blow, the barbarian fell backward, crushing the lizardmen behind it.

Still Bell did not stop. Drawing Hakugen, he fell on the collapsed monsters. The shocked Lyu followed suit by picking up the sword she'd dropped and diving onto the monsters like she was one of their own.

"GYAAAA!"

"GA?! GO?! GI?!"

"…, …, …?!"

Spattered with fountains of blood, the monsters screamed cease-lessly.

Ignoring their cries, Bell and Lyu brought their sharp blades down again and again on the torsos of their enemies. They knew they could not let a single one rise again. The vision of the two adventur-ers furiously stabbing the monsters over and over had not a shred of refinement to it; it was primitive, even bizarre.

Their cheeks painted with the blood of their enemies and their eyes opened wide, they moved with frantic desperation. They could not afford to leave any stone unturned in this battle that they had risked their lives on.

When the arms of the last monster had finished convulsing and finally lay still…the passageway was silent aside from the panting of the two adventurers.

The pair of sky-blue eyes and the pair of rubellite ones reflected the bedraggled adventurers.

Lyu slowly parted her lips.

"Let's rest a little…"

"The Juggernaut?"

Sitting with my back against a wall, I repeat the name.

We are in a small room with a single doorway. The room's odd shape is as far from a cube as you can get—a rock cave would be a more accurate analogy. After damaging the walls, Lyu and I rest for the second time since arriving on the thirty-seventh floor.

"Yes, I heard that's what it's called…after it was all over, of course."

As we keep an eye out for monsters, our conversation turns to the horrible monster from the twenty-seventh floor—the one with the hid-eous claws that followed us down here.

"It was after I had lost my friends and gotten revenge…around when Syr took me in. A figure in black appeared before me…prob-ably a mage."

Her description startles me. A mage in black...that's got to be Fels. So Fels was in contact with Lyu years ago?

Gale Wind...you must never speak of the Juggernaut you encountered in the Dungeon.

The two had spoken in a back alley on a dark, rainy night. Fels had come to warn her, addressing her by her nickname. At the time, no one knew her true identity.

It must never be summoned again. If you keep your promise...we will let you go free. We will take your achievements in Astrea Familia *into account and not prosecute your crimes.*

Did "we" mean the upper echelons of the Guild...or even Lord Ouranos?

Was she saying that thanks to Ouranos's edict, the Guild had only fulfilled its basic duty of blacklisting her, but had not tried to track her down?

According to Lyu, she had nodded silently in response to the warning, and Fels had melted into the darkness.

"If the mage was a private messenger, that means the Guild knew about the existence of the monster. Most likely they were acting under the mandate of the god Ouranos, who prays to the Dungeon..."

Lyu seems to have guessed Fels's true identity. I glance over at her as she leans against the wall, exhausted. I'm lost in my own thoughts. So even Fels was worried about that monster...that calamity that appeared before Lyu twice.

"The Juggernaut..."

I stroke my mangled left arm as I whisper its name. As I think back on that being so much more terrifying than any other monster I've encountered, the question on my mind swells to the point where I can't hide it anymore.

"...Ms. Lyu. The thing the man named Jura said..."

It's been bothering me ever since I heard the tamer say it.

To save your precious self!

By sacrificing your friends, you were finally able to drive off the monster!

I'm sure that's what he said.

What happened on that day when all of *Astrea Familia* died except Lyu? How did she survive? What happened to the Juggernaut she encountered that time? Did she kill it? Jura said she "drove it off"— did that mean it might still be alive?

These are the questions circling my mind when I ask her what happened. I can't help asking.

"…"

Lyu does not answer. Her sealed lips return only silence, although her fist begins to tremble from being clenched so tight.

"…Mr. Cranell, enemies."

Multiple roars echo down the passage from a distance. From behind, I watch Lyu stand. I follow silently, unable to ask my question a second time.

He was wandering.

He exhaled hot breath. Pieces of his shell flaked off his body and fell to the ground.

The claws on his left paw caught the faint phosphorescence on the wall, glittering a weird purplish-blue.

The dark maze was quiet now.

The other monsters held their collective breath in fear of him, making sure not to cross his path. Only the sound of his footsteps shook the air.

The monster that the deities and adventurers called Juggernaut was roaming the thirty-seventh floor.

His wounds were deep.

Within him existed a complete intelligence that one could call thought.

He quietly looked over his body with those intelligent eyes.

The reverse joint on his right leg had been sliced through. He could still jump, but his mobility had plunged compared to when he was in prime shape. The extreme speed that terrified the adventurers was no longer possible.

His right arm had been blown off with that enormous flare. Not a trace of it was left. The deadly threat that had spelled the end of his arm had impacted the entire right side of his body, and half of the magic-reflection shell that served as his armor was flaking off. Half of his tail was missing, too.

His whole body was damaged.

His wounds were severe.

Eventually, he would be immobilized.

He didn't care.

He would disintegrate anyway.

Without anyone telling him, he was aware of that. He understood it.

Juggernauts are short-lived creatures.

Their greatest peculiarity—the thing that set them apart from other monsters—was their lack of a magic stone.

Perhaps their whole self could be thought of as one enormous magic stone. Their unparalleled strength and agility were products of this. Their potential varied according to the zone on which they emerged; the deeper the floor, the stronger the individual. Some were so strong they could wipe out a whole familia like *Astrea Familia*, or crush a whole party of first-tier adventurers. Even if a Juggernaut lost its head in battle or was pierced through the chest, it would continue to destroy. Only when its entire body was crushed would its life finally come to an end.

The price for this extraordinary strength was natural disintegration after a certain period of time. Like sculptures made of ice, they shattered noisily.

The first Juggernaut may have been male, or it may have been female. Unknown to the human race, this child of calamity retreated to a corner after slaughtering *Astrea Familia* and turned to ash. Their lives came with an expiration date. They were a fleeting species of monster destined to burn themselves out like shooting stars.

And so the schemes of the tamer Jura, who attempted to bring a Juggernaut under his control, too, were destined to go unfulfilled...

The Juggernaut would leave behind neither a magic stone nor any drop items. Not a single trace of its life would remain. Born in service to its mother, it would eradicate the elements threatening her and then vanish from the world and from the memory of its people.

Therefore, massacre was the only thing that gave its existence meaning.

The Juggernaut did not think of his life as empty. Nor did he see himself as pitiable. The emotions to feel these things did not exist within this newborn creature.

But—his body burned with the flames of hell.

That white prey.

That being who always rose again, no matter how many times it was crushed.

That male who lost its own blood and flesh only to turn and begin to destroy him.

Those white flames that had taught him to fear.

He could not forgive this. He could not accept it. Allowing it would be the same as denying the meaning of his own existence. He would lose the very reason for having been born into this world. That alone he understood instinctively.

It was awful, awful, awful.

It was the one thing he could not stand. He might be forgotten by the world, his life might vanish in a flash, but he must fulfill the purpose of his birth.

His hopes were warped, his prayers twisted.

But for the Juggernaut, they were everything.

As if in sympathy with his thoughts, the circlet fastened around his neck pulsed with light.

It fed his destructive impulses, as if it were driving his emotions or making him run wild. The voice of his mother was distant now. He ignored that voice, which repeatedly begged something of him. He put his own will first.

This was the side effect of Jura's magic item.

Although it should not have been so in a being who served as antibody to the invading virus, his sense of self was fierce. The apostle of murder whose sole purpose was massacre did not realize that self-interest now controlled him. The powerful murderous intent now focused on a single prey was enough to render him independent. The current Juggernaut, who was no slave to his mother's will, was prepared to die in the line of duty.

He had been set free.

Free from Jura's dying wish, but more than that, free from the voice of the Dungeon.

The apostle of murder eradicating foreign matter from the Dungeon had been reborn as a monster whose purpose was to pursue a single human to the point of insanity, and kill him.

And so.

He would kill that thing, if nothing else.

He absolutely, without question, would kill him.

With that fervent desire burning at the core of his being, the Juggernaut slowly but surely approached his prey.

At the same time, his intention sparked an irregularity that even the Dungeon had not foreseen, an irregularity so great it went beyond his given abilities to the realm of evolution.

He had no right arm. In this state, he could not kill the white prey.

He needed an arm. He needed claws to murder that thing.

The Juggernaut's crimson eyes pulsated faintly.

The next instant, he was attacking his own kind.

A chorus of screams was followed by the reverberations of destruction, and then the sound of mastication.

The noises echoed ominously through the writhing darkness of the Dungeon.

SPECIAL CHAPTER
REMINISCENCE OF JUSTICE

"Ideal and reality? What, Leon? Has Alize or Kaguya been putting strange ideas in your head again?"

The girl was sitting in a chair, swinging her short legs in evident enjoyment.

Several days had passed since Lyu's argument with Kaguya. After stewing over it for a while on her own, the elf had brought it up with her fellow familia member Lyra.

The prum, who measured less than 120 celches, had spread a collection of strange instruments on the table. She was in the process of disassembling and repairing them, and her nimble fingers worked incessantly. Without lifting her head to look at Lyu, she offered her a silly grin.

"Instead of making that serious expression, you should just nod and smile. If you jump in bed pretending you've figured it all out, the strange thing is that all your worries simply up and vanish!"

"Come on, Lyra, I'm being serious. Just because Kaguya is so confrontational doesn't mean I should ignore what she says. That only narrows my own view. Alize's words really stuck with me, too. I feel like I need to hear more opinions if I'm ever going to sort this out…"

"Oh man, are elves ever annoying…"

Lyra rudely brushed away Lyu's concerns. The prum's words were incredibly out of sync with her tender, innocent eyes. Surprisingly, she was two years older than Lyu. Her short hair was dyed peach (which was "super-cool," according to the prum herself), and a crafty smile constantly played on her lips.

As her appearance and behavior suggested, Lyra the prum was quite the cynic.

"Why do you have to be the one who has to come up with an answer anyway? Let alone an answer other people think is correct."

At first glance, she seemed a poor match for this elf who was the very picture of an upright soul, but whenever Lyu was troubled by something, she tended to go to Alize first, then Lyra. Lyra's opinions were always honest and unreserved, and sometimes unexpected for Lyu. Within the familia, her sharp words were always respected.

Although Lyra didn't seem serious about life on the surface, Lyu was frequently startled by the perceptive way she got to the heart of things, and unconsciously found herself depending on the prum quite often.

"Just take everything with a grain of salt. That goes for what Kaguya says as well as Alize."

"Lyra, that's a bit…"

"The truth completely changes depending on the person."

"!"

"Ultimately, you are the one who decides what is true. You are the one who creates your own truth. Take everything with a grain of salt, think about it all, and fashion yourself a truth you can be satisfied with."

It was unlike Lyra to sound so much like a walking proverb. Perhaps that was because for once this master liar was actually speaking her own truth.

"…I wish you always talked to me like that."

"What are you talking about, Leon? I'm the most serious and kind person around here!"

"I'd like you to put your hand on your heart and think back on what you've taught me in the past before you make a claim like that…"

It was true.

The prum was always teaching Lyu the most unrespectable things.

Skills like how to see through a lie were fine, but then there were things like the art of using blackmail to negotiate, lessons in intimidation, and to top it all off, she also taught Lyu how to always win at gambling as well as how to cheat.

If you're gonna beat the scumbags, you've gotta understand how they think…Pretty words won't do much in the fight for justice… Lyra's teachings may have had some logic behind them, but they certainly weren't befitting the familia of justice.

After five years in the familia, Lyu had acquired more than her share of unnecessary knowledge.

"I've been looking after you since you're such an innocent little elf."

"If we're comparing me to you, I can't argue with that…"

Lyra smiled teasingly and finally looked up at Lyu, who was standing beside her.

"Listen, Leon. Knowledge is a weapon. Information is a meal ticket. What I've taught you may have been improper and random, but it will all be helpful one day. Remember it all and use it all."

Remember it all and use it all.

That was Lyra's favorite saying.

"Use your brain until blood comes out your ears. If you don't have equipment or items, scavenge what you need from the Dungeon, and if that's not possible, rely on drop items. Make your own substitutions. Even if something is useless on its own, it might be incredibly useful in combination with something else."

"Use your head, right…?"

"It may not come easy to you but study the subtleties of human nature. They're not just key for negotiating—they're incredibly important in the Dungeon."

The characteristics of monsters, improvised weapon-crafting, survival skills, the inner workings of her party members…That day, Lyra had boasted that by knowing all these things and using them in conjunction, it was possible to obtain something important for succeeding in the Dungeon.

She had spoken teasingly, but she was dead serious about planting this seed in Lyu.

"All this random knowledge might have been annoying and time-consuming for you to learn, but it's better than being ignorant. It might take a while, but now you have to turn what you know into wisdom."

"Turn knowledge into wisdom…?"

"Once you can do that, you'll be able to help someone beside yourself. You'll be a crazy-strong elf that everyone looks up to. Not even Kaguya will be able to call you green, then."

Lyra looked part mischievous child, part big sister.

"…Is that how you got so strong?"

"Yep. I mean, if I don't use my head, I'll die. I'm a prum, after all."

"…"

"Anyway, take this with a grain of salt, too. Just remember what's useful to you."

The little prum, who was physically weaker than Lyu, ended her speech with a shrug of her narrow shoulders. Lyu never forgot a single word she said that day.

"It's not proof of anything, but look at me. Here I am, a respected Level Three adventurer, and I got to where I am through cunning and fast-talking easy prey like you. I'm a rising star among the prums."

"I have a feeling you just said something very important."

"It won't be long before Finn Deimne, that budding hero of my race, will be dropping to his knees with a proposal ready. Hee-hee-hee…"

"If I remember correctly, Braver was avoiding you recently…"

Lyu sighed as her friend, who dreamed of marrying into wealth, laughed wickedly.

That, too, was a scene from a bygone era.

Among the most important memories that rose in Lyu's mind, this was a more sentimental one. Lyra's words and all she had taught her were rooted deeply in Lyu's heart.

All the words of her companions, all the assets of *Astrea Familia*, were alive and well within Lyu.

But…

Lyu wasn't sure if she had properly inherited their will.

She didn't know if it had survived in her after all her loss—after the loss of justice.

CHAPTER 12
FORLORN HOPE IN THE DUNGEON

© Suzuhito Yasuda

The sound of sword fighting was ceaseless.

In the maze shadowed dark as night, countless sparks flew.

The panting of the adventurers intertwined with the battle cries of monsters.

"—!!"

"...?!"

A sword the milky white color of the Dungeon swung down ferociously.

Bell blocked the attack of the skeleton warrior by a hairbreadth.

"Spartois..."

Like the skull sheep, these, too, were skeleton monsters. Their bodies of white bone were Bell's height or taller. Each one carried a sword or lance of bone, which they wielded murderously. The pack of spartois had surrounded Bell and Lyu along with other types of warrior monsters.

It had been a sudden surprise attack.

Bell and Lyu, who had been watching carefully for signs of monsters, had heard a cracking sound. The fissure had run not along the wall but instead along the floor, spawning spartois from beneath the feet of the flabbergasted adventurers like undead rising from the grave to attack them.

Caught off guard and surrounded, they had been unable to flee. To the contrary, the sound of battle had begun to draw other monsters to them. They were trapped in a net.

"OOOOOOOOOOOOOOOOOO!!"

Bell could not conceal his panic as the spartoi lunged at him fiercely, sword in one hand and kite shield–like protector in the other.

This one was stronger than the others Bell had encountered so far. Despite the fact that it lacked skin and muscle, the monster was stronger than a lizardman elite or a loup-garou, and more agile by far than a barbarian. It moved with a skill that brought to mind an adventurer rather than a monster, making Bell realize this was a formidable enemy indeed. When he aimed the sword of the dead adventurer at the magic stone he could glimpse between its ribs, it swiftly countered the would-be lethal thrust with its own bone sword.

He was no match for this level of defense.

His attempts at landing a single deadly blow as Lyu had taught him failed again and again. If Bell were fighting monsters one-on-one, his Level 4 status meant he could win reliably. But this was the Dungeon. Numbers were her greatest weapon. If Bell took too much time fighting one monster, he was soon swamped by several others.

The status required for the thirty-seventh floor was Level 4, and the basic ability rating was D or higher. And that assumed adventurers were in a party. Strangely enough, the feeling Bell was having in the deep levels—that there was a point to these floor standards set by the Guild—was exactly what Welf and the others were experiencing in the lower levels.

I can't lead its movements…!!

The worst thing was that tactics weren't working.

By cooperating, the spartois blocked his attempts to limit their movements by leading them where he wanted. They had an outstanding command of battle skills that made use of their various weapons, be they swords, shields, lances, or axes. When Bell tried to advance, he met a shield, and when he tried to retreat, he met a sword. In all his journeys through the upper, middle, and lower levels, he had never encountered a species that worked together so well. The fact that they were fighting in a wide passageway that offered no useful terrain didn't help, either.

He could not control the battlefield as he wanted.

"Oof…!"

"Ms. Lyu?!"

The spartois were threatening Lyu, too, who was fighting back-to-back with Bell. She was at even greater risk than he since she could not move with full freedom. She was managing to fend off the attacks with her quick-draw skills, but she was unable to avoid them fully, and her white skin bloomed with cuts.

"—*Firebolt!*"

Unable to hold out any longer, Bell decided to use his magic.

The firebolt hurtled forward, shaving away precious mental strength as it did. His strategy was to blow back enough enemies to break out of the net surrounding them. The decision took courage when the option of conserving his mental strength was also flickering before him, and even Lyu felt it was the right choice.

As long as *that* monster was not among the pack of enemies.

"What?!"

But no sooner had Bell glimpsed what looked like a black rock peeking out from behind another monster than the electrical fire weakened, just before exploding into its target. The drop was as dramatic as a shell turning suddenly into a bullet.

"Shit—an obsidian soldier?!"

Its distorted form shone glossy jet-black like a precious stone. In the spot where a head would normally be, a purple light glowed eerily like a cyclops eye.

Obsidian soldiers. These rock monsters had bodies made of solidified lava and moved with less agility than warrior monsters; their sole forte was defense. Said to be among the poorest fighters on the thirty-seventh floor, their most distinctive characteristic was their ability to counteract magic. Their obsidian bodies, which were highly valued as drop items, deactivated magic as effectively as amulet stones.

With Bell's attempt to break through the pack of monsters reduced to merely pushing them back slightly, Lyu furrowed her brows and Bell grimaced. It felt like the Dungeon was using every trick it knew to counter Bell's growth. Having discovered it could not crush him with brute force, it was now taking advantage of his weaknesses.

The maze had given them a glimpse of an abyss that could not be conquered by ordinary adventurers.

"OROOOOOooon!"

The Dungeon's barrage continued. A new monster had appeared.

"Peludas?!"

Lyu's shout sounded very close to a scream.

The monsters had long, thin bodies, like a snake with four legs. Their skin was a nauseating dark green, and their backs were covered with countless spines, like a porcupine. At a glance they resembled lizards, but in fact they belonged to a well-recognized species of dragon.

Peludas...were those the things Lyu mentioned?!

Along with the spartois, they were one of the species she had named as the most dangerous on the thirty-seventh floor. Their special weapon was potent poison.

"You must not allow them to pierce you with their spines!"

The volume of Lyu's shout communicated the degree of threat well. Bell gaped at the three peludas that had appeared. The spines on their backs quivered as if they were absorbing power, then shot out in unison.

"Ah!!"

Bell pulled Lyu to him as the barrage of spines darted toward them, dashing straight toward a spartoi holding a kite shield. The point of its sword ripped Bell's skin, but the important thing was that they were able to shelter behind the shield.

The spines collided against the front of the protective gear with a loud *rat-a-tat-tat*.

At the same time, a pair of bloodcurdling screams split the air.

"GAAAAAAAAAAAAAAAA?!"

"GE, GUEE—?!"

A lizardman and a loup-garou had been pierced by the poisonous spines. An instant later they toppled over. Their skin turned black, they began to convulse, and blood spewed from every orifice. Even the blood was black. Bell turned white at the sight.

The poisoned spines of a peluda could easily penetrate the defensive ability of even an upper-tier adventurer.

They were incredibly potent as well; even a minor scrape would plunge the unfortunate adventurer into a hell of pain and coughing up blood. The only treatment was a high-quality antidote or detoxifying magic. Given their poorly equipped state, getting shot by one of the spines would spell death for Bell or Lyu.

"Umph!"

As the rain of poisonous spines continued unabated, Lyu broke the spartoi's arm with pure strength and Bell stole its large shield.

The rapid-fire barrage of spines had thrown the monsters' "net" into chaos. All Lyu and Bell could do was hunch under the shield like turtles. The only monsters that could keep moving after being shot were the obsidian soldier and the spartois. But with their eye sockets and joints pierced by spines, even the few remaining monsters could not approach Bell and Lyu as they wished.

Rat-a-tat-tat! The shield shook from the pounding of spines against it.

Pressed up against Lyu's body, Bell gritted his teeth and weathered the storm of spines.

"GOoooooooooooooo!"

Perhaps becoming frustrated that their attack was not having its desired effect, or perhaps because they had run out of spines, the peludas turned to another strategy. Befitting their dragon bloodline, the monsters transformed their surroundings into a sea of fire with their scorching breath.

As the flames licked around the adventurers and the undead alike, Lyu thrust her hand into her pouch.

"Mr. Cranell, I'm going to use this!"

She threw the Inferno Stone she had pulled from her bag into the sea of flames. Bell reflexively dropped to his haunches and strengthened his hold on the shield. The next instant, a massive explosion rocked the ground.

"~~~~~~~~~~~~~~~~~~~~~~~~~~~~~~~~ooo?!"

Monsters screamed in their death throes.

Bell and Lyu were blown backward, shield and all, as the spartois and the obsidian soldier exploded into countless shards. The three peludas, too, were swallowed up in the ball of flames.

Bell and Lyu rolled across the floor before finally pulling their battered bodies into an upright position.

"Did that do it…?"

"…At the very least, the monsters nearest to us were taken out."

Crimson flames illuminated Bell's face as the shield in his hand crumbled. Flames were still raging in the crater that the explosion had carved out. Countless bones and chunks of obsidian—drop items, it seemed—littered the ground.

Only when he saw the three flaming dragons in the distance did Bell take a breath.

At the very same moment, he heard a dull thud.

A *long spine* was protruding from his left shoulder.

Lyu froze as Bell looked behind them.

His gaze landed on a monster clinging to the maze wall like a lizard, smoke rising from the back that had just fired a spine.

The fourth peluda.

By the time he realized there had not just been three of them, it was too late.

"‼"

"GUGEEI?!"

Lyu snapped into action and threw her knife.

Pinned to the wall like a scientific specimen with a knife through its magic stone, the peluda collapsed into a pile of ash.

At the same time, Bell collapsed to the ground.

"Mr. Cranell?!"

Even Bell could hear the despair in Lyu's scream. His pierced left shoulder was distorted by the eddy of poison attempting to invade and rot every organ in his body and destroy him in seconds.

It was leading him toward the same end the dead adventurers had met.

As Lyu dropped to her knees, her face ghostly white, Bell yanked the spine from his shoulder, his eyes bulging.

"Uhh!"

The next moment, he had plunged the knife he held in his right hand *into the wound*.

This time he was attacking himself. For a moment Lyu questioned his sanity, but then she widened her blue eyes in surprise.

"The knife is stained black...It can't have...?!"

The sparkling white knife he had sunk into his left shoulder was covered in black liquid.

It was Hakugen, the longknife Welf had made from unicorn horn, a rare drop item. The horn was prized for use in recovery-type items, and had the ability to neutralize many different poisons. It would be logical to expect, then, that Hakugen had antidote properties. Bell had remembered the origins of his knife and swiftly stabbed it into his wound.

Sure enough, the unicorn-horn knife sucked the black poison from Bell's wound. The sooty black particles gathered at the center of the blade and eventually melted away, purified. As they did, the pain receded from Bell's body like a wave, reversing his hurtle toward death.

When the knife had finally drawn away all the poison, it glinted in the darkness, having returned to its original sparkling white state.

"Ow...!"

Bell pulled Hakugen from the wound with a sucking sound and collapsed listlessly onto his side. As Lyu looked on in shock, he pressed his right hand, still gripping the knife, to his forehead.

Oh, Welf, Welf...!!

Over and over, he silently called the name of his companion who had made the weapon. If the smith had been here now, Bell would have liked to hug him. He would have liked to rest his head on his chest like a brother and wail pitifully. Because he could not, he murmured his unending thanks to the smith who had saved him from such a close brush with death.

"...Mr. Cranell, let's get that wound fixed up."

Having watched Bell shiver for a few minutes, Lyu finally spoke to him in a cool voice. The poison may have been gone, but since blood was still pulsing from Bell's left shoulder, she made him drink the last of the potion. She had decided that if he didn't use it now, he might never stand up.

Still flopped sluggishly on the ground, he pressed his hand to the wound and desperately tried to calm his breath. Thankfully, the string of encounters with monsters had ended, and he was able to take time to recover while keeping a watchful eye on the sea of flames.

"..."

As Bell tried to regain his strength, Lyu forced herself to switch gears. Now that they had used up the last of their items, they had to move on. She drew a scroll from her hip—the map they had received from the dead adventurers.

Since she had been marking their route as they advanced, the map was now nearly filled with the complex lines of the maze.

We've already come to a number of dead ends...Given Mr. Cranell's physical condition, we'd better find the main route and fast.

She glanced at Bell, and then back down at the map. Although its previous owner had mapped quite a bit for them, they still did not have a complete grasp on their surroundings. Every time they started down a branch in the road that wasn't on the map, they would run into a dead end or a pack of monsters and be forced to reverse course.

Given the distance, it's not a good idea for us to go back to the last side passage we didn't take. That leaves us with this route marked as being blocked by corpses...

Lyu's finger traced a line she had not drawn.

Clinging to the path forged by their predecessors was their only choice.

But why did they *reverse course* on this route...?

The adventurers had been killed by poison. Like Bell, Lyu had decided that was certain. Up till now, she had assumed that they had fallen victim to the potent poison as they were advancing down this last road, and therefore retreated to the small room where she and Bell discovered them.

When she really thought about it, however, she realized that would have been an unnatural thing to do.

If upper-tier adventurers were poisoned and had no way to

counteract the substance, would they really leave their course to return to a base far away?

If Lyu were in their situation, she would have continued forward. Without any items, she would be in a race against time with the poison eating at her flesh, so returning to base would be almost the same as cutting off all hope of escape. That was all the truer if she did not expect a rescue party.

She would take a chance on pioneering a way forward to try to find the main route. And assuming that party was made up of upper-tier adventurers capable of making their way here to the deep levels, wouldn't they bet their lives on that adventure, too?

...*Or was there* something *on this route that forced them to give up...?*

A jolt of fear flashed across the back of Lyu's mind.

"Ms. Lyu, what do we do now...?"

"...We'll follow the map to the route ahead of us."

Bell was finally breathing normally again. Lyu answered him curtly as he looked up at her.

No other option existed.

Lyu leaned against Bell's shoulder, and they began to walk forward again.

"...?"

They had been walking for a while when the passage they were in began to change.

The staircases now led only upward. Unlike before, when each climb had been balanced by an equal descent, they came to one set of stairs after another stretching upward. The thirty-seventh floor did have a multilayer structure, but nevertheless it was unusual to move so consistently upward.

At first Lyu had been puzzled, but with every moment she grew more suspicious.

This terrain...it can't be...

The staircases were unbroken. They continued up and up.

She felt as if she was being led toward the hangman's platform or the executioner's block.

Her suspicion became certain conviction.

A drop of sweat colder than any she had felt since being plunged into the deep levels rolled down her cheek.

—So this is what happened.

It seemed the Dungeon was overwhelmingly bent on killing them.

As Lyu realized where they were and where this route they were taking led, she felt so hopeless she wanted to laugh.

"Ms. Lyu?"

"…I'm fine, I'm fine."

She took care not to spread her despair to Bell, who had noticed her expression.

It took all she had to keep the hopelessness off her face.

"I figured out where we are."

"…! Really?!"

"Yes. Please continue along this passage. We should be coming to a large staircase."

She told him only the facts.

Eventually, as she had said, a large, milky white staircase appeared with irregular distances between each step.

"If we climb these stairs and get past what's on the other side… we'll be on the main route."

Bell's face brightened at her words. He suddenly began to charge energetically up the stairs. In contrast, Lyu's mouth tightened as she thought about the single choice she had been forced to give him.

Bell would have done well to think about the situation more carefully.

He should have asked himself why Lyu had been able to figure out their location even though they weren't on the main route yet. How had she been able to guess when the thirty-seventh floor was as big as all of Orario? The only possible answer was that they had stumbled upon an important point in the maze—or an area that must be regarded with the greatest caution.

But Bell did not realize Lyu remembered this place because it was a danger spot to be avoided at all costs. Only when he mounted the final stair did a terrible shiver run down his spine.

"—"

He was facing an enormous room.

But it was clearly different from the rooms in other areas of the floor.

To start with, there was a gulf of fifty meders between where Bell stood at the room's entryway and its floor. Far below, he could make out sharp rocks sticking up from the ground, packed as tightly as if an invisible army were holding their spears at the ready. The rocks covered the entire floor. A fall would mean death, even for an upper-tier adventurer.

The sole path across the room was a long bridge that began immediately in front of Bell. It reached far into the dim center of the room, where he could see some sort of large structure. Wavering shadows—most likely monsters—were circling the structure in large numbers. The chorus of battle cries that reached Bell's ears came from more mouths than he could count, announcing a despair-inducing level of material superiority on the part of the Dungeon.

Standing beside him, Lyu stripped all emotion from her voice as she spoke.

"The Colosseum…this is a place of slaughter where *monsters are spawned without limit*."

The Colosseum.

There was only one room of its type known to exist on the thirty-seventh floor.

Although the sprawling space was far larger than any other room on the floor, its exact dimensions were not known. This was because it was so dangerous adventurers had given up on measuring it.

To Bell, it looked about the same size as the cavern on the twenty-fifth floor, or perhaps larger. As elsewhere on the floor, the ceiling was hidden in the darkness, making its height impossible to judge. Air must have been circulating in the room, because a whistling sound like dry, cold wind rushing down a narrow ravine came from the distant, rocky floor. Bell trembled at the scale.

The colossal structure rising like an island in the center of the room was especially noteworthy. It reminded Bell of a certain structure in Orario.

"The Amphitheatrum...?"

The huge round structure looked exactly the same. It threw off a dim phosphorescence so that it seemed to float in the darkness.

Even now battle cries echoed ceaselessly from the milky white form to which the bridge in front of Bell led.

"To be clear, the Colosseum isn't this whole area—it's just that structure in the middle. It's called that because...no matter how many monsters you slaughter, the supply never runs out," Lyu said.

At her urging, both she and Bell had lain stomach-down on the ground so the monsters wouldn't notice them.

"In this room, the instant the number of monsters falls, more are spawned from that Colosseum. There is no way to reduce the upper limit. In other words, the supply is *infinite*."

"...!!"

"Perhaps you could call this room a miniature version of the Dungeon itself."

Bell knew about this place.

Eina had told him there was an area in the deep levels where monsters spawned endlessly to maintain a certain predetermined population. But as he looked out on the real thing and heard Lyu describe the reality they faced, he felt despair eating at his heart. Now that he was an upper-tier adventurer, he understood the full meaning of that reality.

Even in the deep levels where the battles came fast and furious, there was always a small break between encounters. But the Colosseum was different. In contrast to ordinary rooms and passageways, there was no end to the monsters no matter how many were killed. The infinite battles continued until the adventurer perished in obscurity.

A "Bottomless Goblet" of monsters.

This was the nickname that trembling, terrified adventurers had given the Colosseum.

"We have come to a danger zone in the thirty-seventh floor that even parties of first-tier adventurers do not dare to approach."

Bell was dumbstruck by Lyu's words.

Even first-tier adventurers—even Aiz and her companions—could not enter this place?

It was the deadliest of "dead spots," on par with or even surpassing in danger the Monster Rex slumbering on this floor.

If they got past this, they would emerge onto the main route.

Bell finally understood the true meaning of the words Lyu had spoken a few minutes earlier.

In order to attain hope, they had to traverse despair as deep as the abyss below them.

He broke out in sweat.

At the same time, he was consumed by an impulse to rip out his hair.

He thought back to the corpses of the adventurers who had died in that little room. The same despair that had broken their spirits now pressed in on Bell. Sweat beaded his forehead. He panted uncontrollably and shifted his eyes restlessly.

"…"

Lyu stole a glance at him. Deep within the torn hood of her long cape, she narrowed her eyes, as if she had made up her mind to take on whatever lay ahead.

"Our only option is to pass through the Colosseum."

They had moved temporarily away from the room's entryway, but Lyu's voice was firm.

"Ms. Lyu, that's—"

"The fact is, turning around isn't an option. We simply don't have the strength or the equipment."

They were midway up the stairs leading to the Colosseum. Lyu was hurriedly pulling items from her backpack and fidgeting restlessly with them without looking at Bell.

What she said was true.

They didn't have the energy left to search for another route. At the very least, if they weren't able to make it to the main route from here, escaping the thirty-seventh floor was extremely unlikely.

To survive, they must pass through the Colosseum towering ahead of them.

"This is the crucial moment...the time to take on the one adventure we cannot avoid."

She looked up and stared at Bell with her sky-blue eyes.

Bell gulped...then nodded.

Sweat was dripping down his body and his heart was pounding, but he trusted Lyu. She had kept him alive this far. Lyu nodded in response to his naked trust.

"But how can we get past the Colosseum? If we have to take on monsters that spawn infinitely no matter how many we kill..."

"Naturally we avoid all battles. We make our way across the room in secret, without their noticing."

Lyu paused in her preparatory work. She held a piece of black cloth outstretched between her hands.

"Is that...?"

"Yes. It's made from skull-sheep robes."

Bell listened in surprise to Lyu's explanation. During the course of their battles thus far, Lyu had been carefully selecting drop items and secreting them away in her backpack. The skull-sheep robes were among them.

She had sewn two of the robes together using a third robe torn into strips for thread and a bone needle. It was just big enough to cover both of them.

"...You mean we're going to use this as camouflage?"

The skull sheep launched their attacks by blending into the dusky darkness that penetrated every corner of the floor. The clandestine movements of the death hermits had given them plenty of trouble on their journey, but now they were going to steal from their playbook. Bell knew from painful experience how well those robes worked. He thought they just might let them deceive the monsters in the Colosseum.

"We'll mask our scent, too. Please rub yourself from head to toe with the monster organs I'm about to mash up."

"Bleh...!"

"I understand your apprehension, but you'll have to put up with it."

Bell reflexively covered his nose as Lyu held up a bag. The reddish-black substance staining the bottom of the bag was a mixture of barbarian hearts and other monster organs. This drop item was normally used like powerful smelling salts, but even through the tightly closed bag, the horrible smell of the unprocessed ingredients was obvious. It would be hard to tolerate even if it did prevent monsters from sniffing them out. Although tears pooled in the corners of her eyes, Lyu's face was as blank as a mask.

Nevertheless, to Bell it seemed like the ultimate strategy.

He knew all too well the power of the gray robe. And they'd be eliminating their scent, too. If they just took care to move silently, they should be able to fool the monsters.

"When we got to the Colosseum I realized where we were."

Lyu had pulled out the map.

"There's only one Colosseum on the thirty-seventh floor, in the Warrior Zone between the Second Wall and the Third Wall. It's in the eastern part of that zone."

She spread the map before Bell, who had gotten down on one knee even as he continued to watch for monsters. Using the blood feather, she drew a large square to indicate the location of the Colosseum.

"There are four doorways in the Colosseum room—north, south, east, and west. The south doorway leads to the main route."

"So if we can just get to the south side...Oh, but if we don't know which way is south..."

"There are several warped columns on the northwest side of the Colosseum in the center of the room. I saw them when we were there a minute ago and figured out our orientation. We're near the northern doorway...which means the south doorway is directly opposite."

Bell looked at the map. The main route was marked at a slight distance from the Colosseum, and opposite it was the doorway where they now crouched. Lyu had combined what she remembered of the Colosseum with the knowledge sleeping within her to determine the most logical way forward.

Bell was filled with admiration. He couldn't help staring at the face of this wise elf who had made one good decision after another in a situation that would have broken many a weaker spirit.

"Ms. Lyu, you're so incredible..."

The words spilled unexpectedly from his lips.

"Mr. Cranell...?"

"Even in a situation like this you stay calm and make the right decision...You've come to my rescue so many times. If you weren't here I'd never be able to get out of the deep levels..."

For just an instant, a guilty look flickered across Lyu's face as she listened silently. But Bell, who was caught up in regret over his inadequacy, did not see it.

"...Mr. Cranell, please turn your knowledge into wisdom."

"Knowledge into wisdom...?"

"Yes. If you tie knowledge to action and learn to apply it, you'll be able to help more people. You'll become a stronger adventurer."

Lyu had paused for a moment before speaking. As she looked at Bell, she seemed to be looking at herself on a day long in the past. Her words sounded as if they were rooted deep within her.

Bell nodded gravely, and Lyu flashed him a quick smile.

"Do you remember the layout of the main route and how to continue the mapping?"

"...? Yes...the main route is a large passageway, and as long as you don't turn down any side roads, you'll get to the connecting passage...and for the mapping, you convert the units from ten to twenty steps..."

"Excellent."

Bell thought over what Lyu had taught him. She had instructed him in mapping during their rest stops, albeit hastily. Lyu narrowed her eyes with apparent satisfaction and held out the pouch that had been tied around her waist.

"We have three Inferno Stones left. You take one."

"But…"

"We don't know what will happen from here on out."

Up to this point, Lyu had supported Bell from the rear guard and managed their items. Now she was splitting them up. She wanted to reduce the risk in case of emergency. Each of them had to be able to respond to any situation they fell into.

Bell was dubious, but nevertheless accepted the pouch. After all, Lyu hadn't said anything he disagreed with. In addition to the Inferno Stone, it held the map with the Colosseum and main route beyond the south side noted on it.

"…"

Bell could not put into words the unease that haunted him. Paying him no mind, Lyu stood up.

"Let's go."

Four bridges led to the Colosseum.

They began at the north, south, east, and west doorways and connected to the central structure like a perfect cross. Each bridge was made of milky white stone and measured about six meders across. Needless to say, there were no railings. A misstep would plunge the hapless adventurer fifty meders to the ground.

Instant death awaited on the tips of the countless stone spears.

"…"

His body pressed close to Lyu's beneath the skull-sheep robe that covered them from head to toe, Bell advanced across the bridge with bated breath.

The real trial would begin when they reached the Colosseum where the monsters skulked. It was impossible to relax. The instant those monsters sensed an invader, Bell and Lyu would be done for.

The Dungeon's infinite material resources would crush them. Of course they were tense. As the stone projectiles covering the floor of the room stared up at them, they slowly moved ahead.

When they looked carefully at the floor, they could make out innumerable writhing forms among the projectiles.

Peludas. Like lizards, they clung close to the rocks, moving around with a slithering sound. This ruled out the option of lowering one-self to the floor and avoiding the Colosseum altogether. A hell of poison and flame awaited anyone who attempted such a strategy.

Bell gagged, having unfortunately glimpsed several skeletons and sets of armor pierced through by the projectiles below the bridge.

In contrast to the central Colosseum, the stone bridge was quiet. But that stillness was a deadly threat to Bell and Lyu.

If they were discovered, their story ended here. They crossed the twisting stone bridge with the utmost care to silence their breath and footsteps. Lyu had poked dozens of holes in the robe with her needle so they could see their way forward, but their narrow view further strained their nerves. They felt as if their very lives were in the hands of this endless journey at a snail's pace.

Lyu could hear Bell's uneven breathing.

Bell could feel Lyu's warm breath caressing his neck.

Suddenly, a handful of small stones fell from the bridge with a clatter. They were chips that had naturally eroded from the structure.

Bell and Lyu froze, holding their breaths.

The noise did not seem to disturb the peludas.

They were okay.

If they had been seen, the monsters would have instantly torn the silence with ferocious howls announcing the pair's death.

So they were okay.

They were still fine.

Their lives were not yet over.

Bell sent that desperate message to his frozen feet and once again began to move forward.

"That's…the Colosseum."

Having neared the end of the seemingly interminable bridge, Bell gulped at the sight of the white stone structure rising up before him. The sheer mass of it was overwhelmingly stately and impressive. The perfectly even circle looked similar in diameter to Babel.

"…Let's go."

"…Right."

At Lyu's urging, they crossed the remaining stretch of the bridge.

They now entered the outer rim of the Colosseum, which connected to the bridges. Only then was Bell able to see the inner structure of the Colosseum, which had been hidden to his view before.

Like the Amphitheatrum, the inside was shaped like an upside-down cone. There were six enormous plates arranged like steps, and at the very bottom, a round field. In terms of the Amphitheatrum, the former equated to the spectator seating and the latter to the arena where battles took place. The field was at the same level as the stone spears outside the Colosseum.

"…!"

As Bell took in the Colosseum's structure, he noticed something else. What he saw below him brought home the true meaning of the structure's name.

"OOOOOOOOOOOOOOOOOOOOOO!"

"_____!"

The Colosseum was packed with a nauseating number of monsters. But it was not this nightmarish cauldron of monsters that shook Bell to the core.

The monsters _were killing one another._

Without a moment's break, they were roaring in outrage and mercilessly ripping one another to pieces.

"…I've heard that aside from the times when someone invades their territory, the monsters in this area are constantly warring among themselves."

Lyu's horrified whisper went in one of Bell's ears and out the other.

In addition to the arena at the bottom, the plates above were also crammed with countless monsters engaged in fierce battle. Near

Bell and Lyu in the fifth plate, a pack of lizardman elites was fighting a pack of spartois. The skeleton warriors had the upper hand over the lizard warriors.

At a diagonal beyond them, a barbarian was roaring as it crushed the head of a loup-garou. A fountain of blood spattered the aggressor, making its hair stand on end. Bell could tell at a glance that the huge, powerful monster was an enhanced species. But even that large-category monster was no match for the herd of skull sheep that rushed it from behind. It screamed in agony as they tore it apart.

The second the monsters fell, cracks appeared at various places in the Colosseum.

A motley assortment of monsters was being spawned constantly from the floors of the plates and walls surrounding the arena. Perhaps the best phrase for the cycle of death and birth was "unending replenishment."

Everything before Bell's eyes spoke to the uniqueness of this area—to the Colosseum's danger and heresy.

"…"

Bell covered his mouth with his hand.

It took all his strength to fight back the unease.

This endless repetition of life and death.

Now more than ever before Bell sensed the mystery of the Dungeon.

Or perhaps he had just been reminded of it—of the horrifying power of the supernatural that defied human understanding and imagination.

"Let's go…we don't have time to stand around in a daze."

"…Right."

The instant this swirling fever of blood thirst turned on them, death was certain. The view before them was enough to drive that point home. Bell nodded faintly in response to Lyu's whispered words.

Somehow peeling their eyes away from the disturbing tableau, the pair began to move forward. They were at the northernmost edge of the Colosseum, where it connected to the northern bridge. This was the sixth plate, the highest and outermost of all. From here they had to reach the southern edge of the Colosseum on the opposite side. Cutting straight across would be fastest, but descending onto the battlefield of the arena would be suicidal. Instead, they planned to skirt the sixth plate.

To their right, on the northwestern side of the Colosseum, were the warped columns Lyu had mentioned. They looked like a grove of enormous stone projectiles. The sixth plate, which formed the outer rim of the structure in other places, was missing in that spot. The bottom three plates were there, but if they descended that far, the monsters would most likely detect them no matter how clandestine their movements. Everything would be over if the edge of the robe got blown back in the aftermath of a fight.

That meant they had to go east around the sixth plate, or left from where they stood.

The monsters are so close…! It's like they're roaring right in our ears!

The aggravating tension was alive and well within Bell. The closer the monsters got, the more strongly he felt he was standing on the border between life and death. Every time a monster passed on the adjacent fifth plate, Bell and Lyu had to freeze.

But fortunately—if that is the right word for it—the Colosseum gave off a horrid smell.

The corpses generated by the endless internecine fighting were left were they fell. Even if their magic stones were gone, chunks of their flesh—drop items—remained, permeating the entire space with an overwhelming stink. There was no way the living monsters could pick up the scent from Bell and Lyu. On the flip side, they struggled to keep from vomiting.

Part of this smell must be coming from the corpses of forgotten adventurers.

If the monsters discover us, will we become just another smear of blood on the wall?

Bell forced his mind away from the gnawing questions that kept bubbling up. He had to focus on keeping himself and Lyu alive.

The constant roars of the monsters reverberated through the torn robe.

…Why…did the Dungeon create a place like this…?

As they crept silently along in utmost secrecy, the question rose in Bell's mind.

According to the Guild's records, the Colosseum had suddenly appeared about thirty years ago. Its existence became known when adventurers reported that what had originally been no more than a very large room with multiple layers of bedrock had changed into its current unique form.

The Bottomless Goblet. Endless war. Monster samsara, where beginnings and endings shared a single origin point.

Was it one of the Dungeon's gimmicks, intended to lure in invading adventurers and kill them?

Or was it a stage created so that monsters could slaughter one another?

Or perhaps it was the product of chance with no deeper meaning behind it.

The sprawling darkness gave Bell no answers.

A howl echoed in his ears, as if to say that the queries of a mere adventurer did not merit response.

"The eastern bridge…"

Finally they reached the first bridge to their left.

Its structure was the same as the northern bridge they had crossed, continuing to the room's wall.

"Ms. Lyu…if we crossed this bridge and left the Colosseum on the left side, would we end up on the main route? If so, maybe we don't have to go all the way to the south side…"

"Unfortunately, you can't get to the main route from the east doorway. The south and west doorways both connect to the maze while skirting the Colosseum itself…but our only option right now is the southern route."

Bell had buckled under the tension and voiced his wishful thinking, only to be categorically denied by Lyu. He was irritated by the fact that they could have used the western doorway if only the huge columns on the northwest side weren't in their way.

Still, they had made it halfway.

If they could just make it through the fan-shaped outer rim stretching from the eastern bridge to the southern bridge, they would reach their goal.

But no sooner had the thought crossed Bell's mind than he recoiled in shock.

"...!!"

Two loup-garous had leaped onto the sixth plate near Bell and Lyu. They were less than ten meders away. Bell crouched and held his breath. His heart pounded as loudly as a drum.

"uuu..."

The wolf-monsters scanned their surroundings.

Lowering their faces to the ground, they twisted their necks several times and snorted.

They seemed to have detected a scent. Fueled by panic, Bell's body temperature skyrocketed. He could sense Lyu grimacing beside him.

Go away, go away, go away...!

Beneath the robe that melted into the dusky darkness, they silently begged, pleaded, and prayed.

And then.

They eyes of a monster met the eyes peering out from the robe.

—

Just when Bell's heart felt like it was about to explode...

"...GURUuu!"

The monsters turned tail and walked away.

Five seconds passed, then ten, and they had still not turned around. They had not seen through Bell and Lyu's clandestine advance. They were in the clear.

Bell abruptly released the tension from his body.

The sudden slackening of strained muscles nearly made him sigh out loud, but fortunately Lyu pressed her hand over his mouth.

Got through that one...

The accelerating pounding of his heart returned to its normal rhythm. Relief flooded his body.

"GYAAAAAAAA...!!"

That very instant, a monster shrieked in a distant part of the

Colosseum. The next moment it had become a pile of ash, its magic stone crushed.

Needless to say, this led a new life to spawn in its place.

The birth cry came from *directly below the two humans.*

"—"

A dense network of cracks split the floor right below Bell's feet.

Time stood still.

Lyu froze.

They did not even have time to react before a white bone arm reached up from the cracked plate.

"OOOOOOOOOOOOOOOOOO!!"

Five bony fingers grasped Bell's leg.

The skeleton warrior that sprang from the floor was a spartoi.

Its hand still clutching Bell's ankle, it lifted him into the air. The camouflage robe dropped to the floor.

Every eye in the Colosseum, every drop of monster bloodlust, zeroed in on the two exposed humans.

"—UAAAAAAAAAAAAAA!"

Letting out a roar that may have been more terror than war cry, Bell cut through the hand of bone wrapped around his ankle with the Hestia Knife.

As he crashed to the ground, Lyu hurled herself against the spartoi shoulder-first, pushing it outside the Colosseum. Its howl was followed by the sound of something shattering.

But it was too late.

"OOOOOOOOOOOOOOOOOOOOOOOOOOOOOOOOOOOOO OOOOOOOOOOOOOOOOOOOOOOOOOOOOOOOOOOOOO OOOOOOOOOOOOOOO!!"

With a chorus of war cries so violent they shook the whole room, the monsters hurtled toward Bell and Lyu.

"Run!!"

The instant Bell heard Lyu's heedless scream, his legs were in motion. Pulling Lyu by the hand, he threw every drop of energy he had into their getaway.

"Huff, puff, huff!"

His breath was ragged, not from running but from the worst-case scenario that had befallen them.

Gripping Lyu's hand as if he would never let it go, he dashed across the southeastern fan of the Colosseum, the only way left open to them.

The unending roars of the monsters, their infinite enmity and blood thirst followed close on the heels of the two humans.

Unable to resist the urge to look behind, Bell turned his head only to grimace convulsively at what he saw.

The silhouettes of countless monsters writhing under the phosphorescence looked like an enormous black comet bearing down on them.

Literally every monster in the Colosseum had its sights set on Bell and Lyu.

An army of monsters was flooding toward the adventurers. Should this muddy torrent engulf them, not a bone would remain to bear witness to their passing.

"GAAAAAAAAA!"

"OOOOOOOU!"

The monsters that had been on the fourth and fifth plates leaped over or scaled the walls, emerging onto the sixth plate.

A forest of monsters blocked their way forward.

In twos and threes, they gathered before the adventurers.

"OUT OF MY WAYYYYYYYYYYYYYYYYY!"

Bell's cry sounded as much like a plea as a scream.

Hakugen plunged into the chest of a lizardman elite that had swung its stone sword down toward him. Before the ash had even settled, the Goliath Scarf wrapped around Bell's left arm was sweeping away the three loup-garous leaping toward them. His recklessly swung fist crashed into them like a huge hammer, crushing their fangs and claws and sending them flying backward.

No sooner were they gone, however, than a pack of spartois charged Bell and Lyu as if to jeer at their struggles.

"…!"

"Don't really fight them!! Just clear a way forward!"

As a chunk of Bell's flesh was gouged out and he stumbled backward, Lyu screamed at him desperately. Leaning forward like some sort of beast herself, she flashed her saber. Guarding her bad leg, she lunged nearly to the ground as she sliced through the spartois' shinbones.

Three of the monsters collapsed on top of one another. Wide-eyed, Bell grasped the hand that Lyu had thrust out at just the right moment and pulled her close to his chest before dashing forward.

Without a glance back at the spartoi's skull he had crushed beneath his boot, Bell thrust his left hand toward the wall of monsters blocking their way.

"Firebolt!!"

Using all the Mind he had stored up, he fired four consecutive shots of Swift-Strike Magic at the line of enemies. As the advancing front gave ground, he and Lyu charged forward with little concern for the aftermath of the flaming wind he had unleashed.

Squeezing their way through the pack of monsters, they forced their way ahead. The claws and nature weapons of the writhing monsters thrashed recklessly at them, ripping and gouging their skin.

Sliding past countless angry howls, they emerged on the far side of this forest of monsters. They fended off the constant barrage of attacks from the scattered swarm with kicks or swipes of the sword of the dead adventurer, sending their attackers flying outside the Colosseum.

The second Lyu sensed that the pursuing horde of enemies was about to catch up with them, she shouted.

"Mr. Cranell!"

"!!"

She threw a sparkling red object behind her.

It was one of their precious Inferno Stones. As the bomb arced through the air, Bell looked behind him, aimed, and shot.

The electrical fire hit its target, setting off a massive explosion.

"~~~~~~

~~~~~~~aaa?!"

Raging petals of flame engulfed not only the monsters but the outer rim of the Colosseum itself, sending crowds of monsters plunging to the ground below. As the plate behind them collapsed with the thundering roar of an avalanche, Bell and Lyu glanced back at the monsters practically on their heels. But…

"AAAAAAAAAAAAAAAA!"

Every time they killed one monster, a new birth cry rang out.

Here was the true power of the Colosseum that even first-tier adventurers feared. An endless flow of monsters. Cracks covered the ground before Bell and Lyu like spiderwebs, sending forth new enemies the instant the adventurers thought they had made a narrow escape.

Destroying the enemy was meaningless.

There was no end to the pursuing hordes.

—*It's impossible.*

Even as Bell parried the monsters that leaped up from the fifth plate and pounced from directly next to them, cold, hard reason whispered the truth in a corner of his mind. Cold blood flowed into his overheated brain, pushing his ash-covered thoughts to their gasping conclusion.

Lyu, her hand still grasping Bell's, could not run at full speed.

If Bell tried to carry her, they would be overtaken.

Even if they managed to escape across the bridge and leave the room, the monsters from the Colosseum might follow them, and that would spell doom. The infinite parade would pursue them until it dealt the final blow.

It was impossible. This was the end. Lyu had said so herself—if they were discovered, everything was over.

There was no point in fleeing.

There was no escape—

"—Not yet!"

Bell screamed as if to push aside the voice of his weak heart.

What he needed to do was put everything he had into fleeing.

Once they crossed the south bridge, he could use his magic to explode it.

There were endless ways to evade pursuit. No matter how impossible they seemed, he would make them reality. No matter how absurd, no matter if they were castles in the air, no matter if they were childish egotism. Because if he didn't, their lives would end.

"Not yet, not yet!"

Screaming, he let go of Lyu's hand and swung his sword wildly at the barbarian blocking their way forward. The sword snaked between the monster's arm and body and sliced off one leg. Pushing away the body of the shrieking giant with his left hand, he proceeded to shatter the obsidian soldiers behind the barbarian.

Lyu grimaced as she watched Bell battle so fiercely.

Unlike the rubellite eyes that desperately sought the future, her own sky-blue eyes strained to see reality. Refusing to turn away from the cruelty of the world, she prepared to make a cold-blooded choice.

Unnoticed by the boy's ears, the scale began to creak.

"*Huff, puff...!* The south bridge...!!"

Bell and Lyu had finally arrived at the Colosseum's southern edge, having suffered so many wounds and paid so heavily in physical and mental strength.

Bell wanted desperately to find hope in the bridge that stretched straight before him, but—

"OOOOOOO—!"

"...?! Monsters coming from outside the Colosseum?"

Perhaps having heard the commotion inside, a pack had appeared at the doorway leading to the main route.

"It can't be...!"

They were caught in a rundown.

One group of foes was already starting down the bridge toward them while the endless hordes pursued them from behind. It was obvious that if they tried to cross the bridge they would be crushed between the two waves of enemies. Even if Bell started charging now and launched a firebolt at the pack in front of them, there were too many to wipe out.

Before they crossed the bridge—before Bell had a chance to bring it crashing down—they would be swallowed up from both sides.

Of course, being caught in a rundown on a bridge with no exit ramp meant certain death.

Bell's face burned with panic.

"…"

That's why he didn't notice.

Directly behind him, Lyu's gaze had grown suddenly distant.

The scale was slowly tipping.

"—Mr. Cranell! Onto the bridge!"

"What?!"

"You destroy the enemy ahead of us! I'll use my magic to take care of the ones at our backs!"

Suddenly Lyu was shouting orders in rapid succession. Bell couldn't believe his ears.

True, if they were pinched between two packs their only choice was to deal with both. But in this case, Lyu was in the rear. If one of them was going to take on infinite enemies, it should be Bell, who could still move normally. He would have a better chance of surviving. He was about to protest when—

"Distant forest sky. Infinite stars inlaid upon the eternal night sky."

Lyu's chant cut him off. She had stopped moving and was fully focused on high-speed recitation. He could not stop her now, but the loss of time could be lethal.

At this point, Bell's only option was to take on the enemy ahead of him.

"Damn…! I'll be back soon!"

He glanced at Lyu, whose back was to him, and the flood of monsters pressing toward them before stepping onto the south bridge. Leaving Lyu at the point where the bridge connected to the Colosseum, he collided with the mass of monsters charging toward him.

"AAAAAAAAAAAAAAAAAAAAAAAAAAAAAAAAAAAAAAAAA AAAA!"

With all his might, he began to slaughter them one by one.

As Lyu had taught him, he landed lethal blows straight to their magic stones and kicked them off the stone bridge. He did not hesitate to use magic as well, raging wildly at his enemies.

"Heed this foolish one's voice, and once more grant the starfire's divine protection. Grant the light of compassion to the one who forsook you..."

From behind, he could hear Lyu chanting rapidly. Her song was as swift as the wind, its melody paying no heed to the threats all around.

"Come, wandering wind, fellow traveler. Cross the skies and sprint through the wilderness, swifter than anything."

The bridge shook beneath Bell's feet as a thundering roar assaulted his ears.

Lyu must have taken advantage of a peluda's fiery breath to ignite the last Inferno Stone and repel the advancing flood of monsters. That, or perhaps she was hiding within the explosion's smoke to escape capture. Either way, the move was ingenious.

Count on Lyu to do something like that. Count on Gale Wind.

She always managed to escape the jaws of death with battle-tested strategies Bell would never think of. As long as he trusted her, he would be able to get through anything. He would even be able to escape the deep levels.

If only he placed his trust in her.

"Imbue the light of stardust and strike down my enemy!"

This was the last line of her chant, the one that announced her magic was complete.

There were still a lot of monsters on the bridge. Bell hadn't yet cleared a path across, but if he didn't turn back now to get Lyu he wouldn't make it in time.

He gritted his teeth and prepared to retreat from the bridge's midpoint.

He glanced back toward the Colosseum.

"—"

His eyes met a pair of sky-blue eyes, and his mind ground to a halt.

He saw *Lyu facing him*, and time froze.

Lyu was not fighting skillfully.

She was using only the bare minimum of attacks and defense. She was covered in wounds.

Her back was to a monster that she should have been fighting off.

For some reason, she was aiming her magic *at the base of the bridge*.

Like a bird shorn of its wings, the battered elf smiled at Bell.

—What was she doing?!

Before the scream could erupt from Bell's throat, Lyu completed her magic in the most beautiful voice he had ever heard.

"Luminous Wind."

An orb of light wrapped in wind appeared on her back and took flight.

The first bullet of light landed on Bell's armor where he stood rooted to the ground, as if to scoop him up from below. Before he moaned at the shock, he felt the wind enveloping his body. The wind enwrapping the orb of light lifted his feet from the bridge and buoyed him into the air. As the monsters craned their necks up at him, he was carried backward in an arc to beyond the end of the bridge.

That is, he was carried out of the Colosseum.

"—"

The next place the stardust magic fell was the bridge.

The remaining orbs of light burst into a chain of explosions that destroyed the bridge in a cloud of dust. The monsters that had been standing on it plummeted to the rocky ground.

As he danced through the air, Bell saw everything.

His eyes wide, he stretched out his right hand even though it could not reach.

It could not reach the elf who, having brought down the bridge of hope, remained alone on the cliff of despair.

"—Ms. Lyu!"

The instant his back hit the ground, the frozen flow of time shattered.

Blown to the passage outside the Colosseum, Bell called Lyu's name. He called it again and again, even as he pressed his hands against his chest to calm his violent coughing.

Far in the distance, he could see Lyu smiling the same smile.

Why! Why did you do it?!

As violent emotions and sorrow thrashed wordlessly in his heart, Lyu parted her lips.

"It is as it should be..."

Her voice did not reach him, but her lips spelled out the words.

Although he did not want to, Bell understood.

Lyu had made a choice.

Unlike himself, who had tried to escape the jaws of death with no viable strategy whatsoever, she had assessed the situation coolly.

She knew that no matter how fiercely they struggled, they would die together, and so she threw away her life.

She threw it away so Bell could live.

"No, no!!"

Bell wailed like a child at Lyu, who had cut him loose.

He screamed at the elf who had protected him like a mother or a sister.

But no matter how he moaned and cried, there was no bridge to bring him to her.

No matter how far he ran before leaping, he could never fly across the gulf separating them.

The river of darkness between them sentenced him to despair and eternal separation.

"Carry on..."

At the very end, he heard those words.

Carry on? With life? With his journey?

Her sky-blue eyes gazed at him until the last, pleading with him to live.

Presently, a monster fell on her from behind her, and she disappeared beyond the curling smoke.

"—Ahhhhhhhhhhhhhhhhhhhhhhhhhhhhhhhhhhhhhhhhhhhhhhhhhh
hhhhhh!!"

With a wail that seemed to cut through his very heart, Bell turned
away from the Colosseum and began to run.

"It is as it should be..."

Lyu squinted at the boy as his screams faded into the distance.

As she had predicted, the Dungeon had finally forced a decision
on them.

It had presented them with a crossroads at which everything
would be lost unless a sacrifice was made.

And so Lyu had made the decision.

She would give up her own life to save Bell's.

She would use his trust in her to achieve what she wanted.

She would use the boy's innocence and tendency to follow her
blindly without ever questioning her orders.

She had been prepared to do it from the start. She had no regrets.

But she did feel guilt. The sole needle in her conscience was the
fact that she had tricked him.

*I've given him the map and the items...I've taught him all I could...
even without me—or rather, without the burden of me, he will be able
to escape the deep levels...*

Lyu understood that her actions would pain the boy.

All the same, she wanted him to live.

Far more than she herself, the sinner, wanted to live.

"OOOOOOOOOOOOOOOOOOOOOOOOOOOOOOOOOOOO
OOOO!"

The monsters roaring behind her gave her no time for sentimentality.

Bell had been set free. No matter how many monsters she slaughtered in the Colosseum, new enemies would rise in their place. There
was no meaning in continued struggle.

Nevertheless, Lyu resisted to the last.

She was an adventurer, and she would not give up her life without exacting a price.

"And…if I don't suffer through to the end, I won't be able to face Alize and the others."

She turned to face the approaching monsters from her position on the southern edge of the sixth plate where the bridge had once connected. She bent her knees and leaped upward.

It was a partial leap since she was protecting her wounded right leg. Still, she made it high enough into the air. As the monsters that had been dashing toward her plunged over the edge onto the pointed rocks below, countless eyes looked up at her.

She landed on the fifth plate but stumbled. As she collapsed to the ground, the shadows fell instantly on her.

A spartoi swung down its cudgel.

She rolled to avoid it and stood, pushing its hand away.

Having fallen farther into the Colosseum, Lyu was pursued by a horde of monsters that was like an enormous serpent, or a whirlpool of beasts closing in around a pitiful sacrificial victim.

She slashed at the loup-garou that lunged at her with the sword of the dead adventurer. She managed to rip open its stomach when the blade bent, and she tossed it away with a word of gratitude for its help.

New enemies appeared. There would be no more reprieve. She fled to the fourth plate but found no escape. Monsters surrounded her. Without even the strength to use her magic, she took a body blow from a lizardman elite.

She fell to the third plate and was grabbed by a waiting barbarian.

"Ah—!"

It kicked her into the air with a leg as big as a tree trunk.

She landed suddenly on the bottom of the Colosseum, that is, in its central arena.

With the breath knocked out of her from the powerful blow on her back, she doubled over in pain.

The monsters surrounded her mercilessly.

It was a scene without hope. She was caught in the center of a many-layered net. She was like a gravely wounded enemy general pursued by an army of ten thousand men. Intent on having her head, every imaginable fang and claw whistled through the air. If a fellow adventurer had been watching from outside the Colosseum, they would almost certainly have abandoned her as a lost cause.

The monsters did not hide their frenzied excitement over this bird who had lost its wings.

They scrambled to be the first to devour her, pushing one another over in a riot of blood and screams.

But that, too, was a trivial matter. The circle around her grew steadily tighter until the monsters were on the verge of trampling her.

"...Aaah...so this is..."

This was the place she would die.

Now she realized it in earnest.

She did feel regret. Her elf's pride screamed out that she should not die like this in a den of monsters. She did not want to be disgraced by monsters, able to leave behind neither her pride nor her dead body.

But she had secured life for one who was important to her.

In the end, she had fulfilled her role as a senior adventurer.

That was enough. Wasn't it?

Because of her shameful yet noble self-sacrifice, he had been saved.

She had not lost what was most important to her.

In response to her whispered words, her heart was silent. Her pesky elf's pride seemed to have been satisfied by her internal arguments.

She smiled fleetingly.

Syr...everyone...

The Benevolent Mistress rose in her mind.

She apologized for disappearing without a word from these friends who had given her a place to feel at home when she had none.

I'm sorry for giving up the life you saved.

Lady Astrea...

Her heart throbbed at the memory of her patron deity.

She lowered her head for those eyes and that sorrowful voice she could no longer remember.

I am sorry for soiling your name and the name of our familia even at the end.

Alize...

How she longed to be reunited.

The death sentence she had longed for at the bottom of her heart, the time of atonement and redemption, had come.

Please, I beg of you, pass judgment on me.

Oblivious to the monsters bearing down on her, Lyu lay her cheek against the ground and smiled.

Just as she had once done in a back alley where she expected to meet death.

She slowly closed her eyes, preparing to welcome her final moment.

But Lyu had made a miscalculation.

She had forgotten.

She had neglected to consider the nature of the life she had cut loose.

She had forgotten that no matter how much he was tricked or injured, the white-haired boy was so simple and good-natured he would insist on rescuing not only humans but even monsters.

She had forgotten that those indomitable rubellite eyes were incapable of leaving anyone behind or parting with anyone—that their owner was a fool who insisted on smashing the scales of choice.

It was just like the time when the girl with the blue-gray hair saved her after she wreaked her revenge.

The person who had gripped her hand so tightly simply would not accept that her life was at its end.

"AAAAAAAAAAAAAAAAAAAAAAAAAAAAAAAAAAAAA AAAAAAAAAAA!!"

The next instant, electrical fire erupted from the Colosseum.

"—"

As the flames roared, swirling sparks drifted down on Lyu where she lay in the center of the arena.

Lyu paid no attention to the stunned monsters, but instead opened her eyes and looked toward the source of the sparks.

She saw white flames.

White flames raging in the midst of horror.

His white hair tousled, his body clothed in flickering flame, a single boy appeared before the monsters.

"Ms. Lyuuuuuuuuuuuuuuuuuuuuuuuuuuuuuuuuuuuuuuuuuuuuuuuuuuuu uuuuu!!"

He was on the sixth plate at the outer rim of the Colosseum.

He was charging ahead, kicking aside the monsters thrown into chaos by his surprise attack. He headed straight for Lyu, who lay facedown in the center of the net of monsters.

"…Why…?"

At first, Lyu didn't know what had happened. But the instant her eyes met his beyond the wall of confused and furious monsters, she screamed her question at the top of her lungs.

"Why?! How?!"

She pushed her trembling hands on the ground and looked up at the scene that was, to her, a nightmare.

Her heart was full of a terrible mess of feelings and doubts.

She was sure Bell had disappeared from the southern side of the Colosseum. So why was he here? How had he gotten here? She had destroyed the bridge. Even an upper-tier adventurer could not leap that far. Less than five minutes had passed, so how—?

Her confused train of thought had gotten that far when she stopped in utter surprise.

"He couldn't have taken…the western bridge?"

He had indeed.

Bell had not given up on rescuing Lyu after he ran out of the room's southern doorway. To save her, he had dashed around to the western doorway. Given the location of the four doorways, all of the terrain surrounding the Colosseum consisted of stairways leading upward.

Even without knowing the exact layout of the passages, he could arrive at his goal by going up at every opportunity. The unique terrain of this area led inexorably toward the Colosseum. And the Colosseum was connected to the western and eastern doorways by mazes. Bell knew all that in advance.

In other words, he used the advice she had given him with the intention of helping him escape to rescue her.

"You idiot...you fool!!"

He was charging downward, from the fifth to the fourth and now the third plate without concern for what Lyu thought.

Why?! Why is he doing this?!

Now it was Lyu's turn to be consumed by violent emotions.

Why was he destroying her wishes? Why would he not listen to her? Now they would both die! Their deaths would be pointless.

I wanted you, at least, to live!

"OOOOOOOOO!"

"Yaa!!"

As he charged straight toward Lyu, spartois and barbarians lashed out at him from every side. He vomited blood, but his momentum carried him forward.

His reckless suicide mission had quickly run him down. His body was damp with blood. Without his knife, he was very nearly killed by monsters. He was like a broken doll.

Enough. Escape! Escape while you still can!

Lyu's lips could not form their heartrending cry in time.

Before she knew it, he had landed in the arena where she lay, having ignored the fountains of blood and the walls of horrid monsters on his way there.

"_____!!"

He gave a now-meaningless bloodthirsty roar and tore toward her.

He crawled like an animal between the monsters' legs, kicked off the ground and flew over their heads when they threatened attack, and when an iron wall of monsters rose before him, he drilled a path forward with his electrical fire.

He did not pay them any real attention. Ignoring the fangs and claws that shaved away his flesh, he dashed toward the center of the living net where Lyu lay.

He became a wedge that split open the wall of monsters, a streak of white flame.

It's no good. It's no use. It means nothing.

Even if Bell made it to Lyu's side, all that awaited was the humiliation of being devoured alive. The two would be shamefully torn to pieces without even the luxury of a few final words. Lyu's wishes had turned to ash.

This was a nasty betrayal indeed. A nasty egotism. A cruel kindness.

Unable to suppress the emotions that rose and fell within her heart, Lyu opened her mouth to scream.

She wanted to curse that incomprehensibly foolish valiant figure to the limits of her strength.

"—"

But before she could, she noticed something.

A fine light was emanating from Bell's right hand.

Particles of white light were converging as a bell chimed.

She saw that he was gripping a crimson sphere in his hand, *and that the particles of light were focusing on it.*

She saw that his rubellite eyes had not given up at all.

No way—!

The right hand that held no knife gripped a bomb.

It was the last of the Inferno Stones, which Lyu had handed over to him.

Bell was charging the stone.

This was wisdom. Bell had taken the advice from Lyu and at great risk had tied together his own knowledge into wisdom.

He had experimented with Argonaut before. He knew that his maximum charge was four minutes, and that he could not charge two places at once, and that it was only effective for actions related to attacks. He also knew that the charge could be applied to magic or his fist, or to a weapon like a knife.

He'd charged weapons like the greatswords and the Hestia Knife quite a few times during battles already. He knew that as long as his hand was touching the weapon, it was possible to boost its power.

Therefore, he should also be able to imbue the Inferno Stone gripped in his hand with the power of his skill. He would charge a drop item that produced explosive flames to start with.

To save a single elf, he would venture the risk.

"AAAAAAAAAAAAAAAAAAAAAAAAAAAAAAAAAAAAA AAAAAAAAAAAA!!"

The blood-soaked rabbit howled, his super-bomb clutched in his hand, and blasted through the wall of monsters.

He had been concurrently charging during the five minutes he spent running from the south to the west side of the Colosseum and then pushing through the net of monsters surrounding Lyu.

A chime rang out. Two hundred and forty seconds had already passed.

He was fully charged.

The red stone where the white particles had gathered glittered sharply as if it were crying out from within.

And then—

"Ms. Lyu!!"

He broke through.

Running with all his might, paying in blood and wounds, and with willingness to die if necessary, he broke through the wall of monsters.

He dashed into the center of the field.

The elf lay prone, illuminated by phosphorescence.

He reached out his left hand, which was wrapped in the Goliath Scarf.

He reached out the hand that was struggling so hard against cruel reality.

"—"

Fragments of memory flitted through Lyu's mind, for which time had frozen.

Memories of debating the nature of justice with her companion in battle.

Of mistaking ideals for the meaning of justice.

When she thought about it, she realized she had stopped pursuing pure justice.

…What if someone really does fulfill their ideals?

A memory from long ago.

A question from long ago.

Don't you know?

That day, her dear, irreplaceable friend had answered.

She was sure of it.

Those are the people we call heroes.

Lyu placed her own hand over the hand that reached out toward her.

"!!"

She was pulled into an embrace.

Into the arms of the boy, and into the heart of an infinite prison filled with monsters' roars.

Monsters closed in on them from all directions. Their escape routes were gone. Fangs and claws flashed before their eyes.

As the flow of time stretched to its limit, a bell chimed within the boy's hand, announcing criticality.

As soon as it did, he threw the stone.

It danced above their heads into the center of the Colosseum.

Due to the nature of his skill, a moment after the charged weapon left Bell's hand, the charge would lose effect and the stored-up particles of light would scatter and dissipate.

But Bell had a fuse that burned faster than that fleeting moment.

"*Firebolt.*"

His Swift-Strike Magic.

Refusing to allow the particles of light to dissipate, the electrical fire raced toward the red stone.

An instant—and it ignited.

Lyu saw the flames expanding outward.

They were not the crimson flames that had swept through the Colosseum twice already, but instead a beautiful white flash of light.

A pure white aurora that blew away everything else.

The monsters craning their necks to look upward, Lyu's own wide-open eyes, the Colosseum itself...everything was illuminated by the blinding brilliance.

And then the brilliance that was like a white sun exploded.

"——————————————————————————————?!"

A white flare engulfed everything.

The monsters' screams were blotted out and the Colosseum's plates crumbled, unable to withstand the shock.

The instant before the glittering light arrived, Lyu had been pressed against the ground, still in Bell's arms, and the world before her eyes, too, had disappeared in a whiteout.

Deafening thunder and waves of heat pounded over her. Powerful shock waves assaulted her body.

Just as her consciousness faded to white, a sensation of floating enveloped her body.

CHAPTER 13
BEYOND A THOUSAND DARKNESSES

It was the same as before.

That day, too, everything began with a powerful explosion.

That fateful day that proclaimed the beginning of calamity.

Endless shaking. The sound of rubble falling in the distance.

Lyu sat up with those sounds still ringing in her ears.

"Huh…?!"

The room was in shambles. Huge holes had been gouged from the walls, and the floor was pocked with craters. Claw marks crosshatched the walls, stubbing out the phosphorescence and plunging the labyrinth into a darkness deep as night.

"Hey, is everyone okay?!"

"That was close!"

"So it was a trap after all…although I've gotta laugh at a plan as crude as burying us alive with bombs…!"

The voices of Alize, Lyra, Kaguya, and the other members of *Astrea Familia* echoed around Lyu. As they climbed over the rubble to stand up, the girls saw that a few of their party had been injured, but it was nothing fatal.

That day, they had descended to the deep levels in pursuit of their longstanding enemy, *Rudra Familia*, and had been lured into a trap. Indiscriminate explosions across a large area, set off by masses of Inferno Stones, had nearly penned them in.

But thanks to the prum Lyra, who had sniffed out the trap and warned everyone, they had escaped disaster by a hairbreadth.

"Why are you still alive, *Astrea Familia* bitches?! How many Inferno Stones do you think we wasted on you?!"

On the far side of the swirling sparks and smoke, Jura Harma was shrieking.

The tamer was still young then, with both ears and both arms intact, and filled with hatred at the sight of his reviled enemies. But terror, too, seeped in at the edges of his rage.

Making allowances for unexpected events, they had scattered more than one hundred explosives in the Dungeon. Judging from the scale of the detonation, this was *Rudra Familia*'s final trap.

Jura and the rest of his familia were clearly cowed by the fact that even this had not managed to wipe out the clan of justice.

"Thank you very much, Jura. But this will be the last of your evil schemes."

"...?!"

"We will put an end to it. To the Evils and to this evil era."

Alize's eloquent words rang out as if she were arraigning the men in court. Lyu and the other members of *Astrea Familia* stood behind her, piercing Jura and his cronies with their eyes as they shrunk away.

Astrea Familia was about to bring the hammer of justice down onto the cornered *Rudra Familia*—when it happened.

The Dungeon cried.

"_____"

This was not the cracking sound of a monster being spawned, nor the shaking that foretold the coming of an Irregular.

It was a piercing, inorganic sound, like a blade being run over a taught silver string.

The instincts of every adventurer present flashed red at this unmistakable lament of the Dungeon.

Lyu was not the only one immobilized by this unfamiliar situation. The other members of *Astrea* and *Rudra* familias froze, too. And then it came.

A loud crack.

A deep, wide, long fissure ran down one of the massive crumbling walls.

A strange purple liquid gushed from the vertical rift.

The opening breathed out scalding steam and something writhed out, as if it was crawling free of a womb.

Lyu's eyes met the piercing crimson eyes nestled inside the fissure.

The next moment, a fierce slash cut through the air, and *Astrea Familia* was split asunder.

"—Huh?"

Before anyone had realized, not even the adventurer herself, a life ended.

The purple claws of destruction flashed mercilessly, and a girl's body was cut in three.

Someone whispered something. The sound of fresh flesh tearing apart.

As if suddenly remembering what they needed to do, the head and torso dancing through the air began to spew blood, then tumbled to the ground where the girl's lower half had collapsed.

The curtain had risen on their tragedy.

"No-Noin?! –Uuuooo?"

Number two.

No sooner had Neze called the dead girl's name than her beast-person torso sprang into the air. This, too, was the work of the glittering purplish-blue claws of destruction.

Number three.

The dwarf Asta thrust forward her shield, only to be crushed by the enormous form that leaped into the air and pounced on her.

The three deaths all took place within the span of a mere handful of seconds.

"—"

Splash!

Warm fluid sprayed Lyu's cheek and long, pointy ear.

The noble blood that should have been flowing through her friend's body now clung to Lyu instead.

It took a moment for her to accept that this was really happening—a moment to realize that her companions would not be coming back.

Lyu's face went white, then as red as her friend's blood with anger.

"—AAAAAAAAAAAAAAAAAAAAAAAAAAAAAAAAAAAA
AAAAAAAAAA!"

Wild with rage at the death of her companions, Lyu flew toward the monster.

"Leon, no!"

Alize's words could not hold her back as she brandished her sword in a frenzy.

Ominous claws wet with the blood of her friend, crimson eyes glittering in the dark, and a huge, bony body that looked like a dinosaur fossil encased in armor.

This was the embodiment of calamity called the Juggernaut.

Lyu roared a thoughtless roar and swung her wooden sword at this apostle of murder sent to massacre foreign bodies in the Dungeon.

"?!"

Her ferocious attack cut through nothing but air.

The monster's reverse joints creaked as it leaped upward, crushing the ground beneath its feet, and disappeared. It had *landed on the ceiling* several dozen meders above Lyu's head. That was only the first in a series of leaps so incredibly fast Lyu did not even have time to be shocked.

Every adventurer in the room stood rooted to the ground as it ricocheted off walls and ceilings like an unending streak of lightning. Lyu stared in a daze at this impossible display of speed by a large-category monster.

Having thoroughly disoriented its prey, the monster then landed behind Lyu.

"!!"

As terror replaced fury, Lyu realized from seeing how her friends died that she had to avoid those claws at all costs. She swiftly dodged the harbingers of destruction, only to find the monster threatening her with an even more incredible attack.

"Aaah!"

Like a third arm, the monster's tail bore down on Lyu, who had barely been able to avoid the previous blow.

The Juggernaut's cudgel-like appendage was plenty capable of delivering a lethal blow. It landed directly on Lyu, sending fissures through every bone in her body. Blood painted her lips red.

As her back crashed against a pile of rubble, Lyu saw light flash before her eyes and then swirl into a whirlpool that crushed her will to go on. Pulled to the ground so hard that she nearly collapsed, she saw the monster approach causally and then mercilessly begin to swing its claws down toward her.

"—Idiot!"

It was Kaguya who saved her.

The price was an arm.

As her friend's right arm flew through the air, raining blood onto Lyu's stunned face, the claws of destruction crashed into the ground, sending both girls flying backward.

"Celty, attack! Together!!"

Lyu, the most bellicose member of the familia, had been knocked down by her intended target, and Kaguya had lost an arm. But *Astrea Familia*'s spirit was far from broken. If anything, its remaining members seethed with a burning desire to exact vengeance for their murdered companions, and so they chanted and activated their magic.

But of course, it only served as more fodder for tragedy.

"?!"

Magic reflection.

The spells that the familia's two sorcerers, Lyana and Celty, had shot at the monster were hurled back at them by its shield—the ability to reflect any and all magic. They horrifically burst into flame.

The Juggernaut was endowed not only with claws that could slaughter an upper-tier adventurer in one swipe, but also with a mobility unheard of in monsters and a shell that could repel magic. As a full picture of this beast specialized entirely in murder developed before the girls of *Astrea Familia*, despair overtook them.

"_____!!"

Its roar was more terrifying and ominous than that of any other monster.

This was the cry of a beast that excelled in killing at first sight.

Its incredible mobility suffered no hand-to-hand combat, and magic was insufficient to defeat it. This monster's potential was enough to wipe out even a party of first-tier adventurers. The Juggernaut was truly a symbol of death.

The five minutes it took them to evade the first round of attacks and pull together the defensive gear they needed to fend off the claws of destruction seemed endless.

Not one of them had what it would take to defeat this nightmare.

"NOOOOOOOOOOOOO!"

"Don't eat meeeeeee!!"

Slaughter, abuse, predation.

Those who revealed cracks in their will to fight were the first to be cruelly massacred.

"Iska, Maryu?!"

Alize's voice rang out. It was pregnant with tears she had never shown before.

And what about Lyu?

She stood beside the groaning Kaguya and witnessed every second of her friends' deaths.

"Ah, aaah…"

The fashionable Amazon was shredded to pieces.

The sisterly human who was such a good cook was devoured from the head down.

Those noble, kind girls were slaughtered so cruelly.

As Lyu watched, she felt something shatter within her.

Their miserable dying screams, the cruel corpses of these friends with whom she had shared so many joys and sorrows, this symbol of calamity that killed everyone—all of it broke her heart.

And when the heart of an upright, proud elf is broken, it becomes fragile. At the very least, more so than other races. Lyu certainly fit that mold. It was one of the reasons Kaguya had called her "weak."

More than anything, *Astrea Familia* was what gave her strength.

These had been her first non-elf friends, and they were everything to her.

"Aaaaaaah…!"

As her companions in battle collapsed, or exploded leaving only their weapons behind, or were eaten alive as they screamed, Lyu's heart was deeply and utterly scarred.

For the first time she felt helpless.

For the first time she felt overwhelming loss.

Despair crushed her proud elven sense of self-worth.

For the first time, she felt afraid.

This elf who had never once given in, no matter how brutal or evil her opponent, now knew terror because of a single monster.

At that moment, a deep wound was carved in her heart.

"Gyaaaaaaaaaaaaaaaaaaaaaaaaaaaaaaaaaaaaaaaaaaaaaaaaaaa!"

Finally, the damage spread to *Rudra Familia*.

Jura's cronies turned to lumps of flesh, and in a span too short to allow comprehension, countless members of his familia succumbed to the claws and tail.

Having turned the tip of its spear toward this large familia, the monster proceeded to mechanically wipe them out as if it was loath to let a single survivor escape.

"...Kaguya, are you okay?"

"If I look okay to you, Captain, you must be blind."

Four members of *Astrea Familia* remained. They were wounded from head to toe. Alize had suffered attacks along with their murdered companions, but all she could do was go on living. Kaguya, of course, had lost her arm. She had used her teeth to rip up her battle clothes and bind the wound, but her face was horribly slick with sweat.

The prum Lyra was there, too.

"...I'm sorry, Alize and Kaguya. It got my eyes..."

"Lyra..."

"I can't see anything..."

Hit by the magic that had been reflected off the monster's hard shell, both eyes were shut tight behind her bangs. There was no hope of recovery. Both her eyeballs and the skin around her eyes had melted. Both of her hands were shaking, perhaps because of the terrible pain from having her nerve endings burned away.

"What the hell is that thing...? Shit, I guess my bad luck ends here..."

The prum's curses rang out in the darkness.

Lyu, who lay facedown on the ground, groggily registered their conversation. Coughs convulsed her. She spat up blood, then shakily looked up.

"—"

Their eyes met.

As the three girls stood before her, one pair of green eyes had glanced swiftly her way. Although she wished otherwise, her gaze met the transient yet beautiful gaze of Alize, so full of decision.

"I'm sorry—Kaguya, Lyra. Please give me your lives."

Alize returned her gaze to the other two girls.

Lyu's own eyes stretched wide.

"I want to save Leon."

It was impossible to describe her despair at that moment.

An emotion far greater than what she felt toward the calamitous monster writhed within her, stopping her breath.

"...From the start, this has been a battle in which we must choose who will survive. We three are already like broken dolls ready to die here."

Ignoring the frozen Lyu, Kaguya confirmed what Alize had said.

"You guys know me. I put my own life first. But I'm the weakest of us all. I'll probably die first anyway...so I may as well go along with your plan."

Lyra smiled resolutely. After all, she wasn't one to make a losing bet.

"But Captain...you must live. As long as you and Lady Astrea remain, justice will live on."

"No, Kaguya. It's like I said before. There are as many kinds of justice as there are people in the world. There is no correct definition of justice."

Alize smiled.

"But I know Leon will make the right choices."

No!!

Lyu's consciousness was crying out.

From outside this memory, the Lyu of the present day who crouched in the darkness contradicted Alize's words.

You're wrong, Alize!

Lyu will be consumed by the flames of vengeance! She will lose her hold on justice!

You're the one who should live!!

Her face contorted, she pointed at herself from that tragic day who lay wretched and immobilized on the ground. But Alize did not hear her desperate shouts. She kneeled beside the Lyu of memory.

"Leon...can you hear me? We need your magic to bring that monster down."

Her final gaze was pure kindness.

"I need you to stay here and chant."

Her final whispered words were pure cruelty.

"We're going to pull off its shell."

Because Lyu couldn't fight anymore. Because an elf with a broken heart would hold them back.

Most of all, because she was Alize Lovell.

To save her friend's life instead of her own, this noble girl pushed Lyu away.

"Please...promise me, Leon."

Those words were a curse.

They were an oath that pinned Lyu to the ground and stole from her the chance to rise.

They were a pledge forcing Lyu to live.

They were a plea not to waste their sacrifice.

Lyu trembled, unable even to cry.

"Leon, are you there? You...will live!"

Wait.

"I'll give you my shortsword. Don't tuck it away like a keepsake—use the hell out of it. Be strong, my first worthy rival."

Don't go.

"Bye, Leon."

Please.

The girls smiled brightly, like offering flowers in parting.

The tears of the Lyu of then and the Lyu of now mingled.

"_____!!"

Having finished with *Rudra Familia*, the Juggernaut announced the resumption of the battle. Alize, Kaguya, and Lyra ran toward it without a backward glance.

"...*Distant forest sky...*"

Lyu began to sing in a trembling voice.

She sang toward their receding figures, in terror and despair.

Lyra was the first to give up her life.

Blinded and unable to move well, she fell at one stroke of the Juggernaut's claws.

"*Infinite stars inlaid upon the eternal night sky.*"

Just before she died, Lyra activated the explosive she held behind her back. It was one of the finest bombs the nimble-fingered girl had made.

It took the Juggernaut's right arm.

"*Heed this foolish one's voice, and once more grant the starfire's divine protection.*"

As the monster howled, Kaguya pounced with her longsword.

Taking advantage of the momentary window Lyra had created, she drove her weapon into its chest at high speed.

Roaring in fury, the Juggernaut swung its claws horizontally through Kaguya's body, sending her flying through the air in pieces.

"*Grant the light of compassion to the one who forsook you.*"

All Lyu could do was sing.

Unable to collect the pieces of her shattered heart, unable to stand, still whimpering, she let the image of her friends being torn apart sear itself into her eyes.

One man was watching her.

Jura had been lucky enough to escape the slaughter of his familia. He smiled mockingly as the elf he hated cried and sang and left her companions to their fate. On his face was a terrified, dark smile.

"*Come, wandering wind, fellow traveler.*"

Alize was last.

"Agris Arvensis!"

As she spoke the name of her magic, flames rose from her body.

Alize Lovell.

She had an unusual skill that gave her strength equal to that of a first-tier adventurer even though she was second-tier. The deities had given her the name Scarlett Harnell because she could use a powerful fire enchantment that sheathed her arms, legs, and sword in an armor of flames.

This time the flames had converged in her boots, and they shattered the ground as the scarlet sword princess dashed forward with ferocious speed.

"Cross the skies and sprint through the wilderness, swifter than anything."

Kaguya had paid with her life to destroy their enemy's knee and its reverse joint, robbing it of rapid movement. As the Juggernaut floundered in confusion, Alize drew near to her opponent for the last time in her life.

"Imbue the light of stardust and strike down my enemy."

The Juggernaut responded with a savage swipe.

What Lyu saw was the back of her dear friend impaled by claws.

For an instant, time froze.

While Lyu was plunged into despair, Alize was burning up her life.

"!!"

She had purposely enticed the monster to pierce her so as to immobilize its hand.

With a roar, she countered by plunging her sword into its body.

"Arvellia!!"

This was the spell key for her enchantment.

The flower of flame burned as red as her hair.

She sent it not onto the surface of the monster's shell but rather underneath it, so that the river of flames cracked the armor-like covering from the inside out, causing it to explode in a rain of shards.

Mixed in with the thundering scream of the Juggernaut was a cry of her own.

Although she did not turn—could not, because she was run through—she spoke the name in a voice that nearly disappeared in the inferno of flame.

"—Aaaaaaaaaaaaaaaaaaaaaaaaaaaaaaaaaaaaaaaaaaaaaaa!"

Tears streaming down her face, her throat trembling, Lyu released her magic.

"Luminous Wind!"

There was a flood of light, a storm of huge glowing orbs.

The light illuminated Jura's face and glinted off Lyu's tears.

The shining wind swallowed up the astonished Juggernaut along with the girl pinned to his hand.

Waves of violent detonations shook the room.

The instant the light swallowed everything, Lyu saw it.

The monster was fleeing.

Having lost its shell and thus the ability to defend itself, the Juggernaut chose retreat in the face of the massive magical assault. Its remaining reverse joint creaking, the monster accelerated. Even as one orb of light after the next hit home, shattering various parts of its body, the monster fled the room with howls of pain and resentment.

After the thundering and shaking had subsided, Lyu looked around, her breath ragged. All that remained where the monster had stood a moment before was the heavily damaged floor.

"Aa, aa…aaaaah…"

Lyu felt neither amazement nor relief at having driven off the monster.

The corpses of her friends and the members of the evil familia lay strewn around her.

Alize was not there. Lyu had blotted her out.

Lyu had taken this friend who burned brightly until the final moment of her life and banished her beyond the light. She had buried her in light.

"Aaaaaaaaaaaaaaaaaaaaaaaaaaaaaaaaaaaaaaaaaaaaaaaaaaaaaa aah…!"

Wails spilled from her as if they were tearing her apart.

A hundred emotions blended in perfect harmony, branding Lyu as a worthless thing.

The howls did not even allow Lyu to feel regret or repentance.

They were synonymous with the shattering of her belief in justice.

By then, Jura was already gone. This did not bother her. She was tossing on the sea of her emotions.

The corpses of Lyra and Kaguya sprawled so mercilessly on the ground would not permit her to die a pointless death.

Dragging her battered body, unable even to collect the remains of her companions, tears streaming from her sky-blue eyes, Lyu fled that place of tragedy.

That was the full story.

Lyu had sacrificed her friends so that she could live. She had sent Alize beyond the light to her death.

This was the true essence of the darkness that still dwelled deep in her heart.

After the incident, Lyu was constantly tormented by loss and guilt. She did not return to Astrea, but rather tended her wounds on the surface and then returned to the Dungeon as swiftly as possible.

The bodies of her friends no longer remained in the room where the tragedy had unfolded. Instead she found signs that they had been devoured by monsters. Their blood-soaked weapons sticking into the ground told her everything. Again, Lyu howled and cried.

Trembling like a baby, fighting desperately against the trauma that had been carved deep into her, she searched for the monster. She wanted to kill the beast that had murdered her friends, but in truth it was also a suicidal act. She had to bring an end to things—both to claim vengeance for her friends, and to pass judgment on herself.

But in the end, she was not able to fulfill her wish.

Deep in the Dungeon, she found a mountain of purplish-blue ash that she thought must be the Juggernaut's remains, as if someone had crushed to powder its magic stone.

Once again, she lost all hope.

Her magic had not killed the monster. Something with no connection to her had occurred. There was nothing now on which her terror and raging emotions and hopes could settle. Denied even the chance to find resolution, Lyu gripped her head in both hands and collapsed to the ground. She was a broken elf, her spirit and body alike split by a thousand cracks.

Afterward, Lyu brought back the mementos her friends had left in the deep levels. She made a grave for them on the eighteenth floor, a place they had loved. Her tears seemed as if they would never run dry. Once they had joked that if they died, they would like to be buried here in the Dungeon's paradise.

Her companions gone, her heart thrust into the depths of disappointment and despair, she stood before the weapons she had driven into the ground like gravestones and questioned herself.

She was the only one left alive.

What should she do?

If only she could vanish.

She wanted to welcome death and disappear from this world.

But there was little chance she would be able to end her life.

How could she throw away the life that Alize and all the others had given her?

That would be the same as rendering their deaths meaningless.

Her mission was to live. Her most ardent wish was to die.

In the narrow space between these fiercely competing emotions, a black flame sprang up.

"I will never forgive him!"

The world distorted like melted candy.

Her pent-up emotions congealed in the vengeance she had forgotten until now, and a voice so dark she hardly recognized it as her own spilled from her lips.

Jura. *Rudra Familia*. Absolute evil.

They had brought on disaster and led Alize and the others to their death. They were detestable. They must not be forgiven. If only they had never existed. Lyu's thoughts converged in this way very quickly. Her black anger burned like hellfire.

All in the name of vengeance.

Lyu justified everything by giving herself over to anger and hatred. They must not be allowed to live. If she let them live, they might call forth another calamity. Letting them run free made no sense. Overlooking their crimes was not even an option. She decided that she would use her life to destroy evil.

This was not for the sake of the city, nor for the citizens who suffered there. This was no noble mission to protect people she had never met.

It was for herself.

She would make them pay for the tragic deaths of her companions.

At the time, Lyu had been unable to think of any other way to use the life they had given her. Or rather, she pretended she was unable to think of any other way.

She carried out her last act of justice.

Of all the justices Alize had spoken of, this was perhaps the ugliest.

In truth, it probably was not justice at all.

This was the end of the elf who wailed tirelessly, her body broken and her wings rotted away.

Black flames consumed Lyu's sword and wings of justice, burning them till nothing remained.

After she decided to walk the path of destruction, Lyu pushed Astrea away.

Given over completely to her raging emotions, she could no longer see herself clearly. Unable to grasp her own heart, she did not want to be seen through by a deity. More than that, though, she did not want to be prevented from exacting revenge.

She did not know what Astrea thought of her when she came to her begging desperately, scraping her forehead on the ground and refusing to meet the deity's eyes. Perhaps she was exhausted by the endless chain of tragedy and hatred, or perhaps she was disappointed by the children's inability to stop fighting.

Lyu could not remember the expression on Astrea's face that day. Her own eyes had been clouded by anger, sorrow, hatred, and resentment.

Before her goddess left, she had spoken with sadness in her voice.

"Lyu...please forget about justice."

Lyu exacted her revenge swiftly.

First she targeted people, then buildings, and finally whole facilities. She did not give the familias that sided with her enemy time to intervene. She struck at night, using surprise attacks and traps. She snuffed out those associated with evil using methods unbefitting an elf.

There was no technique she would not resort to. She struck those who were evil along with those who were suspicious. It didn't matter if they were shopkeepers or Guild employees. These were reprisals carried too far, but also a judgment passed on herself.

If you were going to kill your enemies, you should have been smarter about it.

Not long after all this happened, Chloe had said those words to her.

Lyu had no response. Instead, the depths of her heart smiled mockingly. Of course she couldn't tell the catgirl she wanted to die from the start.

She could not forgive Jura and his cronies for bringing on disaster.

She would not forgive herself for letting her friends die.

It was a dark and reckless time for Lyu.

She sincerely sought death.

Revenge had nearly run its course. Lyu was preparing to attack *Rudra Familia*'s hideout.

Many familia members still remained there. Jura, too, was there, tormented by fear.

Lyu remembered those events only dimly. She remembered roaring like an animal and slashing again and again at the tamer. She had cast off coolness and followed the commands of her raging emotions as she sliced off his arm and then his ear, her dagger flashing countless times.

She didn't leave a single member of the familia alive. After she killed their leader, she used her magic to burn their hideout to the ground with all their corpses still inside.

Immediately after it ended, as the smoke was still rising from the ruins, the deity Rudra appeared before Lyu from wherever he had been hiding.

Even at that point in her life Lyu could not bring herself to kill a deity. But no one remained to protect him, and after Lyu left, the Guild decided to capture and expel him. This dropout of the mortal realm stood before Lyu encircled by raging red flames and roared with laughter.

And then he spoke to Lyu.

"When I saw you just now, I wanted to invite you into our familia."

The face reflected in his eyes was that of a well-worn demon of revenge.

Lyu destroyed twenty-seven organizations, including businesses and bands of outlaw mercenaries.

Lyu's actions led to four sacred columns piercing the heavens.

Lyu's dark impulses drew in many others along with her.

Ironically, they triggered the end of the city's dark days.

But contrary to her wishes, Lyu herself survived.

When her revenge was complete, she had finished everything she wanted to do.

What she attained by crushing those who stole her friends and those who sided with them was not a feeling of accomplishment, but instead a terrible emptiness.

She could remember neither the smiles of her friends nor their wretched faces as they met their ends.

The tears that had overflowed from her eyes and the wails that had erupted from her throat vanished.

She made her way to a back alley where no one ever set foot. Empty and drained of all energy, Lyu waited for death.

Are you okay?

After that, it was as she told Bell.

Lyu was taken from the rainy back alley by Syr, saved against her will. She pulled her back onto the path of the living.

Thank you for fighting for us.

When Syr said those words to her, she felt as if she'd been forgiven. At the same time, she felt she had to live—to live for Alize and her other companions. All this was thanks to Syr and The Benevolent Mistress.

But she was not able to wipe the old feelings from the depths of her heart.

The thirst to be sentenced for her sins continued to smolder.

She did not confess her crimes to Syr or the others.

The pain and loss from losing her irreplaceable friends could never heal.

Even if the wounds had closed, they would suddenly begin to throb when she least expected it, invoking a terrible loneliness.

The blame that never disappeared hounded her heart for having chosen the path of life.

It always had, and it still did.

Lyu stepped out of the forest of reminiscence and stood perfectly still in the darkness.

Suddenly, there was a blinding light, and she turned toward it.

It was the same scene she had witnessed many times before.

Beyond the white light, her friends were standing with their backs to her. Among them was the girl with the red hair.

They were on the far shore of the light, where Lyu had driven them. The far shore, where the dead are.

She could call them till she went hoarse and yearn for them from the bottom of her heart, but they would never look back toward her.

As if to say, *This is your punishment.*

Only when she reached their sides and was welcomed into their fold would she truly be forgiven.

Lyu believed that, and she was sad that once again she had failed to reach them. As that sadness washed over her, the white light blotted out the world and swallowed her up.

Consciousness returned.

But Lyu did not know if she was in reality or in a continuation of her dream.

She was aware only of a darkness like a swamp. Her other senses were not working properly. Her ability to interpret her surroundings stolen by vestiges of the past, her eyelids fluttered. She opened her eyes—and saw a pair of bloodshot eyes right in front of her own.

"!"

Astonishment brought her instantly back to her senses. The owner of the eyes was writhing in the darkness.

She heard a scraping sound coming from all around her.

It took a moment for her to realize that someone was digging her out of a pile of rubble.

And another to recognize that the bloodshot eyes were the color of rubellite.

Eventually, a cool draft blew over her wound-covered skin, and a pair of bloody hands grabbed her. Without allowing her a word in the matter, the hands pulled her body onto a thin back.

"……Cra…nell…?"

"…Yes."

The voice of the boy who had returned for her was so faint and mixed with exhaled breath that it almost disappeared.

Suddenly everything came back to Lyu in a rush, and she looked around at her surroundings with wide eyes.

The straight path ahead had become a mountain of dirt and rubble. The path was completely blocked off behind them, leaving only the option of moving forward.

She looked up and saw that the bedrock was repairing itself. The holes were nearly closed already. For a brief moment, she saw the vast darkness that veiled the ceiling and unfurled through the Colosseum.

Did the floor of the Colosseum collapse…and I fell through with Mr. Cranell?

As if to confirm her guess, the body parts of dead monsters were sticking up here and there from the mountain of rubble. There was a lizardman crushed by rock, a loup-garou with a broken neck, and a dismembered spartoi. They must have been swept up in the collapsing floor. Corpses lay everywhere.

Like the Water Capital, the thirty-seventh floor had a multi-layered structure.

The power of Bell's fully charged bomb had caused the floor to fall, plunging Lyu, Bell, and the monsters into a passageway that apparently existed directly below.

There was a passage like this beneath the Colosseum…? Anyway, I need to focus on other things right now…

Lyu returned her eyes with a start to the boy who was still carrying her on his back.

Bell was *on the verge of death*.

His breathing was so ragged it was peculiar he was still able to move.

His irregular gasps made Lyu want to cover her ears. He sounded like a broken instrument or a dying animal. Little red bubbles foamed from the edges of his mouth, and then, as if remembering to do something, he spit up a red glob.

His body was riddled with holes.

Droplets of his life were draining away at this very moment. Warm red liquid dampened Lyu's chest as it pressed against his back.

He must have shielded her as the massive charge reverberated and their footing caved in. His entire body was stained with blood, and the protective gear he had gotten from the dead adventurers was deformed beyond recognition.

Most of the nails on the fingers gripping Lyu were either cracked or missing.

"You idiot…you idiot!!"

Lyu screamed at him as he carried her swaying on his back.

"Mr. Cranell, why did you save me?! Why didn't you desert me?!"

She was so angry at him for coming back to the Colosseum. The hair right in front of her nose—that hair white as virgin snow that she had so loved to gaze at from afar—was now a dirty bloodred. As she looked at it, she felt her eyes brim with illogical tears.

"Answer me!"

"...Ms. Lyu, I mean..."

Lyu's eyes were squeezed shut as she barked at him. He barely managed to squeeze out a few words in response between his shallow breaths.

"Ms. Lyu...you would...surely do the same."

Lyu was at a loss for words. Her lips trembled at the certainty in the boy's voice, the conviction that she would take the same risk in his place.

"...No I wouldn't. I wouldn't...save you!"

"...Liar."

Bell rejected the words that she spit out with such sorrow and pain. She could tell from his voice that his lips were curled slightly. In a smile.

Lyu hated lies. Lyu was an elf who would not stand for lies.

Bell was smiling because this lie-hating elf had lied for his sake.

Lyu's face distorted like a baby about to wail.

"Enough! Put me down at once...!"

"...I don't want to."

Bell flatly refused.

"I won't let you die..."

"You will die yourself!"

She replied to his whisper with a shriek.

She willed herself to break free of his hold.

But she could not make herself do it.

That was because she knew who he was struggling so long and hard for—the same person Alize and the others had fought to save.

There was no strength in the two legs that walked forward.

He stumbled many times, until Lyu was not even sure he was still conscious.

Nevertheless, Bell continued to walk forward with Lyu on his back as if he was possessed.

Bell was struggling for Lyu. He was burning up his life for her.

"Please stop…!"

Stop.

Stop!

Why do you have to save me like Alize and the others did?

I'm not worth it!

I wasn't able to save anyone!

"…Mr. Cranell."

Lacking the strength to scream anymore, Lyu laid her face limply against Bell's neck. She was like a living corpse that had lost hope and everything else.

"I…let my friends die before my eyes…"

"…!"

"It's like Jura said…to save my precious self, I…killed my friend Alize with these two hands…"

Lyu whispered her confession into Bell's ear.

She was finally revealing to him what he had asked her about before.

She did it so he would abandon her.

For the first time, Bell's shivering body showed signs that he was upset.

"I'm not the pure elf you think I am…I'm a criminal, soiled beyond belief…"

She laid bare her true feelings. These were the dregs at the bottom of her soul. This was the mark of failure branded into her heart.

"The elf you are trying to rescue…is not worth saving…"

That was the true content of Lyu's heart.

If she closed her eyes, she could see it.

Her friends' dying moments. Her miserable self. Alize, killed by these very hands. The endless sorrow and despair she had seen in her dream was eating away at her.

"I have no right to speak of justice…justice has been lost for me…"

Lyu realized that she was muttering deliriously.

She thought of the commandments of the familia that had meant everything to her, and the ties to the friends who could never be replaced. For the five years since that day, there had been a hollow place inside Lyu. The hole could not be filled by all of Syr's comforting words or by the welcoming embrace of The Benevolent Mistress. This was the loss at her very core that she had tried so hard to keep hidden.

Even now, the "blessing" of justice carved into her back throbbed like a curse.

You have no right to carry the burden of justice. Her delusional mind spoke to her in the voice of Astrea.

Lyu's face was blank.

In its place, her frozen heart cried quietly.

She looked down as she spoke her next words.

"For me…justice no longer exists."

Her dejected words echoed in the darkness.

Bell's steps became sluggish. The strength drained from the hands supporting Lyu, as if they had reached their limit. He coughed up a few drops of blood, which fell onto Lyu's limp arm.

"I…don't know anything about justice."

But.

"But…you've given me so much."

His nearly broken legs stepped once more onto the ground. His quivering arms did not let go of Lyu. He clenched his teeth inside his bloodstained mouth.

"So…"

He spoke as if to prove Lyu's existence—as if to sweep the darkness from her.

"You do have justice within you."

"—"

Lyu's eyes opened wide.

"You've saved other adventurers."

That was on the eighteenth floor. The elf had thrown herself before the Goliath and saved many lives.

"You saved our deity…and Lilly, and Welf…"

That was in the war games. Lyu had run to their aid in the face of Apollo's absurd Will.

"You saved me…!"

That was in so many tight spots he couldn't count.

Lyu's hands had led Bell forward so many times when he was hurt or lost or frozen.

Lyu's advice, her words, had always given him courage.

"You were always like a hero…always right, always on the side of justice…!"

Bell's simple words shook Lyu deeply. Her sky-blue eyes wavered and grew hot. His honest, unvarnished voice pierced her heart, just like Alize's words had.

"No…you're wrong! I was wrong! I lost my hold on justice…!"

She could not allow him to offer affirmation to the self that had abandoned Alize and the others in their time of need, and so she desperately contradicted him.

But…

"You, wrong? I won't let anyone deny your worth…!"

"!"

"Not even you…!"

Bell contradicted Lyu's contradiction.

Drops of red liquid were pooling at their feet. Despite that, Bell's steps were growing more forceful and his words more impassioned.

"…I don't know the old Lyu…but…"

His words evoked the elf possessed by flames of vengeance. All the same, he argued that justice still dwelled in her.

"…I know the Lyu who is more just than anyone…"

Bell had changed. As Lyu had sensed several times before, he had grown beyond recognition. Meeting the Xenos had changed him. Foolishness and hypocrisy. Good and bad. Caught between these poles, he had suffered wounds and mental anguish. Now he was trying to teach Lyu something. He was trying to give something back to the elf who had saved him so many times.

"Ah…"

Lyu understood already.

There were three people whom she had allowed to take her hand.

Three people whom her heart had accepted and respected as righteous.

Alize had led her.

Syr had healed her.

And Bell—

"Justice…is alive within you."

Like a mirror, he reflected back the justice she had given him.

If Bell was just, then Lyu, who had given him so much, must be just as well.

"Yes…! There is justice! Within you!"

A tear fell from Lyu's eye.

It was a vestige of the justice that remained inside her, which Bell had shown her.

Lyu had stepped off the path once. That was certain.

The flames of vengeance had charred her body and soul.

Still, within the burned-up sword and wings, the ashes of justice remained.

This was the starting point for the Lyu who had not turned her back on all those people, but instead had saved them.

But I know Leon will make the right choices.

Alize's words came back to her.

Bell and many others could attest to the same thing.

If she looked back, she should be able to see it.

Many smiles blossomed in the tracks she left behind.

This was Lyu's accomplishment.

This was the accomplishment of justice that had continued to exist even as ash.

The ash at the bottom of her heart swirled up to fill the hole inside her.

Her elven heart was empty no more.

Tears spilled endlessly from the eyes that had been wavering like pools of water.

"I…I…!"

Unable to deny the truth any longer, unable even to wipe her tears away, Lyu grasped for words. She did not know what this feeling overflowing her heart was. She had no idea what the boy, who was looking straight ahead, his warm body so close to her own, was trying to give her.

"For me right now, justice is…returning alive with you."

There was no good or bad in the Dungeon.

There was only life and death, only the strong devouring the weak.

If justice existed in the Dungeon, then, it was to return alive.

Returning alive from this infinite maze was the adventurer's royal road, and their justice.

"Returning to the surface…to where the deities are, to where Syr and our other friends are…!"

Let us talk of justice.

Let us do what is just.

The only justice that existed for them, and for them alone at this moment.

"So…I will never let you go!"

Like dew falling from a leaf struck by rain, a droplet fell from Lyu's once-dry heart, spreading ripples through it.

In all likelihood, these horrendous lower levels would not let them go free. Lyu knew that.

But she wanted to live—if only a little, if only for a few seconds more.

She wanted to return alive with Bell to Syr and all the others. She couldn't help it.

"Uuu…!"

And then, as if to squash that feeling—a black form appeared before them, jeering at their hopes.

"…?! A barbarian…!"

Both Bell and Lyu were stunned to find a panting, snorting large-category monster blocking their way forward. The barbarian was injured. Most likely it had survived the fall from the Colosseum, like Bell and Lyu. Flakes of stone stuck out of the bulging muscles on its shoulders and arms like scales. One corner of its head was bent in as well. Rage colored the blood-drenched monster's eyes as it glared at the adventurers with something resembling vengeance.

"Uh-oh…!"

They were standing in a straight, narrow passage. There was no place to run. The barbarian's eyes flashed viscously at Bell as he stood rooted to the ground.

"GAAAAA!"

"Ah!"

The massive form raised its cudgel and charged toward them. Bell had no way to parry the attack. He threw Lyu aside an instant before the earth-crushing blow launched him backward like a piece of paper.

"Oof…! Mr Cranell!"

As Lyu hit the ground, Bell flew through the air, bounced off the ground, rolled a meder or two, and came to a halt.

He lay completely still. Not a drop of strength remained in his battered arms and legs. The shadow of his bangs hid his eyes, and Lyu couldn't even see his chest rising and falling with breath. Sorrow spread over her face as she once again stood on the brink of despair.

"—Mr. Cranell! Please get up!" she screamed.

She tried to summon the strength to stand up, but her body would not budge. Her wounded right leg slipped repeatedly, bringing her back down. She could not peel herself from the ground.

Ignoring this elf shorn of her wings, the barbarian turned toward Bell.

"Mr. Cranell…Bell!! Answer me!"

Lyu did not notice the change in her voice as she called him.

She did not notice how upset she was.

She simply continued to call his name, having jettisoned her usual cool composure.

But Bell, who lay facedown on the ground, did not answer.

The monster strode slowly but mercilessly toward him, intent on delivering the final blow.

"Bell, Bell! …Please…answer me…"

Her voice grew weak. In Bell's prostrate body, she saw the forms of her bygone friends.

No, no.

I don't want to lose any more.

She did not want to let go of the feeling in her heart.

She could lose anything…anything except him.

How ironic that this should happen just as something inside her had been about to change.

Her wishes were in vain, however. The barbarian stopped above Bell.

It probably intended to bite right into him. It grabbed his head in one hand and lifted him up.

"No, don't, wait…"

She shook her head sluggishly, tears pooling in her eyes, and stretched out her shaking hands.

Mocked by despair, Gale Wind's mask cracked and fell away.

Lyu's true self was laid bare.

This was not the feared elf Gale Wind. This was a weak girl who cried as someone important was about to be stolen from her. This was the real Lyu who had been hidden beneath the adventurer's armor and mask.

Forgetting her usual way of speaking, she pleaded vainly in the words of a powerless little girl.

"Please…stop…"

Bell's body swayed limply as it hung suspended above the ground.

The monster jaws opened wide, revealing its hideous teeth.

"Bell!!"

Just as the tears began to spill from her eyes—

"—!!"

The rubellite eyes veiled by his bangs sprang open and he drew the knife at his hip.

He drove Hakugen's sparkling white blade into the monster's chest.

"GAAA?!"

Stabbed at close range, its magic stone pierced, the barbarian's astonished grunt became its final utterance.

Bell dropped to the ground amid a thick swirl of ash.

For Lyu, time stood still.

"Huh...?"

Beyond the swirling ash and scant wisp of smoke, she saw the boy rise shakily. Before she could comprehend what had happened, he walked slowly toward her.

"I'm sorry Ms. Lyu...I had to draw the monster to me..."

"Ah..."

At those words, Lyu understood.

It had all been a strategy to kill the monster.

Lyu had taught him to deliver a single lethal blow aimed at the magic stone. Without the energy left to raise his arm, Bell had waited for the barbarian to come to him. To land a blow on its chest, he had played the role of helpless prey.

It was literally his final gamble.

"I heard you, but...I'm sorry."

He kneeled in front of her and pulled her up. She sat in a daze at eye level with him...blushing far redder than the circumstances merited.

He'd heard her pleading like a little girl.

He'd heard that pitiful voice.

Bell looked somewhat uncomfortable.

Helped by her embarrassment, Lyu forced her teary eyes to glare fiercely and raised her hand. Bell closed his eyes, and she was about to slap his cheek...but in the end, she lowered her hand without doing anything.

Giving in to relief, she buried her face in Bell's chest as if she was about to dissolve into tears.

"I'm begging you...never do that again..." she muttered, pressing her forehead to his chest.

"…I'm sorry."

Bell's apology for making Lyu worry fell onto her hair. The heartbeat that reached her ear told her he really was alive, and because of that, she forgave everything.

After a few moments, Bell lifted Lyu onto his back. They started down the dim passage.

Bell's steps were as unreliable as a boat made of sand, but to her they were fantastically reassuring—even if they were the extension of a mission that might cost them their lives.

…I don't sense any monsters. Aren't there any around here…?

Although the dimly lit passage was littered with rubble and monster corpses, no eyes peered at them and no bloodthirsty animosity lurked in the shadows. The barbarian from a few minutes earlier had come from the Colosseum. Lyu's exhausted mind concluded it must be sheer luck that monsters were n⸋t spawning nearby.

Just then, Bell paused.

In the dusky darkness ahead of them, the passage turned.

A faint blue light spilled from around the corner.

In the Dungeon, changes in scenery signaled danger. Not that turning back was an option, of course. The path behind them was blocked by rubble. Bell and Lyu continued nervously toward the turn.

"—!!"

Lyu gasped at the scene that was suddenly revealed. Although the passage remained the same width, water was running down the center.

"A river…?"

Bell was right. A pure blue stream began right before their eyes.

Water bubbled up like a pedestal from the bedrock and continued as far down the straight passage as they could see.

"A spring on the thirty-seventh floor…?"

Lyu had never heard of such a thing.

Acquiring food and water in the White Palace made of milky white stone was extremely difficult. This was one reason why she viewed escaping the lower levels as of the utmost importance. Even

Lyu, who had made it all the way to the forty-first floor with *Astrea Familia*, had not known that a place like this existed.

"To think that this was here below the Colosseum…I guess it was never discovered because no one dared to go near the Colosseum…?"

As Lyu mumbled doubtfully, Bell moved ahead. Whatever else this signified, it was the water they had been wishing for. He stepped toward the river's edge, planning to sooth his parched throat.

"…!"

Suddenly, however, his legs buckled beneath him. The strength strangely drained from his legs, he lost his balance, pitching forward into the water with Lyu still on his back. The impact of the fall knocked his green longsword loose, and it danced through the air.

"…B-Bell!"

Lyu planted her hands on the shore and looked up. Bell was underwater beside her, and did not answer. Through the clear water she could see that his eyes were closed as if he had been drained of his final strength. Bubbles broke the water's surface.

Fortunately, the stream was shallow. Nevertheless, Bell was bleeding, and the blue water soon turned pink. Lyu reached toward him in a panic.

Unable to stand thanks to her injured leg, she remained sitting on the streambed and wrapped her arms around his waist to pull his head out of the water.

"I sing now of a distant forest. A familiar melody of life!"

She began to chant, clinging to the white-faced boy. This was the last of her mental strength, her last gamble. She knew full well that she might suffer a Mind Down and end up toppling into the water with him, but she activated her healing magic anyway.

"Noa Heal…!"

A warm green color enveloped Bell's body.

Lyu felt the strength draining from her fingertips as her consciousness flickered, but she bit down on her lip. The healing was very slow. His wounds would not close. Life seeped from his body second by second.

It was no good. She had to stop the bleeding. She refused to let him die.

She squeezed every last drop of magic from every corner of her body, half cursing herself as she did, and funneled it toward him.

The edge of the green light spread outward, carrying a warmth like sunlight filtering through the trees.

Finally, the light converged.

Bell's wounds were all closed.

"…Bell."

She whispered his name so faintly her voice could have been blown out like a candle.

Clinging desperately to consciousness, she scooped water in her hand and brought it to her lips. Only after confirming that it was safe to drink did she scoop some up for Bell.

"Please drink…drink," she whispered again, so that he could live.

Supporting his head with her left hand, she brought her right hand to his mouth.

The clear water cupped in her palm quivered. Her fingers touched his lips, which were glued together with blood.

As if she was praying, she continued to moisten his lips. Again, and again.

Although darkness enveloped them from above, the pure glittering water illuminated his face. He looked as ephemeral, silent, and noble as a statue of the pietà.

Only the hushed Dungeon watched over the elf in her vigil.

Finally, Bell coughed and opened his eyes slightly.

The stream gurgled quietly.

The sound of the thirty-seventh floor's lone spring was a song unconnected to battlefields.

There was no phosphorescence on either the walls or ceiling.

But the pure stream that ran down the center of the passage shone, itself a light source illuminating the passage with mysterious blue light. The shore on either side was about four meders wide. It was not rocky but rather as smooth as an iceberg.

Lyu and Bell sat on one shore, resting with their backs against the wall as they had done up to this point.

"...How does your body feel?" Lyu whispered, a rustling sound coming from her nearly motionless form.

"Fine. I slept for quite a while...and I drank that water."

For Bell and Lyu, finding water was lifesaving. The combination of the harsh environment and the merciless string of battles had pushed Bell to the edge of dehydration. The stream was the water of life.

They had already spent nearly an hour by the river.

Without any monsters to fight, they were able to get a full rest. That was unprecedented given their five-minute breaks up to this point.

"   "
...
"   "
...

Both Lyu and Bell fell silent.

Properly speaking, whatever they talked about, the exchange ended quickly, so that conversation amounted to a succession of short bursts. They looked at the river, not meeting each other's eyes.

To get to the point, they were half-naked.

"   "
......
"   "
......

Their soaked clothes and equipment had been pitilessly robbing them of body heat—all the more so because they were so tired. They had consequently decided to take their clothes off. It was the obvious choice.

No matter how much they understood the logic, however, their emotions were another matter.

The serious, upright elf and the inexperienced human were both thrown into a panic. They blushed, each unable to ignore the presence of the other, as they desperately tried to quiet their pounding hearts.

That was the situation.

"........."

"........."

Lyu was naked on top but wore her long cape, which had escaped a soaking. From the waist down, she wore only a thin pair of underwear.

Bell was also naked on top and wore a pair of black long underwear rolled up to the knees. The repeated inadequate healing had glued the underwear to his leg wounds, and pulling it off by force would have opened the wounds again. He'd compromised by leaving them on. On balance, though, he was still more exposed than Lyu.

At first, she had covered her chest with her arms and insisted, eyes averted and cheeks flaming, that he wrap himself in her cape, but he had managed to convince her to keep it for herself.

"..."

Unable to fight off the feelings bubbling up in her chest, Lyu was squirming subtly but repeatedly, and the cape rustled against her skin. Every time she did, Bell held his breath and stiffened.

This is so embarrassing...even though I know I shouldn't care right now.

Lyu muttered quietly to herself, her satiny legs hugged close to her chest. If she stole a glance at Bell, she could see even in the dim light that his face was pink. So was her own. She could feel the heat to the tips of her long ears.

Their clothes and equipment were scattered on the ground. She hadn't folded her battle clothes because she wanted them to dry, and her long boots were bent over messily.

For some reason she did not comprehend at all, the scene struck her as faintly immoral. She couldn't tolerate it, perhaps because those things belonged to her, an elf. Bell, too, was studiously avoiding looking at them.

Lyu being Lyu, she also couldn't bring herself to look at the clothes Bell had taken off.

They were caught in a negative cycle of contagious tension.

The gap between their shoulders spoke vividly of their embarrassment.

Why am I so hyperaware of him?

No answer came in response to the simple question she asked her heart. Was it because he had saved her? Because they had been tied together? Because he had comforted her by saying she was just? Because he had held her and told her he would never abandon her?

She continued to question herself, but found no answers. Her heart simply continued to beat as irregularly as before.

In the first place, she hadn't felt like this when he'd seen her bathing that time—

"...!!"

She cut her thoughts off there. Blood had rushed to her face at the memory of what happened on the eighteenth floor. She looked down, determined not to let Bell see her looking so horrid.

She succeeded in evading his notice, but he recoiled.

I never thought I'd end up in this situation in the Dungeon...in the deep levels, of all places...

She didn't have time for a farce like this.

It wasn't just that she was half-naked. She didn't have much energy left, either. If a monster attacked at this point they'd be done for. She had to forget her embarrassment and do what she could.

But for some reason...she had a feeling no monsters were going to show up.

She guessed that Bell thought the same.

She couldn't put it into words, but this whole area around the stream lacked the Dungeon's usual tense atmosphere. She didn't sense any monsters or hear any breath, or even feel any eyes on them. All she heard was the gurgling stream.

The fact that they'd been able to rest for a whole hour backed up what her instincts told her. She even felt that time moved more slowly in this place.

"..."

But the current situation couldn't go on.

Here they were wasting a good rest by being so nervous they couldn't regain their strength, Lyu told herself.

"...There's something I have to ask you about."

"Uh…oh, of course. What is it?"

Lyu wanted to ease the tension, but she had also been wondering about this incessantly. She looked at him as she asked the question.

"Why did you come back that time?"

By "that time," she meant when she was in the Colosseum.

Her decision had not been mistaken. She wasn't trying to glorify self-sacrifice; that situation had demanded a choice. The options had to be placed on a scale. There was no way to know in advance that things would turn out like they had.

"If you'd taken one wrong step—or even if you hadn't—we both could have died," she continued.

"…"

"Did you know this space existed under the Colosseum?"

"No…"

"Then why did you do it?"

She had set aside her emotions and was asking as an adventurer.

Bell returned Lyu's serious gaze unflinchingly.

"I didn't want to let anyone else die…that's why I did it."

His words were simple. The feeling motivating his behavior was unsullied and straightforward.

But was there really no more to it? Was that the only reason he had saved Lyu?

That much seemed clear. There had been no calculation or goal to his actions other than saving her life. He had destroyed the scale that forced choices on them for the sake of his own ideals. He had used all his strength and wit, paid with his own blood, and struggled against the world.

"…"

He had left everything to chance.

They were more than lucky the floor of the Colosseum had caved in; if it hadn't—

…If it hadn't, he probably would have fought off the surviving monsters, carried me off, and saved me anyway. Knowing Bell, I don't doubt it.

At this point, Lyu couldn't help coming to that conclusion.

"Bell…will you listen to me?"

She was asking without really having intended to. But just like that day in the Dungeon's paradise, she told all to the boy beside her. She told him what had happened to her and to the rest of *Astrea Familia*—all the details of the story she had always hid from everyone.

"—That's what Jura meant by 'sacrifice.'"

"…"

Having finished her story, Lyu looked at the ground as if to escape. The wounds she had revealed by her own choice were throbbing. She was terrified of what Bell would say next.

He slowly parted his lips.

"In that case…it sounds like you have to go on living…" he said, smiling. "The people who cared about you fought because they wanted you to live."

"Ah…"

"Even an idiot like me can see that. If you died now…Alize and the rest would definitely be mad."

He spoke slowly, like he was explaining something to a young child. He was not looking down on her or reprimanding her. But he did sound a little angry, as if he would not forgive her if she did the same thing again. He sounded like Syr, and the look in his eyes reminded her of Alize.

He arched his brows as if he was going to smile cynically again. Pulled into his rubellite eyes, Lyu placed her hands on her chest. Her heart was pounding.

At least, she felt like it was. Obviously, it was just a feeling.

And this impulse to reach out and touch him was definitely just her imagination.

She looked down and clenched her fists.

"B-Bell."

"…?"

"I-I think we should……get a little closer."

"What?"

Bell had already been giving her a strange look, and now he

clammed up. After a long pause, during which he must have understood what she was trying to say, his cheeks began to flush. Lyu, who was red to the tips of her ears as well, stumbled over her next words.

"Wh-what we're doing right now…isn't e-efficient. If you really want me to return alive…we have to warm each other up s-skin to skin…!"

"Uh, um, but…?!" Bell stuttered.

"Now is no time to be shy…can't you feel how cold I am?"

Bell's eyes popped open as Lyu gripped his hand. Her own was white and cold as ice. As for Bell, he had lost quite a lot of blood. Now was no time to tough out the situation in a show of upper-tier-adventurer strength.

Lyu was embarrassed, too, but her point was well taken. She was genuinely concerned for his well-being.

"B-but you're an elf, Ms. Lyu…"

"Don't worry about that. In emergency situations…I'd even be willing to hug a dwarf…"

She quickly shut down Bell's concern about race issues. He was out of arguments.

"B-but, Bell…don't get any nasty ideas in your head."

"…What?"

"If you do, I-I won't be able to stop myself from slapping you."

Lyu was dying of embarrassment even though she was the one who started listing rules in the first place. Bell had a blank look on his face.

"I-I mean, given my body type, I doubt you'd be interested anyway… I mean…!"

She was now more flustered and redder than ever, unable to escape her upright elf's nature.

"Uh…ha-ha-ha. A-owww…"

"What are you laughing at…?"

Bell had broken out laughing. The sight of him holding his stomach in pain, seemingly from the strain of laughing, upset Lyu even more. As she was steaming over the fact that he wasn't taking her seriously, he went on with a smile.

"I'm very sorry. Please don't worry...because you're Ms. Lyu, after all."

In other words, she may be acting strange, but she was still the elf he knew and liked. Lyu gaped at him for a moment, then pressed her lips together. She felt like even more hot blood was rushing to her face, and she was getting itchy to boot.

Bell, who was still doubled over from the pain of laughing, glanced at her cautiously.

"Um, so...what should we do...?"

" ... "

"Hugging would be awkward since we're not wearing clothes, I think, so, um..."

Lyu broke off and was silent for a few seconds before standing up. Dragging her bad leg, she moved in front of Bell and turned her back to him. Then she slipped off her cape.

"—"

The garment fell to the ground with a swoosh.

Below the white nape of her neck, her naked back was fresh and youthful. Drops of water traced a path from her neck to her slim waist, where they were absorbed by her single garment—her panties.

Bell gulped. His whole body was extremely tense. Even with her back to him, Lyu was blushing. Logically, he couldn't see anything from behind, but she hugged her arms to her chest anyway as she sat on the ground.

The silence only lasted a few seconds, but to Lyu it felt like an eternity. She looked down, and her meaning must somehow have gotten through, because she could sense Bell steeling his will behind her.

He crouched down.

Lyu's heart skipped a beat.

Very timidly, he wrapped both arms around her from behind.

Her shoulders shivered.

The space between them disappeared.

" ... "

" ... "

Bell hugged Lyu to his breast from behind. He could feel her back and thin chest. He crossed his arms in front of her upper body, which was as naked as the day she was born.

The burning embarrassment only lasted a few seconds. Their bodies began to warm each other. Cold skin lost its chill and warmth spread through Lyu. Bell's furiously beating heart slowed and became calm, knocking against her back. The comforting rhythm rocked her like a cradle, relaxing her heart.

The stiffness melted from their bodies.

The sound of their heartbeats melded into one.

They relaxed into this feeling as if it were entirely natural.

Bell leaned against Lyu's back as she rested against his chest.

"Are you warm now?"

"Yes, very…"

"Good…"

"Yeah…"

"……"

"……"

As usual, their conversation didn't last very long. But the silence this time wasn't uncomfortable. The gurgling of the stream added to the peaceful feeling. Bell widened his legs a little so that Lyu could fit fully between them. Lyu was very warm, but she thought Bell must be cold. She told him to put on her cape and he wrapped it around both of them. His face was right next to hers. His easy breath tickled her ear and neck a little, caressing her thin ear over and over.

"I didn't realize…"

"…?"

"I didn't realize you were so small…"

"I'm not much shorter than you."

"I know, but…I can't explain it."

"What?"

"…Nothing."

"…Tell me."

"It's nothing."

"Um—"

"Hurry up."

"…You're so slender and soft…it makes me realize you're a woman."

"…"

"It's like I understand that feeling men have…of wanting to protect women."

"…You're very sly," Lyu muttered softly.

She repositioned herself so that her back was pressed more firmly to him, as if she was seeking him out. He responded by firming his chest muscles.

He let out a shaky sigh. For some reason, it struck her as sweet.

…*It's not fair.*

Lyu was trying not to think of the girl with the blue-gray hair.

The elf in the corner of her heart criticized her for being contemptible.

She wanted to be forgiven.

Just for this one short moment.

She didn't know what she was asking forgiveness for. She didn't understand who she was apologizing to. She was simply obeying her emotions.

Her heart whispered that it wanted her to turn around.

Her chest burned for her to meet the gaze of the beautiful rubellite eyes behind her.

She wanted to lock eyes with that boy whose face was so close it was practically touching her own.

But she was afraid.

She was afraid that something would change irreversibly between them.

She felt she would not be able to turn back.

And so she resisted the desire.

She grasped her slender upper arms and let the upright elf inside her come to the rescue. She scolded the self who was neither an elf nor a tavern waitress nor Gale Wind, but simply Lyu.

It was sad and painful, but it reassured her.

"Ms. Lyu…"

"Yes…"

"What do you want to do when you get back…?"

"…I want to eat a warm meal made by Mama Mia."

"Ah, me too…Let's go together, then."

"But before I do that, I'm sure I'll get an earful from Syr and the others…"

"Ha-ha-ha…"

"…What about you?"

"I want to go back home with Welf and the rest of my party, walk into my house, and say 'I'm back!' to our deity…"

"That's a good plan. You should value your familia…"

"I will. I'll value them forever, just like you…"

"…Thank you."

They leaned into each other as they whispered back and forth.

They were like lovers sharing pillow talk.

At the same time, though, there was a fleeting feeling to the moment that they could not wipe away.

There was a peaceful danger in their faint smiles and in their voices so soft the slightest breeze could blow them away, like a candle flame about to flicker out.

They closed their eyes and slept like travelers through space.

They held each other, drawing ever closer in their own private world.

Beside them, the pure stream sparkled blue, as if it were giving them this quiet moment.

Several hours had passed since Lyu and Bell's rest began.

Their deep sleep had restored them in both mind and body.

Setting aside their physical wounds, the recovery of their mental strength was incredibly important. Their stubborn headaches and lethargy had vanished. Compared to their condition before the rest, it was like night and day.

As soon as they opened their eyes, they swung into action.

"Thank you, Bell, for using your precious mental strength to start a fire."

"It's fine, I rested well…I can handle that level of firepower."

The sound of a crackling fire blended with that of the babbling stream. The bonfire illuminated their faces. Lyu, somewhat revitalized now, had gathered the kindling and Bell had shot a firebolt into it. Starting a fire in such a damp location without proper fuel or tools was extremely difficult.

They had used drop items as kindling. Lyu had returned along the passage to the pile of rubble and corpses from the Colosseum to gather monster skins—especially the oily hair of the barbarians. Just like that of the heretical barbarian Bell and the children from the orphanage had encountered in the secret passage below Daedalus Street, the hair burned extremely well.

"Bell, how strong do you feel?"

"A lot better, but my hands still shake like this if I'm not paying attention…"

Since they'd lit a fire, Bell and Lyu were no long embracing. Instead, they were sitting side by side in front of the flames. Lyu stared at Bell's quivering hand, which he was holding in front of his chest.

The stream was a safe zone.

Lyu was sure of it.

As if the sparkling blue water was an amulet warding them off, no monster had attacked. It was likely the sole "paradise" on the thirty-seventh floor. As long as they stayed here they would shed no blood and could rest as long as they liked.

Holing up down here is one option…but we don't have the all-important rations for that.

There was plenty of water. However, there was not a crumb to eat.

Second-tier adventurers might be a far cry from ordinary people, but they still relied on nutrition to function. This was why they would never fully recover no matter how long they rested here.

All that awaited them in this passage was a gentle death. That was the unspoken message of Bell's shaking hands.

Even if a rescue party had been dispatched, it would never make it here before they died. She was certain of that.

To start with, the chances of rescuers stumbling on Lyu and Bell in a floor as big as Orario were slim to none. Adventurers who lost their way in the deep levels were as good as dead. At least, that's how the Guild treated them.

The Dungeon does not let those who stop moving return to the surface alive...

No one wanted to suffer through more brutality.

But accepting the heart's yearning for peace was the same as losing to the Dungeon.

The image of the adventurers-turned-skeletons flickered across Lyu's mind. If they settled into this peaceful paradise, Lyu and Bell would meet the same end.

They had to press on.

They had to risk another adventure—if they were adventurers.

Lyu made her decision.

"Bell...let's rest a little more and then leave this place."

"...Right."

Bell nodded in response to Lyu's hushed voice. Drawing on her revived mental strength, she used Noa Heal to fully restore Bell's physical well-being. That is, with the exception of his left arm and lost blood, neither of which could be brought back with instant healing.

Lyu also healed her own right leg. When she had enough mental strength, her magic could fix broken bones. The only problem was that despite having stabilized the fracture with her knife hilt, she had been moving around so much that the bones didn't fit back together quite right. This was the price she paid for not being a real healer.

Her movement might still be somewhat compromised, but at least she could get around on her own now. There was no question Bell's burden would be lightened, since he had been supporting her this whole time. When she got back to the surface, she could have a real healer fix it for her.

After Lyu finished with the healing and took another short rest to replenish her Mind, she and Bell collected their garments. Thanks to the bonfire, the battle clothes were nearly dry. Turning their backs on each other, they started putting their gear back on. By now they weren't overly flustered by the situation, but they still weren't used to the sound of the clothes rustling around.

They finished getting dressed and put out the fire.

Just before they set off, Lyu realized she felt reluctant to leave.

...It's only a temporary weakness. The exhaustion must have gotten to me.

Enveloped in Bell's warmth, she had experienced the illusion that her mind and body were one. She had never experienced a peace like that before.

However, she would not permit herself to drown in that feeling. She was a noble elf through and through. She pretended she did not notice the feelings budding in her heart, telling herself they were mere false attachments.

"Shall we go?"

"Yes, I'm ready."

She and Bell set out walking side by side. Turning their backs on the place that had allowed them a brief respite, they began to move ahead once again.

They walked down the passage with the stream for what felt like an eternity.

As they had suspected, it appeared to be free of monsters, and they were able to advance safely.

"Is this an 'unexplored area'?"

"Yes, in the sense that it hasn't been mapped. But...I feel like this is a special place."

Bell peered around as he talked with Lyu. As it was elsewhere, the walls were milky white stone, but because of the light given off by the stream running down the center of the floor, the passage itself seemed to have a blue tint. Thanks to the water, it felt moist and cool. Diminutive lily-like flowers bloomed along the boundary between the walls and the ground. Some of the petite white blossoms swayed with the passing of the river water.

These undiscovered flowers, absent from the illustrated guides detailing the Dungeon kept at the Guild, were quite likely the only plants in the White Palace. Lyu stopped at Bell's suggestion and plucked a flower, then tasted it.

It was sweet. She offered one for Bell to try. She was right—it had a faint, nectarlike flavor that melted on his tongue. Even if he stuffed his mouth with them, he suspected he would regain very little of his stamina. Still, they were a temporary solace, and better than nothing. In fact, for someone like Bell who hadn't tasted sugar in ages, they were a delicious treat.

Then he looked up and noticed that the ceilings were lower than anywhere else on the thirty-seventh floor. He could see the uneven surface clearly. It reminded him of a rocky cave.

The place felt like a groundwater vein, or a ravine with the sky blocked out overhead. Those were the impressions the passage gave him.

"This passage goes on forever...all I can hear is the water..."

The passage and its stream stretched out before them like a blue pathway.

Compared to the Under Resort on the eighteenth floor or the Water Capital on the twenty-fifth floor, the scene was incredibly bland. But to Bell and Lyu, who had been wandering the dark world of the deep levels, the glowing blue stream was more precious and mysterious than anything they could imagine.

This, too, was the Dungeon.

It bared its cruel fangs to adventurers, but it also showed them fantastical landscapes like this one. This was the Dungeon's one act of mercy within its endless darkness, or so it seemed to Bell.

"…"

"…"

The blue road stretched on interminably.

Inevitably, conversation had dried up between Bell and Lyu. The journey was long. Where would it end? What awaited them ahead? Now and then Bell stumbled, the price of his blood loss. Would he be able to escape the deep levels in this condition? Anxiety was always with him.

But he and Lyu held onto hope as they continued down the blue road. Presently…

"A dead end…"

Beyond the end of the road was a small spring. An uneven circular space announced the end of the passage. Unlike the clear spring in the center of the passage where water bubbled up, here the water was sucked into the bottom of the spring, as if completing a cycle in the Dungeon.

There were no tunnels or stairways in sight. As Lyu looked around wondering if they really would have to retrace their steps, she noticed something.

"That stone…its composition is different from the others."

The pure white ore brought to mind quartz more than stone.

With a tense look on his face, Bell drew the Hestia Knife and thrust it into the mass Lyu was pointing at. No sooner had a crack spread across its surface than the entire lump of ore shattered. Beyond it was a cave and a stairway leading up.

Bell and Lyu exchanged glances, nodded, and crawled through the cave. They could hear the mineral repairing itself behind them. The cave was just wide enough to fit two people shoulder-to-shoulder, and pitch black. Lyu took out one of the jars she had filled with water from the stream. It gave off a faint blue glow. Using it as a lantern, they climbed step by step.

When they had climbed about one hundred steps, they came to a ceiling blocked by the same ore that had been at the cave's mouth. Bell boldly broke through it.

"This is…"

They were looking into a room on the thirty-seventh floor.

It was a cul-de-sac with only one doorway. The ground was littered with rocks as tall as Bell. The chunk of ore leading to the passage with the stream was hidden among these rocks.

They could sense monsters in the maze beyond.

Adjusting to the fact that they were now back in the Dungeon's cruel reality, they stepped out of the room with every nerve on high alert.

Contrary to their expectations, however, they did not encounter any monsters in the straight, unbranching passage before them.

Presently they came to a larger passage. Immediately, a huge wall sprang into view.

"...Ms. Lyu, that's not..."

"Yes...a Ring Wall."

As Bell craned his neck to peer at the looming wall, Lyu confirmed his guess. There was no doubt about it, the enormous, smooth surface was one of the White Palace's five Ring Walls. It was perhaps one hundred meders beyond the point where Lyu and Bell had come from the side passage into the larger passage.

On top of that...

"This passage...yes, I'm sure of it. It's the main route."

"!"

"That Ring Wall is gray. In other words, it's the Fourth Wall."

As she spoke, Lyu looked around like she was piecing together a puzzle made of memories. When *Astrea Familia* was still alive and well, Lyu had come to the deep levels a number of times. Although she did not have a full picture of the sprawling floor in her mind, her body knew the main route instinctively because she had traveled it so often on her way to and from the surface.

The Colosseum was situated on the inside of the Third Wall, which meant the stream directly below it—the Blue Road—led straight to the Fourth Wall.

Bell and Lyu had suffered greatly, but their suffering had brought them incredible good fortune.

"S-so if we get past that wall...!"

"Yes, only the Fifth Wall will remain. And if we get past that, there is no maze between there and the connecting passage to the thirty-sixth floor."

Beyond the Fifth Wall lay a vast wasteland. It was quite a distance to the southern edge of the floor, where the passage was located, but if they got that far there would be no chance of losing their way. Only the White Palace within the Ring Walls had a maze structure.

For the first time since Bell had been plunged into the deep levels, true hope illuminated his face. Lyu's expression was forbidding, but she, too, felt the same.

It was as if a lighthouse had shone its beam on a ship pummeled by the rough waves of a storm. That single beam of light was more than enough for them to cling to.

"Let's go! While there are no monsters around!"

"…Yes!"

As Bell said, no monsters were to be seen. This was a perfect opportunity.

The darkness peered down on them from far above as they headed straight ahead toward the Ring Wall.

We sure are lucky…! No—we snatched luck ourselves because we didn't give up!

Bell did not commit the fool's crime of making a racket in his rush. Advancing with even more caution than they had so far, he stepped boldly forward. One step behind him, Lyu, too, looked around warily as she bounded energetically ahead.

The maze between the Fourth and Fifth Walls is called the Beast Zone…If we can just get through here…!

The region between the Second and Third Walls, where the Colosseum was, was the Warrior Zone. The area they were currently traversing was the Soldier Zone. Aside from a few spots, the main route on the thirty-seventh floor was several dozen meders wide. Once they got onto it, they wouldn't likely lose their way, unless they encountered some irregularity.

As Bell racked his brain for bits of information Eina had taught him, he ground his molars together as if to squeeze out an extra drop or two of energy.

I can go home...I will go home! To the surface! To where my friends are! With Lyu...!

Bell was running toward the future. He blended into the dusky darkness, moving ever farther from the monsters lurking nearby.

He did not let down his guard.

Neither did Lyu.

Still, they should have realized.

As they frantically tried to take advantage of their good fortune, they should have thought about that luck more deeply.

Why *weren't they* encountering any monsters?

Why hadn't the monsters they had sensed as they emerged from the Blue Road found them yet?

Why were they hiding as if they were afraid of something?

"The Fourth Wall...! ...We made it!"

Having arrived at the towering wall, Bell and Lyu squeezed into the squared-off hole at its base. They pressed forward without hesitation toward the faint phosphorescence beyond the pitch-black tunnel.

They stepped out.

They were on the other side of the Fourth Wall.

They were in the last maze between them and the connecting passage to the lower levels.

They were in the Beast Zone, *the final battlefield.*

"—"

Bell sensed it.

As soon as he emerged from the Ring Wall, he knew.

He sensed it the second he stepped into that zone.

A piece of rock fell with a soft patter from above.

A gaze pierced his head.

The crimson, murderous gaze of calamity.

"—"

The monster was there.

Far above Bell's head.

Clinging by those terrible claws to the towering Ring Wall.

Waiting for its sole target to come walking beneath it.

Waiting for its prey—that is, Bell and Lyu—to pass through the Fourth Wall and enter the Beast Zone.

The grotesque form pulled its claws from the wall and silently descended.

Giving the adventurers little time to track its movements, it kicked off the ground.

As the claws of destruction closed in, Bell grabbed Lyu's hand and leaped with all his might.

"OOOOOOOOOOOOOOOOOOOOOOOOOOOOOOOOOOOOOO OOOOOOO!!"

An explosion.

As if it had been struck by a meteor, the ground where Lyu and Bell had stood an instant before shattered. Bedrock fractured, stone shards hailed down, and a brutal dust cloud swirled. They tumbled awkwardly over the ground. When he finally stopped rolling, Bell snapped his head up, dumbfounded.

"ooo…!"

The purplish-blue shell glowed faintly.

There was that distinctive form, reminiscent of a dinosaur fossil in armor. The monster of calamity had wandered in search of the prey that got away and eventually settled in here to lay in wait for it.

"The Jugger…naut…!"

Looking once again at that unforgettable nightmare, Bell uttered its name for the first time. As if responding to his call, the monster turned its left side, which was shrouded in darkness, toward Bell and pulled its glittering purplish-black claws from the ground. Its presence was all the more overwhelming since it was injured; there could be no greater symbol of death for Lyu and Bell.

"Aaa…!"

The trauma dwelling within Lyu rose again at the breathtaking sight.

As she struggled fiercely against the terror, Bell grimaced.

Of all the times…!

Surging emotions roiled his chest as his left arm recalled the hell it had been through. His flesh throbbing with hot pain beneath the scarf wrapped around it, Bell drew the Hestia Knife.

He neither gave in to absurd anger nor moaned uselessly, but instead prepared to fight back so he could live.

The Juggernaut narrowed its eyes at this prey that still had not lost the will to fight, its piercing eyes glowing in the dark. The claws on its feet screeching across the floor of the maze, it slowly rotated its body so it was facing Bell.

"Wha—?"

Bell could not believe his eyes.

"It has its right arm?"

The right half of its body was turned toward Bell.

Through the veil of dusky darkness, the silhouette of its right arm was clearly visible.

What was going on? During their deadly fight on the twenty-seventh floor, Bell had risked his life to take that arm. He had used Argo Vesta, his lethal skill, to erase the arm along with its claws of destruction—or so he thought.

But now that he looked closely, he saw that the Juggernaut's tail was back to its original length as well, despite having been severed during the fight.

Had it self-regenerated? Did it have the same ability as the Black Goliath?

As Bell was lost in confusion over the regeneration of the arm he had stolen at such great cost, he heard a noise.

"…?"

Something was writhing in the darkness.

It was coming from where the monster's right arm was, from the shoulder down.

Perhaps the Juggernaut was making the unpleasant creaking sound intentionally. It reminded Bell of insects devouring one another inside a jar. That, or two gears that didn't quite fit being forced to turn with a chunk of meat stuck between them.

A subconscious alarm bell began to ring in Bell's mind.

Finally, the monster called calamity took a thundering step forward.

Beneath the phosphorescence, it shook off the darkness.

"—"

Time stopped for Bell.

Lyu, too, froze.

The now-exposed right arm—*was made of countless masks of bone.*

"…Skull sheep…?"

From the monster's shoulders all down the side of its body, sheep skulls were packed close together. The sheep of death that Bell had fought so many times on this floor *had become part of the Juggernaut's body.*

"No way. It…"

Lyu's lips quivered as she shuddered uncontrollably. Bell spoke the abominable words that she could not.

"…Ate those monsters…?"

That was the answer.

It was different from an enhanced species.

It had not eaten only magic stones.

It had eaten those monsters alive from top to bottom.

And by eating them, it had absorbed their bodies.

It shouldn't have been possible. It was incomprehensible.

But there was no other way to explain the monster before them.

It was an Irregular like none before it.

It was an unknown being unforeseen by even the Dungeon herself.

Adventurers, monsters, maze.

When she spoke, Lyu expressed the horror that possessed all that existed in that place.

"It's impossible…it can't be…!"

The Juggernaut simply raised its grotesque arm as if to show it off. The right arm made of white bone contrasted eerily with the purplish-blue armor covering the rest of the monster's body. Innumerable sheep ribs, femurs, and twisting horns fit together like a puzzle into a warped curve. Pink scraps of muscle showed through here and there.

Most likely, the large sinews, still glossy with blood, came from barbarians.

The humanlike skeletons mixed in among the assortment of bony parts were without question spartois.

The sizable scales covering the long, curving tail belonged to lizardmen.

The chunks of stone reinforcing the severely cracked magic-reflecting shell came from obsidian soldiers.

Skull sheep were not the only monsters the Juggernaut had incorporated. Lacking a magic stone of its own, it had taken in every type of monster inhabiting the deep levels and made their bodies its own.

The hideous form had grown even larger than before.

Every monster Bell had fought on this floor had become a single being that now loomed in front of him.

A chimera.

Bell couldn't help thinking of that monster that appeared only in made-up stories—that fairy-tale monster that contained the bodies of a hundred beasts, that powerful goblin he had believed was only a product of inventive imaginations.

But now that nightmare had taken on the form of the Juggernaut and appeared before him.

"Haaa…!"

The Juggernaut breathed out a gust of white mist that could have been mistaken for steam, as if the monster could not contain the billowing volume of heat produced within its trunk.

With a hiss, some of the bones making up the right arm melted out. Bell's and Lyu's faces twitched as skull-sheep heads coated in sticky liquid rolled toward them.

It was like a human body rejecting a transplant.

The monsters were resisting their unnatural fusion.

To Bell, the sound of the various parts rubbing against one another with terrible creaks and groans sounded like screaming—like living monsters sobbing in pain.

The Juggernaut, too, was likely suffering from this armor of persistence. By devouring its fellow monsters and using their bodies in place of its own, it had gained a new weapon.

The sole purpose of that weapon was to kill the white prey—that is, Bell.

"OOOOOOOOOOOOOOOOOOOOOOOOOOOOOOOOOOOOOOOOOOO OOOOOO!!"

The Juggernaut signaled the start of the battle, shattering Bell and Lyu's moment of shuddering horror. Bending its left reverse joint, it leaped abruptly toward Bell.

"Whoa!"

As the Juggernaut sped through the air like a bullet, Bell shielded Lyu behind his back and repelled the claws of destruction in the nick of time. He'd used the Goliath Scarf. Sparks flew and pain shot through his brain, but at this point he couldn't complain.

His enemy's mobility had declined. He was quite sure of it.

Aside from crushing the reverse joint in its knee, Argo Vesta had severely damaged its entire lower body, reducing its jump speed to the point that even in his depleted state Bell could follow the monster with his eyes and parry its attacks.

But...

"HAA!"

The Juggernaut landed on the passage wall and stuck out its composite right arm. As if imitating Bell's Firebolt, it *fired off* several pointy white bones.

"—"

A total of four white javelins flew from various sections of its right arm. Bell gaped as the sharp projectiles soared in an arc toward him.

"Pila—?!"

He and Lyu narrowly managed to evade the deadly weapons.

Bam-bam-bam-bam!! The four javelins pounded noisily into the ground.

Bell, whose right shoulder had been grazed, could not hide his agitation.

"Were those skull-sheep pila…?!"

Bell was flabbergasted. It seemed his enemy had acquired the attack methods of the monsters it absorbed, including the pila the skull sheep had tormented him with.

Bel returned the monster's glare with his own shuddering gaze.

"_____!!"

The Juggernaut's fierce offense had begun.

With a rolling thunder, it shot off pila from its spot on the passage wall. Sixteen of them. Each was a different size and drew its own arc through the air as it raced toward the Juggernaut's prey. As Bell and Lyu contorted their bodies to escape harm, the rapid-fire barrage of sharp projectiles crashed into the floor, sending up a rain of stone.

The crimson eyes tracked the two adventurers on the other side of the dust cloud as they dashed frantically back and forth. Suddenly, the Juggernaut bent its knee and flew forward.

"?!"

Shifting from shooting to direct attack, the monster turned itself into a shell hurtling forward.

Bell moved to defend himself from the huge, rapidly approaching form. Although he managed to narrowly evade the surprise attack with skill and tactics, the monster began shooting pila again the instant it landed.

Bell didn't have time to catch his breath, let alone feel shock.

The elongating pila were coming both from the ground and the air following jumps. They flew toward Bell at like a phalanx rushing forward with the force of an angry wave. Bell was forced onto the defensive by the constant threat of a deadly blow from the terrible claws combined with the Juggernaut's insistence on piercing him like a piece of grilled chicken.

He couldn't use a Firebolt because he feared the monster's magic reflection.

"It's using projectiles...!"

Lyu narrowed her eyes at the spectacle before her.

Under normal circumstances, the pila would be worse than useless for the Juggernaut. Missiles that moved more slowly than its legs would be nothing but baggage. But since Bell had crushed its reverse joint, they were the ideal weapon for making up the deficiency.

Hard as it was to believe, the monster was carrying out a hit-and-run made up of repeated missile attacks followed by lunges at Bell. It had come up with a strategy to beat the adventurers at their own game.

The massive body of the Juggernaut zigzagged across their field of vision along with countless flying pila.

They're too fast!

I can't track them—!!

As the glowing red eyes streaked through the darkness trailing a tail of light, Bell and Lyu screamed out silently. The pila were coming from every direction, including above their heads, in a ferocious three-dimensional attack. Forced to intercept them, Bell was tossed from left to right, up and down.

The terrain was unfavorable for them as well.

The passage was wide, with no obstacles. The Juggernaut was able to leap freely in all directions around the space as wide as a room, breeding chaos. Even if its astounding jump speed was somewhat reduced, a closed-in space would have allowed Bell to track it more easily.

The wavelike attacks lapped closer to the adventurers with each passing second. Although it scattered shards of its shell with every leap and shed melted-off monster parts, the Juggernaut did not ease up. With its hideous roars and flashing claws, its unbendable determination to kill was clear.

Even without its incredible mobility, the Juggernaut was a slaughterer. Clad in an "armor of persistence" made from countless other monsters, it was carrying out a new, unprecedented campaign of destruction.

Faced with this deadly calamity, the adventurers recalled their despair. The apostle of murder had blotted out the light of hope.

My hands are shaking. This calamity is terrifying...!

Lyu's spirit was the first to be worn down. Although the situation now was different, the Juggernaut's insane behavior, so unlike that of any ordinary monster, summoned a gray scene to her mind—*Astrea Familia*, trampled, stripped from her, lost. That same trauma still tortured her.

The past hounded her. The nightmare was trying to rise from the ashes.

She could not stand it. She could lose anything but Bell. Determined to ward off the return of tragedy, she tried desperately to infuse her terrified limbs with the will to fight.

"HAAA!!"

But the Juggernaut did not wait for her limbs to respond. It pushed its cruelty to the limit in a drive to slaughter the enemy that had escaped its grasp before.

"Ah!!"

As it dropped to the ground, it swung down its scale-covered tail, throwing both Lyu and Bell backward. As the white rabbit's stance crumbled, the monster roared triumphantly.

Its bony right arm crashed to the ground.

Its palm smacked down.

The ground shook.

Deep fissures raced across the stone at lightning speed.

The instant the cracks reached Bell and Lyu's feet, *they exploded.*

"—"

A great thicket of bone stakes rose from the ground directly beneath them.

Two rubellite eyes and two sky-blue eyes were glued to the mountain of enormous needles that burst through the ground.

The Juggernaut had fired its bony javelins through the ground.

There were so many of these pila—or rather reverse pila—that they could not count them.

Bell's and Lyu's gazes had been focused upward because of the rain of pila launched a minute earlier. Now they were coming from below. It was a surprise attack intended to catch them off guard. They had become accustomed to looking up for incoming attacks when they lost their footing, and so they were not able to dodge this one.

"Eeeeeeeeeeeeeeeeeeeeeeeeeeeeeeeeeeeeeeeeeeeeeeeeeaa!"

It was like a super-sized land mine. The tsunami of pila thundered ominously as it exploded around them.

They shaved away strips of Bell's side armor, arm, and cheeks.

They gouged out pieces of Lyu's mantle, right leg, and ear.

The hideous mountain of swords swallowed up the two adventurers.

Damn—this is the floor boss Udaeus's attack—

Lyu shuddered as time spun out to its limit like a revolving lantern.

A new level of despair descended on her as she wondered if their enemy was equal to the Monster Rex of the thirty-seventh floor. Even as she thought this, pila continued to shoot up like grave markers, gouging her skin as they formed an ever-denser mountain.

"_____!!"

The Juggernaut thundered its terrible roar, not lightening its attack in the least. It shot one barrage of pila after the next in a continuous attack.

Within the hideous armor, "he" uttered a monologue.

—Look.

The prey is struggling uselessly, using what protective gear it has left, spraying red sweat. It will not succumb willingly to the spikes. It will fight to the end.

I know, I know. That's what they're like.

They are supreme prey, refusing to die no matter how I crush them. All the more reason, all the more reason—

The monster of calamity howled and continued to produce its deadly pila.

On went the thunder of firing so loud it made ears meaningless.

On flew the pila that sent up their rain of blood and flesh.

Finally…

"—Rgh."

The final "reverse pilum" hit Bell.

Beneath the tattered side armor with its broken clasps, it found his stomach.

The pointy crimson projectile pierced his flesh.

The artillery fire had been concentrated on him.

The clutch of pila aimed at the white prey that had stolen the Juggernaut's right arm did not let that prey escape.

Time froze for Lyu, who was also covered in wounds.

As Bell hovered unnaturally in midair and the pilum fell to the ground, she reached toward him.

But she could not rewind time.

Instead, as if to shatter the frozen flow of minutes, blood began to seep from the hole in his stomach.

Blood bubbled from his mouth, staining his lips red.

It was a perfectly lethal wound.

An irreversible, decisive blow.

———

Bell responded correctly to this worst of all possible situations.

Before his guts spilled pitifully from the hole, he acted.

He made the immediate decision to *close the wound*.

"—Firebolt!!"

As he pressed his left hand to the opening, a small explosion erupted.

His stomach was burning.

The pain was hellish, a flash of light running across his field of vision followed by the sensation of his insides on fire.

His eyes were so bloodshot it was like they had turned into pomegranates.

Lyu gaped and the monster stiffened.

His stomach smoking, Bell raised his left hand and *fired wildly*.

"GAAAAAAAAAAAAAAAAAAAAAAAAAAAAAAAAAAAAAA
AAAAAAAAA!!"

The first and second shots hit the ground.

The third shot on went into the air directly in front of him.

A wave of heat and wind billowed out as the ground exploded. Abandoning his usual habit of stomping down to withstand the recoil, he grabbed Lyu's outstretched hand and they both shot backward.

Pulling the surprised elf along with him, he flew far from the sword-mountain, as if that had been his plan all along.

"!!"

For a second, the Juggernaut was caught off guard.

Billows of smoke swirled in the air, a curtain concealing the prey. From beyond this veil, flames streaked wildly toward the monster. Magic reflection was meaningless if it didn't know where the prey was. Worse, its attempts to reflect the shots nailed the monster in place.

The space between the monster and its prey widened.

"AAAAAAAAAAAAAAAAAAAAAAAAAAAAA?!"

Bell was shooting off firebolts indiscriminately as he flew through the air.

The price of searing his stomach was an inability to aim properly. Sparks filled his field of vision. It was like he was broken, simply releasing his magic in the blind hope that it would keep his enemy away, buying time and distance.

After a second or two he and Lyu crashed to the ground and tumbled over and over.

"Bell?!"

They had been blown to the edge of the large passage. Lyu screamed as she stood up.

Convulsing from the extreme pain, Bell flickered in and out of consciousness.

"…Hrk!"

Lyu only paused for an instant.

She saw the smoke swirling behind them and understood their high-risk escape. Dragging Bell behind her, she dashed toward a side passage she could see in the distance.

"—!!"

The instant the electrical fire ended, the Juggernaut roared in fury. The huge purplish-blue form hurtled toward the adventurers.

Lyu kicked off the ground even harder as the monster broke through the smoke and raced toward them. Just as the claws reached her long cape and ripped into it, she dove into the side passage.

It was about two meders wide, enough to fit two adventurers but not an extra-large-category monster. The three-meder-high Juggernaut could not squeeze itself into the tunnel. In terms of width, the parts it had absorbed from other monsters turned out to be its curse.

"OOOOOOO!"

"…?!"

All the same, it twisted and turned, trying to catch the adventurers. Its left arm reached forward, yearning to shred Bell and Lyu where they lay collapsed on the ground. But it could not quite reach. It was like a rampaging giant attempting to rake a dwarf from the hole into which it had fled. Lyu felt the purplish-blue claws persistently scraping the tips of her boots.

Shivering at the tremendous noise of claws attempting to break through walls and ground, she lashed herself into standing. Now it was she who supported Bell. Sweating from head to toe and breathing raggedly, on the verge of stumbling and falling at any moment, she fled deeper into the tunnel, away from the crimson eyes tracking their every move.

The path was straight and unbranching. She felt as if the walls on either side were closing in on her. The ceiling, however, was so high she could not see it, making the passage feel like an alley at night.

"GAAAAAA!"

"OOU, OOOUN!"

Lizardman elites, loup-garous, and spartois blocked their way forward.

The monsters might have been cowering as they instinctively hid from their calamitous kin, but if an adventurer landed at their feet they would show no mercy. Lyu and Bell could not turn back; the only road to salvation lay ahead. Lyu brandished her shortsword, grimacing.

"—!!"

At that very moment, however, the Juggernaut—whose left arm had been plumbing the tunnel—stepped back and beat the adjacent wall with its bony right arm. The passage shuddered as deep fissures spread through it.

Dozens of pila shot through the wall to the right of Lyu and Bell.

"?!"

"Ahh!"

The hellish javelins targeted adventurers and monsters alike.

The lizardmen, loup-garous, and spartois were all torn to shreds. Lyu's right leg and hand, which was gripping the shortsword, were pierced and the nape of her neck was gouged. Red splotches swam before her eyes as she collapsed to the ground beside the ripped-open monster corpses.

Fresh blood splattered the walls of the tunnel and pooled like springs on the ground. Lyu and Bell were both as red as if they'd bathed in blood. The passage looked like the scene of a brutal murder. The monster corpses stank terribly. Bell and Lyu were drowning in a revolting sea of intestines and flesh—as if they themselves were corpses.

"…!"

Pila were still shooting through the wall to their right and battering the wall to their left. However, they did not reach Bell and Lyu where they lay. The angle was off.

Eventually, the Juggernaut stopped its barrage, as if it had realized the projectiles were not reaching their target.

The crimson eyes stared down the tunnel.

After observing the perfectly still lake of blood for several moments, the monster vanished silently into the darkness.

"……Ugh, ahh."

Lyu, who had not moved at all, exhaled with a soft moan.

She was still alive.

Ironically, the pack of monsters that had intended to kill them had become a wall that protected them from lethal wounds.

Lyu stopped playing dead and opened her eyes. All she saw was red. Tepid, nauseating bodily fluids and soft lumps violated her senses. The powerful stench made her want to vomit even though her stomach was empty.

Her wounds were open again. Signals were flashing from her whole body, telling her if she didn't do something she would die.

She had to use her recovery magic—no, it was no use.

She'd lost too much blood. Her magic could not bring that back. Even if they survived this particular moment, they were—

"…Bell…"

Steeling herself against the picture of hell surrounding her, Lyu turned her head. Her eyes fell on Bell, who lay faceup beside her. He must have heard her, because his finger twitched slightly.

"*Cough, cough…! …*Ms. Lyu?"

He began to convulse again, as if he had forgotten for a moment and then remembered again, and coughed violently several times. He flopped his head to the side and looked at Lyu, who was lying on her stomach.

"…Did the Juggernaut…?"

"It's gone…it's not in here…"

Their voices in this red world were so faint they nearly vanished.

His gaze still locked with Lyu's, Bell turned the corners of his mouth up ever so slightly. His smile didn't even look like a smile.

"So it's given up on us…"

"…Yes."

No.

In all likelihood it had not given up but rather was looking for its next opportunity. The Juggernaut would not stop pursuing them until it had killed them with its own hands. Lyu sensed its persistence and understood that terrible truth.

"So…we can go home now, right…?"

Bell probably understood as well. But he was pretending he did not so that he could lie to Lyu.

He was pretending they could return to the surface—that they could overcome the darkness of the maze and bask in the warm sunlight.

"You can go back...to Syr and your other friends..."

Their odds of returning home were worse than terrible.

As long as the Juggernaut remained, Lyu and Bell would never be able to leave the thirty-seventh floor.

Bell understood, but he told Lyu a kindhearted lie.

He promised her a future in which they walked together through the door of The Benevolent Mistress, were greeted by an angry Syr, punished mildly, and then spent the evening laughing and talking together.

He promised her so she would not be afraid even though she had lost *Astrea Familia*.

What a kind lie it was.

What a happy dream.

Lyu smiled.

A light sheen of tears gathered in the corners of her eyes as she smiled peacefully.

"Yes...we can go home now..."

The lie tricked her.

As she lay on the boundary of life and death, sinking in a pool of blood beneath the gaze of the darkness, she drowned in a happy dream.

The boy and the elf smiled at each other.

"Bell..."

"Yes..."

"...Will you hold me?"

At the very, very, end, she had finally grown honest. She was finally able to lay bare her feelings for her friend, and her elf's pride, and the heart that she had kept concealed for so long.

Bell looked surprised at first, but then he reached a shaking hand toward her. Lyu reached her own hand toward him and he drew her into his arms.

He's so warm...

She smiled as they prayed and held on to each other.

She basked in his warmth and let the tears spill from her eyes.

The world truly was cruel.

Of all the people in the world, Bell was the one she hoped would live on, and yet the Dungeon had made him her companion on this journey. Her heart had been broken, her hopes eaten away by that monster. She could struggle no more.

She could not let go of this warmth.

She pressed her cheek to his bloody chest. He smelled of iron. She saw a vision of pure white snow. She saw the two of them embracing as the snow buried them.

When she pulled her face away, the beautiful snowy field disappeared and all that remained were the two of them wet with each other's blood.

I wasn't able to do anything, and yet these last moments...are so tender.

Lyu could not help feeling that way.

At this moment, she was closer to him than anyone else.

No matter what anyone said, she could tell them this with confidence.

Right now, for this one brief moment, Bell and Lyu were tied more closely together than anyone in the world.

She was so glad of it, and so sad.

So happy, and so lonely.

"Bell...I'm going to sleep, just a little..."

Slowly, she closed her heavy eyelids.

Was she bidding life farewell?

Or when she opened her eyes, would she still be here in this cold, dark reality, the warmth vanished from beside her?

Or would she meet Bell once again, on the far shore of the light, beside Alize and the others?

"Okay...I'll wake you up soon."

Bell's voice caressed her gouged ear gently.

She pulled his hands to her chest so that she would not forget the warmth, and drifted off to sleep like a baby.

…
Lyu slept.

Bell smiled faintly as he watched her drift off.

She had let him fool her.

This way, he was sure she wouldn't have any nightmares.

That was all he wished for.

He wanted her to dream sweet dreams until *everything was over*.

She has suffered so much already…

As she had suspected, he had lied to her.

But it was not a kindly lie. To the contrary, it was a terrible betrayal prompted by self-righteous egotism.

Bell had not given up on returning alive.

I remember the look on her face when she told me everything…

He had not forgotten the expression of long-suffering pain on the face of this elf who had lost her companions.

That was why he did it.

"…!"

The wretched spasms were already subsiding. In their place came unbelievable pain.

He touched the stomach wound that he had seared shut.

Sparks danced before his eyes.

Pain. Pain. Pain.

He wanted to scream and wail and break into a hundred pieces.

He wanted to howl until all his energy was gone.

But if he could feel pain, then *he could move*.

If his body was screaming that it would die, then he had the energy he needed to cling to life.

If his heart was insisting with its rapid beat that he run from death, then he had the strength left to escape.

He would not use that strength to escape death—he would use it to defeat death.

"!!"

He heard his instincts screaming. He ignored them.

He heard his body shouting a warning. He ignored it.

He heard his heart sniffling that it was impossible. He ignored it.

His whole self, every element that made up that human called Bell Cranell, was fighting against his decision. He ignored it.

He heard his soul crying for him to stand up. He affirmed it.

"Aaaaaaaaaaaaaaa…!!"

He gave the cry of an animal.

The adventurer became a beast and chewed up the shards of life so it could stand.

As light flashed before his eyes, what remained of his human rationality recalled a story.

It was the tale of Belius the Guard.

The elf's guardian was a sorrowful and unyielding knight loved by an elf of the lake. A martyr to love till the very end, he died in her arms.

Bell begged the elf's hero to give him the strength to protect what was important to him.

…I have no light to concentrate. Most likely I only have one charge left. I cannot summon the heroic blow.

But the desire to be a hero is here in my heart.

He stroked Lyu's hair softly, his smile gone.

The lone male stood.

The Juggernaut was moving.

Having given up on penetrating the passage Lyu and Bell were in from its entrance, it circled around to the exit. The Juggernaut had exquisitely refined senses. This immune ability was a gift from its mother, the Dungeon, to enable it to exterminate foreign viruses. It was able to rapidly track any adventurer on the same floor as it. This was one reason the "banquet of calamity" had unfolded with such speed on the twenty-seventh floor.

Here on the thirty-seventh floor, it knew where Bell and Lyu were. The reason it chose to lay in wait in the Beast Zone was because it disliked narrower passages and did not want to risk letting its prey escape.

The Juggernaut—he—also knew that Bell and Lyu were still alive.

He would crush them when they came out the exit thinking he had disappeared. This was the plan he had concocted with his hunter's instinct. With a speed out of proportion to his large size, he raced to a large room adjacent to the main route. There were four doorways in the room, and he hovered by the one that led to the passage his prey had fled into.

He still sensed life inside. From his position, he would be able to send pila through the walls to where they were, which meant he would be able to smoke them out. He exhaled a hot breath and peered down the passage with his red eyes.

"—Firebolt!"

The next instant, a river of flame erupted from the darkness.

"‼"

He jumped backward, his left reverse joint creaking. Electrical flames erupted from the passage and carved a path of raging fire to the middle of the room.

Slowly, the boy followed in this path of flame.

Trailing swirls of sparks, his white hair swaying, the adventurer appeared.

He stopped close enough for the Juggernaut to reach him at a single leap. Then he let out a war cry and lunged forward.

"_____"

In the middle of his lunge, he froze.

The prey looked up and smiled.

A dark, fleeting smile.

That body so battered it was hard to find a place without a wound was displaying a smile that seemed ready to flicker out at any moment.

The shadow of death was on the boy.

The god of death had drawn near and given the boy his gift.

In other words, the promised end.

Victory or defeat mattered little to the prey before the Juggernaut.

Even if he, the monster, did not deliver the final blow, this human would—

"—OOOOOO!!"

But it didn't matter.

Even if the boy were fated to die anyway, he would slaughter him with the full brunt of his strength.

The Grim Reaper's scythe would not take the prey's life—his own claws of destruction would.

He would throw all he had against this human.

That was the raison d'être of the Juggernaut now that it was free of the Dungeon.

"…I will end you."

But neither would the boy embrace a meaningless death with open arms.

"I will return to the surface…with Ms. Lyu…"

If he did not win—if he did not return to her—she would die.

So he had to win. He could not lose.

He brandished his jet-black knife, his breast full of unspoken feelings.

The monster understood neither his words nor his feelings.

What it understood was his will.

The boy was intent on killing him. He would try to beat him.

He would turn the Juggernaut to white flame and burn him to ash.

The monster's breast quivered.

A monster of calamity who spread massacre mechanistically wherever he went should not have felt that emotion.

Joy.

The Juggernaut gave thanks for having met this human.

He was moved deeply by the fact that this male was offering himself up.

"Let's do this."

The monster welcomed the boy's words with a roar of joy that split the heavens.

When Lyu woke up, she was sitting in the darkness.

It was a familiar darkness.

This was the darkness that had tormented her for the past five years. This was the boundary between life and death where she had been stalled.

No one was beside her. That person was gone. She felt that was a pity.

She did not know why. She could not remember anything. But her cold hands struck her as sad.

Suddenly, light pierced the darkness.

Beyond the light, she saw her irreplaceable companions.

Astrea Familia.

Alize, Kaguya, Lyra, and all the others were standing with their backs to her.

No matter how she shouted, they would not turn toward her. Lyu knew that. The gulf between her in the darkness and them on the far shore of the light was too wide.

Suddenly, she realized she could walk forward.

She could walk out of the darkness. She could walk to the source of the light, to the place where the companions she longed for so deeply were standing.

Joy filled her.

No matter how much she called to them or how bitterly she cried, they would never turn toward her. But if Lyu walked toward them, they would welcome her.

At first they would be angry. Kaguya would scold her and Lyra might crossly pull on her ear. Maryu and the others would probably push her around. Alize would definitely stick her finger in the air and give her a half-baked sermon.

And then, she was certain, they would break into smiles.

They would all gather round to welcome her back and praise her for how she had soldiered through these five years.

They would throw their arms around her shoulders and stroke her head.

Her wish would finally be granted.

Her sins would finally be atoned for.

She would finally be able to pass away.

Lyu began walking toward the light, searching for salvation.

One step, two steps, three steps.

She passed the boundary of the darkness. Only a little farther now until she reached the distant shore—

You can't.

At that very moment, one of the forms that had never before turned toward her finally showed her face.

"—"

The red hair swayed and the green eyes pierced Lyu.

She had been seeking the light, but now her feet stopped.

Leon, you can't come here. We won't let you.

The eyebrows rose in flat rejection.

The lips that were always so just denied her.

Alize spoke as if she were trying to make Lyu realize something.

You must not run away.

Alize's gaze skipped past Lyu into the darkness beyond.

The monster's horrible roar pounded against Lyu's back. It was the same roar of despair that terrified her, robbed her of the mask of wind, and turned her into a wretched elf.

But within that hair-raising roar was the sound of resistance—a brave war cry like raging flames.

If you come here, you will regret it!

Alize's powerful voice made Lyu's hands shake.

Finally she was able to go beyond the light where she had so longed to go, but now she was beginning to question her decision.

Her dried-out heart that yearned for her friends was competing fiercely with the mad desire to seek out that battle cry of flame.

"I can't do it anymore…"

Lyu's voice was quiet now. To stop the fight in her heart, to give up on everything, she spoke in the unfeigned voice of her heart.

"I just can't, Alize…I can't fight anymore. I can't resist the past."

The Juggernaut. It was the beginning of everything, the source of all misfortune. A symbol of the past that tormented Lyu. She knew that if she returned to the darkness, harsh reality awaited her. It terrified her. She was crippled by her fear of facing the past.

Lyu gave a miserable bleat and hung her head.

Liar.

But Alize responded with a single word.

"—"

Lyu opened her sky-blue eyes and looked up. Her friend's face was before her, with its firm gaze that saw right through her.

You claim you don't want to lose hold of justice.

Alize did not explain anything. She did not admonish Lyu. She did not lead her.

She simply presented her with the truth.

Her words shook Lyu to the core, sending out ripples in her heart.

Justice is still alive within you!

What was "justice"? What was "right"?

Lyu had never known. She had never been able to find an answer.

All she knew was that Astrea had told her to forget about justice. She assumed that she had lost all right to it.

But Bell had told her something different.

He had said she still had justice within her.

Now Alize, too, was confirming Lyu's justice.

The words of the boy and the girl linked up in her mind so that finally she understood their meaning.

Your justice—your hope has not died yet!

It was true.

The justice Lyu had been seeking since the day her companions died was hope.

When Syr saved her, she decided to live so she could make sure the justice of her companions was fulfilled. She wanted to believe that what *Astrea Familia* had bequeathed her would connect to hope. She wanted to believe it would bring order and peace to Orario and smiles to the faces of its people. Lyu had been pursuing that vision since the day they died.

It was like Bell had said:

Lyu had brought them help and salvation and hope.

Lyu's actions had led to hope for someone.

That's what Bell had been saying all along.

There was no such thing as universal justice.

But this was Lyu's justice.

A hope that illuminated the future, not the past.

Finally, finally, Lyu realized what the justice that lived within her meant.

As she did, the other members of *Astrea Familia* turned toward her, as if to compound the change in her heart.

Go.

Next to Alize, Kaguya shooed Lyu toward the dark.

Don't run away!

Lyra smiled spitefully, her hands laced behind her head.

Do your best.

Beat 'em!

Each of her familia members had their own words of encouragement for Lyu.

Unable to bear their words and kind gazes, Lyu frowned and shouted back at them.

"I…I've wanted to apologize for so long! I wanted to say sorry to you all!"

At long last she spoke the words weighing on her mind.

This was the true wish she had harbored since the day she lost everything.

"I stood by and watched while you died, and I didn't do a thing. I wanted you to judge me! I wanted you to blame me and curse me and condemn me!"

On the far shore of the light, neither Kaguya nor any of the others spoke a word.

They simply looked back kindly at her as if to say, *But you knew!*

Yes, she did know.

She knew they would not have blamed her.

It was only Lyu who could not forgive herself. She could not accept her past.

By thinking of it as a crime, she was trying to punish herself so she could stop suffering.

Lyu's fists relaxed and hung limply at her sides.

Leon!

The voice of the girl she loved so dearly rang out high and clear.

What does justice mean to you?

Lyu's throat quivered.

Before she realized it, she was weeping uncontrollably.

Desperately holding back her wails, she answered with her truest desire.

"I want...to save him..."

Not the gentle light on the far shore, but the depths of darkness where cruelty awaited her.

Not by the sides of Alize and the others, but by the side of the boy who was alive now.

"I want to go back to the tavern with him...to where Syr is!"

Not to the past where her familia was, but to the future.

Alize smiled.

Her smile was like the sun telling her she had done well.

Leon, you must not run away! You must not let go!

Lyu smiled.

Tears rolled down her cheeks.

There was no sorrow in her sobs, and no darkness.

She turned her back on her companions and walked toward the darkness.

We will meet another day, Leon.

Their words sent her softly on her way.

She would go, and come back one day.

I loved you, my dear friends.

"—!!"

Lyu opened her eyes.

The first sensations she felt were a burning pain and a will-crushing lethargy. Then the loneliness of having been left by herself. The warmth that had enveloped her was gone.

Bell had vanished. In his place, in the darkness at the end of the passage, was a fierce song of battle.

Bell had not given up in the least.

He was thinking of Lyu and trying to fulfill her hopes.

He did not want her justice to be lost.

"Bell…!"

Lyu drew together her strength and made a fist.

She knew what she had to do.

The vision was gone. The hallucination had vanished. Alize and the others were nowhere to be found. Perhaps everything she had seen on the far shore of the light was no more than a delusion that suited her own fancy.

Still, they had taught her something.

Justice was alive within her.

She must not throw it aside. She must seek hope.

Lyu planted her shaking hands on the ground and peeled herself off it.

"Aaaaaa…!!"

In the pool of blood, she gave a newborn cry.

She broke with the self that had huddled in the shadow of her departed companions, imprisoned by the past, and gave birth to a new self.

She had to face it.

She had to face that past she had hid from for so long.

She had to fight.

She had to fight the symbol of her past she had feared all these years.

The Juggernaut, the monster of calamity, was her past personified.

If she wanted a future, she had to overcome that past.

If she was determined not to lose anyone else, and to live out her justice and hope, then she had no other choice.

"Aaaaaaa!!"

She stood up.

She grabbed a weapon from the pool of blood—the skeletal sword of a spartoi—and thrust it into the ground.

Pushing the pain away, she took a step forward. That step gave birth to another, stronger step. She called forth the strength to move ahead.

Ignoring her screaming body, Lyu walked down the dusky path.

She walked toward the song of battle.

Toward the place where the roars of the monster and the war cries of a human reverberated.

Beneath the phosphorescence that illuminated the darkness, Lyu threw herself toward the place where calamity and cruelty waited.

"———————————————————————!!"

"OOOOOOOOOOOOOOOOOOOOOOO!!"

Beyond the passage, a fight to the death was under way.

In the center of the room, the monster and the human were clashing, intent on killing each other. Bell was crossing swords with the Juggernaut. Where did that strength come from? It was as if he was literally pouring the last dregs of his life itself into their fight.

He had pulled the monster into a pure contest of strength.

With the gleaming white knife in his right hand, he was fending off every pilum the monster shot at him as they ricocheted relentlessly off the walls, floor, and ceiling.

The enemy's pila were slower than iguaçu. Of course, that meant he could counter them. He had faced a storm of those murderous swallows before, and now Hakugen knocked down the barrage of evil pila without missing a single one.

When the Juggernaut, with its hatefully joyous roars, shifted to close combat, Bell switched to the Hestia Knife. It was a high-speed weapon with a double edge. By alternating between the dark purple blade and the sparkling white one in his right hand, Bell successfully shut down the monster's hit-and-run strategy. He even found time to slash its tail and slice off some of the lizardman scales.

There was a regular pattern to his enemy's jumps now that it could not move with complete freedom. With his adventurer's instincts, Bell registered the relationship between the angle at which it landed and the time needed to prepare for its next jump, and by doing so he managed to withstand the savage attacks.

Determined to use his earlier loss as the basis for victory this time around, Bell roared and launched a counterattack.

The knife and the claws flashed purplish-blue, drawing countless arcs through the air. Sparks swirled amidst the deafening clatter. It was a circle dance of fiercely clashing light.

To Lyu, it looked like one raw life force being hurled against another.

"—! Ms. Lyu?!"

Bell had noticed her presence.

At the same time, the Juggernaut twirled around and looked straight at her.

Her chest shuddered. She could not hide it. Her trauma creaked with fear.

But now there was something that scared her more than having her past wounds opened afresh.

That was the prospect of once again losing something irreplaceable.

For a brief second of concentrated time, her heart was calm.

This perfect stillness was followed by a tempestuous gale wind.

This was the wind of her will driving her forward.

"—!!"

Lyu leaned forward and took off running.

She kicked off the ground, danced through the air, and landed a terrific blow on the astonished Juggernaut.

She plunged the blade of white bone into the monster's raised right arm, above its protective armor.

"Bell! I…can't be the elf of the lake."

Knocked aside by her enemy's forearm, she hit the ground rolling and shouted at the dazed Bell. Since he liked heroic tales, she was sure he was familiar with the one she'd mentioned. Elves respected the story greatly. Young elven girls dreamed of living that story. But Lyu was rejecting it.

Bell stared at her.

"I will not allow those who I care about to protect me while I sit by and do nothing! I will not let you walk into the jaws of death alone!"

Bell smiled as her strong words reached him. He nodded back to her with his bloody, scarred head. The hieroglyphs on the Divine Knife gripped in his hand pulsated with light, as if it was burning with a renewed passion to fight.

Standing shoulder to shoulder, the human and the elf launched their counterattack.

"AAAAAA!!"

The Juggernaut was wild with rage.

He was terribly put out to have his fight to the death with Bell spoiled.

The clock was ticking for this monster who had incorporated so many of its own kind and now wore its unnatural "armor of persistence." He had decided to pour every last remaining second of his life into the battle against this one male. He absolutely must kill the white-haired boy.

This worthless being was interfering with his reason for existing despite being nothing but a distraction. At the whim of his anger, the Juggernaut prepared to squash the offending bug.

"!!"

"!"

But Lyu dodged. And that was not all; she fought back.

Her movements were incomparable to those of a few moments before. It was hard to believe they came from the same adventurer. Blood was still flowing from her right arm and right leg, and indeed from her entire body. She was wounded from head to toe yet still she had found the courage to face her past, her trauma. Gale Wind was back to her old outstanding self. More than that, she was set on overcoming her past limits.

The beauty with which she fought set her apart from the rabble the Juggernaut had slaughtered so far.

"I will end you!!"

She screamed the same words as the white-haired boy, with the same look in her eyes and the same will.

The Juggernaut had recognized this before. Like the boy, the elf was worth hunting. She was worth giving of himself body and soul to massacre.

Therefore, he would kill both of them together.

The Juggernaut gave a fearsome battle cry and devoted every ounce of his being to murdering them.

"Ahhh…!"

The accelerated onslaught consisting of a series of jumps and a storm of pila pushed Bell to the limit.

Five minutes had passed since the battle began. But in their tattered state, it would not have been surprising for either Bell or Lyu to lose their equilibrium at any moment. Their bodies were well beyond their capacity. When their flames of life had flickered out, the journey would end. Although the Juggernaut was paying for its transformation into a chimera through the rejection of body parts, the physical strength of this nonstandard monster exceeded that of the adventurers. When the waiting game was over, it would destroy them.

When Bell was fighting alone, he had constantly been on the lookout for a chance to land his lethal blow. The Juggernaut, however, seemed aware of this. The evidence lay in the fact that while it still used its claws, the pila were now its main weapon.

In the current stage of the battle, there was no such thing as a decisive blow.

"Distant forest sky. Infinite stars inlaid upon the eternal night sky."

Against this backdrop, Lyu began to chant.

"!"

"!"

Both Bell and the Juggernaut had the same reaction to the elf as she began to sing in the midst of running and brandishing her sword.

Concurrent chanting.

By carrying out attacks, movement, evasion, and chanting at the same time, the user called forth the necessary moment for a lethal blow.

"Heed this foolish one's voice, and once more grant the starfire's divine protection."

It was also a song of regret.

Lyu had sung the same song as she allowed Alize and the others to protect her without saving them in return. Succumbing to despair and terror, she had frozen, able to move only her lips.

"Grant the light of compassion to the one who forsook you."

Now she sang that detestable song as she fought.

She was determined not to lose what she cared most about. This time, she would not only be protected, she would protect in return.

"...!"

Bell sensed the intention behind her actions, as well as their strategic meaning.

The removal of the Juggernaut's shell.

The shell that still remained on the left side of its body was endowed not only with magic reflection, but also with the stone body of the obsidian soldiers it had incorporated. Lyu's Luminous Wind could not deal a lethal blow as long as their enemy wore this stony armor capable of reducing the strength of magic. And she did not have the mental strength left for two attacks.

"...!"

The Juggernaut interpreted the cutthroat speed of Lyu's chanting as a threat. Given the compromised state of its armor, there was a slim chance the attack could hit home. There was a small possibility this could open the door to defeat. Thus the Juggernaut was determined to destroy Lyu first, before her magic swelled to its full strength.

"—*Firebolt!*"

Bell fired off a shot—not at the monster, but at his own black knife.

"!"

The electrical fire converged on the blade, followed immediately by the sound of a chime. He was preparing to activate Argo Vesta. He was summoning what strength he had left to charge for the last time.

The Juggernaut could not help reacting to this omen signaling the same attack that had taken his right arm. There was no way he could ignore the lethal blow that had almost killed him.

This was what Bell had been aiming for.

In front of the monster was a human carrying out a concurrent charge; behind him was an elf chanting as she ran. The one in front was clearly a decoy, yet he could not ignore it. His attention split, the Juggernaut stopped moving for a second.

"Come, wandering wind, fellow traveler."

Behind the monster, Lyu belted out her chant.

In front of it, Bell charged forward with his flaming knife.

Their plan was to strip the Juggernaut of its shell and then blast it with magic.

The monster of calamity reacted by slamming its right arm against the ground.

"—!!"

Pila erupted from below—but not only in one spot. They formed a circle measuring ten meders in radius around the adventurers.

"Shit!!"

"Ahh!"

By sending the bone javelins underground, the monster had managed to attack Lyu and Bell at the same time. The sword mountain rose with the monster at its center, injuring both adventurers. Lyu's shoulder was torn and Bell's thigh gouged. With one strike, the Juggernaut had shaved away at both of their lives. It intended to finish them off by skewering them on another batch of pila.

"Cross the skies and sprint through the wilderness..."

But Lyu did not stop chanting. With an indomitable spirit, she maintained control over her magic and seized a chance at victory.

Because she did, Bell did, too.

Even as blood spilled from his mouth, he narrowed his eyes and hit the ground with his right hand.

"Argo Vesta!!"

He had charged for seven seconds.

The lethal blow was not aimed at the Juggernaut itself, but instead at the pila boring through the earth.

"?!"

The ground exploded with a thundering roar as the reverberations shook the world before the Juggernaut's eyes. The underground flare blasted every one of the bone javelins into dust. The supply of pila had been cut off.

That was not all, however. The power and impact of the sacred fire was transmitted through the pila to the Juggernaut's right arm. The limb made of the bodies of countless monsters shattered.

"_____?!"

The Juggernaut screamed as its right arm exploded from the inside out. As Argo Vesta sent cracks racing across the floor and the entire room shook, the monster stumbled. For a moment, its guard was down.

Bell did not let the opportunity slip past. He charged.

Without the strength left to keep a solid grip on his weapon, the Hestia Knife spun into the air. He closed his hand into a fist instead, intending to dive into the monster's chest.

"Damn—!"

But he was far too late.

Using Argonaut to carry out his last concurrent charge had robbed him of his remaining mental and physical strength. Even though he cursed his collapsing knees and braved a close press, the threat was no match for a monster specialized in agility. In the final moment, the limits of Bell's physical body betrayed him.

Having bounced back from the damage inflicted on him, the Juggernaut turned his outraged red eyes on Bell.

He anticipated no trouble in intercepting the ragged rabbit that was flying toward his chest. He raised his left arm, brandishing his six purplish-blue claws.

Raised at an angle above its head, the claws of destruction were without question intended to finish off Bell by skewering him. No doubt they would color the world red when they pierced his chest and exited his back. Just as Bell imagined they would. Just like the attack that had stolen Lyu's friends five years earlier.

"—AAAAAAAAAAAAAAAAAAAAAAAAAAAAAAAAAAAAA
AAAAAAA!!"

Blocked from regaining her footing by the damage from the pila as well as the impact of Bell's attack, Lyu howled.

To overcome the tragedy that had been seared into her eyes, she became the wind and flew through space. She kicked her left foot against the ground and pierced the air like a flash of light arcing toward the monster. Approaching from the side, she soared directly to his upraised left arm.

"?!"

With Futaba already drawn, she used her two shortswords to dissect the claws of destruction. The blades sliced through his wrist and finger joints.

Time stopped for the Juggernaut as it realized Lyu had just stolen its most potent weapon, those claws so sharp they could be mistaken for fangs.

If I'd only done the same on that other day—

Within the still pool of time, memories of the past rose in Lyu's mind.

Again she saw Alize, her back pierced by those claws that she had welcomed in order to protect Lyu.

If only Lyu had stood up.

If only she had fought beside them like she was fighting now.

—she would not have been defeated!

Regret and pain seared her body as her heart let out a scream that ripped through her chest.

She knew she could not bring back the past.

Still, she looked back on that moment when she had been saved and cried out with a heart full of a hundred different emotions.

All of this while she sailed past the dazed Juggernaut.

"—OOOOOOOOOOOOOOOOOOOOOOOOOOOOOOOOOO
OOOOOOOO!"

The next instant, Bell hurtled into the Juggernaut.

Lyu's support had allowed him to make the final leap toward the monster's breast.

The enormous skeleton froze as the space between Bell and him vanished and the boy's right fist pounded down on his right side.

"*FIIIREBOOOOOOOOOOOOOOOOOOOOLT!*"

The cry came an instant later. Swift-Strike Magic exploded into his body.

There was just one shot.

But one shot was enough.

The final dregs of Bell's magic raced through the Juggernaut's poorly defended body, ruthlessly exploding it from the inside.

"?!"

The remaining shell on its left side flew off its body as the electrical fire detonated. The obsidian soldier's armor, too, shattered to the ground in a swirl of sparks.

A single weak Firebolt did not have the force to take down the Juggernaut altogether. Without a magic stone to be shattered, the unique monster remained standing. However, the massive form was now completely naked and without armor.

"*—swifter than anything.*"

The elf's song rang out, a beautiful melody of wind.

From the Juggernaut's perspective, she was on his right side. Having stolen his claws, she now lay on the ground with both legs pressed into it.

She thrust her right hand toward the frozen Juggernaut and prepared to release a torrent of magic.

"*Imbue the light of stardust and strike down my enemy!*"

This was the final line, the one that announced the spell's completion.

Bell had been thrown backward by his own attack. Astonishment filled the monster's red eyes.

Lyu fired.

"*Luminous Wind!*"

The magic was activated.

Huge orbs of light swathed in green wind materialized.

Forty-seven of them.

The magic attack into which she had poured every drop of her mental strength had begun.

"_____!!"

The stream of light-orbs flew toward the monster.

There was no escape from this storm of destruction.

Yet the Juggernaut did escape.

"What?!"

Bell stared in disbelief.

The monster had leaped with such power it seemed his right knee would shatter as it bent. The orbs of light swallowed up his tail and blew off his right leg from the shin down, yet still he flew into the air.

Having lost their target, the storm of glowing orbs blasted past Bell as he screamed in frustration and crashed into the wall of the room.

The monster had evaded Lyu's lethal blow.

Bell grimaced as reverberations shook the air. But not Lyu.

"I know your speed *better than anyone else in the world.*"

She had *kept* ten of the forty-seven orbs by her side.

She had predicted this.

She had guessed that the monster of calamity would probably evade even the most powerful magic released at the ideal moment.

Even with the sacrifice of her closest friend she had not been able to fully take down the previous Juggernaut. She had looked at the current situation with coolheaded realism and fully anticipated the monster's ability to evade her attack.

From its position on the far wall of the room, the Juggernaut stared along with Bell below him at the ten glowing orbs.

Ten.

That was a special number for Lyu.

The number of irreplaceable battle companions she had lost.

These orbs, larger than all the others she had produced, hovered around her back.

"—Let's go."

With that, she dashed forward.

"?!"

She did not fire the orbs she had held in reserve but instead pulled them forward with her toward the Juggernaut.

This would not be a long- or mid-range attack.

Just before Bell used Argo Vesta on the twenty-seventh floor, the monster had leaped into the air. If Bell hadn't used the Goliath Scarf to pull him back, his blow would not have hit its mark. Likewise, if Lyu didn't release her attack from extremely close range, the Juggernaut would not be destroyed.

Lyu had learned from her repeated fights against the Juggernaut, and she chose a "zero-range attack."

Although she could not accelerate as fast as she would have liked because a pilum had wounded her thigh, she leaped forward with a scream.

"Noin, Neze!"

As if responding to the names, two of the glowing orbs exploded into *the soles of Lyu's boots.*

"Huh?!"

The sound of the light slipped into Bell's ears as Lyu accelerated with explosive speed. The wind-wrapped orbs of light had given her incredible forward momentum. Lyu became a gale wind that cut through the air so quickly it left both the shuddering Bell and the astonished Juggernaut in the dust. As if she was kicking off from the two orbs of light, she hurtled straight toward the monster.

"?!"

The Juggernaut scrambled to thrust its right arm, which was now missing its lower half, toward the flying elf.

A pilum volley erupted from the joint between its arm and its body.

"Asta, Lyana!"

Lyu once again howled the names of her companions and shot forth two large orbs of light. One was released from her side and landed on her left arm, which she held close to her, thereby changing her course midair.

"?!"

She turned at a near right angle, evading the rain of pila in the nick of time.

Immediately, the second glowing orb exploded into the sole of her right shoe, and once again she flew forward.

The arc she drew through the air was like a bolt of lightning.

As the space between Lyu and the Juggernaut vanished almost instantly, the monster kicked off the wall with its left foot in an attempt to escape.

"No way!!"

She followed.

Ignoring head wind and the law of inertia alike, she twisted her creaking body around by pure force of will, landed on the wall where the monster had been a second earlier, and took off flying again.

The Juggernaut's gaze wavered as it took in the form roaring toward it.

She was using her magic like never before to move through the air.

Her high-speed leap beat the astonished Juggernaut at its own game.

Of course, her reckless strategy of changing her magic into propellant force was unlikely to lack consequences. The heels of her boots flaked off, exposing the blazing red soles of her feet. The left arm she had blasted an orb into in order to change directions was fractured as well.

Her body was not broken, however.

It might take all the abilities she had to withstand its evil power, but she would not permit herself to die until she had shot that monster dead.

She shot herself with her own magic, making her flesh smoke and her skin burn, and yet the "flight of the elf" continued.

—*Friends, give me strength.*

Together with her familia, she would shoot their enemy.

"OOOOOOOOOOOOOOOOOOOOOOOOOOOOOOOOOOOOO OOOOOOO!"

Correctly perceiving Lyu's intention, the destroyer sounded a blaring alarm.

Throwing caution to the wind, it shot all its remaining pila.

Having lost a great deal of its mobility, it was desperately trying to prevent the elf from drawing near.

"Celty, Iska, Maryu!"

As if they were lending her a hand, the three orbs whose names had been called redirected Lyu diagonally and smashed the pila speeding toward her.

As Lyu flew through the air buffeted by powerful wind pressure, she saw the faces of her companions in war.

Her ten sisters in justice flew beside her, raising their voices with her in a battle cry.

It was a hallucination. A mere sentimental delusion.

A mirage to suit her whims.

She knew that.

And so she transformed that vision into the strength that drove her forward.

"—AAAAAAAAAAAAAAAAAAAAAAAAAAAAAAAAAAAA AAAAAAAA!!"

The elf's roar shook the air.

Strangely enough, this was a dogfight between two wingless opponents.

As if drawn upward by this scene unfolding like stardust criss-crossing the night sky, Bell rose to his feet. His eyes wide, he was like an animal unable to do more than stare up at the stars in the heavens.

He saw:

The track of the elf as she danced through the air guided by ten orbs of light.

Her long cape fluttering like wings spread wide, truly a vision of the wings of justice.

The sword was the girl herself striving to overtake the monster.

At last, this girl with the name of Astrea, the goddess of justice, carved in her back had the monster of calamity in her grasp.

"AAAAAAAAAAAAAA?!"

Strangely enough, all this was unfolding in midair in the center of the room.

As the monster raised its right arm of bone to intercept this pursuit that had left it no escape route, Lyu released one of the three remaining orbs.

"Kaguya!"

As if responding to the cry of a companion in arms, the orb raced forward like a fencer throwing off cutting wind.

The orb pulverized the monster's last remaining section of arm, its last weapon.

"—"

The impact of the explosion sent the monster's trunk swimming through space.

Lyu soared very close to it and then overtook it, dancing over its head. The instant her powerful momentum vanished...her body slowly rotated, as if time had been cut away from that patch of air.

Her legs were stretched toward the heavens, her head toward the ground.

The Juggernaut twisted its massive body so that it was looking up at her from directly below her eyes.

"Lyra."

She called forth the glowing orb quietly and it approached her feet as she began to fall. It was like an older sister pushing her forward with a smile.

Tears gathered in Lyu's eyes, and the next moment the impact hit her feet. She became a shooting star falling downward.

And last:

"Alize."

The final orb of light flew to Lyu's palm.

She had wanted judgment.

She had wanted redemption.

She had wanted to die and join her friends.

She had been afraid to overcome the past.

She had been terrified of forgetting the past.

If she could have, she would have taken back her past and made it right.

But now.

Now she wanted the future.

For its sake—

The monster's huge form was approaching. It had lost both arms, but its red eyes still stared up at her in a daze.

Like her, this symbol of her past was battered from top to bottom. Lyu held the orb of light in her right hand and raised it.

She was sure that in the light of the beautiful glowing sphere, she saw her friend's hand on top of her own. A tear fell from her sky-blue eyes as she spoke with quivering lips.

"—Good-bye."

Good-bye to the lingering shadow of her friends.

Good-bye to those bygone days.

Good-bye to the past that she must overcome.

Lyu said her farewell to everything, and then she roared.

"Luvia!!"

A violent explosion.

"_____"

The huge glowing sphere crashed into the monster's chest.

As if it were receiving all the skill of the girl who had protected Lyu and saved her, it flowered into a circle of light.

Unable to defend itself, without even a dying scream or a roar of fury or resentment, the Juggernaut burst quietly into pieces. A piercing melody of light and wind rang out as the monster's body transformed into innumerable fragments.

Lyu watched the falling shards turn to ash like any other monster and then closed her eyes, drained of every last bit of energy.

Her tears scattered into the air.

"Ms. Lyu?!"

Lyu and the remnants of the Juggernaut drifted down into the center of the room like a meteor shower. As the monster's ash swirled in a smoky haze, Bell watched, unable in his injured state to dash to Lyu's side. Instead he dragged himself slowly to the center of the room and gazed at the purplish smoke hanging in the air.

"Aah…!"

He saw an elven form hovering at a distance. Gradually its silhouette came into focus and the figure stepped forward out of the smoke.

It was the battered Lyu.

She met his eyes and curved her lips up ever so slightly. Bell smiled back in relief.

The room was entirely still aside from the two of them.

They had beaten the calamity.

Still smiling, they walked forward slowly, as if they were seeking each other out.

But before they reached each other, Bell stumbled.

His body tilted forward.

Lyu's did the same.

Although they were only steps apart, their knees buckled and with a crash they tumbled to the ground.

"……"
"……"

Blood was erupting from their bodies, which were no more than walking wounds.

Their breathing was shallow.

They could hardly feel their hands and feet.

They could hardly see the hazy world.

They were close enough for Lyu to place her right hand over Bell's right hand.

They lay facedown on the cold Dungeon floor.

"…We won, didn't we?"

"…Yes."

"…And now we can go home."

"…Yes."

Their voices were faint.

They did not look at each other as they formed smiles that were not really smiles.

A future in which they returned to the surface had become no more than a dream that they shared, its boundary with reality blurred.

No adventurers remained in that room.

There was only burned-out ash.

They were like birds that had flown to the heavens and back only to lose their wings.

White embers and the fading vestiges of an elf.

That was all.

The howls of monsters echoed in the distance. As if the stillness that the monster of calamity had presided over was a lie, the darkness thundered. The pounding of countless feet twined with roars heading toward the room where Bell and Lyu lay.

They could not stand. They could not move a muscle. The darkness stared down at them.

"…Bell."

"…Yes."

"…I…you…"

"……"

Lyu did not finish her thought.

The light faded from their eyes as they gazed to the side.

As if they were going to sleep, they closed their eyes.

By the time the roaring monsters reached the room, their bodies had ceased moving.

Their adventures had ended.

They had beat the calamity but lost to the Dungeon.

They had failed to escape the maze.

Like many adventurers before them, Lyu and Bell were swallowed up by the darkness of the deep levels—

"—, —chi, —llucchi!!"

Or so it had seemed.

"—Bellucchi!!"

The volley of the monsters' roars—the roars that sounded exactly like monsters communicating with companions some distance away—turned into words in human language.

Within the dimness of his world, Bell sensed a shadow falling over his body.

His eyelids fluttered open as his body was lifted in someone's arms.

"He's alive, he's alive!!"

"Tell the humans!"

Following an explosion of joyful roars, familiar voices echoed in his ears.

Bell understood that he had been turned on his back, and a pair of eyes was peering down at him.

Those very same round amber eyes that he had wanted to see for so long.

"Bell, Bell!"

Tears spilled from the amber eyes and dampened Bell's cheeks. The sparkling red stone in the girl's forehead glistened as if it, too, was crying. Bell tried to brush the tears from her face, only to remember that he could not move at all. He tried at least to smile, but failed at that as well. Finally he managed to move the muscles in his cheeks and raise the corners of his mouth very slightly. The girl with the amber eyes responded with a huge grin.

"Mr. Bell!"

"Bell!!"

"Lyu!"

"She's over there, meow!"

Bell could hear other familiar voices in the distance.

The voices of their friends who had found them.

The curtain had fallen on their adventure; they had lost to the Dungeon.

But Lyu's hopes had not been crushed.

She and Bell had not given up hope. Instead they had risked death to fight the monster, and that fight had called their companions to their side. The ties of friendship they had pulled toward them had beaten the Dungeon.

Moving quicky, the monsters who had gathered at their sides hurried away. Their jobs were done, although they would continue to watch over the pair from the shadows. Their presence remained near, as if to whisper their reassurances.

The only two Xenos who remained with the adventurers were the dragon girl and the harpy disguised in hoods and robes. The harpy lifted Lyu and held her close.

"…Bell."

"…Yes."

The tearful, joyful voices of the friends who had called their names drew closer.

Lyu looked Bell in the eye and smiled.

"We can…go home."

EPILOGUE **YOU'LL BE BACK II**

You can still come back.

Someone said that to me once.

And they were right.

I did overcome the past—and now I return to a place where the light shines.

"……"

Lyu felt tears pooling beneath her eyelids. She frowned, trying not to let them spill over.

"Where am I…?"

She opened her eyes a little but closed them right away after seeing blinding light.

Even a magic-stone lantern was too much for those sky-blue eyes that had grown overly accustomed to the darkness of the labyrinth. As she grimaced, unable even to blink, she heard a surprised voice coming from immediately beside her.

"Lyu, are you okay?!"

She looked up at the form leaning over her.

The blurry shape eventually came into focus and the colors become clearer. She made out blue-gray hair and eyes. Lyu parted her lips as the exhausted face peered down at her.

"Syr…"

Her voice was terribly hoarse, as if her throat had forgotten how it was like to talk. Nevertheless, as soon as she spoke the name, the face above her lit up with happiness. Seemingly overcome with emotion, the girl fell onto Lyu.

"Lyu! Oh, Lyu!! I'm so glad…!"

She buried her face in Lyu's neck and hugged her softly like a sister or a mother. Lyu could feel the familiar, kind warmth of her body through the blanket. Her heart was so full she could not speak.

"Meow!! Lyu opened her eyes, meow!"

"Now please tell us how you feel about troubling us by sleeping for three days straight!"

"Damn, I was worried about you!"

Suddenly, Lyu was surrounded by chaos. Ahnya threw her hands up and pranced around like a child while Chloe teased her with a smile and Runoa's happy face contradicted her cross words.

Tears spilled from Lyu's eyes as she took in the smiles adorning the faces of her most treasured friends.

"...I've never seen you cry before, meow."

Lyu smiled back faintly at the grinning Ahnya. Her mind was still blank as an untouched sheet of paper, but she whispered the only words that she could think of: "Thank you."

"You're in such a daze we really ought to explain what's going on. You're in a clinic run by the Guild inside Babel, meow."

"You were brought here as soon as you got back to the surface."

"We tried various items and magic on you as we were rushing through the Dungeon but you just wouldn't wake up. We were so worried about you, meow!"

As Chloe tugged on the elf's gauze-wrapped ear, Runoa and Ahnya finished her explanation. It was a bit hard for Lyu to make sense of everything since she had just woken up a few minutes earlier, but the distinctive smell of antiseptics and the clean white room helped her to understand.

As Syr slapped Chloe's hand away from Lyu's ear, Ahnya leaned over her.

"Lyu, how much do you remember, meow?"

"...I heard your voices in the deep levels...and I knew I could go home, with him..."

She had gotten that far when the image of Bell's face rose in her memory and she opened her eyes wide. A second later the white vision vanished and she leaped up, fully awake.

"What about him?! What about Bell?!"

"Meow! Calm down, meow!"

"Lyu, you'll hurt yourself!"

Chloe panicked as Lyu's face changed color and Syr desperately tried to calm her. Lyu doubled over, her body screaming in protest at the sudden movement, but she ignored the pain and grabbed Syr's shoulder.

"Syr, tell me! Is he all right?!"

"Mr. Bell is fine! He woke up before you did!"

"Yes, yes, meow! The white-haired kid is alive and well in a room down the hall! Now calm down and take a nap, meow!"

"Idiot…!"

Ignoring Syr's soothing words, Ahnya prattled on until she had given away more information than she should have, sending Runoa into a panic. As she feared, Lyu leaped out of bed the instant she had learned Bell's whereabouts. With a speed that caught her friends off guard given her injured condition, she flew out of her sickroom.

"Lyu, Lyu?! You can't leave dressed like that!"

Ignoring Syr's attempts to stop her, Lyu raced down the white hallway. Glimpses through the windows of the blue sky she had so longed for didn't slow her down, either. An animal person walking toward her—most likely some familia's healer serving at the clinic by request of the Guild—gave her a shocked look, but Lyu didn't even register her presence.

Bell…Bell!

All she cared about at the moment was her companion's safety.

Stumbling now and then, she steadied herself by propping a gauze-wrapped hand against the wall and continued to the end of the hallway. At the place where the path intersected with another hallway, she found the special-care room Ahnya had been referring to and burst through the door.

"Bell!"

Sure enough, he was there.

He was sitting up on a bed pushed against the wall, wearing a sleeveless gown as someone palpated his tightly wrapped left arm.

A beautiful silver-haired girl was examining him. Hestia and Lilly sat on either side of the bed. Beside them the god Miach and his follower Nahza stood watching.

As Bell looked up in surprise, relief flooded Lyu's face.

"Ms. Lyu! Wait!"

Bell had started to smile back at Lyu, but then his face flushed. She followed his gaze and looked down at her own body—and then she realized.

She wasn't wearing anything that could be properly called clothes. Just very thin pieces of cloth. Frankly speaking, clinic underwear.

A pair of white short shorts on the bottom and a midriff-baring shirt on top.

The bandages wrapped around her arms and one thigh did a poor job of concealing her supple skin. Lyu was standing wide-eyed, her face growing increasingly red, when yet another tragedy befell her.

Perhaps because of her rapid movement, the thin strap tied at her shoulder had come undone...

As the top fell to the ground with a rustle, Lyu shrieked like a little girl.

"Eeeeeeeeeeeeeeeeeeeeeeeeeeeek!"

""Don't look!!""

"Ouch!"

Ignoring Lyu as she sank to the ground with her arms crossed over her chest, the blushing Hestia and Lilly both slapped Bell's head at the same time. To add to the uproar, Nahza reprimanded her patron deity with a sharp shout of "You can't either, Lord Miach!" He whined as she dug her elbow into his side.

"How dare you hit a critically injured patient!!!!!!!!!!"

With that, the beautiful silver-haired girl—Amid Teasanare, the *Dian Cecht Familia* healer—thundered at the group.

After the fuss died down, Amid sent Lyu back to her room, where she was relegated to strict bed rest. Little by little, she heard the whole story from the visitors who streamed in and out.

*　　　*　　　*

"I heard from the Xenos that it was amazing you were still alive."

That she learned from Welf.

"Lady Lyu, we are so happy you made it."

"Thank you for saving Sir Bell."

The smith, who was accompanied on his visit by the fully recovered Mikoto and Haruhime, recounted his conversation with the lizardman Lido.

"The thought of spending days in a place like that without proper equipment makes even a monster like me shudder."

This was after they had collected Lyu and Bell and rushed back to the lower-level safety point to take refuge. Welf had overheard the Xenos saying similar things to what Lido told him.

Four days.

That was how long Bell and Lyu had spent wandering the thirty-seventh floor after the wormwell carried them there. It had taken Welf and the rest of their party the same amount of time to fight the Amphisbaena, join up with the Xenos, and make their way down to the thirty-seventh floor.

"Honestly, I thought we were in deep trouble when we got Ouranos's message from Fels telling us to head to the thirty-seventh floor."

While they rested briefly at the safety point and Lilly, Ahnya, and several others tried to heal Bell and Lyu, Welf met with the Xenos in a place where Bors wouldn't find them.

They had been able to determine what floor Bell and Lyu were on thanks to directions from the wizened god, who spoke to them through Lido's oculus. Although even the Dungeon could not control the Juggernaut, the god had sensed its abnormal behavior, in particular its independent battle cries, and immediately dispatched the rescue team to the thirty-seventh floor.

"On top of the fact that there's nothing to eat down there, that floor is incredibly huge, and our fellow monsters are very violent. We almost never spend time there. Plus, there's no village caretaker like Gryu or Mari down there…"

"I can believe it. The passages and walls and everything are all so huge it made me dizzy. I had no idea how we'd ever find Bell and Lyu."

"We can thank Bell and Lyu for making it to what you adventurers call the 'main route.' We wouldn't have found them if they'd been lost in that impenetrable maze."

Since the Xenos didn't know where on the thirty-seventh floor Bell and Lyu were, all they could do was charge frantically down the main route. That's when they heard the sounds of the titanic struggle against the Juggernaut and were ultimately able to locate them. In large part, their rescue was the result of Bell and Lyu's refusal to give up on returning to the surface.

"Thanks to you guys, we were able to save Bell. Pass on our thanks to that mermaid, too."

In addition to regular potions, they'd used mermaid lifeblood, a drop item, on an emergency basis. Mari, who was unable to leave the water's edge, had cut herself and collected blood to hand over to Lido's party. She hadn't been able to provide much, since she had recently used her lifeblood to heal Bell during the battle on the twenty-seventh floor—and in fact, Lido had had to stop her from stubbornly trying to give too much when she nearly fainted—but it had nevertheless played a key role in keeping the heavily wounded Bell and Lyu alive.

Lido had furtively handed the bottles of lifeblood to Welf, and according to Lilly and Aisha, Lyu's and Bell's lives would have been in danger if they hadn't received it during their journey to the surface.

"Don't worry about that…But am I right that some of the humans with you don't know about us? I mean, is everything okay?"

"Well, setting aside the head of Rivira and the tavern waitresses, I think the big guy and his friends probably figured it out…But their patron deity is a good guy. I'll leave it up to their familia to decide how to deal with it from here on out."

In all likelihood, some party members had noticed monsters helping *Hestia Familia* starting with the big clash on the twenty-seventh floor. However, it seemed Ouka and his familia members had gotten some hints even before that, starting with Cassandra's mysterious babbling about her prophetic dream around the time of the battle at

Daedalus Street. Meanwhile, Aisha and Tsubaki already knew about the Xenos. The main problem would be explaining things to Daphne, but Welf had decided to leave that task to Miach and Takemikazuchi.

All in all, the public seemed unlikely to get wind of the Xenos as a result of the most recent events, so *Hestia Familia* had little grounds to worry they'd be labeled "enemies of humanity."

"Um, Welf…the elf and Bell, will they be all right?"

The vouivre Wiene had approached him with deep concern just before leaving the safety point.

"…Yeah. I'll make sure they're healed and Bell is able to see you again. And I'll send the elf along as a bodyguard when he does."

It seems Welf was unable to resist making a promise to the gentle dragon girl.

After they made it past the twenty-fifth floor, which was still scarred by claw marks, the adventurers had parted ways with the Xenos and rushed to the surface without a single rest, according to the young smith.

"Anyway, she already said it, but…thanks for taking care of Bell."

Gesturing to Haruhime, Welf expressed his bashful gratitude to Lyu, who still lay in bed. Hestia and Lilly had visited earlier and said the same thing. She tried to protest that she was the one who had gotten him involved to start with, and that it was he who had saved her, but Welf wouldn't have it.

"You've saved his butt more than once or twice. I've never properly thanked someone like this…so just assume I've taken all that into consideration and accept my gratitude."

It was like he was offering proof of the "justice" within her that Bell had talked about.

And so, it was in this way that Welf and the rest of *Hestia Familia* expressed their heartfelt gratitude to Lyu.

"Jura Harma…and what other survivors of *Rudra Familia* finally kicked the bucket. *And Gale Wind died along with them. That's how the story goes.*"

Aisha visited alone to tell Lyu how the whole incident shook out on the surface.

"You've been cleared of suspicion for the murder in Rivira. Looks like that was a false accusation to start with…but anyway, everyone seems satisfied with the explanation that the irregularities on the twenty-seventh floor were also the work of the trainer Jura Harma. You can thank a big-mouthed oaf for that."

Apparently, there had been a quarrel at the Guild after Lyu and Bell were taken to the clinic.

"Listen, Gale Wind showed up! But she tried to protect us, and then she croaked! Gale Wind is really dead this time around!"

"Uh, um, can you please explain that more coherently…?!"

"What the hell are you talking about?!"

The half-healed Bors had charged to the Guild's reception desk, it seems. He'd grabbed hold of a half-elf employee who simply wanted to confirm the safety of her charge, along with her receptionist friend, and blabbed the news so loudly a number of other adventurers at the Guild had overheard.

"A crazy number of my fellow adventurers bought the farm this time around. But it wasn't Gale Wind's fault! It was those pieces of shit from *Rudra Familia*! The elf tried to protect us to the last!"

Bors slammed a piece of Gale Wind's broken wooden sword onto the counter and carried on with his tirade.

According to Aisha, this was his unique way of repaying her for saving his life. Apparently, he was trying to protect Lyu, who still had a bounty on her head, as well as the honor of Gale Wind's name. His words bore more weight than Aisha had expected. As a second-tier adventurer and head of Rivira, he seemed to have convinced most of the rogues and hooligans that his story was true. At first, the residents of Rivira and adventurers in general were suspicious of his sudden change of heart, especially since he had led the charge for the issuing of Lyu's bounty in the first place, but in the end they believed him as one of the few survivors of the incident.

More to the point, adventurers trying to repay their debt couldn't say much about his words or actions since they hinted at a resolution to the whole affair. Plus, it seemed word had gotten out in Rivira that the elf who helped kill the Black Goliath was actually Gale Wind.

At this point, Gale Wind was starting to be seen as a friend of justice who had tried to foil the schemes of the Evils. Lots of people thought it was all an exaggerated tale, but others believed the stories and were grateful.

Lyu found herself blinking in surprise, but according to Aisha that was how things had played out.

That wasn't quite the end of the commotion at the Guild, though.

"By the way…she did have a bounty on her head, and I've got some of her property right here. If you take into consideration the prize money for Jura Harma, I'd say a third would be fair. Hey, I'd even be happy with a tenth…"

"Um, I would say that is out of the question…"

"I agree. Your logic is insane…"

"Damn it all!!!!!!!!!!"

Oddly, Lyu felt reassured when she heard about Bors's argument with the receptionist over his attempt to slyly squeeze some cash out of the whole affair.

The upper echelons of the Guild accepted the convenient report of Gale Wind's death with remarkably few questions, as if the will of the deity in charge of the organization were behind it all. An official announcement was supposed to be made soon. The Guild also placed a strict gag order on anything concerning the Juggernaut that had killed so many upper-tier adventurers, as well as the Amphisbaena that had appeared without regard for the regular spawn interval. As for the Juggernaut, few people even knew it existed, and even the adventurers who had been in Rivira when the tragedy occurred had apparently blamed everything on the floor boss.

In any case, this marked the end, by and large, to Lyu's ties with Gale Wind.

"It all worked out nicely, didn't it, old friend of justice? Anyone who still hates you is likely to give up for real this time, and your violent acts of the past have been whitewashed."

Since Lyu had been ordered to avoid all strenuous activities, all she could do in response to the Amazon's taunting grin was tolerate it with a cold look on her face.

*   *   *

And then there was The Benevolent Mistress.

"Mama Mia sure is mad at Ahnya, Chloe, and Runoa for taking off to rescue you."

On another day, Syr came to see her. Apparently, the rescue team hadn't had a day off work since they got back, which explained why they hadn't come by the clinic since the day Lyu woke up. Lyu felt a little nervous about meeting a similar fate herself not too far into the future.

"Also, I have a message for you."

The girl with the blue-gray hair, who had snuck out while her miserably overworked companions weren't looking, broke into a smile.

"Mama Mia says to tell you we made too much risotto, so you'd better come help us eat it soon."

Lyu felt a very, very small urge to cry.

To walk under the blue sky.

To Lyu, that simple act seemed like an incredible luxury and joy. Simply to feel the sunshine pour down on her and the wind blow against her skin.

"The light of the sun…"

"Yes, it feels amazing…and so warm."

As Lyu shaded her eyes with one hand and looked up at the sky, her companion replied. The boy, who was also looking up at the sky, smiled shyly when she realized she was looking at him.

Lyu was walking through Orario at Bell's side.

It sounded funny to say they had been discharged, but since their treatment was finished, they had been allowed to leave Babel. Given that they had spent so many days alone together wandering the Dungeon, Bell's familia and Lyu's coworkers had thoughtfully decided to give them some space. It only seemed right that the pair that had overcome hardship together should walk on the surface again for the first time together.

Lyu was very happy they had done so. She hoped Bell felt the same.

"Ms. Lyu, are those clothes…?"

"Yes, they're Syr's...Strange, right?"

"Not at all! They look great."

"O-of course they do, because they're Syr's."

Syr had been kind enough to leave a change of clothes when she came to visit, since she realized Lyu probably wouldn't want to leave the clinic wearing her waitress uniform. The simple white dress decorated with flowery lace suited the elf Lyu well.

Lyu pressed the hem down around her knees as she answered Bell brusquely—although in a high-pitched, excited voice.

"Is your left arm all right?"

"Yes. They told me not to exercise it, but it has the same range of movement as before. It's like it was never even injured..."

Bell looked down at his arm as he walked. What had been a horrible mess before was now back to its original shape. At the very least, it seemed to have healed perfectly as far as Lyu could tell. The bandage was gone and in its place were metal restraints at his elbow, wrist, and finger joints. It reminded her of a gauntlet with parts cut out, or an incomplete artificial arm.

"Actually, they said they couldn't fix it...*so they practically had to remake the whole thing.*"

"...I didn't know they could do that."

"Apparently they can..."

The medical staff had only been able to do so because all bones and everything else making up his arm were all preserved inside the scarf he'd wrapped around it in place of a bandage. If he'd lost any of that, he would have had to replace it with an artificial arm like Nahza.

"My arm is still the same length, too," he said, holding both arms together and looking at them. Lyu recalled Amid's face and thought that she wasn't called the best healer in the city for nothing.

"By the way, how much did it cost?"

"Um...there were about eight zeroes in a row..."

"...!!"

"Oh, no, it's fine. The Guild, or I think probably Ouranos, covered it because it was an emergency! And Hermes had his familia gather the materials for the brace...!"

As Bell hurried to explain the situation to the shocked Lyu, they continued to walk through the city side by side.

The wind brushing against their cheeks felt lovely.

The sunlight seemed to be washing their bodies clean after spending so much time in the darkness.

The smiles of the children passing by were contagious.

The peaceful noises of the street mingled with the gentle atmosphere of the surface.

They took it all in with their whole bodies, wandering wherever their fancy led them. Passing through the tangle of streets, they crossed a bridge spanning a canal and then climbed a back-alley stairway, finally emerging onto a hilltop that overlooked western Orario.

"I never knew this place was here…"

"Yes…I used to come here with Alize."

Alize Lovell enjoyed high places.

She had often taken Lyu to hilltops like this or climbed onto the rooftops of buildings where they would talk surrounded by blue sky. Just like Bell and Lyu were doing now.

"…Five years ago, Lady Astrea told me to forget about justice."

Lyu spoke quietly as she stood by the banister and looked out on the city. She was speaking both to Bell, who listened quietly, and to the endless blue sky, where her voice carried on the wind.

"I thought she was excommunicating me. I thought she'd lost hope in me after seeing how consumed I was by vengeance…that she'd only let me keep the mark of her Blessing on my back out of pity."

That was how Lyu had interpreted it at the time, thinking she was accepting her deity's will. She thought the fact that Astrea had disappeared from the city and only sent her an occasional short letter meant that she, Lyu, had been stripped of the right to act in the name of justice.

Bell leaned forward as if to say something, but Lyu's next words stopped him.

"But…I was wrong."

She stared off into the distance, a smile on her lips.

She was right.

Astrea had not abandoned Lyu.

She had been watching over her body and soul.

Vengeance could never be justice. But the will to put an end to vengeance and break the cycle of hatred could become justice.

If Astrea had told Lyu that vengeance never created anything, however, what would have happened to Lyu?

She would certainly have fallen apart.

Unable to claim revenge, unable to forgive herself, she would have given in to the desire to end her miserable life.

The goddess must have known that from the beginning. Certainly she understood it better than Lyu did. And so she had gone so far as to forsake the justice she presided over for the sake of protecting Lyu.

"She told me to forget about justice for my own sake..."

The pillar of the familia had turned against her own truth for the sake of her follower. She had carried half the burden of Lyu's vengeance.

But that was not all.

The goddess had believed that when the flames of vengeance had burned out and turned to ash, Lyu would rise again like a fairy spreading her wings as she rose from the dead. She had believed that justice would come to live once again in Lyu's breast.

"I have you to thank for everything."

"Huh?"

Lyu turned slowly from the banister and faced Bell. She narrowed her eyes at the wide-eyed Bell.

"You told me I still had justice within me. You showed me the ties to Astrea that still remain inside...and you showed me what my familia left for me."

Bell had helped her realize.

The justice that persisted within her still connected her to Astrea and the rest of her familia.

He had helped her remember.

When the haze of regret cleared from her memories, she recalled that on a certain day five years earlier when they parted ways, her goddess had cried, and smiled.

That was how Lyu knew she was not wrong.

"Alize protected me, Syr rescued me...and you opened my eyes."

Alize had led her forward.

Syr had saved her when she was charred by the flames of vengeance and had shown her the future that her familia members had left her.

And Bell...he had given her the courage to face the past she had not been able to cut loose. He had stood by and supported her the whole time.

Everything was ongoing.

The people who had taken her hands in theirs were the ones she had to thank for her life. She no longer tried to conceal the feelings of gratitude overflowing from her heart.

"There's something I still haven't told you."

Beneath the warm sunlight and the clear blue sky, she turned toward Bell.

"Thank you, Bell."

And then she smiled.

"You're a human I can respect."

A smile blossomed like a beautiful white flower on her petite lips.

Bell stared at her as the elf's smile pulled him in.

A wind blew around them, rustling the pure-white hem of her dress and tousling his white hair. A smile spread over his face. He blushed shyly as kindness filled his eyes.

"Your smile is so beautiful right now," he said.

"Huh...?"

"More beautiful than ever before. Much more than that other time."

He was thinking back to the day when Lyu had stood before the *Astrea Familia* grave markers, surrounded by forest and crystal. Lost in reminiscence, he smiled like an innocent child.

"It makes me so happy to see you smile like that."

Bell's words were as pure as snow. He was as happy as if the change had been his own.

Lyu felt her heart leap as she looked at him. Her face grew hot. She looked down, although she was unsure why she did.

"...Lyu, Ms. Lyu...?"

Noticing her strange behavior, Bell leaned toward her and spoke worriedly into her ear.

That was enough to make her heart leap again.

Strange. I'm having palpitations. What is going on?

Flustered by her unruly emotions and failing to think clearly, she blurted out the honest truth.

"I-I can't look you in the face..."

"Huh? Why?!"

"I-I don't know..."

That was the honest truth.

Why did her cheeks grow hot when she looked at him?

Why was her heart abuzz?

She had no idea why she couldn't look directly at those rubellite eyes.

"B-Bell! I'll see you later!"

Unable to tolerate it any longer, she took off running.

Left behind in surprise, Bell soon took his leave as well.

It was no good.

Even though she ran and ran, pressing both hands to her chest like an innocent girl, she could not hide the excitement rumbling deep in her heart.

"What in the world...?!"

Lyu hadn't noticed.

When had her lips begun to call his name?

When had her white skin begun to flush so red?

What was this feeling blossoming in her heart?

"Oh, Alize, what in the world should I do...?!"

Her face beet red, she ran with the wind through the busy city streets, begging her beloved friend for advice.

Don't let him escape!

From beyond the blue sky, she thought she heard the bright voice of a smiling, confident girl answer her.

© Suzuhito Yasuda

【BELL・CRANELL】

BELONGS TO: *HESTIA FAMILIA*
RACE: HUMAN
JOB: ADVENTURER
DUNGEON RANGE: THIRTY-SEVENTH FLOOR
WEAPONS: HESTIA KNIFE, HAKUGEN
CURRENT FUNDS: 340 VALIS

《THE ADVENTURER'S HEIRLOOM SWORD》

• 90-CELCH ONE-HANDED SWORD

• ALTHOUGH THE BLADE IS CHIPPED IN PLACES, IT WAS THE WEAPON OF AN UPPER-CLASS ADVENTURER WHO WAS DEVOTED TO EXPLORING THE DEEP LEVELS, AND THEREFORE STILL FUNCTIONS WELL.

• APPEARS TO BE ENGRAVED WITH A FAMILIA EMBLEM, ALTHOUGH IT IS BLOODSTAINED AND ILLEGIBLE.

Lv. **4**

STRENGTH: IO   DEFENSE: IO   DEXTERITY: IO   AGILITY: IO
MAGIC: IO   LUCK: G   IMMUNITY: H   ESCAPE: I

《MAGIC》

【FIREBOLT】   • SWIFT-STRIKE MAGIC

《SKILL》

【LIARIS FREESE】
- RAPID GROWTH
- CONTINUED DESIRE RESULTS IN CONTINUED GROWTH
- STRONGER DESIRE RESULTS IN STRONGER GROWTH

【ARGONAUT】
- CHARGES AUTOMATICALLY WITH ACTIVE ACTION

【OX SLAYER】
- ALL ABILITIES ARE DRASTICALLY ENHANCED WHEN FIGHTING MINOTAURS

《THE ADVENTURER'S HEIRLOOM POTION》

- SPOILED.

- ORIGINALLY A HIGH POTION. SIGNIFICANTLY RESTORES PHYSICAL STRENGTH.

- IF THE USER DOES NOT HAVE IMMUNITY, GUARANTEED TO CAUSE VOMITING AND DIARRHEA.

- IF HESTIA DRINKS IT, SHE WILL BE PLUNGED INTO A HELLISH FAST FOR SEVEN DAYS AND SEVEN NIGHTS.

Afterword

Before writing this manuscript, I went to Awamura Akamitsu at GA Bunko for advice on a number of points.

"It's always so hard to portray battles with giant monsters... Do you have any ideas for a nasty attack from an enemy boss?" I asked him.

"In *Mon**** Hun****, it's rough when giant enemies fly around or come falling down from overhead."

Ooh, I can use that.

I was already ignoring the cheerful explanation from my predecessor in this craft and jotting down ideas on the pages of my heart.

This volume is the fourteenth in the series. First, let me apologize sincerely for the belated publication. The delay is entirely my fault. At the same time, I express my deep gratitude to everyone who picked this book up after such a long wait.

This time I have a lot to say in the afterword. All of it involves spoilers, so consider yourself forewarned.

First, about the battle in the first half.

My favorite weapon in a certain classic manga is the armor magic sword that lets its user go "Amudo!" and my next favorite is probably the light wand of a certain demon king. When the strongest demon king possesses this, it quickly transforms into the strongest possible weapon, but I could never help wondering, what if a novice adventurer got ahold of it?

I find weapons that become stronger in tandem with the amount of power the user can summon to be extremely fascinating and appealing. That is one reason why I gave the hero of this story the goddess knife.

I also knew within myself that his partner, the creator of magic swords, would ultimately have to arrive at the same answer.

I think the fact that he said, "Weapons become a part of their wielder" in the fourth volume of this series clinched it. What he meant was that if they're part of your body, you've got to become stronger together. The solution the smith came up with in this volume was surely only one of many possibilities, which gives me great hope that in a future volume, he will go on to exceed the expectations of the hero as well as the author and invent many more incredible weapons.

I'd also like to touch on the prophetess of tragedy. Many readers probably realized that her character is based on a famous queen in Greek mythology whose ill fate is to never be believed no matter what she does or says. I once had the honor of receiving the following praise from Ryohgo Narita, the author of *Baccano!* and *Durarara!*:

"Cassandra and her friend Daphne are so great! I'm sure that at the very end Daphne will be the only one who believes her!"

"Huh?"

"Huh?"

That was about how our conversation went.

Of course, that was my intention from the start! And that's why I was able to wait until the time was ripe in this volume to properly portray their friendship!! ...But jokes aside, it was thanks to this so-called "encounter" that I decided to dig deeper into the prophetess of tragedy's character. As this story and the one I told at the beginning of this afterword illustrate, the *Is It Wrong* series is the result of many people's contributions. My sincere thanks go out to all the other authors who never hesitate to offer their casual opinions and advice.

*   *   *

And now for the battle in the second half.

There's a certain firefighter manga that I like just as much as my favorite classic adventure manga.

When I was a little boy, my father—who was a firefighter—would buy me comics, and I would get very excited about Daigo and Amakasu and Gomi-san. Oh, and Kanda-san, too.

For the final section of this volume, I initially came up with a lot of crazy plots like having Bell and Lyu recapture the lambton and intentionally get swallowed by it in order to escape the deep levels, but as I was depicting their friends in the fight in the first half, I decided to do it like *Megumi no Daigo*, the comic about the Megumi fire brigade in old Edo.

Rather than making the main character an out-of-this-world fighter who dominates everyone around him, I wanted to make this a story about the main character working so hard to overcome the challenges set before him that he nearly dies, as well as saving people who are important to him and being saved by them in turn. That, it seems to me, is what a Dungeon tale, or an adventurer's tale, is all about. He pushed himself past his limits at least three times and got completely pounded in the process. Every time he thought he had become stronger I put him through another trial. Sorry about that, Bell.

The reason I decided to model the episode on *Megumi no Daigo*, or at least one of the reasons, is that I had a friend who loved that manga and who used to talk about it with me all the time and get super excited. That person recently passed away due to heart failure. As I'm writing this afterword in 2018, I am not yet thirty, and this friend wouldn't have reached that age yet, either.

A lot of thoughts crossed my mind, like how could I call him a close friend when we hadn't seen each other in over five years, and why had I waited until the fourteenth volume, and I guess this is what they mean by your mind going blank from an overly abrupt idea, but ultimately, I just cried a lot. Aside from this friend, I lost a lot of relatives this year, and I was kind of becoming a useless human being, having thoughts like *Maybe Volume 13 cursed me* and

Geez, I don't want to write about the elf's past in Volume 14. I'm fine now, don't worry. My personal feelings and words didn't seep into the scenes between the elven heroine and her best friend. For this one volume, I simply wanted to try bringing out the themes of our favorite comic. That does have a bit to do with my personal feelings, and I apologize for that.

As for where I'm going with all this, well dear readers, please take good care of yourselves.

I've gotten off track, but finally, I'd like to talk about the elven heroine.

Since this was her moment in the spotlight, I wanted to attempt a romantic comedy in a fight-to-the-death setting, but I genuinely almost failed. I've actually never played a dating sim, but this time I tried out all kinds of plots only for them to all crash and burn. The elven heroine refused to smile. She refused to cry. She refused to flirt. She showed no sign of sitting down beneath that tree from the famous legend.

Where were the flags?! Where were the choices?! Couldn't she be more likeable? In this state, I tried and failed with at least thirty plots. Finally, after great struggles, I reached a good ending.

To tell the truth, I was tempted to end the whole series with this elven heroine's story, but I held back. Our hero still has a lot of girls to rescue. My apologies to you, elven heroine. If the folks at GA Bunko let me, I'd like to write about you again some time. On the other hand, if this elf was such a struggle, I wonder how things will go with other characters who have been stuck in the shadows so far. For now, I'm doing my utmost to avoid thinking about that.

And now, at long last, my acknowledgements.

To my editor Matsumoto and head editor Kitamura, whom I once again put through a great deal of trouble, thank you. To Suzuhito Yasuda, the man behind the wonderful illustrations in this book, I apologize for writing a book this long...And to everyone else who played a role in producing this book, I express my deepest gratitude.

Thank you, readers, for sticking with me this far. I went through some tough times while I was writing this book, but your fan letters kept me going. I am truly grateful.

I intend for the next volume to deal with everyday life. I'll do my best to get it to you as quickly as possible, so I do hope you'll wait.

Thank you, and good-bye for now.

Fujino Omori

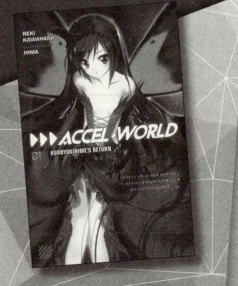

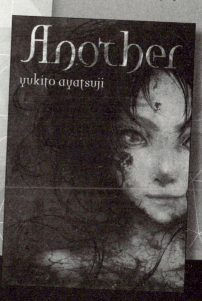

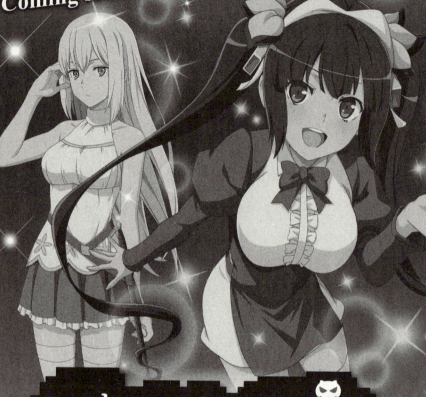